"Don't you know, sweetheart, that you should never go riding without your groom?"

He edged his Cavalier closer. "Or talk to strange men?"

"Then you may find your own way," she said tartly, and gathered up her reins.

"Oh, I shall," said Jack. Before she realized what he was about, he had dropped Cavalier's reins and put his hands on her shoulders. Her mouth opened slightly in alarm or indignation, but before she could express either Jack had his arms well around her and was kissing her firmly and thoroughly.

Also by Rosemary Edghill:

TURKISH DELIGHT

TWO OF A KIND:

An English Trifle

Rosemary Edghill

FAWCETT CREST • NEW YORK

A Fawcett Crest Book
Published by Ballantine Books
Copyright © 1988 by Rosemary Edghill

Library of Congress Catalog Card Number: 88-1853

ISBN 0-449-21708-6

This edition published by arrangement with St. Martin's Press, Inc.

Manufactured in the United States of America

First Ballantine Books Edition: August 1989

To Anne Elizabeth Zeek and Sara Campbell:
Jacks or better.

Chapter

ONE

The coach jounced and jostled appallingly. Lady Juliette Devereaux's head ached, a most unaccustomed and disagreeable sensation. Tucked into her reticule, out of sight but not out of mind, was yet another thick missive from Great-aunt Solange that Juliette, usually no coward, had not dared to read. It would only be an even more imperative summons for her to attend Madame Solange Devereaux at Fakenham at once—a fate Juliette intended to put off as long as humanly possible.

As Lady Juliette was a young woman of great determination and organizational ability, she had already put off the fatal meeting since her disastrous come-out ball in April. It was now mid-September, and she hoped to postpone the event still longer.

Juliette frowned, sighed, and rubbed her forehead fretfully. She still was not sure what had gone wrong in her assault on the *ton*; she had made her plans carefully (Juliette always made her plans carefully and then carried them out forthrightly), and she had tailored her expectations to fit her circumstances. After all, she consoled herself, she had always known she couldn't expect to rival Mama, whose Season had been the most brilliant of triumphal progresses.

On the other hand, Juliette, who not only possessed a mirror but believed in looking at things practically, knew that she was quite pretty indeed, and more important, was the heiress to Chaceley, with the considerable "all" that appertained thereto.

Juliette's ancestors, the Comtes de Devereaux, a French family of great antiquity and uncommon sense, had spent the past two hundred years intermarrying with their English connections. As a result, when the first rumblings of Revolution shook Paris the Devereaux family simply decamped for their English estates, leaving the danger zone long before it was fashionable to become a wistful emigré. (As no one in the neighborhood of Chaceley was quite sure what the proper mode of address was for the granddaughter of a Comte de Devereaux, the daughter of the house was universally referred to in the English style as Lady Juliette.)

Juliette had been chatelaine of Chaceley since she'd entered her 'teens, and had done, in her father's words, "damned well by the place." Juliette had thanked him kindly, thinking privately that all it had really required was a little application and management. In Juliette's opinion, all one need do was have a proper plan and a little sense, and things would invariably fall out as desired.

It was a simple philosophy, and one which had never before been proven wanting—until her London Season. Juliette sighed once more.

"What's the matter, lovey? Have ye got the headache, then? And sure and I'm not surprised, what with bouncing about like this. Do take off your bonnet, Miss Julie, and be comfortable-like."

Juliette turned her attention to her abigail, Matilda, who was watching her anxiously from the seat beside her. "No, no, Mattie," she lied. Juliette knew from experience that otherwise Mattie would fuss and worry unendingly, lest she be proving as delicate as Mama. "I suppose I'm a trifle blue-deviled, that's all."

Matilda sniffed. "And what have you got to be blue-deviled about, Miss?"

"Nothing," said Juliette without much conviction. "I—oh, Mattie, whatever went wrong?" she demanded with sudden indignation. "I had my Season all planned—but now there's been all that trouble and expense, and nothing to show for it, and—"

"Fiddle," said Mattie comfortably. "Ye was the prettiest thing in London, Miss Julie—well-nigh the image of Miss Sophia. And the young men at your feet and all—"

Frowning, Juliette ceased to listen and turned back to the window. She'd heard all this before; Mattie was an unthinking and uncritical partisan of the perfect Miss Sophia Halford's daughter. But Juliette, who prided herself on her clear thinking, knew better.

On the evening of her twentieth birthday Juliette had realized she could put off her search for a proper lord and master for Chaceley no longer. Being a sensible, forthright, and decisive girl, she had straightaway sat down and written to Cousin Euphemia Templeton, who would surely sponsor her and who had the added advantage of bringing out her own daughter, Deborah, that Season. Euphemia had been delighted to sponsor Lady Juliette as well, and matters had all been well in train before Juliette had written to inform Great-aunt Solange of the arrangements.

So much had gone smoothly. But the measles had laid the Templeton household low and deprived Juliette of her sponsor. Rather than wait once her course of action had been decided upon, Juliette had handed her instructions for running Chaceley to her father and to the estate agent, kissed her father good-bye (though not the estate agent), taken Mattie and gone up to Town. There Juliette had promptly and efficiently hired a chaperon and a house, acquired a wardrobe, and sent out invitations for a ball.

But from the moment of her come-out ball she'd realized she had somehow been labeled as not quite good *ton*. She had refused to retire from Town or to respond to Madame Solange's increasingly vehement demands that she come to Fakenham at once, and took what solace she might in Mattie's unstinting admiration and Mrs. Basingstoke's unsophisticated flatteries.

It had never occurred to Juliette, accustomed to ruling the roast at Chaceley for years, that she might stand in need of guidance, nor that the brilliantly hued dresses that she had succumbed to were hardly suitable to a girl in her first Season, no matter how dazzling her mama had looked in green silk at her come-out twenty-five years before. Matilda, who had been a good stout nursemaid during the legendary Miss Sophia's reign, was a good plain country abigail under Juliette's, and could not judge. Mrs. Basingstoke, a good-hearted but not high-bred lady, could not say no to Juliette, so beautiful, so rich, and so obviously intoxicated with London! Poor Mrs. Basingstoke had quite wept at parting with dear Juliette at the Season's end, and could never understand why the sweet child seemed not to have had even one Offer!

However, Offers or no, Juliette had managed to make enough friends to make London bearable enough, and to provide a means of escaping Madame Solange's urgent summonses. Juliette had quite happily spent July in Brighton with Sir Gerald and Lady Lockridge, and August in Bath with Mr. and Mrs. Lucas Markham, who had the added virtue of being distant cousins of Juliette's. But these visits had inevitably come to an end, and Juliette had cast about desperately for some new means of avoiding Great-aunt Solange Devereaux's draconian lair.

Just as Fakenham and doom had loomed large in her future, Juliette had received reprieve in the form of an invitation to a September house party at Duckmanton, in Sussex. It was true that Juliette's presence was desired because she was an heiress and Lady Ralph Candlesby had a son, but Duckmanton was situated close by Temple Down, home of Lord and Lady Templeton. Juliette, who had no interest in Douglas Candlesby, had a great deal of interest in Lord Templeton's bloodstock.

And if the Templetons invited her to stop with them, as they very well might—the measles being long since departed—there was every chance for Juliette to go from Temple Down straightaway home to Chaceley, avoiding Madame until next spring at the earliest.

So Juliette had eagerly accepted Lady Ralph's kind invitation, regardless of entanglements. Douglas Candlesby would be no problem; Juliette had no intention of encouraging that amiable fribble. He was not at all the kind of man to take care of such an estate as Chaceley!

Which brought poor Juliette's thoughts around full circle to her unfortunate Season and its biggest disappointment: it had failed utterly to produce the man of her dreams, that still-undiscovered paragon who would be her partner as the custodian and cultivator of the Devereaux estates. Juliette's dreams were as yet rather unformed, as the pleasant vice of novel-reading was one of the many in which she did not waste her time by indulging. However, she had been certain before her Season that London would hold someone she could find agreeable.

Juliette sighed and shifted uncomfortably on the hard coach seat. Hands full of sawdust and minds on their clothes! She had quickly realized that the would-be Brummels she'd met in the drawing-rooms and ballrooms of London saw their lands merely as a useful commodity to be wrung dry to finance their pleasuring—or, occasionally, as an equally useful bolthole to retire to when the duns became too heavy. Furthermore, not one of them could hold a sensible conversation, let alone hold household!

And as for the older men who could—well, not only were the desirable ones long-married already, but those who were still fancy-free were totally ineligible. And while she had no desire that her husband live under the sign of the cat's foot, she would allow no man to ride roughshod over her, either! Nor had Juliette any particular desire to marry a man twice her age only to be early-widowed. There wouldn't be much help for Chaceley in that—

"—and furthermore, I look a perfect fright in black!" she finished crossly, rubbing her forehead again.

Matilda instantly began to scold lovingly about poor Miss Julie getting burnt to the socket and to

6

proffer all manner of sovereign remedies for the headache, when the coach topped a low rise.

"Never mind that now, Mattie . . . here's Duckmanton, at last!" Juliette said with real relief.

Duckmanton, country seat of Lord Ralph Candlesby, had been presented to Lord Ralph as an engagement present by his father, the Duke of Birdwell. It had been enriched by a Palladian portico when Lord Ralph had taken his wife, and Italianate gardens when his wife had taken a notion. Still more additions had been made from time to time, most notably the Gothic folly in the aforementioned gardens, and it was only through the great good fortune of being blessed with an exceedingly expensive and rackety heir that Lord Ralph had recently been able to stop making improvements to the estate.

Lady Juliette's coach came to a halt before Duckmanton's impressive bronze doors, which had been imported from Venice four years before. Lady Ralph Candlesby was on the steps to greet her as Juliette thankfully descended from the coach.

"My dear! How well you look—considering the dreadful strain you must have been under!" Lady Ralph amended hastily. "And how *is* your dear papa?"

Juliette had been Lady Ralph's guest many times in London this past Season and so knew how to interpret her hostess's remarks. "Father is well, thank you—at least I assume so, or Wharton would have written. He is the estate agent for Chaceley, you know, and sends me regular reports. For my own part, I must admit that the journey was dreadfully tiring—but I always find it so, when I am not in the saddle."

"Oh, yes!" Lady Ralph, who never rode when she could be driven, and who was rumored not even to own a hack, nodded enthusiastically. "I *always* find it so, and indeed, Douglas has remarked to me many times that he feels precisely the same. And here he is now to greet you—Douglas!" Her ladyship's voice rose as she summoned her only son.

"Lady Juliette! So you did come! How splendid!" A slender young man in fawn pantaloons and tobacco-colored coat bounded forward to grasp Juliette's hands.

Mr. Douglas Warwick Candlesby was, at four-and-twenty, considered quite an eligible *parti*—providing, of course, that one did not require overmuch intellect in a husband. Mr. Candlesby was a creature of Fashion, and, Fashion being so very fleeting, it could only be accounted an asset that he could not hold one thought in his head above two minutes together. He had advantages other than intellect, however: he was a handsome young man, good-natured enough to dance with any young lady presented to him as a desireable partner, no matter how plain she be, and he was the grandson of a Duke.

Unfortunately for his and Lady Juliette's peace of mind, during the past Season he had taken it into his head that to be truly *au courant* one must be possessed of a violent unreciprocated passion. Since he was not, as his friends kindly informed him, a *complete* idiot, he had made Lady Juliette Devereaux the object of these strong passions. Juliette had paid no heed, but Lady Ralph had. Lady Ralph, a good-natured woman, but, as she had informed her spouse, a Lioness in Defense of her Child, was willing to overlook Juliette's faults and mounted a campaign to match Juliette's money with Douglas's proven ability to spend it, and was not to be deterred by such insignificant considerations as the mutual indifference of the two young people involved.

Douglas, having clutched Juliette's hands in the obligatory rapture of ecstasy, abruptly abandoned Romance in favor of more important matters. "I say, since you've brought your horses, Lady Juliette—oh, I forgot to say they arrived yesterday, and in prime twig! Anyway, I thought we might ride over to Temple Down tomorrow—Lord Templeton's minded to sell some of his stock, and we can have a look at them before the sales!"

"Douglas, really!" said Lady Ralph reprovingly, but Juliette smiled.

"Indeed, Mr. Candlesby, I shall be delighted to ride over—I'm quite longing to see the Templetons again. You are lucky to be so close to Temple Down." And as he was, Juliette considered it ridiculous that Douglas Candlesby was not mounted better. Tomorrow she would look over the Templeton stock and recommend several possible remounts for his purchase.

Douglas, looking at the quelling expression on his mama's face and the thoughtful one on Juliette's, found them equally alarming and discovered urgent business elsewhere. Juliette was left to Lady Ralph's attentions.

"You mustn't mind Douglas, Lady Juliette; I am sure he merely does not wish to embarrass you by too particular an attention. Young people can *not* be too careful, you know. Oh, and I have invited a number of your particular friends—dear Douglas was invaluable in making up a list for me—and we shall have a quiet, comfortable party . . . at least, we shall if nothing too dreadful happens," Lady

Ralph amended cheerfully and continued without pause for breath.

"Now, my dear child, you must treat Duckmanton precisely as you would your own home, since after all . . . well, I must not run ahead of myself, since nothing is at all settled, of course, and you will have plenty of time to refresh yourself before dinner, since it is most important to the digestion that one not be over tired, and . . . well, never mind that now. Most of the rest of the party is here, but dinner will be time enough for them of course. Mind you, I rely on you for all the gossip—is Mrs. Markham's condition improved? And one does hear about poor dear Lady Lockridge's headaches."

The vivacious Pamela Lockridge might very well suffer headaches in Lady Ralph's presence; Juliette only knew that that most delightful of hostesses had not been afflicted by one during all of July. But she said only, "I promise I shall tell you everything, Lady Ralph, though I am persuaded that Douglas will already have told you most of my poor news."

And after a further exchange of courtesies, which did nothing to help Juliette's own headache, she was finally allowed to attain the sanctuary of her room.

"My dear Madam," Juliette wrote some time later, as Mattie bustled about the room behind her setting all to rights. Juliette, cleansed from the dust of the road, plied with a soothing *tisane* which had, in fact, relieved her aching temples, and wrapped in a frilly coquelicot-colored dressing gown lavishly embellished with knots of pale cream ribbons at the shoulders, was now faced with Duty. Time enough after that to venture on who her fellow guests might be—just such a tedious lot as she had had about her in Town, she supposed. Oh well, there *were* the Templeton sales. She chewed the end of her pen reflectively. Great-aunt Solange had tracked her down at the Markhams'; Juliette had cravenly refrained from unsealing the thick letter until now and was sorry she had ever opened it. She had the distinct feeling that Madame's letter would set Duckmanton itself afire were it not safely housed in the grate. She was only surprised it had not burned through her reticule.

However, some reply must be made. Juliette stopped nibbling on her pen and set it to paper once more.

"I am stopping at Duckmanton in Sussex, near Temple Down, as Lady Ralph Candlesby so kindly invited me. This will give me the opportunity to view the Templeton horses before the autumn sales, for, as you know, we need some new blood for the Chaceley stock."

That was all very well, as far as it went, but Juliette knew it would hardly mollify Madame. She bit her pen again, then continued hastily. "I do not know if I shall be able to come to you next, or if duty will call me back to Chaceley. Perhaps, dear Madame, we will have the felicity of seeing you at Christmas—" This was a safe enough wish; Madame hadn't left Fakenham in ten years; and if, heaven forbid, Madame *did* come, it would be hunting season and Juliette would simply ride out with Squire Alworthy's pack every day she could.

". . . and do give my fondest love to Cousin Tony, and I shall write again soon, when you shall receive the fullest budget of gossip with which Lady Ralph can invest me—and I remain, your very affectionate grandniece, Juliette."

Madame Solange would infinitely prefer an obedient grandniece, but Juliette decided to let it stand, and quickly sealed it with a wafer before she changed her mind. It could go off with tomorrow's post, and if all went well she would be safe at Chaceley by this time next month. Surely Papa could be persuaded that duty called his gadabout daughter home—especially as he would wish nothing to interfere with his hunting. Juliette only hoped Madame Solange hadn't sent Papa a letter too, as she truly *was* a dutiful daughter and had no wish that his life be made hideous as well!

Her task completed, Juliette turned to watch Matilda at work. The abigail was methodically emptying the trunks of their contents, brushing out dresses and riding habits carefully before hanging them in the towering oak wardrobe. Brushes and silver-topped bottles lined the dressing table in orderly rows; the jewel-case was precisely centered.

It was a great pity that Life could not always be as orderly as Mattie's unpacking. Years of overseeing the management of extensive estates had given Juliette a firm taste for definite answers, definitely expressed, on definite subjects. She had, not unnaturally, found Society disorderly at best; Juliette liked to have everything out in the open and clearly stated. Society favored ambiguous hints that could mean anything.

Take Lady Ralph Candlesby, for example. In Juliette's opinion, if Lady Ralph thought Douglas was going to offer for her, Lady Ralph should simply say so. Juliette could then tell her frankly that it was no such thing, and they could go on about their business without all this confusion. It seemed so simple to Juliette that she could not understand why everyone else took such delight in being mysterious.

"—but say what you will, Miss, it's a *lovely* bonnet, and that I will hold to!" Mattie held up the object in question, and Juliette realized that she had been air-dreaming just as surely as if she'd been thinking of her nonexistent ideal husband.

"Well, I must say that I think so too," Juliette confessed, rising and going over to take the gaudy green watered silk confection from Mattie's hands. She turned it this way and that, admiring its ostrich plumes and the artificial cherries and flowers that trimmed its extravagant poke. "But do you know, Mattie, Miss Fonthill said it was not-at-all the thing, and I confess I cannot see why."

"Tush, Miss Julie—it's jealous Miss Fonthill likely was, for it's home truth *she* couldn't be a-wearing the color, not for ever so! But it do look a treat on you, and just what your dear mama would like to see you in, God rest her soul."

Juliette found it hard to doubt in the face of Matilda's sublime confidence. Why, she'd even gone to the same modiste Mattie said Mama had used, and that venerable establishment charged dearly enough for her dressing, heaven knew! But she'd known she would only be doing her come-out Season once, and hadn't been able to resist any of the glowing fabrics or dazzling dresses paraded for her delectation. No, nothing could be wrong with her clothes. Still ... Juliette regarded the bonnet in her hands doubtfully. Althea Fonthill *had* said—

Something in her expression made Mattie snatch the poke bonnet back from her charge's unworthy hands and replace it tenderly in its nest of silver paper.

"Next you'll be a-saying your amethyst satin

13

tisn't fit to be seen in—and Madame Lambourne slaving over it day and night to have it ready for you, just as she always did for Miss Sophia!"

"Nonsense, it's lovely," said Juliette briskly. Normally she was willing to listen as long as Matilda chose to talk about how things had been in Miss Sophia's day, but for some heretical reason now she found it just a bit tedious. So to cut the conversation short, Juliette added, "In fact, I'll wear it to dinner tonight. Now, you may lay out a riding habit for me, Mattie dear. I'm sure a good gallop will shake the last of the headache away."

"Miss Julie, you'll never go riding *now*! And how'm I to turn you out a credit to Miss Sophia with you dashing about on horseback at all hours?"

"Nonsense, I shall be back in plenty of time to dress—and I simply must have some exercise after being cooped up in that coach all day! I shall just ride over towards Temple Down—yes, the green habit will do very well—what a pity Gussie Templeton is gone to Russia. He hasn't a brain in his head, of course, but he's never dull and he *does* know horses." With that doubtful encomium upon the absent Mr. Templeton, Juliette allowed Matilda to help her out of the dressing gown and into a habit of green Melton cloth and impeccable cut that not even the most severe arbiter of taste could have faulted. A small round beaver hat with a dull gold buckle and a veil of Urling's net, and black boots and gloves completed the ensemble. A brisk gallop was just what she needed to set her up before an evening spent dancing attendance on some of Douglas's impossible friends.

"Mattie, while I'm gone can you find out who else Lady Ralph has invited and which of them will be at dinner? I don't like to ask Lady Ralph, or I'll hear that they've all suffered hideous tragedies, but it would be nice to know before I'm seated with them."

"Just you leave that to me, miss, and mind you, you're to be back in good time for me to brush the snarls out of your hair—and put the embrocation on your bruises!"

"Oh, do be serious, Mattie," said Juliette mildly. "You know I never fall."

"That's as may be, miss," the abigail observed darkly, "but there's a first time for all, is my motto."

The Duckmanton stables were clean and spacious but woefully under-stocked. Fewer than half the stalls were filled, and those with horses of what Juliette considered decidedly inferior quality. Hence Juliette had prudently written to Chaceley before she left Bath and had Tom Perkins bring two of her own horses to Duckmanton.

Juliette regarded the stable disapprovingly, tapping her crop against her boot. Tom Perkins appeared from a nearby stall, brush in hand. He did not look happy.

"Good afternoon, Miss Julie. I've just gotten the carriage horses rubbed down and settled in, if you're wishful to look at them. But if it's Dulcinea you're wanting . . ."

"What's wrong with her?" Juliette demanded, more sharply than she'd intended.

Perkins shook his head. "She's gone lame again, miss."

Juliette sighed. She had hunted Dulcinea last season, with but indifferent success, and then decided to keep her for a hack. But the unfortunate season in the hunting field had left the mare in no good shape for that either—at least in Dulcinea's opinion.

"Well, if she is, there's no help for it, and I know you've done all you can. Saddle Skylark for me, then, and send to Chaceley for Thunderbolt. I warrant there isn't a horse in these stables I want to try!"

"There's the truth with no bark on it—add the beasts I brought from Chaceley and you'll still have the right of it." Perkins expressed himself with the privileged freedom of one who had tossed Lady Juliette up onto her first pony and later felt he had made a mistake.

"Nonsense! Skylark's perfectly safe for a decent rider, and I hope you will own I am that, at least. Why people *will* say a horse is a bad horse when *they* are only bad riders is quite beyond me! Please bring him around."

"As you say, miss, but he's a nervy one at best, and in strange country like this . . ."

"I hope I may be trusted to sit a horse even if he *is* nervous. And I don't need to be lapped in cotton-wool!" A muscle in Juliette's jaw jumped as she clamped her teeth tightly shut over further remarks. There was no point in flaying her servants merely because she was out-of-temper after that letter from Madame!

Perkins, defeated, soon had Skylark ready. The horse was a burly gray gelding, with a hard mouth and uncertain temper, and Juliette had bought him at Tattersall's primarily because her escort, whom she had browbeaten into the indiscretion of taking her there, had made the further error of stating that the gray was no horse for a lady. It was Juliette's opinion, now that Skylark was in her own stables, that he was a perfectly trustworthy mount as long as he was carefully ridden.

Perkins tossed Juliette lightly into the saddle and turned to his own mount. But before he had foot in the stirrup or could open his mouth to remonstrate with her, Juliette had spurred the indignant Skylark and galloped off alone.

Chapter
T W O

In the late afternoon it began to rain. The Marquess of Barham raised petitioning eyes to the gloomy heavens, but found no reason for optimism there. It had lacked only this.

This would teach him, Jack Barham thought ruefully, to trust in that invariably fatal epilogue to directions, "—but you can't miss it." At this rate he'd be lucky to reach Duckmanton by tomorrow morning. "Blast Candlesby anyway," he said to his patient mount. "I've half a mind to give him the go-bye and head for Doncaster direct. What d'you think, old boy?" He patted Cavalier's neck, and the horse snorted and shook his head.

"No?" Jack grinned wryly, stroking Cavalier's wet black neck once more. The old cavalry charger had more good sense than he did; Duckmanton it must be. Both he and Cavalier needed at least a short repairing lease before pushing on again—and there was always the possibility of coaxing more of Douglas Candlesby's golden guineas into Jack's own pockets. Besides, young Candlesby was a free-spending and well-breeched young idiot, likable enough, and inclined to look with admiration upon Bad Jack Barham. This was fortunate indeed for a man who had, over the last five years, developed a reputation that caused less trustful souls than Douglas Candlesby to give him a wide berth.

Oh, there were still plenty of men—and women, too—willing to aid a man in his efforts to go to the devil in the most expeditious possible fashion, a course which Jack Barham had been energetically following since he'd returned home from the wars.

He'd enlisted in a youthful burst of patriotism shortly after Jena. His infuriated father, the Duke of Owlsthorne, had responded by striking his only child's name from the family Bible. His Grace then changed his will, bequeathing anything unentailed elsewhere, and began a course of actions nicely calculated to completely ruin the remaining properties. Her Grace of Owlsthorne was well-served for attempting to reason with His Grace by having all communication with her son cut off. Her Grace was carried off by grief and the influenza three years later and the news of her death reached Jack by sheerest chance some months afterward, along with the information that he was popularly supposed to have refused to go to his dying mother.

After Waterloo Jack discovered that his resources consisted of a dark, piratical handsomeness, a sturdy but aging cavalry mount, a pile of dragoon's debts, and an ancestral home almost ruined by deliberate malice and barred to him by parental decree. The Marquess of Barham, with a reckless disregard for consequences ill-suited to his new civilian status, had retaliated as best he might by going to the devil in as blatant a fashion as possible. If his father were going to ruin the Owlsthorne properties, Jack had thought bitterly, then he would see the name ruined along with it. And the world was full of people eager to oblige him in his efforts.

But now that Jack was nearing thirty, he no longer, somehow, found the devil so amusing a fellow as once he was. As for his cohorts in sin and wickedness—well, they were not only ill-bred, but tedious, and not half so clever as they liked to think themselves.

But all this cogitation wasn't getting him any nearer to the elusive Duckmanton, and it had begun to rain harder now. He shrugged deeper into the capes of his riding coat and urged Cavalier forward through a gap in a nearby hedge. As he pushed through it, Cavalier pricked up his ears and whickered, then threw back his head and neighed loudly. An answering whinny greeted him, and Jack spurred Cavalier towards the sound.

There was a young woman on a gray horse in the next clearing. She wore an exquisitely cut riding habit of dark green; it perfectly displayed both her elegant figure and the whiteness of her skin. A saucy little hat perched at a rakish angle on her raven's-wing curls, a wayward wisp of veiling plastered damply against her cheek serving only to accentuate the incredible emerald of her eyes. One tiny toe peeped roguishly from beneath the skirts of the habit, and as Jack rode up she regarded him with an imperious and arrogant look.

Jack smiled and pulled Cavalier up. The fair unknown did not flinch under his scrutiny; rather, she returned stare for stare. Jack's lazy smile widened; he reached up and swept off his hat. "Fair wood-nymph, will you take pity on a lost stranger?"

The wood-nymph continued to stare; then a wave of rose-petal pink swept over her cheeks. "If—if you are lost, sir, the main road is that way." She gestured with her riding whip. "I cannot imagine how you managed to stray from it, but—but I daresay you are unused to this country." The rose still stained her cheeks; her gray sidled under her as if agitated.

Jack set his hat back on his now soaking hair. "I was bewitched, no doubt, by—shall I say, the natural beauty of the landscape?"

She frowned, as if puzzling out this utterance, then turned even pinker. "Nonsense, sir—you have only just this minute seen me, and—and you shouldn't say such things, you know."

Jack laughed and moved Cavalier up to the nervous gray. "And you shouldn't listen to them, young lady." He raised his eyebrows as if scandalized. "Don't you know, sweetheart, that you should never go riding without your groom?" He edged Cavalier even closer; the gray fidgeted, but didn't move. "Or talk to strange men?"

"Then you may find your own way," she said tartly, and gathered up her reins.

"Oh, I shall," said Jack. Before she realized what he was about, he had dropped Cavalier's reins and put his hands on her shoulders. Raindrops glinted on her thick dark lashes; her green eyes looked enormous. Her mouth opened slightly in alarm or indignation, but before she could express either Jack had his arms well around her and was kissing her firmly and thoroughly.

There was a stunned moment of stiffness, and her hand came up to push against his chest. Her eyes closed and she swayed against him, her warm, rain-wet lips softening to his . . .

Then the gray danced impatiently and she began to slide from her sidesaddle. Jack put a hand to her

21

horse's reins, but the spell had been broken. She cried out and wrenched herself away, slashing at Jack with her riding whip. The high-strung gray shied violently and then bolted, with his mistress's complete encouragement, clearing a low stone wall like a winged thing and disappearing into the trees.

Jack sat back on Cavalier and gazed after her, fingering the welt that burned like fire on his cheek. That particular little wood-nymph had a strong arm on her, for all her elfin beauty, and he must admit he'd certainly deserved it. All things considered it was a small price to pay for one of the sweetest kisses of his experience.

And when he reached Duckmanton he'd turn young Candlesby upside down until he found out which of the neighborhood households harbored this rare gem. Perhaps she was the daughter of the local squire—but her dress and her manner bespoke higher origins than that. In any case—Jack gathered up Cavalier's reins and laughed.

"In any case, I'll wager it's a long time until that young miss gives her groom the slip again, eh, boy?"

Cavalier sneezed and shook his head vigorously, showering droplets from his mane. Jack grinned, swatted Cavalier's neck companionably, and resumed his search for the manor of Duckmanton.

Althea Fonthill hummed contentedly to herself as she oversaw the unpacking of the trunks. Mama, whose rooms were elsewhere, had retired to lie down after the rigors of the journey, and Isobel, butterfly-quick and deft as Tib-o'-the-buttery when it came to avoiding disagreeable toil, had attached herself to Lady Ralph to be shown everything about

Duckmanton, leaving Althea to oversee the ordering of their wardrobe.

Althea looked about the room she was to share with her sister. Lady Ralph Candlesby judged her guests' social standing to a nicety; Lady Juliette Devereaux might well have a private room in the new wing by virtue of her papa's bank balance and Lady Ralph's matrimonial ambitions, but the Misses Fonthill shared a room in the original bedroom wing of the house where it was necessary to step up over the sill to enter. At least Lady Ralph did not accord such unimportant guests the grudging hospitality of some less good-natured hostesses, Althea thought, looking about the quaint, old-fashioned room; it might be old and small, but a bright coal-fire burned in the grate to take away the September chill and damp.

Althea was quite looking forward to seeing Lady Juliette again. She had first encountered Lady Juliette at one of Lady Vane's parties, and, drawn together by their mutual lack of social success, Miss Fonthill and Lady Juliette had become bosom-bows in no time at all, despite the fact that Juliette was a great heiress and Mrs. Fonthill and her two daughters were churchmouse-poor. The late Mr. Fonthill had invested unwisely upon 'Change, and his loving family was left to reap the reward.

Althea Fonthill had a pleasing, if plump, figure, soft mouse-blond hair, wide gray eyes, and no particular dowry. She was instantly relegated to the background whenever her sister appeared; golden Isobel, as vividly English pink-and-gold as Juliette was fairy-tale ebony-and-snow. The two beauties made a striking picture when they were together, though Althea knew Juliette dismissed Isobel as just another empty-headed damsel. Empty-headed or no—and Althea loyally refused to so label her lighthearted sister—it was upon Isobel that family hopes were firmly pinned. It was not unreasonable that such a pretty girl as Isobel should make quite a good match, even without a decent dowry, and Althea, having had a fruitless Season to herself, was now willing to step back and allow Isobel the center stage.

It had been very pleasant for Althea to have a friend of her own age, and though Juliette had her faults, condescension was not among them. Unhappily for this promising friendship, Isobel, for all her great blue eyes and guinea-gold curls, was herself hardly noticeable in a Season that boasted almost an embarrassment of young ladies possessed of both face *and* fortune. Mrs. Fonthill had therefore, in the interests of economy, cut short their stay in London, retiring with her daughters to visit a distant cousin near Harrowgate. Althea had been left to follow the course of Juliette's ignominious progress through the medium of a number of hastily scrawled letters rife with dark hints of Madame's displeasure, and had been genuinely surprised to receive an invitation to Duckmanton, by reason of the family being such especial friends of Lady Juliette's. Lady Ralph must be sure of her prey indeed, Althea thought irreverently, to invite not one but two unmarried females to a party meant to attach Douglas Candlesby's affections irredeemably to Lady Juliette Devereaux.

Still, it was no concern of hers, Althea reflected, for not only had she no hope of attaching the feckless and improvident Mr. Candlesby, she had not the slightest desire to do so. She had seen quite enough of him during the bit of the London Season she had shared with Juliette—during which he had written Juliette sonnets and Juliette had kindly corrected their grammar—to see that such a manageable man was not for Althea Fonthill. At two-and-twenty she was not quite on the shelf—though another Season or so would surely see her there—but even the terrors of a life spent as a charge on the grudging charity of relatives could not quite reconcile her to the thought of marrying without even fondness present. Althea kept these heretical notions entirely to herself; there was no reason to fuss Mama with her vaporings, nor to distract Mama's attention from Isobel. Let Isobel only find fondness and fortune together, and Althea would quite happily propose herself upon her sister to live out her days in virtuous spinsterhood.

Perhaps next season would see them more fortunate, Althea considered, seating herself in a chair next to the grate and taking up her needlepoint. Just as soon as everything was in order here, she would go out for a walk—perhaps Lady Juliette would have returned from her ride—and they could have a comfortable coze before dinner. Lady Ralph had been coy to the point of mysteriousness about her other houseguests, but undoubtedly Isobel would have charmed the list out of her by now.

She must have been quite, quite mad. This was the only conclusion that made any sense whatsoever to Juliette as she urged Skylark on in his efforts to emulate his avian namesake. How *could* she have—have—Oh, whatever must that appalling man have thought of her?

Juliette finally pulled Skylark to a walk, not without some argument. She couldn't go back to Duckmanton looking all no-how, nor could she bring Skylark in lathered to foam. Matilda would talk, and Tom Perkins would look, and Juliette couldn't possibly bear it!

How could she—and how dare he! Juliette put a gloved hand to her lips, which still seemed to tingle oddly. Yes, how *dare* he come riding out of the rain like that, and smile at her with those eyes like warm amber and then take outrageous liberties with her!

The very thought of those outrageous liberties made her cheeks burn. It had been bad enough for that—that rake, for he could be nothing less, to be kissing any stray female that crossed his path—to have made such advances. But for her, Juliette Devereaux, to have allowed him—to have practically fallen into his arms—well, that was the outside of enough!

However, Juliette prided herself on her good sense; it was obvious that such a man was not one she would ever meet again—not beneath any respectable roof, at any rate! And he, of course, had no idea who she was. So nothing had really happened, no one would ever know, and she would never see him again.

So cheered was Lady Juliette by this clear thinking that she frowned and rapped Skylark firmly with her crop. As a result, they reached the Duckmanton stables again in record time—and Tom Perkins did look—but, being wise in the ways of safety, said nothing.

Matilda did talk, but Juliette was oddly distracted, staring dreamily at herself in the dressing table mirror and paying little attention to her abigail's fussing. After a while, Mattie simply set her mouth and devoted herself to arranging Juliette's gleaming black curls, eventually interrupting her mistress's reverie by setting the brush down with a sharp clatter.

"Something's got into you tonight, Miss Julie," Mattie pronounced. "You look like mischief and no mistake!"

Juliette started guiltily. "I—I don't know what you're talking about, Mattie." She was angrily aware that she was blushing, and moved to the offensive. "Now see to my dress, or I'll be late."

Mattie sniffed, but softened when the amethyst satin was slipped over Juliette's head. "You do look a treat, and that's the truth, lovey," Mattie said as she fastened up the bodice.

Juliette surveyed herself in the pier glass. She'd fallen in love with the damasked satin at first sight and bought the entire bolt on the spot, ignoring Miss Althea Fonthill's efforts to interest her in a demure sprigged muslin instead. The obliging Madame Lambourne had made it up to Juliette's order: a short round dress over a sarsnet slip in a deeper violet, trimmed in crepe rouleaux edged with gilt tassels, finished with a demi-train. Juliette nodded with satisfaction and reached for the ostrich-plume ornament for her hair.

Then she paused. She didn't know a great deal about fashion; she knew only what she liked. But this was a country house party, no matter how fashionable. Perhaps a slightly simpler mode . . . ?

"The pearls, do you think, Mattie?" said Juliette hesitantly, setting down the feathers.

"Pearls!" cried Mattie, outraged. "With that lovely purple dress? Why, I'd die o'shame to turn you out so! What you wants with that is a bit o'color, Miss Juliette, and no argufying!" The abigail pulled a velvet box from the array on the dressing table. "There you are—Miss Sophia's amethysts.

Now you just slip those on and you'll be turned out all right and tight quick's the cat can lick her ear. And we'll hear no more about pearls, if you please, miss!"

Juliette stood docilely as Matilda fixed the ostrich plume aigrette in her hair and bedecked her with the amethyst set. Mattie was right, of course; the dress looked much better with the sparkling stones than it would have with the milky pearls. Juliette had dutifully studied the various periodicals during the past Season, but had been totally unable to see much difference between those outfits eulogized as bang up to the knocker and those apostrophized as perfect quizzes. But Matilda and Mrs. Basingstoke had approved every stitch of her wardrobe; it was no business of Juliette's to worry over it.

By the time the Fonthill trunks had been unpacked, Juliette had returned from her ride and was dressing for dinner, as Althea discovered upon venturing out to the stables—the surest place, in Althea's experience, to find Lady Juliette at almost any time. Upon receiving this intelligence, and knowing from harsh experience how taxing one of Lady Juliettes *grandes toilettes* could be, she did not bother to seek out her friend, but prolonged her sojourn in the open air. There was more than enough time for one who followed a simpler mode to dress before dinner, and she was somehow loathe to return to the house. She would rather brave the uncertain weather for a space.

A house party was a delicate thing, and Althea, veteran of many, was not quite confident that Lady Ralph was clever enough to carry this one off—not with the incendiary Lady Juliette right in the middle. It would hardly matter who else Lady Ralph invited; and though Althea had been absent from Town for the later part of the Season, there had been nothing in Juliette's letters to indicate that she had formed a *tendre* for the shatterbrained Douglas Candlesby. Unfortunately, Althea was certain Juliette would not hesitate to say so—even, or possibly especially, to Douglas's doting mother. And that way lay only strife. If only Juliette were not so—so—out of the common way, Althea finished lamely. Ah, well, if talking paid no toll, how very much less use must thinking be?

While Althea stood lost in thought beneath the eaves of the stableyard mews, the faint drizzle had turned to an earnest soaking rain. By the time she was aware of this, it was far too late to cross the courtyard and preserve her slippers of glazed kid. As for her flowered muslin round dress and felt pelisse, they would require many hours of toil to return to their best looks. As Althea hesitated, trying to decide if waiting would gain her anything, a man on horseback appeared, making his way toward the stable with the dogged speed of the delayed guest. Althea ducked back inside to avoid being splashed by his passage and tucked herself out of the way as the newcomer rode in through the door.

He wore a soaking high-crowned beaver and had a muffler swathed about his face to protect him from the mud of the road. He vaulted down from the chestnut gelding's back and made vague gestures to the stablehands. Then he turned around.

"Good lord, Julie—what are you doing here?" the apparition demanded.

Althea drew back with a startled squeak.

"Oh, lord," said the stranger mournfully. "I thought you were my cousin." He removed his hat and shook it. Drops of water flew every which way.

He then unwound the sodden muffler, revealing spectacles solidly fogged by the weather. "Blast this rain! It makes it impossible to see anything. On closer inspection," he continued smoothly, removing the spectacles, "I see that you cannot possibly be my cousin Juliette, though I confess myself at a loss as to what any other female might be doing in the Duckmanton stables in this weather. I am Anthony Devereaux, by the way; Lady Juliette is my cousin." He blinked at her with mild blue eyes and appeared to await further developments.

"*You* are Juliette's cousin Anthony?" Althea blurted out before she could help herself. Cousin Anthony had figured in Juliette's disjointed narratives as a harmless yet inoffensive lunatic given to bizarre pursuits. To hear his cousin tell it, he existed only to devil Juliette with his good example, and was so nondescript as to be almost invisible to the naked eye.

Althea saw that she had allowed Lady Juliette's prejudices to mislead her; though she could not on this acquaintance pronounce with any certainty on his sanity, to Althea's eyes Mr. Anthony Percival St. Devereaux Devereaux was quite a well-looking man indeed. The blond hair plastered wetly to his high broad forehead with rain was the unimpeachable yellow of flax, his eyes were of a pellucid Wedgewood blue, and the mud-spattered boots and the well-used riding coat visible beneath the cape were of excellent quality, yet commonplace. Any interesting eccentricities he might possess were disguised, at least for the moment.

Althea sighed again, this time with relief.

Mr. Devereaux also sighed, with resignation. "By your air of stunned surprise, I gather that you know Lady Juliette and she has once again been telling tales of her idiot cousin. Tell me, has she arrived yet? I came on ahead of my coach, hoping to arrive before she did and, er, head her off; but perhaps I'm too late. Oh, and delighted to make your acquaintance, Miss—?"

"I am Miss Fonthill," said Althea. "Althea Fonthill—my mama and sister and I are Lady Ralph's guests—and I am so very glad to make your acquaintance, Mr. Devereaux."

"Oh, dear," said Mr. Devereaux, lines of worry creasing his brow. "I'd be flattered, but I've been acquainted with my cousin Juliette since she was born. In fact, I arrive upon the wings of wrath—not to mention the express wishes of Madame Solange Devereaux, of whom you may also have heard—to restore my erring cousin to the familial bosom before Juliette develops another pressing engagement. Now I know I am going to be sorry I asked, but isn't that why I'm here?"

"I—of course it is," said Althea, a bit staggered by all this airy persiflage. "And Juliette is here—that is, she is dressing for dinner, and. . . . You did hear about Juliette's Season, did you not?"

Mr. Devereaux seemed to take this conversational detour in good part. "Miss Fonthill, I shall be brutally frank," said Mr. Devereaux setting his still-dripping hat back upon his lank hair. "I am an abject coward, and when I heard that Juliette was to make her come-out this Season, I straightaway discovered a project that would take me to the far end of the country for at least six months. I managed to remain in blissful ignorance until Madame—that is, our Great-aunt Solange—wrote to me at Chaceley a fortnight since, having ferreted out— if one may apply such a word to one's relative— Juliette's current location and demanded Juliette's immediate retrieval. One doesn't lightly disobey the royal command, so here I am."

"Oh my," said Althea inadequately, having formed a good idea of Juliette's probable response to such a plan. "But—oh!—you are soaked, and it *is* time to change for dinner. That is—"

"Oh, I imagine I am expected, Miss Fonthill. Madame did write, and put the fear of God into Lady Ralph, I daresay. Let us go up to the house; I would offer you my arm, but you'd be soaked."

"I shall be soaked anyway by the time we reach the house, Mr. Devereaux," said Althea as she took his arm, "so you see you need have no qualms."

Mr. Devereaux looked as if he most sincerely doubted that statement, but forebore to say so, and meekly allowed Miss Fonthill to escort him from the stables.

Lady Ralph, it developed, had been expecting Anthony Devereaux while hoping he wouldn't arrive— since his arrival meant, perforce, a truncation of her matrimonial campaign. Still, she bore his presence in good part, and had even provided accommodation for him in the dizzying heights of bachelor country. Anthony, looking even more apprehensive, allowed himself to be taken away for drying, hoping that his trunks would arrive soon, and Althea went off to dress for dinner, hoping she could contrive a moment to warn Juliette of her cousin's arrival.

By the time the Marquess of Barham reached Duckmanton he had almost convinced himself that he was the damndest fool in Christendom—and probably in heathen lands as well. Had he had the least sense, he would have ridden up to the beautiful young lady, said, "Forgive the intrusion, ma'am, but do you know the way to Duckmanton?"—and, ten to one, been here an hour ago.

Yes, it was high time he began behaving less like a character from the pages of a lurid novel. Of course, if he hadn't, he would have denied himself a very pleasant moment's diversion indeed. So which was, in fact, the foolish course? Jack decided to let the question stand for the time being, and bent his energies to the task of persuading the lackey who opened the doors of Duckmanton—and very peculiar doors they were, too, looking more suitable for a Venetian palazzo than an English manor—that he was, indeed, expected. The footman, apparently unnerved by the sight of a dripping wet Figure of Romance on the threshold, promptly referred the matter to that most impressive personage, the butler, whose business it properly was to deal with the unexpected.

Jack's assurance, his title, and his signet ring had been reason enough for the butler to grant him the honor of a parlor with a fire, even if his lordship *had* chosen to ride up sopping wet and with his luggage tied on behind his saddle. The Quality were well-known belowstairs to be eccentric.

Within a very few minutes Douglas Candlesby bounded into the room, volubly protesting his delight at Jack's arrival.

"Barham! By heaven—here you are! What an amazing piece of luck!"

"Considering your directions, I call it a miracle," said Jack, continuing to warm his hands at the cheerful fire.

Douglas disregarded this, rambling on happily. "Good thing you took me up on my invitation, Barham—devilish good. Mama's gotten another maggot into her head about getting me spliced—she takes that notion every once in a while, you know—and she's invited a houseful of people *and* the Devereaux. Thinks she'll catch me on the sly, home turf and all—all very well, if you like being dictated to as if you were a dashed troop of horse, Barham, which I don't above half! Mind, she's very pretty and all that if you like that sort of thing, but damme, Barham, a fellow's got to stand up for himself, and I don't want any wife of mine always giving orders as if she knows best. Not that she doesn't," Douglas added fairmindedly. "Juliette, I mean—knows a great deal—farming, mostly, though, and I *ask* you, Barham—At any rate, I've got a plan in train that'll nobble her conkers, so to speak. Mama, that is. Don't think Juliette fancies me above half, you know."

"How odd in her," said Jack dryly. He hadn't followed more than a few words of Douglas's speech, but those had been quite enough. A highly respectable house party, complete with hopeful damsels! Good God, Douglas must have been mad to invite him here at such a time. Jack didn't wish to put Lady Ralph Candlesby to the disagreeable task of ordering him out of her house. "Well, I shan't stand between you and any conker-nobbling you have in mind, Candlesby. Just give me a bed for the night and I'll be on my way tomorrow."

"What? But you've just arrived! Can't be running off like that."

Jack sighed. "Candlesby, do try thinking some time—I'm sure it would be good for you. I won't be wanted if there's to be a houseful of young ladies—*and* an heiress, too."

"But why not?" It was one of Mr. Candlesby's more—and less—endearing characteristics that any information he found unwelcome or uninteresting could not be imparted to him by any act of will whatsoever. After a long day in the saddle, the Marquess of Barham felt unequal to the task of trying to explain why the presence of such a notorious personage as himself would be in the least unwelcome to Mr. Candlesby's mama and her guests.

A practical man, Jack abandoned the attempt. "What can I be but thankful for your kindness, then? Oh—and speaking of young ladies, I met a little piece of perfection hacking cross-country near here. Little bit of a thing, big green eyes, perilously high in the instep, rides a nervy gray screw—"

"Near here?" Douglas's brow furrowed. "Well—"

"Oh, come now, man, think! She must live around here somewhere!"

After some contemplation, Douglas shook his head. "No one like that around here—unless you mean Deb Templeton—but she ain't even out yet—and I wouldn't say she's a little bit of a thing, myself. Besides, her eyes are blue."

Jack reconsidered his previous notion of turning Mr. Candlesby upside down and shaking him until something sensible was produced, then acknowledged defeat, at least for the moment. "It's my dryad or nothing, Candlesby," he said lightly, rejecting the unknown Deborah Templeton out of hand. "And I never romance schoolgirls, especially if their eyes are blue. As I'm staying, can I prevail upon you to either find me a room or get me a brandy? I'm chilled to the bone."

"Oh, by jove! Yes, at once—you'll have to dress for dinner, you know—won't Mama be pleased?"

"Oh, by jove, won't she just?" Jack murmured

sardonically, but sarcasm was wasted on the impervious Mr. Candlesby. He strolled after Douglas into the main hallway, absently noting out of the corner of his eye that a woman in a hideous purple satin dress was descending the stairs. As he put a hand on the banister and his foot on the first stair, a soft gasp made him pause and look up.

There on the stairs above him, poised between one step and the next, gloved hand to her mouth, green eyes wide with horror, was his enchanting little wood-nymph.

"Oh, what luck!" said Douglas Candlesby happily. "Lady Juliette, I want you to meet a most particular friend of mine—Marquess of Barham. Jack, let me make you known to Lady Juliette Devereaux—one I was telling you about," he added in a confidential undertone.

Juliette stared.

Jack smiled.

Juliette, trapped, had no choice but to descend. She came slowly down the steps, feeling a hot tide of color sweep over her face as the Marquess of Barham's lazy, knowing smile widened and he looked her over carefully. No gentleman should look at a lady like that; it gave her the oddest feeling—as if she wore nothing but her chemise.

She reached the foot of the stairs and Barham bent over her kid-gloved hand, carrying it to his lips. "Well met, fair—"

Alarmed, Juliette tried to extract her hand from his grasp, but without success; his grip was too firm.

"—Lady Juliette," he finished smoothly, kissing her hand and then releasing it.

Warm amber eyes seemed to mock her consternation; the dark brigand's face, so far above her own that she had to tilt back her head to look at him, made Juliette, normally the least fanciful of women, think giddily of Elizabethan privateers. And the relaxed yet competent way he moved, for all his muscular height, put her forcibly in mind of a large, lazy tomcat.

"Now you say 'good evening, Lord Barham,' " he prompted helpfully.

Juliette blushed again, and was startled by an unladylike impulse to laugh. "Good—good evening, Lord Barham," she said, feeling rather short of breath.

"I call this a considerable improvement on our first, er, conversation, don't you?" Barham grinned and lightly touched his cheek, and Juliette suddenly realized that the livid welt under his fingers must have been made by her riding crop, and that this was indeed the man who had mishandled her so vilely.

"You deserved it," she responded, stiffening.

Barham looked at her contemplatively. "It was worth it," he said at last.

Juliette's indignant gasp was covered by Douglas Candlesby's sudden contribution to the discussion. "D'you know Lady Juliette already, Barham? But—" Douglas stared at Juliette as if seeing her for the first time. Then, suddenly struck, he said, "I say, Barham, you don't mean to say that all that rot about dryads—well, I mean to say, Lady Juliette's got green eyes, but she don't live around here!"

Barham, obviously in the grip of some strong emotion, regarded young Mr. Candlesby for a moment, then sighed. "*If* I said, Candlesby, that while riding I saw a beautiful young lady at a distance and wished that it were proper for me to discover her direction, and *if*, further, I so far forgot myself as to remark that she seemed—at a distance—to be as graceful as a wood-nymph, propriety dictates that such a conversation be forgotten when the lady in question is discovered to be a fellow house-guest." He paused, then added warily, "Is it too much to hope that that's quite clear?"

"What?" Douglas thought for a moment, then his brow cleared. "Oh, by jove, yes. Mum's the word, Barham!"

Juliette was once more torn between consternation and a fit of the giggles. However, alarm won out. "Do you mean to say—"

"That I, too, am residing under this hospitable roof? I'm afraid so, Lady Juliette." Barham looked her up and down once more, raising his eyebrows as he did so. "However, I'm sure we can contrive to be comfortable together."

Douglas enthusiastically seconded this. "Barham's ripping good fun, Lady Juliette, and just the fellow you want for—well, that is to say, *you* wouldn't particularly—but on the other hand—"

Barham gently shouldered Douglas out of the way and tucked Juliette's hand through his arm. "And yet he's been allowed to grow up," he said, grinning down at Juliette. "The age of miracles is still with us. Shall we join the others? I'm sure it won't make the least difference to your mother, Candlesby, if I don't change for dinner."

In the drawing room, Lady Ralph Candlesby was so appalled by the sight of Juliette's escort that she could spare Juliette's plumes and parure only one incredulous glance before taking firm possession of her and whisking her away from the Marquess of Barham. Once fixed on a settee by the fire, however, Lady Ralph became oddly reticent.

"Lady Ralph, did you wish to speak to me?" Juliette said at last.

"Well, my dear—and you know I do not wish to meddle, but . . ." Here Lady Ralph fidgeted with her fan a great deal. ". . . but as you've no mother to advise you—well—I'm truly sorry to have to say this, but . . ." Lady Ralph's voice dropped, as if she were about to reveal high treason, or worse. ". . . but I'm very much afraid that Lord Barham is, well, not good *ton*. I fear I cannot, with propriety, tell you more. Of course, he is a duke's son, but when one considers—I cannot imagine what in heaven's name Douglas was about, to invite him here— But as you know already, Lady Juliette, my Douglas has an open, generous heart and is too charitable to see defects in others."

Juliette thought, rather, that Douglas was too shatterbrained to see anything whatsoever. However, she was too intrigued to argue the point; when Lady Ralph Candlesby refused to speak ill of a person, his sins must be black indeed. But when she pressed her hostess for more information, that good lady only shook her head sadly.

"You know I abhor gossip, my dear, so I will only say that Lord Barham has brought most of his misfortunes upon himself, and his poor father—well, Owlsthorne has risen above it, and I can only be truly thankful that *my* son is no such thing— although I'm sure I should never cast him off even if he *were*!"

Juliette untangled this speech, then gazed wide-eyed at Lady Ralph. "But—good heavens, ma'am, do you mean that he is 'Bad Barham'? His Grace of Owlsthorne's son? However did Douglas make his acquaintance?"

"It was in Town, of course—as if I hadn't told

Lord Ralph that no good would come of sending such an innocent boy up to Town alone. But heaven knows I don't wish to keep him in leading-strings at his age!" Lady Ralph sighed heavily. "Little did I realize the dear boy's natural high-mindedness would leave him prey to the most ineligible—it is obvious, my dear, that he cries out for a woman's care—and meanwhile the Marquess of Barham is among us, and who knows what he may do?"

Juliette's glance flew, unbidden, across the room to where the Marquess of Barham was deep in conversation with Douglas Candlesby. As if he felt her gaze, Barham looked up and regarded her with that smile that hinted so disconcertingly of lazy warmth and strange delights. Furious with herself, Juliette jerked her chin in the air and turned her attention back to her hostess. Yes, Juliette knew very well what the Marquess of Barham might do.

Anything.

And it was exceedingly vexatious to find the thought so exciting.

Jack, wryly conscious of Lady Ralph's well-bred horror, had fully appreciated her strategic removal of temptation from his path. "So that's the Devereaux heiress—and you won't have her?" said Jack. "You astound me, Candlesby."

"She won't have me, come to that," Douglas said firmly. "As for why not, I've told you already—addresses you as if you were a public meeting and gives you the devil of a lecture. Too headstrong by half—galloping in the park—and that's not the worst of it."

"I look forward to hearing every detail," said Jack. "And if the worst isn't her clothes, it should be. Why the devil is she dressed up like St. Audrey's Fair?"

"Dresses like a Cit puffing off her blunt," Douglas agreed. "But can't criticize a lady's clothes—not the thing. She wouldn't like it. None of my business, anyway."

"Well, someone should make it their business. It's a shame to wrap a face like that in tinsel garlands. Christian charity alone demands the instant removal of Lady Juliette's clothes—for the purest of motives, of course," Jack finished smoothly.

"Here, now, Barham . . ." Douglas began uncomfortably.

"My profuse and insincere apologies," said Jack. "But by heaven, purple satin and plumes—!"

"Not so loud!" Douglas begged. "Once she takes an idea in her head there's nothing for it but she carries it out—and you, too, if you're standing too near!"

Jack looked over to Lady Juliette, her Dresden-delicate figure outraged by that hideous dress. At that moment she glanced towards him, her expression intrigued. Knowing what sort of scandalous gossip must have engendered that look, Jack smiled; Juliette ostentatiously turned her back. Jack raised his eyebrows. "I think it would be very amusing to give Lady Juliette ideas, Candlesby."

At this interesting juncture, however, Lord Ralph Candlesby arrived, bearing still more members of the house party with him in the pious hope they might all go in to dinner soon. His wife, their much-tried hostess, promptly rose to her feet and rushed to greet them, talking all the while. Lady Ralph's air was that of one flustered and buffeted by circumstance, but gamely attempting to deal with harsh blows of uncertain fate. "Here you all are!"

she exclaimed brightly. "Not to say that *all* for I'm sure I don't know where he might be, Lady Juliette—and I'm sure we all know each other, but let me make you known to Mr. and Miss Gressingham, Lord Barham, for I am sure you will have a great deal in common!"

The introduction of Miss Gressingham drove whatever questions Lady Ralph's effusion might have raised from Juliette's mind; Juliette put her fan to her lips and uttered a very faintly audible groan.

Miss Jerusha Gressingham was the sole support and protection of her young and innocent brother Robert, as anyone unacquainted with her tragic story was sure to discover within a very few moments of making her acquaintance.

Robert Gressingham was perhaps better-known in some circles as "Lightfoot Bobby," due to his rather eccentric habit of taking to the rooftops when in his cups. This taste for steeplejacking had won him a certain amount of fame in London club-land, but its indulgence had done nothing to render more stable an already volatile and erratic temperament. Many people—even Mr. Bartholomew Rainford, that dedicated bachelor and arbiter of true elegance—had said that a good marriage would be the making of him, but it was unlikely that Lightfoot Bobby wished to be so made, and there was no one to compel him. Mr. Gressingham's father, a dedicated soldier, had been carried off in the same Peninsular battle that took the life of his sister Jerusha's betrothed; Mrs. Gressingham, who had followed her husband, was carried off soon after of the cholera.

Miss Jerusha Gressingham, then aged twenty-four, had instantly abandoned all ambitions for herself and devoted herself to her young brother, discouraging all offers for her hand and heart so that she might make a home for him. It was difficult to remember now that Jerusha was only six years Robert's senior, so firmly had she embraced the spinster state. Her glossy dark hair was pulled firmly back under unbecoming caps; now that her mourning, which had lasted a full two years, was long over she favored for her gowns a shade some wag had dubbed "Gressingham Green"—a trying shade of chartreuse that turned her slightly sallow complexion quite yellow. In fairness to Miss Gressingham, the color had been all the crack some eight seasons before; Miss Gressingham's wardrobe, loyal, as was Miss Gressingham, to the past, was expensively and aggressively dowdy.

Nothing could be more uplifting than the sight of Jerusha Gressingham's devotion to her brother—and nothing safer than Jerusha herself—to an anxious mama wishful of filling a house party with a proper balance of ages and sexes without putting overmuch temptation before a wayward son. Thus Lady Ralph had reasoned when Douglas has proposed the inclusion of his great friend Bobs Gressingham. Lady Ralph had included both Gressinghams on her guest list with only a momentary pang over Jerusha's decidedly Methodistic leanings.

Never, however, had Lady Ralph expected to be actively grateful for Miss Gressingham's presence. But with the Marquess of Barham looming among them in a fashion that—well! Lady Ralph was sure she didn't know *how* to describe it—and the man hadn't even dressed for dinner, which she was sure was understandable, but still—well, she was exceedingly thankful that she would have dear Jerusha's undoubted virtue to help her bear up under this trial. So it was with a note of real relief that Lady Ralph greeted the new arrivals.

"Oh, and *here* is dear Mr. Devereaux and dear Miss Fonthill," Lady Ralph gushed on happily. "*Now* we may all perhaps be a little comfortable!"

Juliette was first stunned, then appalled, to meet the eyes of her cousin Tony. Juliette instantly and correctly assessed the reason for Anthony's presence. And to see him with Althea Fonthill, whom she had accounted her friend, on his arm—! The accusing look she sent the traitorous Althea was quite enough to make that damsel blush. Reckless of the proprieties, Juliette swept to Anthony's side in the midst of the bustle of going in to dinner, cutting across Jerusha's bow in much the same fashion that a racing yacht will outmaneuver a ship of state. The burning look Miss Gressingham directed at Juliette's back was lost on no one but Juliette herself.

"Tony! What are you doing here?" Juliette demanded in a preemptory undertone.

Mr. Devereaux's eyes widened slightly at the sight of Juliette's *toilette*. "Why Anthony," he said, "how lovely to see you again. Hello, Julie; I see you're keeping—ahem!—well."

"Oh, do be serious! You cannot have come to take me to Fakenham—say you have not! I won't go!"

"For heaven's sake, Julie—keep your voice down. How long did you expect to fox Madame, anyway? But we can talk about it later—now run along to dinner like a good girl—I daresay Candlesby is perishing to escort you!" Removing Althea's hand temporarily from his arm, he turned Juliette around toward Douglas and gave her an encouraging push.

But it was somehow Barham's arm she ended on, and not Douglas's. Unaccountably Mr. Candlesby had so far forgot himself as to company Miss Isobel, who everyone knew had no fortune to speak of, and Jack was not slow to take advantage of this lapse. Juliette, defeated, looked wildly about for aid, but Jack tightened his grasp on her arm and hurried her on before rescue could arrive.

Dinner was a difficult meal. Mr. Gressingham, upon discovering Barham's identity, promptly embarked upon a recitation of the notable incidents of the Marquess's career—without regard for the fact that most of them were far too warm for mixed company.

Anthony Devereaux responded to this solecism with a line of amiable chatter that might be witty, but was definitely incomprehensible; Lightfoot Bobby did not attempt to respond in kind, but continued on his own blithely damning conversational path. Lady Ralph was horrified; Miss Gressingham made vain efforts to curb her brother; Juliette stared at her plate and tried to pretend that she wasn't in the least interested in the scandalous exploits of the Marquess of Barham.

Fortunately for the sensibilities of the ladies, Mr. Candlesby soon added his contribution to the discussion by attempting to correct what he considered Mr. Gressingham's misapprehensions concerning certain of the events being retailed. But as Mr. Candlesby promptly became entangled in contradictions, second thoughts, and self-corrections, he was quite unable to finish even one sentence, making it possible for Lord Ralph to turn the conversation to the safer topic of Barham's military service.

"Yes, I must admit I was with Wellington in Portugal," Jack said in response to Lord Ralph's query.

"Joined early in '07—well, sir, it was that or Oxford, so I cravenly chose the easier course."

"Rode with the Lights, didn't you?" said Mr. Gressingham eagerly. "I wish I'd been there to see the fun!"

At a generous estimate, Jack thought that the carefree Mr. Gressingham would have lasted about fifteen minutes in the horror that had been Wellington's Peninsular campaign. However, he mildly agreed that it was the devil of a shame that life was so boring nowadays.

"The Lights?" Lord Ralph frowned. "You can't be serious, Barham—you must ride about eighteen, surely?"

"I lied about my weight," said Jack with a perfectly straight face.

Lord Ralph looked taken aback, then laughed. "Lied about his weight, did he—very witty, eh, Helena?"

"Very," said Lady Ralph weakly.

"If it's Barham's wit we're talking about," Mr. Gressingham began portentously, "there's a tale I heard from—"

There was a faint gasp from the much-tried Lady Ralph. "Robert, dear . . ." Miss Gressingham said in gentle reproof.

"No, no, very funny, nothing to distress anyone in it." Robert Gressingham leaned forward confidentially. "Anyway, it was at the Newmarket races last year, and—"

Jack set down his wineglass and looked hard at Mr. Gressingham, who subsided, flushing quite red. "All common knowledge, old man," he muttered.

"In that case, it hardly needs repetition, does it?" said Jack, and continued smoothly, "Speaking of the races, do you favor Wrangler or Sultan in the

St. Leger next week, Mr. Gressingham? I fancy you must have some interest in the outcome."

As the St. Leger, which was to be run in Doncaster on September 20th, promised to be one of the most hotly-contested events of the year, this was proved a most effective diversion. The merits of the two rival racing stallions were fiercely debated by all save Lady Ralph and Miss Gressingham, even including Anthony Devereaux, who defended Sultan's supremacy with a great deal of common sensicality. The race carried the diners through the second course and the dessert, and deposited them safely at the end of the meal, when the ladies retired to the quiet of the drawing room.

There Miss Gressingham pounced upon her hostess. "Lady Ralph, I do sincerely feel for you! You may imagine my surprise at seeing Lord Barham under *this* roof." She smiled graciously, which did not appreciably lighten her habitually wistful expression. "But then I realized how it must have been. Young men are so thoughtless, are they not? My Robert is just the same."

Lady Ralph was plainly torn between agreeing with Miss Gressingham and defending her son from all charges, and Juliette saw her chance. She wanted more information about Lord Barham, and Miss Gressingham, who went everywhere, knew everyone, and told everything, would provide it. Abandoning Althea and Isobel, she made her way to Miss Gressingham's side.

"I, too, was surprised to see Lord Barham here," she said, with perfect truth.

"When one considers . . ." Miss Gressingham cast a sidelong glance at her hostess.

Juliette hastily added, "But of course I know very little about him—although one does hear tales . . ."

Miss Isobel, divining Juliette's plan, added her encouragement to Juliette's, despite a minatory look from Althea.

Miss Gressingham rose to the lure, leaning forward confidentially in her chair as the ladies clustered about her. "My dear Lady Juliette—and Miss Fonthill, of course—I'm sure none of them are fit for our ears," she began, then went on, with no apparent notion of incongruity, to retail as much of the scandalous history of the notorious Marquess of Barham as was possible in a few minutes. "Well, to begin with, you must know that Barham stole his mother's jewels to buy his colors! At least, so I have heard, although I quite forget where. I have the wretchedest memory! However, I *do* know that he was sent down from Eton, and ran off in the most unfeeling way to enlist in the army. It killed his poor mother—they say she died of a broken heart—and though she begged him to come to her on her deathbed, he refused."

"Oh, but my dear! You must not say such things—even if they are true." Lady Ralph looked quite distrait.

Miss Gressingham sighed, and looked penitent. "I am sorry, Lady Ralph, but you know I never mean anything I say—and certainly none of it can be a secret, for all the world knows I cannot remember to keep one!" Miss Gressingham prided herself on her frankness. "But I am very worried on Robert's account—such a dissipated influence cannot be good for him. And he is so headstrong," she finished with another sigh. "Oh, and you, too, should have a care, Lady Juliette. Lord Barham is notorious for his attentions—and you do have a great deal of money."

This shattering lack of tact made Lady Ralph

flutter nervously. Miss Gressingham meekly apologized, then added, as if in duty bound, "So of course it is very easy to understand what Lord Barham is doing here, after all."

"You mean he is a fortune-hunter, as well as a rake, I suppose," said Juliette flatly. She was tired of roundaboutations and sly hints; Jerusha's tale was too lurid to ring completely true to one so hard-headed as Juliette.

"And that, of course," Miss Gressingham finished dolefully, and with a complete lack of consideration for her hostess's sensibilities, "is why he is not received by the best families."

"Or even by my own," drawled a sardonically amused voice. Lord Barham strolled into the room, regarding the tableau-like grouping of the ladies with an expression that made Juliette wonder just how long he'd been listening. He paused just behind Juliette's chair, looked Jerusha Gressingham up and down, and added, "Although many people are still delighted to receive me with open . . . arms."

Miss Gressingham turned an unbecoming shade of scarlet, and hastily opened her fan to shield herself against the contamination of Lord Barham's gaze. Lady Ralph uttered something confused and unintelligible, and Barham's mouth quirked as he looked down at Juliette.

"Of course," he went on with a rueful smile, "not everyone has such excellent taste." Here he raised his fingers to the mark her whip had left on his face.

Juliette grew hot at this reminder of their encounter in the woods; she looked down at her hands, then up, and saw the spark she had known would be there catch and kindle in his golden eyes.

"Oh, Douglas, there you are! Do go and tell Wiggins to set up the table—I fancy a game of whist will be just the diversion we need!" Lady Ralph's breathlessly agitated voice was a rude shock.

"Oh, absolutely," Barham agreed blandly, turning to his harassed hostess. Juliette wondered if she imagined the undertone of laughter.

"Although it will only be a *friendly* game, Lord Barham, and not at all what you are used to!" finished Lady Ralph valiantly.

"That, dear lady," said Barham, turning from Juliette to bow low over Lady Ralph's hand, "is more than I dare to hope."

Juliette might have stayed to carry the fight to the foe, but Althea pinched her quite hard on the arm and carried the three of them off to the safety of the pianoforte. Once safely established on the piano bench, far from the eyes of the wicked Marquess, Althea rounded on her friend.

"Oh, Juliette," she said, "how could you?"

"I am sure I do not know what you mean," said Juliette, with a guilty toss of the head. Althea sighed.

"You know very well that encouraging Miss Gressingham to gossip—and on such a topic—can only do the greatest of harm. And to have Lord Barham himself overhear—I was ready to sink! Had Mama known he was to be here, we would not have come, but it is too late now, and I suppose we need not be much in his company, after all," Althea finished philosophically. "But what *do* you suppose he is doing here?"

"Lord Barham is a great friend of Doug—of Mr. Candlesby—or so I have heard," Isobel offered.

"We shall have to avoid him without causing Lady Ralph any more distress than she must already feel." Althea paused, regarding Juliette curiously. "I saw you go in to dinner with him, Juliette. You must be on your guard. Miss Gressingham for once spoke no more than the truth when she called him a fortune-hunter. Everyone knows he is that close to being ruined."

"I do not think Lady Ralph wished to see him here," said Juliette considering.

"I have never met a rake before," piped up Isobel happily.

"No," said Althea cuttingly, "and you never shall. A shared roof need not constitute a formal introduction, after all. Belle, do be sensible," she added coaxingly. "You would not wish to know a person such as Lord Barham."

"He is so very handsome!" said Isobel provocatively, as if considering the matter carefully.

"Well, it is plain that he thinks so," said Juliette sharply. "He looks just like Lord Byron's Corsair," she added, as if this were a major failing on Lord Barham's part. "His eyes are quite golden. It is very odd."

Althea looked surprised at this poetical reference from Juliette; Isobel said eagerly, "Does he have 'a laughing devil in his sneer'? Oh, how exciting!"

"He does," snapped Juliette, flushing slightly. "And—and he is the most vexing and vile man alive!" she said roundly.

Althea Fonthill regarded her friend intently for a moment. "Juliette, you cannot—you positively cannot—have formed a *tendre* for him!"

"Althea! I don't know what you mean," said Juliette, tossing her head. "He is a shameless, despicable creature, and I'm sure I dislike him more than anyone else I've ever met!"

Miss Fonthill did not look much reassured by

this, but merely said in her quiet way, "Well, if he is so disagreeable, then he cannot be a very *successful* rake, surely, and we have nothing to worry about. And besides, while Belle is very lovely indeed, I am not, and so shall be perfectly safe from the wicked Marquess. But you and Belle had best have trays in your rooms from now on," she finished with a mischievous smile that crinkled the corners of her eyes and made her look quite pretty herself.

"I shall not have a tray in my room!" said Isobel hotly. "I shall attach the wicked Marquess and bring him to his knees!"

"Oh, hush, Belle—if Mama heard you going on in that fashion it would bring on a spasm for certain! Attach the wicked Marquess—what fustian! Let us talk of something pleasant, rather. How nice it is to see you again, Juliette; we did not hope for that, did we, Belle? When Mama had the invitation from Lady Ralph, it was to make up a party of young people—as she said it—to amuse Mr. Candlesby. I think it was to keep him from going to Doncaster, for he can hardly be loitering about the racing course if he is here."

"Oh, you know it is only my fortune that makes me a desirable guest, and *I* think the truth of the matter is that Lady Ralph actually thinks I might marry Douglas! And I confess I was delighted to be asked here! Oh, Thea, I have the most famous news!"

"Marry—marry Douglas?" Isobel said, her voice quavering a trifle. "Is—is that your news, Lady Juliette?"

"Certainly not, for *he* is quite the silliest young man I have ever met! But it is known that Marcus Templeton is selling off a number of his young horses, and I am going there tomorrow to buy stock for Chaceley! Do say you wish to go with me!"

Althea, wise in the ways of Juliette Devereaux, braved this suggestion without a quiver. "I think not, Juliette—for it would not be very kind if we were all to desert Lady Ralph in her hour of need. But is not your cousin Anthony come to take you home? Surely you will not have time to buy horses."

Juliette set her jaw. "Tony may try if he likes to drag me off—but I am not going. And I will tell him so, just as soon as possible!"

At this juncture Lady Ralph, observing her guests having an interesting time in a corner, descended upon them with the news that Douglas was desolate for lack of company, but too high-minded to force himself on them. The result of this was that Isobel bounced up, announcing herself ready to bear Douglas's company, and Lady Ralph, after looking hopefully and in vain at Lady Juliette, was forced to accompany quite the wrong person back to her beloved son's side.

Althea and Juliette, left to themselves, spoke of the Season and other matters of concern to unmarried young ladies. The Fonthills had rusticated in Harrowgate until the end of the Season drove the upper Ten Thousand back to their estates; they had then followed much the same course as Juliette, visiting among such of their connections as could welcome into complaisance the company of an impoverished widow with two marriageable daughters.

"And Mama is cross as crabs about poor Isobel," observed Althea in an undertone, "for it was the purest ill-fortune that she should make her come-out in a Season with so many beautiful heiresses on the marriage mart. But talking pays no toll, and we must hope to make a better showing next year."

"Poor Isobel," said Juliette sympathetically. "But how can you bear to talk of your sister as if she were a blood mare to be shown to advantage to fetch the highest price?"

Althea sighed. She was fond of Lady Juliette, but there was no denying that she was, at times, far too forthright. However, she merely said, "It is Mama who worries, Juliette, for she thinks it only fair that I marry before Isobel, and says I do not take enough trouble with myself. But it is the way of the world is it not, that there are more women to marry than men to marry them?"

"But dearest Althea—you have been out for two Seasons—you must have had offers?"

"Yes," said Miss Fonthill simply. "But you know, dear Juliette, that if I marry I must marry well."

Juliette set her chin firmly. "Well, and there is no reason you should not. You would make any man the best of wives."

Althea smiled, and looked across the room at Isobel, and shook her head. Lady Juliette Devereaux, with beauty and rich estates, deferred to from her cradle by the local gentry surrounding Chaceley, could not possibly understand the painstaking lures and stratagems practiced by a family whose only hope of recouping their fortunes was to marry a pretty daughter to advantage. Nor could she understand how little chance a girl like Althea, who had little to recommend her in the way of looks, and nothing at all in the way of fortune, had of attracting the interest of any man she could possibly bear to marry.

Juliette looked thoughtful, an expression that alarmed Althea; it usually presaged one of Lady

Juliette's attempts at solving problems with what she called practical common sense. "Oh, yes, you shall," she said with decision. "Someone may fall in love with you, after all."

"Oh, really Juliette!" said Althea tartly. "Whom do you suggest? Your Lord Barham? Do, I beg of you, have some sense! And if you are proposing yourself as matchmaker—well, if no one will look at me when Belle is beside me, how much less will they see me if you take her place?"

Juliette's mouth dropped open in honest surprise. "But Thea, I—oh, how does anyone ever marry?" she said in despair.

"I daresay it is arranged by their parents, as such things usually are. If Papa were still alive, perhaps both Belle and I should be brides by now." Althea did not look particularly cast down by the absence of this turn of events.

"We shall find someone for you, Althea, see if we don't," Juliette prophesied.

Althea looked both skeptical and slightly alarmed, but prudently said nothing more.

Juliette had intended to deal with Anthony this very evening, and not have him hanging over her visit to Duckmanton like a bird of ill-omen, but she found that her maddening cousin refused to be dealt with, closeting himself with the gentlemen of the party in a way that Juliette found most inconvenient. Juliette, never a one for late hours, found that the day's excitements had taken their toll and she was yawning before the tea-tray had been brought. Her hostess, seeing this, bundled her off to bed with a particularity Juliette was too sleepy to object to. She would deal with Anthony tomorrow.

Chapter
THREE

The next day dawned bright and clear, and Matilda, who brought gossip as an indispensable ancillary to morning chocolate and biscuits, presented Juliette with the intelligence that the rest of the Duckmanton house party was to arrive today and consist of a Lady Hawkchurch and her son—and was it true what Mr. Tony had told her, that they were to leave for Fakenham almost at once?

"No such thing," said Juliette roundly. "Tony has got it all muddled again, as usual. We shall be here some time—just as we planned."

She could easily imagine the look of horror on Madame's face upon beholding the Marquess of Barham making free of Duckmanton hospitality, and had no desire to be scolded for what was so patently not her fault in addition to what was. There must be some way to make Tony relent in his madcap scheme of dragging her back to Madame, and she would hit upon it while delaying her fate as long as possible. The day held other hopes than these, however, so Juliette hastily drank her chocolate and commanded Mattie to discover whether Mr. Candlesby was yet awake. "—for we are to ride to

Temple Down today, and I will not have him leaving me behind!"

At the breakfast table Juliette found herself with only Lady Ralph for company. Upon hearing her plan for the day, Lady Ralph pronounced the expedition to Temple Down just the thing to amuse "you two young people" and a blear-eyed and staring Douglas Candlesby was soon produced. It was plain to Juliette, at least, that much of the plan's charm lay in the extended period Juliette would be spending in Douglas's sole company.

"Mr. Candlesby, shouldn't we ask Mr. and Miss Gressingham and Lord Barham if they wish to inspect the Templeton stock as well?" said Juliette, crumbling a small bit of toast into a pile of even smaller crumbs. She had no desire for her cousin's company and hoped the omission of Anthony's name would not be noticed.

"I *very* much fear, Lady Juliette, that—well—" Lady Ralph sighed. "Lord Barham did not retire until *very* late, and you may trust me when I say that poor Mr. Gressingham—such an unhappy boy, and such a trial to his sister—will certainly not wish to be inspecting horses today. So you will have Douglas all to yourself, Lady Juliette, unless of course your cousin. . . ?"

"Oh, Anthony doesn't care particularly for horses—but how very disagreeable for you," said Juliette, hastily and slightly incoherently, as if her hostess's mode of speech were contagious. It took no great brainpower to interpret Lady Ralph's disclosures: the gentlemen had gone to bed very late and very foxed; doubtless they had been gaming as well. "But surely Miss Gressingham—?"

"Miss Gressingham," said Lady Ralph with great dignity, "cannot, of course, leave her brother. But

I am sure you will find adequate company in Douglas, and his great good sense can only be an asset to you." She beamed impartially upon the pair of them.

Juliette and Douglas regarded each other with identical blank expressions, equally outraged by the statement that Douglas had sense.

Due in large part to Lady Ralph's determination that Douglas should have Juliette all to himself, their departure from Duckmanton was accomplished with all the speed and efficiency even Juliette could have desired. As it was Dulcinea's conviction that she was still lame, and as Skylark was not at his best in strange company, it was decided to make the trip to Temple Down in one of the gigs. It did not take the strong-willed Juliette long to persuade Douglas that she should take the ribbons; she had much to say on the way and had no wish to be driven into a ditch while the amiable but absent-minded Mr. Candlesby considered his replies.

Once out of sight of the house, Juliette allowed the horse to slow its pace a trifle and tried subtly to broach a topic she found, if truth were to be told, even more engrossing than the prospect of obtaining some of the Templeton horses for Chaceley. But try though she might, it seemed impossible to introduce the subject casually; eventually Juliette abandoned the attempt in favor of a frontal attack.

"I have been wishing to ask you, Mr. Candlesby," she said abruptly, "how it is that you are on such terms with—with Lord Barham." It sounded awkward even to her own ears, and she was sure she was blushing; for the first time she was thankful for Douglas Candlesby's skimble-skamble brain.

"Barham? Oh, nothing odd in that." Douglas attempted to look wise. "I was by way of being able to help him out of what you might call a tight spot a couple of years back—and he hasn't forgotten. Jack's a decent chap."

"A tight spot?" Juliette echoed. "What sort of tight spot, Mr. Candlesby?"

Douglas waved a hand airily. "Oh, just the usual sort, don't you know. Nothing important—besides, nothing a lady should bother her pretty little head with."

"Oh, I see," said Juliette dryly. Her Season, unsatisfactory though it might have been, had at least taught her what vital topics men tended to consider both trivial and unfit for female ears. "You loaned him money."

"Good God!" said Douglas indignantly. "Of course I didn't! Besides, hadn't any to lend—m'father keeps me so devilish short. You'd think he hadn't an idea of the expenses a gentleman incurs keeping up a decent establishment, but no, he— At any rate, all I did was sign a couple of notes for him. Jack, I mean. So you see."

"Notes?" said Juliette uneasily. "But what kind of notes?"

Douglas shrugged. "Oh, some sort of annuity, that sort of thing. Forget the name, but you only pay the interest now, you see, and the rest don't come due for years—actually, not until m'father— which *will* be years, since he's in prime twig. But females," he finished grandly, "never understand finances."

Juliette, who understood them very well indeed, pulled up sharply, bringing the gig to a rocking halt. "Douglas!" she gasped. "You haven't signed *post-obit bonds*?"

"Here, now, watch what you're about!" said Douglas, grasping the side of the gig inelegantly. "Why yes, that's it. Of course, Jack'll settle 'em if he steps into his father's shoes first, and he's bound to. Besides, when Duckmanton's mine I'll have plenty of scratch," he finished cheerfully.

Juliette stared at him in horror. Douglas had signed post-obit bonds for the Marquess of Barham. That meant that Douglas Candlesby had guaranteed an annuity to a moneylender in exchange for a lump sum in cash paid to Jack; Douglas would pay only the interest on the amount during his father's lifetime, but upon Lord Ralph's death the entire principal would fall due at once. It was the most ruinous of courses, and all too common. Juliette's father had once roused himself from his books long enough to lecture her severely and unnecessarily on the wickedness of selling annuities for cash—for unless one bought back the note, the unwary borrower found himself paying annuities that cost many times the original amount obtained.

With a sinking heart, Juliette realized why the infamous Marquess of Barham tolerated an engaging nonentity like Douglas Candlesby. Douglas was too idiotically innocent to realize that he was facing complete bankruptcy; he seemed to have escaped the nearly universal knowledge that the only thing Barham would inherit from his father would be ruinous debts. Barham had callously allowed Douglas to sign away his birthright, and Juliette would not have thought it of him—

Her eyes stung, and she shook her head angrily, suddenly and furiously aware that she had, half-unknowing, been indulging in the most foolish of fancies. One could not reform a rake, all the world knew that—and to be cozened by an engaging smile and a certain warmth in the eyes— Well, doubtless many others had felt the same, to their scathe, but Lady Juliette Devereaux would not swell their number!

She took a deep breath, about to order Douglas to reveal all this to his father immediately, when hooves drumming on the hard turf behind them made them both turn.

Lord Barham was bearing down on them, his face like a thundercloud.

The Marquess of Barham had spent a very bad night, and the day did not promise to be any more appealing. He had, quite without intending it, made a grievous mistake, and one that he saw no way of rectifying. Jack didn't care overmuch for the feeling.

God knew he was no angel; he'd ruined men before, and killed a number, too. Arriving home after five years of war to find his mother dead and his father intent on bankrupting the estates, had sent the young idiot Jack felt himself to have been off on a course of dissipation and excesses that had finished off what was left of his reputation as a gentleman. A proper son of a proper father, in Jack's opinion.

When he'd talked Douglas Candlesby into standing surety for those damned post-obits, he'd thought the young fool quite as plump in the pocket as he seemed, quite capable of standing the expense as a salutary lesson in the untrustworthiness of strangers.

The size and luxury of Duckmanton had done nothing to disabuse Jack of this notion; apparently

Douglas, indulged grandson of the Duke of Birdwell, could stand the nonsense. But then Jack had spoken to Lord Ralph Candlesby during the seemingly interminable games of whist last night; Lord Ralph, already fairly well to live, didn't realize the point of Jack's conversation, or how much information he had conveyed in response to Jack's sallies.

Drink or no, Jack had sobered rapidly. Far from being as well-breeched as expected, Douglas would be inheriting merely a small but well-managed estate and a tidy competence. And payment of the amount Douglas had so blithely pledged would ruin him past praying for.

Jack, although much in favor of the salutary lessoning of fools, had always drawn the line at the ruination of innocents, male or female. But there was nothing he could do; he had no possible way of redeeming those damned notes either. He would not see one penny from the Owlsthorne estates even if his father were so obliging as to stick his spoon in the wall tomorrow, and no amount of luck with cards or dice-cup could bring him about this time. Jack had pressing duns of his own, and his little capital was currently invested on Sultan in the St. Leger.

At this point, Jack had obliged his host by matching him two and three drinks for one. Brooding over the matter through a haze of brandy, Jack finally decided that the only solution was for Douglas to go to Lord Ralph and confess all. Jack would be cast in the role of villain, hardly a new experience; Lord Ralph, forewarned, would be able to apply to his father or elder brothers and could surely raise the blunt required to appease the moneylenders.

Jack had rolled into bed shortly before dawn convinced that a word in Douglas's ear would solve the entire matter. But when he managed to remove himself from his bed a few hours later and descend in search of that young man, it was to discover, from an infuriatingly arch Lady Ralph, that Mr. Candlesby was squiring Lady Juliette Devereaux to Temple Down and was not, on that account, to be expected before tea.

Jack swore, Lady Ralph gasped, and Jack, hastily apologizing, had quitted the house and was flinging himself aboard Cavalier not ten minutes later. He sent the horse out of the stableyard at a speed that made the stableboys scramble out of the way and the grooms raise their eyebrows.

Juliette's first impulse was to whip up the horse; however, as she certainly couldn't outrace Lord Barham with a gig, and could hardly pretend she hadn't noticed him, she perforce remained where she was.

"Why, there's Barham now," said Mr. Candlesby happily. "What a piece of luck!"

"Yes, isn't it," Juliette responded hollowly. The sudden appearance of Lord Barham had brought her face to face with a confusion of ideas, and she had no notion how to deal with them. That she had been instantly attracted to the Marquess she was honest enough to admit. But Douglas Candlesby's revelations had rudely shattered the hazy dreams in which she now realized she had been indulging; such a man as the Marquess of Barham, one who could cold-bloodedly ruin the inoffensive Mr. Candlesby and who doubtless would have looked as warmly upon any well-off young lady as he had at her, was one who could inspire no other emotion than dislike.

So Juliette told herself firmly as the Marquess pulled Cavalier up beside the gig and swept off his hat, raising his eyebrows at the sight of Juliette in possession of the reins.

"Good morning, Lady Juliette," he said lightly. "Tell me, is there nothing beyond your infinite capacities?"

"Good morning, Lord Barham," Juliette responded in a colorless voice, lifting her chin and regarding him coldly.

"Oh, I say, Barham, how splendid of you to join us," said Douglas, blissfully unaware of any emotional undercurrents. "D've asked you m'self, but Mama said you were dished."

Barham raised his brows. "Too kind by far, Candlesby. Dare I hope, then, that my untimely appearance as chaperon is not too unwelcome?"

"Chaperon?" said Douglas in patent astonishment. "You?"

Despite her newly acquired distaste for Lord Barham's company, Juliette almost found herself laughing once more. She did wish the man would not make everything sound so ridiculous; it made it difficult to remember that he was dangerous and that one must hold him at arm's length.

Barham grinned. "As Lady Ralph was quite sure that the two of you wished only to be alone—"

"Alone?" said Mr. Candlesby blankly. "No such thing, Barham—must've misunderstood her. We're off to see the Templeton horses. Thought that was why you caught us up."

"Doubtless it was," said Barham, apparently abandoning unworthy game. He smiled at Juliette. "Lead on, then, to these famous horses."

Juliette dropped her hands and urged the horse forward. Any awkwardness she might have feared, however, was covered by Mr. Candlesby's stream of praise for the Temple Down stock.

"Firedrake nearly won the Derby this year," Douglas confided, as Barham kept Cavalier to an easy trot beside the gig. "And you know the Templeton hunters are the best blood-and-bone this side of Ireland. Got a lot of spirit," he added helpfully. Then he frowned. "Not horses for the ladies, though."

"Nonsense!" Juliette retorted. "A spirited mount is safer than a timid one." She made the tactical error of looking to Lord Barham for confirmation of this sweeping statement.

"So," said the Marquess, eyes glinting golden, "I have always thought, Lady Juliette."

Juliette bit her lip, and abruptly touched her horse with the whip, sending the gig forward at a pace that made the startled Mr. Candlesby grab at the seat for support.

All other matters were forgotten, however, when they rattled into the yard at Temple Down. Juliette drew the gig up, a stablehand came forward to take the horse's head, and Juliette leapt down before either Barham or Mr. Candlesby could move to assist her.

"Lord Templeton!" she exclaimed in delight, holding out her hands to the man who strode stiffly to greet them.

Although nearly sixty, Marcus Templeton was still a handsome man. Tight watchsprings of silver dusted his dark curls, but his figure was strong and vigorous, although he had recently been forced to abandon the hunt field after a fall that many thought would be the end of him. Now he walked with a cane and rode but seldom, devoting his energies almost entirely to the family avocation of horse-breeding. His first wife, Georgiana Halford, had been cousin to Juliette's mother; the families had always visited frequently, and the connection had been kept up even after Georgiana's death and Marcus's subsequent remarriage to Lady Euphemia Darwen. Marcus's first marriage had resulted in two sons, George and Harry; the second had added Augustus, Deborah, Emily, Anabel, Sophie, Margaret, and Lucius to the Templeton family.

"Oh, how glad I am to see you again!" Juliette went on, as Marcus Templeton clasped her hands and bent to kiss her cheek.

"Me, or my horses?" Marcus Templeton smiled. "Well, no matter. It's good to see you again, my dear child. When we heard you were to visit at Duckmanton, I thought you might spare a moment to come to us."

"Well, of course I wish to see you all as well," said Juliette, dimpling in a fashion that made Lord Barham stare.

Lord Templeton raised his heavy dark eyebrows in mock surprise. "Indeed? You flatter us, child. But you must wait to pay your respects to Lady Templeton and Deborah, as I tyrannically insist upon showing off my horses first." He tucked Juliette's arm through his and turned to the others. "Mr. Candlesby, how pleasant to see you in our midst once more. And—?"

Upon being introduced to the Marquess, Lord Templeton showed no signs of surprise or alarm, merely commenting, "Lord Barham? Then I believe you know my son Henry."

It was Juliette's turn to stare, as Barham smiled with unfeigned and unalloyed pleasure.

"Don't tell me you're 'Hell-bent Harry's' father!"

he exclaimed. "I'm pleased to make your acquaintance, sir. Harry spoke of you often enough—and wished he had your horses with him more often, I daresay."

Lord Templeton laughed. "Well, he has them now, at least. He's home on leave, and recuperating from the measles. But you may see him later; we mustn't keep Lady Juliette standing here when the horses await." He patted Juliette's hand, and, leaning lightly on his cane, led them off towards the secondary stable where the sale horses were being groomed for display.

A securely fenced paddock stood to one side of the lane that led to their goal. As they strolled along, a magnificent blood bay stallion galloped madly over to the fence, then followed them along it, stamping and snorting and shaking his head.

"Prometheus, as you see," said Lord Templeton as Juliette stopped to admire the stallion. "I'm afraid he's become fat and lazy now that that scamp Augustus isn't here to ride him. And before you ask, no, I will *not* loan him to you—as I've had occasion to tell Deborah, he is not a lady's hack."

Juliette jerked her chin. "I am not so indifferent a horsewoman as that, you know!" she said aggrievedly, but Lord Templeton merely smiled, refusing to be drawn.

"Prometheus aside," he went on calmly, "what do you hope to find among our sale stock? And don't sulk, child, it will have no effect on my decision."

"I never sulk," said Juliette indignantly. "You know I don't, sir! Well, if you will not loan me Prometheus, you will not—but I did so wish to find a new stud for Chaceley, so perhaps if I promise most straitly not to ride him, you will reconsider the matter?"

"Perhaps," said Lord Templeton noncommitally.

Juliette set her mouth in a way that promised further argument; Barham laughed. " 'Perhaps,' " he said, "is a word women invariably translate as 'of course.' Mr. Candlesby, shall we lay a small wager on the outcome?"

Douglas Candlesby stopped his vain efforts to pat Prometheus without losing his very-well-tailored sleeve. "Wager? Not about a lady, surely, old chap."

Without indicating that he'd noticed this byplay, Lord Templeton went on, "But come, Juliette, surely you need something other than breeding stock—at least you do if you're still riding that brown mare."

Juliette sighed, and allowed that he was right. "For you said there was bad blood in Dulcinea, and I must admit, she's been lame more often than not. I'm afraid there's nothing for it but to sell her, for she's of no use to me—and she *may* make someone else a decent hack," she added dubiously. "So I would like, if you please, at least one bang-up hunter, and perhaps a hack or two."

Marcus Templeton smiled. "I'm afraid the sale will be mostly of youngsters and of no interest to you, but you shall have first pick of the stock," he promised. "And then you must come up to the house and give Euphemia all your news. How is Madame Solange, for example?"

"Oh—well—" Juliette stammered, looking very guilty. "I have not spoken with her in—in some time, you know."

"But you've heard from her, I'll dare swear?" said Lord Templeton with dismaying accuracy.

Juliette, defeated, demanded with great dignity that the promised horses be produced for viewing immediately, and Marcus Templeton laughed. "Very well, my dear child, here we are."

Lord Templeton then shepherded his three guests from stall to stall, naming each horse and giving its breeding. As he'd told Juliette, most of the sale stock was yearlings and two-year-olds, unbroken and too young to ride as yet. Still, one must have a prudent eye to the future; Juliette had made up her mind to make an offer for several of the young horses, and had just opened her mouth to do so, when a dull, heavy thudding noise diverted her attention.

She looked inquiringly up at Lord Templeton. The lines about his mouth were sharp-cut with disappointment. "Ah, yes," he said. "That is the prize of my sale—Vulcan."

"Vulcan!" exclaimed Douglas Candlesby. "Here, sir, you can't be serious!"

"But I thought he was to be destroyed!" Juliette added.

The Marquess of Barham looked from one to the other, baffled. The tempo of the banging increased.

Lord Templeton sighed, and shrugged. "You will find it odd, when even Augustus urged that course upon me, but I had not the heart. He *is* a splendid animal—in his fashion. But I make no secret of his manners and temper. If he finds a buyer, it will not be through ignorance."

"I take it there is yet another horse for the sale?" said Barham, considerably intrigued.

Marcus Templeton's eyes sparked with weary amusement. "Oh, yes. These two young people already know him, but you, my lord, have not yet had the pleasure. Allow me to make the introduction."

* * *

Upon closer investigation, the steady banging proved to be coming from an iron-barred loose-box at the far end of the stable. Lord Templeton slid open a peephole, and Jack looked through with some interest.

"This is Vulcan. He's something of a legend in these parts. I made the error of breeding Witchfire to Snapdragon, rather than to Torchlight, a few years ago, and Vulcan was the result. Salamander was his grandsire, and Vulcan has inherited all his temper."

"Hasn't he just!" said Mr. Candlesby indignantly. "Last summer he got loose and chased me nearly two miles—had to drive the gig into the lake to be rid of him—Mama wasn't half pleased!"

"I daresay the style of your cravat offended him," said Jack absently, studying Vulcan through the peephole. He saw a huge, heavily-muscled red stallion, ramping fretfully in a loose-box that seemed far too small for him. His coat was dusty, and his mane and tail matted and full of straw. His eye, however, was bright and lively. The thudding noise was made by his hooves as they struck the walls. As Jack studied him, the big horse suddenly stopped dead and flung up his head, staring at the door, almost as if inspecting the Marquess in his turn, before resuming his restless attempts to flatten his stall.

"I admit Lady Ralph had a great deal to do with my decision to be rid of him, and she was quite right, too," said Lord Templeton, sounding a trifle regretful. "He cannot be kept confined, and he cannot be ridden—not easily, at any rate. And as I can no longer ride myself, I wish him gone from Temple Down."

Jack turned to look questioningly at Lord Templeton, who explained ruefully, "I love my children, Lord Barham, but common sense is not one of their outstanding traits. I want Vulcan gone before Harry—or even Deb or Emily, heaven help me!—decides to risk his neck in a misguided attempt at taming him." He shook his head. "No, Vulcan must go."

Lady Juliette had been looking more and more agitated as Marcus Templeton spoke, as he finished, she burst out, "Then sell him to me! Why, he's precisely what we need to add some spirit to our bloodlines at Chaceley! Do tell me his price, Lord Templeton!"

The three men looked at her in horror. Mr. Candlesby found his voice first. "Dash it, Lady Juliette, it's you ought to be locked up! How would you *get* the dashed beast to Chaceley in the first place?"

"Out of the mouths of babes," drawled Jack. "But I doubt you need worry, Candlesby; I have faith in Lord Templeton."

Lady Juliette glared at them. Marcus Templeton shook his head. "You may put that notion out of your mind at once, Juliette. I could square it with neither Euphemia nor my conscience if I sold him to you, nor can I think it any improvement to have him ravaging Buckingham rather than Sussex. If you're a good girl, I will send Prometheus to stand at Chaceley in the spring—provided you give me your solemn oath that you'll not put a saddle on his back!"

"Lord Templeton, you know I could ride him!" Juliette protested.

"Not sidesaddle you couldn't," said Lord Templeton patiently. "And if you contemplate riding astride, my dear child, I beg you will spare our masculine blushes and not say so." He patted her hand.

"Now come along and I'll show you something that will be more to your taste than Vulcan here."

So saying, Lord Templeton led them away from the close-box. The tempo of the pounding hooves increased, as if the big stallion objected to losing his audience. Jack looked back over his shoulder; it was too bad to waste such a magnificent animal, but he was forced to admit he couldn't see what else Lord Templeton could do.

As they entered the main stableyard once more a groom rode up on a brown hack leading one of the most perfect mares Barham had ever seen. A vivid chestnut, with snowy stockings and a wide splash of white down her forehead, her silken coat flamed molten copper in the sunlight as she stepped delicately across the flagstones, ears flicking back and forth. Every sleek line of her proclaimed flawless breeding.

Lady Juliette gasped in surprise. "Oriflamme!" she cried, turning eagerly to Lord Templeton. "Never say you're selling Oriflamme, sir!"

"I'm afraid so," Lord Templeton responded. "She's too wild for any of the girls, so she's wasted here—"

"Wild? Why, Oriflamme's a perfect darling! Just because Deb's cow-handed—"

"—but I thought you might be persuaded to take an interest in her," Lord Templeton finished, ignoring Juliette's comments. "She's got a great deal of spirit, of course, but—"

At this point Oriflamme, distracted by the novel sight of humans in her stableyard, planted her gleaming hooves and refused to move. Two ostlers ran up to aid the groom in urging her on; a brisk fracas ensued that ended only when one of the men managed to fling a cloth over the young mare's eyes to stop her plunging.

"Spirit!" exclaimed Douglas Candlesby indignantly. "Ain't she the mare that's had everyone off in the duck pond and goes through her fences instead of over them? Well, Lady Juliette, if that's your idea of *spirit*—"

"Apparently it is," said Jack, amused by the almost greedy look of anticipation on Lady Juliette's face as she gazed at Oriflamme—rather like a kitten about to pounce on a particularly choice goldfish, not realizing it would become thoroughly drenched in the process.

"Well, of course she's a bit high-couraged," said Lady Juliette reasonably. "She's one of Witchfire's foals, you know, and half-sister to Prometheus and Vulcan—"

"A great recommendation, that, to be sure," Jack said. "And might I suggest the green habit, Lady Juliette? Oh, a bit obvious, you may say, but I feel sure it will set you both off to perfection."

Lady Juliette looked uncertain, plainly trying to decide whether this was a compliment or arrant provocation. Barham kindly settled the matter by grinning at her; Lady Juliette lifted her chin and turned back to Lord Templeton.

"—and I have *so* wanted one of Witchfire's foals for years," she went on, ignoring Barham with great dignity. "You will not sell her to anyone else, sir—say you will not!"

Lord Templeton smiled and shook his head. "Well, I will not tease you, Juliette; you may have her if you wish. But mind, when you're up to your neck in the nearest lake, don't come crying to me."

Lady Juliette most reprehensibly flung her arms around Lord Templeton and tugged him down to kiss his cheek. "Oh, I shan't! Thank you!" she cried, and abandoned them to go and make much of the now-quiet Oriflamme, who submitted to this adulation as if it were only her due.

"*Caveat emptor*, I take it?" said Jack as an aside to Lord Templeton.

"Lady Juliette," said Marcus Templeton dryly, "is a young lady who knows her own mind—"

"And who likes spirit in a horse?" the Marquess interjected, with a slight lift of his eyebrows.

"And is an excellent horsewoman," Lord Templeton finished. "I'm sure she and Oriflamme will deal very well together."

"Won't they just!" put in Mr. Candlesby with feeling. "Both like their own way—won't have any other."

Lord Barham looked across the stableyard. Oriflamme and Lady Juliette made a pretty picture indeed; the two seemed in a fine way to becoming a mutual admiration society. "That," he said, watching the young mare's playful attempts to see what, if anything, Lady Juliette might have concealed about her person that would be of interest to Oriflamme, "remains to be seen."

Lord Templeton shot a sharp look at the Marquess, but said only, "And now I must persuade my goddaughter to abandon the stables for the time being. Lady Templeton is expecting us."

Despite the early hour, a generous informal repast was spread in the Blue Parlor, where Lady Templeton presided, her eldest daughter seated demurely beside her.

Euphemia Templeton, a Darwen by birth, was a well-enough-looking woman, with sandy-red hair that time had softened to an attractive sugared cinnamon. The Honorable Deborah Mary Templeton, however, took after her father, as did most of the Templeton offspring, and was a vivacious-looking brunette, with eyes of a stormy blue. She greeted Lady Juliette with glad cries, and looked inquiringly at the Marquess of Barham, interest and admiration both plain; Miss Templeton, having been deprived of her first Season by the measles, had been denied the opportunity to learn the fashionable accomplishment of dissembling.

She was to be denied an introduction to this intriguing stranger, however. A quick, wordless communication flashed between Lord and Lady Templeton as Juliette returned Deborah's greetings; Lady Templeton glanced at Lord Barham, and said quietly, "Deborah, dear, do go upstairs and help Nurse with Meg and little Lucius. He is inclined to fuss," she added as an aside to her guests.

Deborah looked startled. "But Mama—"

"You heard your mother, my dear," said Lord Templeton mildly. Young Miss Templeton's fine eyes flashed mutinously, but she obeyed, contenting herself with a speaking glance at Lady Juliette before she flounced out of the room.

The dismissal was not lost on the Marquess of Barham, nor was its cause. Lord and Lady Templeton might receive the notorious Lord Barham politely—they had had little choice, after all. But they would not introduce him to their daughters.

The Marquess looked at Lady Juliette, who appeared slightly puzzled. Then, as understanding apparently sunk in, the color heightened in her cheeks and she slanted a glance at the Marquess. Their eyes met; Jack grinned at her. Juliette looked quickly away again and began talking to Lady Templeton with great animation.

At that moment the door to the Blue Parlor burst open and yet another of the numerous Templeton offspring strode into the room: a tall, broad-shouldered young man who was the very image of a proud British dragoon, down to the ferocious moustaches affected by the cavalry fraternity.

"Jack!" Captain the Honorable Harry Templeton stopped dead upon seeing the Marquess. "Well, I'll be—tell me what you're doing here!" Harry glanced quickly around the room; he caught sight of Juliette, and added, "On second thought, don't. Hello, Juliette—Douglas. What the devil are you doing in Sussex, Jack? I'd heard you sold out, mind, but—" Here Captain Templeton stopped abruptly.

"Yes, I sold out some time ago," the Marquess said before the silence became too awkward, wondering as he did so why he was taking pity on Harry. It had been impossible to miss Harry's instant search for Deborah and his expression of relief when he found she wasn't in the room. Well, Jack had known his brilliant career was unlikely to win him any partisans, but it was somehow increasingly galling that men who would drink and gamble and roister with him would then bar him from their homes. Did the sanctimonious hypocrites think his mere presence would contaminate their womenfolk?

"As for what I'm doing in Sussex . . ." Jack shrugged elegantly. "You see before you a veritable reformed character, Harry; I stop for a few days at the ultra-respectable Duckmanton. I'm such a mild fellow that I soon shan't be able to afford knowing a wild man like you."

"Oh, aye, mild as Vulcan," Harry agreed, and there was a general murmur of amusement from

76

the little company; apparently "mild as Vulcan" was a family catch-phrase.

The conversation then became general and harmless, giving Jack the leisure to think gloomily that his reputation was little better than Vulcan's and to wonder what would become of that noble beast.

It was arrant folly on his part to worry about Vulcan's fate; his own was quite uncertain enough as it stood. But Marcus Templeton did not strike Jack as a self-deluding man; he must know that Vulcan's chances of finding a decent buyer were slim indeed. No man in his right mind wanted an unmanageable, unridable full-grown stallion, and Jack himself wouldn't sell a horse to any man who did.

But he was willing to bet that Vulcan could be ridden—by the right person. He'd make Lord Templeton an offer for the stallion—

With what? Unless Lord Templeton gave him the animal, he couldn't afford him—and if he had him, he couldn't afford to keep him.

No, thought Jack ruefully, watching as the morning sunlight slanting through the windows struck raven-wing flashes on Lady Juliette's ebony curls, Vulcan, like so much in life these days, was—perhaps fortunately—beyond his reach.

CHAPTER
FOUR

The day that had dawned so gloriously for Lady Juliette Devereaux also shone favorably on Althea Fonthill. Mama felt entirely recovered from the travails of travel and had come down to breakfast. There Lady Ralph had greeted the Fonthills—for some mysterious reason the rest of the house party was not yet risen, though the hour was quite advanced—with the news that dear Douglas had taken Lady Juliette out driving quite early, with the object of visiting the Templetons.

"For as you know, dear Marcus stands almost as a father to Lady Juliette, and I am sure that is why she wished him to meet Douglas."

"*I* am sure I know who took whom driving," Isobel muttered under her breath. "Poor Douglas!"

Breakfast was complicated by the arrival of Jerusha Gressingham in search of soothing *tisanes* for her brother, but she could be on no account persuaded to leave his side in his hour of anguish—"Just what he will want, in his condition," muttered Isobel again, and was soundly kicked beneath the table by Althea.

Lady Ralph, wearing a rather forced smile, announced that the rest of the house party would be joining them today, and suggested that in the absence of other entertainment, dear Clothilde would wish to see her garden before nuncheon.

Mrs. Fonthill instantly fell in with this agreeable plan, and Isobel, spurning all offers of sisterly company, announced it her intention to write letters. As Belle was a notoriously bad correspondent, Althea suspected a number of things into which it was better not to enquire and took the opportunity to dawdle over a second cup of tea in the warmth of the breakfast room.

She was reluctantly deciding to leave the comfort of that cheerful parlor, with its view of the ornamental water and the Gothic folly, when the doors opened and Mr. Anthony Devereaux made his appearance.

His trunks, Althea instantly perceived, had made their appearance in the night, for he had never borrowed that cheerfully comfortable-looking coat and trousers from Douglas Candlesby, and his boots, while well-brushed, owed nothing to the Duckmanton bootblack's over-earnest ministrations. He peered round the door as if searching for someone, and Althea said, "Lady Juliette is not here, Mr. Devereaux; she has gone driving."

"Ah, I had hoped so, Miss Fonthill. Might I join you in breakfast? I see you have already finished, but my valet refused to allow me downstairs until I had rejected at least three coats. The fellow does have his standards to consider, poor fellow—and it seems there isn't a decent champagne in the place for the formulation of my bootblack."

"Oh, Mr. Devereaux, you don't really?" Althea said with a startled giggle, remembering the tale still told of the Beau, that Brummell had had his boots blacked with champagne froth and apricot jam.

"No, Miss Fonthill, I don't, really—what a figure of fun I would be as a Pink of the Ton, though Petersby would revel in it, I imagine," Mr. Devereaux said. He rang for the butler and seated himself, and when tea had been brought and poured he turned to Althea.

"I'll confess now, and trust to be forgiven; I was particularly hoping to see you, Miss Fonthill, and induce you to confide in me the tale of Juliette's Season, so that I can decide if the best course of action is to induce Julie to go home with me, or simply stop trying to serve both God and Madame and ride off Land's End. You cannot imagine what a quaking coward I am; there was talk of marriage hot in the air as I left."

"Marriage?" said Althea.

"Mine—to Juliette. Madame thinks it would be a capital idea, and of course it would keep the money—such as it is—in the family, but I think that Juliette requires a braver husband than I, and I confess my hopes lie in other directions."

"Such as?" said Althea, willing to be drawn by this amiable madman.

"Peace and quiet," said Anthony, buttering toast. "Now, Miss Fonthill. I am utterly at your mercy. Tell me about Juliette's Season."

"Well," said Althea, "To begin with, you must know that Lady Juliette went to town with a hired chaperon. Mrs. Basingstoke is a worthy woman, and she meant well . . ."

"Oh, lord! No, no, do go on, Miss Fonthill."

"And she was the soul of kindness, but . . ." But Mrs. Hector Basingstoke, dazzled by Lady Juliete Devereaux's beauty and openhandedness, had encouraged her charge to think very well of herself indeed and to indulge in all manner of extravagant and unbecoming follies. Juliette had been permitted to deck herself out like a dashing matron of thirty—and who could truly blame her? Juliette had spent her youth in sturdy gowns and sober riding habits; how could she have resisted the bird-of-paradise lures spread out by the old-fashioned modiste she had insisted on patronizing because her mother had?

So Juliette had done just as she chose, secure in Mrs. Basingstoke's eager approval, and disregarded all attempts at criticism. For was it not her chaperon's opinion that all such strictures were merely the carping of those jealous of her beauty, birth, and fortune? Althea sighed, trying to think how to put all this, and Anthony raised a hand.

"No, Miss Fonthill, do not pause to spare a cousin's feelings, I implore you. Rather, press on, staunch in virtue, and hope we shall come to a safe haven at last."

"Well," Althea began again, "Perhaps your cousin's Season was not—not quite the triumph she wished, but I have found that so much depends upon those sharing the Season with one, and that one has no control over. But after the Season, she was invited to make up a number of house parties—"

"And accepted with alacrity, fleeing the wrath of Madame, no doubt." Anthony shook his head. "Never try to be tactful, Miss Fonthill, especially to one who knows Julie well. Let me see . . . from your admirable reticence, I collect that my cousin did exactly as she pleased in Town, ran roughshod over Mrs. Basingstoke, received no offers worthy of Chaceley—and a good thing too, all things considered—and was invited to Duckmanton chiefly because Lady Ralph wants her to marry Douglas Candlesby, who is only notable for overspending an exceedingly generous allowance. Juliette remained in blissful ignorance of this intention for the longest time, and upon discovering it, told Lady Ralph she would not marry Douglas if he were the last man on earth. Following that—"

"Oh, stop!" Althea put her hands over her ears. There had been nothing but a sort of disinterested affection in Mr. Devereaux's tone as he recited his dismayingly accurate analysis, but Althea could not bear to hear her friend so accurately pilloried.

"I am sorry; I would not distress you for the world, Miss Fonthill; only I have known Julie all my life, and I cannot bear to see people who love her try to be kind. It never does the least good, you know—it is all Uncle Sebastian's fault."

"Uncle Sebastian?"

"Julie's father. Someday I shall tell you the whole shocking tale of the Devereaux *ménage*, including how I, a grown man, continue as a charge upon my great-aunt, of whom, you may have noticed, both Julie and I go in mortal dread. But what of Candlesby? Julie's still here; never say she means to accept him?"

"No. . . . In fact, she has told me—in strict confidence, Mr. Devereaux—that he is quite silly. But she did wish to stop at Duckmanton—"

"For the Templeton sales. Say no more, Miss Fonthill—Julie's entire devious plan is laid before me. Lady Ralph invited her here to fix Candlesby's affections, and Julie's mind was on only two things—evading Madame and seeing the Templeton stud. So she is still ignorant of Lady Ralph's intentions for her?"

"You do her an injustice, Mr. Devereaux," said

Althea, attempting to remain grave in the face of Juliette's cousin's droll humor. "She is wide awake to Lady Ralph's intentions, but is sure that a moment's reflection will bring her hostess to her senses—and as I am sure Mr. Candlesby has no intention of pursuing her—"

"Not being a complete idiot," Mr. Devereaux confirmed.

"Well," said Althea brightly. "You see."

"I see nothing but trouble," Mr. Devereaux said, "since I must continue to attempt to steer between Julie and Madame."

Much to Juliette's relief, when she and Douglas Candlesby finally left Temple Down, the Marquess of Barham had elected to ride off to spend the afternoon in Harry Templeton's company. She did not know how much longer she could have held her peace over the matter of the bonds he had made Douglas Candlesby sign.

It was inconceivable to Juliette, who had been raised almost from babyhood to understand the importance of figures in a ledger, that young Mr. Candlesby should be unaware of the enormity of his plight. Well, she would make him aware, and Lord Barham simply must be made to repay his debts. However, as Juliette could not, at the moment, see any hope of convincing either the ingenuous Mr. Candlesby nor the recalcitrant Lord Barham of either of these necessary things, she contented herself with driving briskly back to Duckmanton, thinking furiously. The first thing she must do was to dissuade Tony from his wrongheaded idea of carrying her off to Fakenham—if she couldn't do that, she'd have very little chance to carry out any of her other hopes. Now . . . what was the best way to convince Tony she must be let to stay here. Juliette's brow furrowed in thought, then cleared. She had it.

She would tell Anthony she intended to marry Douglas. Then he would *have* to stop interfering.

On arriving at the Duckmanton stables, Juliette handed the gig over to a groom and hastened into the house to change her severe driving habit for something more suited to telling faradiddles to her cousin. It was not much past two of the clock when Juliette Devereaux, attired in a bright primrose-yellow gown of Circassian cloth, with a ruff made up high at the neck, and a great deal of passementerie trim about the bodice and sleeves which made jewelry almost unnecessary, brushed a splash of Florida water through her hair and sallied forth in search of the other members of the Duckmanton house party.

The first person she met was Althea, fresh from a happy morning spent in Mr. Anthony ("—Percival St. Devereaux Devereaux, and what a pity there isn't an 'of Devereuax at Devereaux in Devereaux' to attach to it; Madame would expire of ecstasy—") Devereaux's company. It was Althea's conviction that Mr. Devereaux had been ill-served by Juliette's report of him; a conviction which would have tried her loyalty to her friend harder if she thought that Mr. Devereaux took the least notice of it. Instead of being a gibbering lunatic, as Juliette had painted him, Althea found him to be a quiet, personable young gentleman, and had fallen quickly into terms of easy intimacy with him—as befit one nearly on the shelf and uninterested in romantic entanglements. But chaste and agreeable thoughts of Juliette's cousin vanished when Juliette herself, clad in a hideous yellow gown covered over with

84

steel-cut beads to which she had added the final insult of a necklace of turquoises, bounded up, cheeks glowing.

"Oh, Thea—I have had the loveliest morning—and she is to be delivered tomorrow! Oh, and where is Tony—I must speak to him and tell him I am in love with Douglas, so he will go away."

"I—Good heavens, Juliette—in love with *Douglas*? Mr. Devereaux will never believe that, especially as I have just spent the morning assuring him it cannot be the case at all. And who is being delivered tomorrow? Have you bought a horse? Mr. Candlesby said something on that head when I saw him a few minutes ago, but I did not perfectly understand."

Lady Juliette, unsurprised that Mr. Candlesby should not have made himself clear, and easily diverted, eagerly began a paean to the glories of Oriflamme, interspersed with promises that Althea should meet this equine paragon as soon as the mare was delivered from Temple Down on the morrow.

Their comfortable coze was interrupted by a distracted Lady Ralph; Douglas had been in the company of Isobel Fonthill for quite half-an-hour and showed no signs of wishing to quit it. This had sent Lady Ralph hurrying over to Lady Juliette and Miss Fonthill to announce mendaciously that dear Douglas had been asking after Juliette, and she was sure that dear Mrs. Fonthill had just requested dear Miss Isobel's company at once.

Althea, wise in the ways of the marriage mart, smoothed over the awkwardness occasioned by Lady Juliette's surprise at these statements. Lady Ralph attached herself to Juliette, leaving Althea to go and remove her sister from Douglas's side, reflecting that Lady Ralph would have had her son at the church door within a month, were her prey any other young lady. Althea had great faith in Lady Juliette's determination. She only hoped Juliette would not confide her newfound *tendre* for Douglas to his mama.

Althea obediently detached Isobel from Douglas, but rather than hurrying off after Lady Juliette as advertised, he bounced off with Robert Gressingham. Lady Ralph, frustrated, attempted to bear Juliette off to sit with Lady Hawkchurch, to keep her safe for Douglas's return, but Juliette, shying away from the very thought, announced a pressing need to find and speak with her cousin Anthony "—for as you know, ma'am, he has come to take me to Fakenham, but I am sure when he has heard what I wish to tell him, he will agree that I should stay here." Juliette, braced for an argument, was agreeably surprised to find that Lady Ralph merely beamed upon her, and directed her toward the library, where Anthony Devereaux had installed himself in solitary splendor.

Anthony Devereaux had spent the morning spying out—as he would put it himself—the lay of the land, and having formed a tolerable notion of the events that had brought his cousin to Duckmanton, could easily understand the impetus for Madame's preemptory demand. Poor Julie! His vivid imagination easily painted the utter hash she had made of her Season—and being Juliette, she had undoubtedly written off the Upper Ten Thousand as a bad lot and would not try her hand in society further. Which left, in the delicate matter of marriage and Juliette's future career, him.

He supposed he would not mind being married to

his cousin overmuch—they would be rather polite and well-bred, and see as little of each other as they could help, and scrape along tolerably. Anthony sighed and closed the book he had been reading. He knew himself for a dull fellow indeed; instead of troubling deaf heaven with his bootless cries—as befit a bachelor with an inconvenient marriage looming before him—or even doing anything about it, he would almost certainly allow Madame to have her way in this, and obediently marry his cousin. It could hardly be more of a matter of indifference to him, for all that he and Juliette were so unsuited; he had as yet found no woman capable of engaging his emotions, and was, at six-and-twenty, young enough to believe that he never would.

He heard the tapping at the door and bade the communicant enter. As if summoned up by his mordant musings, Juliette herself appeared, garbed in yet another costume of exquisite awfulness. Anthony braced himself for the inevitable, assumed an expression of meek insipidity, and beckoned a welcome.

Juliette strode into the Duckmanton library and hesitated. Propriety dictated that an unmarried woman should not be behind closed doors with a gentleman; but Juliette thought that silly, no matter how often Mrs. Basingstoke had repeated it. Besides, Tony was her cousin, and so respectable that no society hostess could possibly make him the focus for her fevered imagination. With a decisive motion, she pushed the door to behind her.

"Oh, bravo, Julie; bravely done," said her cousin.

Juliette made an irritated face before recalling that her intention was to make Anthony fall in with her plans. "I do not see why you are always teasing me, Tony—oh, I know very well that I ought to leave the door open, but it is only you, after all."

"A little more than kin, and less than kind, yes, I know," Anthony agreed elliptically. "And let me say I am as happy to be here on this commission as you are to see me, but there's no hope for it. Trust in Madame; she will provide. We shall stay out the week, if you like, but—"

"Oh, but Tony—you cannot possibly be serious! After all, I—I—I—am to marry Douglas, so I cannot possibly leave!"

Anthony removed his spectacles from a pocket and peered at them as if trying to decide whether they might be at fault for his sudden lapse of hearing. Deciding not, he put them away again.

"Fell off your horse this morning, did you, Julie?" he enquired kindly.

"I am!" Juliette insisted. Then as Anthony made no further comment, her sense of the ridiculous took possession of her and she laughed. "Oh, not really—Douglas is the most cake-brained thing in nature," she confided, flouncing into a seat. "In fact, I cannot imagine why *anyone* would want Douglas, though his mama is convinced he is a prime good 'un and has us all but wed. But you must see, Tony, that I cannot possibly go to Fakenham; not possibly!"

"And neither can I—if I don't return bearing you. Cheer up, cousin; what's a little scold?"

"Oh, Tony, you never did have any sense!"

"More sense than you, at any rate. I saw you at dinner last night—whatever possessed you to cozy up to Bad Barham that way—and for that matter, what could Lady Ralph have been thinking of?"

"Why, as to that," said Juliette, glad of the diversion, "she was not thinking at all—I mean, it was Douglas who did the thinking, what there was

of it. He invited Lord Barham to visit at Duckmanton any time he pleased, and so he has come at a
most inconvenient moment—"

"—for Lady Ralph," interrupted Anthony know-
ingly. "See here, Julie, it is very too bad of you to
raise a hopeful mama's expectations this way—since
you'd hardly do for Douglas, all things considered.
You ought not have come."

"Well, Lady Ralph did invite me, Tony, and I
wished to view the Templeton stock—oh, Tony, I
have bought the loveliest mare; she is one of Witchfire's foals, and—"

"And nothing to the point," Anthony interrupted
brutally. "Well, it is no matter now; we shall just
swiftly and silently vanish away, and Lady Ralph
can husband her shattered hopes against the offing
of some other hopeful damsel. I shall let her know
that Family Duty beckons and you are called home
to Fakenham by the end of the week."

"Oh, Tony, I can't!" The real distress in Juliette's voice caused Anthony to regard her
strangely. "No," she rushed on, "there's something
important—it's about Barham—and Douglas needs
me—and—I can't tell you about it just yet, but—
Don't ask me to leave them all alone in such dreadful trouble—I can't!"

"That Barham's in dreadful trouble I can believe,
Ju'—and can remain there for all of me—*and* you.
But what's this about Candlesby?"

Juliette sat mum and mutinous before her cousin's limpid cerulean gaze. Finally he sighed. "Oh
very well. I don't suppose even Madame can expect
me to behave like a brute in a Gothic romance and
drag you off, but when she hears Barham's here—
and she will—she will *not* be best pleased. Don't
expect me to get you out of this one, Julie—this isn't

a matter of one or two of Farmer Graythorpe's ewes."

Juliette snorted. "That was entirely different! *This* is a matter that simply requires the application of a bit of common sense," she said, dismissing the "dreadful trouble" of a few moments before now that she had won her point. Once she settled the matter of the post-obit bonds, surely she could think of some way of avoiding Fakenham!

"Was there anything else, cousin?" said Anthony, feeling the matrimonial bonds close inexorably around him. Juliette sniffed dismissively, announced she would trouble him no further as he was so *very* busy, and skipped out of the room.

"—and of course they are cousins, Lady Hawkchurch, and certainly on the terms of the greatest intimacy—cousins often are, you know, and nothing the least exceptionable in it—but I always feel that breeding is all important, and a regard for one's hostess—of course, I did not mean you, Lady Ralph—and—oh, there you are, Lady Juliette; did you enjoy your conversation with your cousin Mr. Devereaux?" Miss Gressingham brought her vague rambling to a smooth close, not at all discomfitted by the appearance of her subject. Miss Gressingham was a forthright person, who never said anything she did not believe to be true, or at least had heard said, and so was rarely in a position to be embarrassed.

Juliette, caught unwary by the tribunal of Lady Ralph, Lady Hawkchurch, and Miss Jerusha Gressingham, hesitated on the doorsill. She had come into the drawing room to find Althea and solicit her advice on the best way of handling Douglas Candlesby, and realized too late that it might be a mistake.

"Lady Juliette, how d'ye do?" said Lady Hawkchurch, contriving to look down her prominent nose although she was already seated. "Come and sit by me. Helena and Miss Gressingham have told me all their news, now you may tell me yours. I was not in Town this Season, you know, so I wish to hear everything, for I feel quite the hermit."

Samantha, Lady Hawkchurch, a formidable widow in her fifties, had, like Helena Candlesby, one son upon whom she doted. She had once been matriarch of a sizable family, but the combined efforts of Bonaparte and the influenza had conspired to carry off all but her youngest, who perforce became the sole recipient of her maternal care. It might be considered surprising that Lady Ralph, with a son she wished to marry well, should include the Hawkchurch family in a party that also contained so very eligible a young lady as Lady Juliette Devereaux. But young Lord Hawkchurch was safely betrothed, and furthermore, he had disposed himself precisely where his mama chose, and without, so rumor had it, ever actually setting eyes on the young lady in question. Such shining examples of filial piety should be always before the eyes of the erring young; the Hawkchurches, *mère et fils*, were in gratifying demand at the most select of gatherings.

"Well . . ." began Juliette obediently.

"Well, m'girl? What's the news, then? I want what I can't get in the *Gazette*, mind."

As this stipulation, coupled with Lady Hawkchurch's round refusal to listen to any of the Season's most fascinating *on-dits*, eliminated every conceivable item of social information, Juliette could not imagine what she was to be permitted to reveal. Something must be said, however, as Lady Hawkchurch was sitting and staring with reptilian patience. Juliette cudgeled her brains, and finally offered, "Well, ma'am, I have just purchased a new hunter from Lord Templeton, and they are all free of the measles now."

"Horses!" said Lady Hawkchurch dismissively. "What about your own plans, girl? Why haven't I seen the announcement of *your* engagement in the *Gazette*?"

Lady Ralph waved her hands, and said with a proprietary air, "Oh, Samantha dear, now you *know* nothing is decided yet . . ."

Juliette swallowed her irritation. "That is because it has not yet appeared there, Lady Hawkchurch."

"Well, why not?" her ladyship demanded. "Can't have you running around Town causing riot and rumpus for another Season—d'you mean to tell me that not one of the dandies made you an offer?"

"No, I don't mean to tell you that," said Juliette crossly. "But Chaceley is a large estate, and I have a responsibility to see that the man I bring to it is no tame marmoset to dance to his matchmaking mama's piping! Nor will I marry a man who knows everything about spending and nothing about management!"

To her surprise, Lady Hawkchurch guffawed and dug her elbow into Lady Ralph's side. "As neat a description of your Douglas as ever I've heard, Helena—Lady Juliette'll go far, mark my words—if someone don't drown her first!"

"Oh, dear, but really, dear Lady Juliette, you *must* not joke so, for now dear Samantha has quite misunderstood you. Why, everyone knows how fond you are of Douglas!"

Juliette, eyes kindling, had drawn breath for a most intemperate reply indeed when a steadying hand on her shoulder forestalled her. She looked up to find the Marquess of Barham gazing down with every indication of polite interest.

"Indeed, Lady Ralph, one need spend only a few moments in Lady Juliette's presence to know exactly what she feels for your son—and do you know, he has told me many times that he feels precisely the same." Barham smiled and removed his hand from Juliette's shoulder. "Forgive the liberty, Lady Juliette, but it was vital to attract your attention; we're handicapping the St. Leger and I know Candlesby will be lost without you."

Jack bowed to the other three ladies as Juliette rose hastily to her feet; he took Juliette's elbow and steered her away from the danger zone with the ease of long practice, bending slightly to murmur for her ears only, "Come along, sweetheart, before you cut up our poor Lady Ralph's peace entirely."

Lady Juliette looked up sharply, her emerald eyes seeming to flash sparks; doubtless it was a trick of the brilliant candlelight. "What are you doing here? I thought you were to spend the day with Harry Templeton."

"And so I did, but I have, as you see, returned. It *is* well past tea-time, and Lady Ralph sets an excellent table for dinner."

"I see," said Lady Juliette doubtfully, as if this were an unheard-of notion.

Jack had indeed been passing the time since his return with the stolid Lord Hawkchurch and the skimble-skamble Mr. Gressingham, but the topic of discussion had not been horses. It had taken no great powers of persuasion to prevail upon Lightfoot Bobby to reveal such facts about Lady Juliette Devereaux's Season as that worthy knew, and Jack had found the tale enlightening. The only daughter of Count Sebastian Devereaux of Chaceley, Bucks, had driven up to Town last March with her maid, engaged Mrs. Hector Basingstoke and her house for the Season, and proceeded to propose herself to the *ton*. She had not received an overwarm welcome, but in these sad days, when even merchants and tradesmen could buy honors and ape their betters, no one with Lady Juliette's prospects was entirely ostracized.

"—little piece of perfection, of course," Mr. Gressingham had said, "and enough blunt to buy an abbey—but lord, that tongue! I mean, you could rip off those clothes, but I ask you, Barham, d'you want a woman who lectures all day long—and all night, too, I dare swear! Too much common sense by half— a fellow don't need a woman with common sense! Look at m'sister—she knows how to treat a chap, and she don't preach at him, neither!"

Jack, who had, after a day's study, pegged Jerusha Gressingham as being as clingingly supportive as ivy and just as destructive, agreed to this without a quiver. Mr. Gressingham, encouraged, continued to regale Jack with a highly colored account of Lady Juliette's Town progress until they were joined by Mr. Candlesby. At that point Jack, stung by the unaccustomed pricking of his conscience, had left the gun-room for the drawing-room, arriving just in time to prevent Lady Juliette from reading Lady Hawkchurch a rousing scold.

"But why do you say I cut up Lady Ralph's

peace?" asked Juliette now, accompanying him docilely enough for all her flashing eyes.

"My dear child, if you don't think informing an overindulgent mama flat out that her only son is a cow-handed young cloudhead would put her out of temper, then I can only bow to your superior understanding of the race of women," said Jack. "Furthermore, my sweet, I'm sure you don't overface your fences in the hunting field; don't do it in the drawing-room! You're no match for Lady Hawkchurch's sort, and won't be for years."

Juliette frowned, tilting her head to look up at him slantwise. "But surely Lady Ralph knows that Douglas has no sense at all!" she protested. "And it would be a kindness to make her believe at last that Douglas will not offer for me, and I would not accept him if he did."

"Then why come to Duckmanton? You must have known, my Cruel Fair, that it would raise false hopes."

Lady Juliette developed a sudden interest in the black-and-white tiles underfoot. "Oh, I do wish people would stop saying that to me! As—as if every house party must naturally end in marriage! There are other reasons for accepting an invitation to stay, Lord Barham!"

"Ah, of course," said Jack, who knew most of them far better than he suspected Lady Juliette ever could. "But I could not imagine that a woman of such high principles as yourself would ever have accepted her invitation, despising Douglas as you do."

Juliette looked up again. "Oh, but I do not despise him, Lord Barham. Indeed, he is a pleasant enough companion—but even you must agree that he would not do as a husband! He is shockingly expensive, and no one to put in the charge of a great estate. And I thought—" She stopped with a wistful sigh.

By now their steps had carried them to yet another of Lady Ralph's fashionable improvements: an orangery, built entirely of glass and leading off the Gothic conservatory. Fruit trees in tubs lined the walls and a fountain of fine Italian marble leapt and rang in the center of the room. Well-tended fireplaces kept the temperature high enough for the plants to flourish and the room was redolent with citrus. Neither Jack nor Juliette paid this exotic luxury much attention.

"But in any case, I do not see that it is any concern of yours, sir," Juliette finished with great dignity.

"Certainly it is not—save that I am fond of my own comforts and dislike abiding in establishments set upon their ears."

"An odd comment from you, my lord!"

"Perhaps," said Jack imperturbably. "But I am considerably more experienced than you, and my advice upon the subject is sound. I can support the taint of scandal, which you, my child, cannot. You should refrain from ruffling the feathers of the older hens; their beaks can be sharper than you think."

Lady Juliette stared up at him, eyes flashing indignantly. "How dare you lecture me upon proper behavior, Lord Barham? When all the world knows that *you*—" She broke off, flushing.

"I dare the most amazing things," said Jack with a grin. "Now be a good girl and I shall restore you to young Candlesby's side with all speed; doubtless he can be persuaded he is longing to see you."

Lady Juliette made a strangled noise that might have been a muffled giggle, but when she answered her voice was steady. "Thank you, Lord Barham, but I have no wish to talk to Mr. Candlesby just yet; in fact I have something most particular to discuss with you."

Jack cocked an eyebrow at her. "My dear—my very dear Lady Juliette! I had no notion—but do you think you ought?"

Lady Juliette's ivory brow furrowed. "What do you mean?"

Abandoning his lightly flirtatious tone, Jack said, "I mean, Lady Juliette, that it is highly incautious of you to converse with a man of my reputation in such a fashion—and in such a secluded place!"

To his surprise, she smiled, a small, grave smile that tucked a dimple into the corner of her mouth. "Because you are a rake, you mean? But that is of no concern to me, sir."

"It isn't?" said Jack blankly.

"Not in the least," Lady Juliette informed him. "For while you must be interested in my fortune, you cannot touch it without marrying me, you know, and even then you would have only an income until my father died, and he is not yet five-and-forty! And you are not at all what I look for in a husband, my lord; I need a man who can manage Chaceley." She looked slightly wistful. "That is why I went to Town this Season—"

"To find a husband for Chaceley?" put in Jack dryly.

Lady Juliette apparently missed the note of mockery, for she merely nodded. "And I thought I should, for while I know I am not so great a beauty as Mama was, I am quite well-looking enough, and brunettes are all the crack just now, you know! And Mattie—my abigail—first came to Chaceley with Mama, and was able to tell me everything about her, so I knew if I went up to Town and did just as she had, I should be a Success too, and find a good man to help me run Chaceley. But for some reason it did not answer, and— But I do not know why I should be telling you this!" she finished rather crossly, as if he had somehow cozened the admission out of her.

"And so you are still heart-whole and fancy-free," Jack said with a smile. "But don't worry, Lady Juliette—surely somewhere in all of England exists the paragon who will be worthy of Chaceley."

Lady Juliette set her chin. "You may scoff, Lord Barham, for it plainly is impossible for you to understand that I do not wish to see my lands given over to some wastrel who will see them only as a source of money for his racing stables and his gaming debts. It is my duty to take care of Chaceley, for the estate is not entailed, and the wrong man might lose it entirely!"

Jack regarded her almost with awe, torn between the desire to laugh, an equally strong desire to shake Lady Juliette until her teeth rattled, and an urge to comfort the troubled expression out of those impossible emerald eyes. Unfortunately, none of these tempting courses would endear him to a girl whose feelings were so obviously smarting from the failure of her carefully planned campaign. He settled for reaching out to take her kid-gloved hand in his. "My dear child," he began, feeling oddly responsible for her disappointment, "has it never occurred to you—"

To his surprise and chagrin, Lady Juliette snatched her hand away, eyes dark and cheeks flaming. "And *you* are worse than they!" she said in a low, passionate voice. "I wonder, my lord, that you can still look yourself in the eye!"

Before the Marquess could rally against this sudden attack, Lady Juliette swept from the orangery without another word, leaving him staring after her in confusion. He hadn't the faintest understanding of the cause of her shift in mood; a new sensation for him with regard to a woman, and one he cared for not at all.

It was high time, in the humble opinion of the Marquess of Barham, that the self-possessed Lady Juliette was taught a lesson. Only a certain indecision as to the object of this lesson, and the necessity of going up to change for dinner, prevented him from following her to adminster it immediately.

How could she be so taken in? This was the question Lady Juliette could not answer. Time and again she would find herself in conversation with the Marquess of Barham, and time and again he would beguile her into forgetting that he was not only heartless and profligate, but the living incarnation of all she despised in men.

Well, she was no longer to be beguiled. She must speak immediately to Douglas Candlesby; if Douglas would not speak to Lord Ralph himself, *she* would explain matters. She dared swear she could do a better job of it than Mr. Candlesby, in any case!

But when she inquired for Douglas, it was discovered that he was down at the kennels with the gentlemen of the house party. That would never do; Juliette must see Douglas alone. Juliette, fuming, went upstairs to dress for dinner.

An hour later, attired in dashing creation of poppy-colored sarcenet trimmed in knots of green ribbons that Mattie said gave Miss Julie a bit of color, Juliette was ready for battle. A green-and-purple Cashemire shawl, to compensate for draughty hallways, was tucked lovingly round her by Mattie, and then Juliette scurried out to lie in wait for the unsuspecting Mr. Candlesby in the long gallery outside his room.

"Douglas! I must speak with you alone!"

"What? Now? I mean, your very obedient, Lady Juliette, but—almost time for dinner, you know!" There was little doubt that Mr. Candlesby had taken particular pains over this evening's toilette: his imposing collar points were of a great height and whiteness, his trousers were a daring shade of pale yellow, and his waistcoat was an almost incandescent confection in embroidered Chinese silk. Juliette, who was up to every nicety of hunt livery, hardly noticed this stunning ensemble.

"Oh, not now, stupid!" she said quickly. "Later. Walk with me after dinner—in the conservatory!"

"But— That is, dash it all, Lady Juliette—"

"Promise!" Juliette hissed fiercely, hearing footsteps at the far end of the gallery and fearing for their privacy.

Douglas, blinking in surprise, agreed.

Juliette paid little attention to the evening meal—even an announcement that a party from Temple Down would be joining them tomorrow evening drew only automatic politenesses from her, and she forgot the information as soon as it was mentioned. She was aware of Lady Hawkchurch's disapproving stare, although what that dowager could find to disapprove of now, Juliette couldn't imagine. In any case, Lady Hawkchurch would do better to reserve that basilisk stare for the Marquess of Barham—instead of positively fawning over the man as she was doing!

After dinner Juliette talked nervously to Althea until the gentlemen finally rose from their wine to join the ladies in the drawing-room. As soon as Douglas Candlesby appeared Juliette leapt to her feet, deserting Althea and snatching Douglas from Isobel Fonthill with no more than a garbled excuse. As Douglas stared bemused, Juliette marched him off to the conservatory.

The conservatory on such a night would have been the perfect trysting-place for lovers. Moonlight streaming through the glass silvered Juliette's ruddy gown and gleamed on her dark hair. Unfortunately, as Juliette prided herself on her practical mind, and Mr. Candlesby had no interest in her charms, this idyllic setting was quite wasted on them.

"Dash it all, Lady Juliette, what was so devilish important that you had to drag me all the way out here?" Douglas demanded. "Belle's wondering if I've run mad!"

"Douglas, you must ask Lord Barham to buy back those annuities you made over to him," Juliette told him flatly. "You know Duckmanton cannot possibly stand such a charge upon it— I daresay there is already a mortgage on the property, and the estate is not large. If you do not make Lord Barham settle what he owes, you will be turned out in your shirt-sleeves when the time comes for you to repay the principal."

Mr. Candlesby stared at her. "Now you've run mad," he finally pronounced.

"Indeed I have not! Lord Barham will not make good the debt, Douglas—even if he intended to, which I doubt; all the world knows he will have nothing when Owlsthorne dies. He *cannot* pay it!"

She waited hopefully as Mr. Candlesby appeared

to consider the matter carefully. "Well," he said finally, "as you say Jack hasn't the money, and no more have I; I shall just have to be ruined, then," he finished with a cheerfulness that left Juliette wishing to wring his neck.

"Oh, do be serious! If you apply directly to the Duke of Owlsthorne he must be constrained by common decency to pay his son's debt. Is he not a crony of your grandfather? You must tell Lord Ralph—"

"M'father! Lord, there's no cause to be dragging him into this! Swear you'll say nothing to him!"

Juliette nearly stamped her foot in frustration. "For heaven's sake, Douglas Candlesby, do you want to be a pauper, or in debtor's prison? You must at least speak to Lord Barham about this!"

At this most reasonable demand, Mr. Candlesby drew himself up with an expression of affronted dignity. "You're not the only one who knows how to go on, Lady Juliette. I daresay others have a tolerable understanding—and the Candlesby brain is well-known to be at its best in dealing with trifles of this nature."

"But—"

"Now promise you'll say nothing to m'father!"

"But Douglas, someone must!"

"Well, even if someone must, it ain't your place to," Douglas told her bluntly, and as honesty compelled Juliette to admit that he was quite right, she was forced to concede.

"Oh, very well! But—"

"Now we'll say no more about it," Mr. Candlesby announced magnanimously. "You've just gotten things all turned 'round and muddled up. Females don't understand business. Just leave it to me and everything'll turn out first-rate. You'll see."

As Juliette marshaled her arguments for another attempt at making him see reason, Douglas bowed, raised her hand to rain kisses six inches above it, and took his leave.

With that Juliette was forced to be content. It was plain now that Douglas Candlesby would continue to do nothing until the bailiffs came to drag him away. It was apparently impossible, short of physical force, to make him see the necessity of action—the Candlesby brain notwithstanding. For her part, Juliette doubted the very existence of the vaunted Candlesby brain, let alone its ability to contend with a matter of this nature.

And while Juliette would have been quite willing to go to Lord Ralph, business of hers or no, she had no real information to impart to him. She could only bear the tale that Douglas had said that he had guaranteed loans for the Marquess of Barham; if Douglas, confronted by his father, chose to deny the whole—

That left only one person who could reveal the matter to Lord Ralph and hope to be effective. Juliette wrapped her shawl more firmly around her and stared unseeing at the glorious vision that was the conservatory by moonlight, her mouth set in a determined line. Her duty was plain; she must confront the Marquess of Barham with her knowledge of the affair and bring him to a sense of his own culpability.

Chapter

FIVE

In point of fact, the Marquess of Barham already felt quite as guilty about the matter of his debts as even Lady Juliette would have liked. It had been a grave mistake to come to Duckmanton at all; Jack would have been far more comfortable never seeing Douglas Candlesby's home, nor talking with Lord and Lady Ralph, whose upbringing had made their well-loved son into the sort of affectionate idiot who had ruined them all with a generous gesture. Douglas Candlesby, ideally suited by nature to idolize an elder brother, had been deprived of that object for his adorations by fate, until he had not unnaturally cast Jack Barham in the role. Jack, who had, to be frank, paid little heed to Douglas save as a convenient soft touch, now wished Candlesby, Duckmanton, and the damned annuities at the devil. A man who led Jack Barham's life couldn't afford to be sentimental, nor to have a conscience.

On the other hand, he could and did think more clearly than those encumbered by such emotional baggage. Since he could not pay the bonds, and it was increasingly obvious that Douglas could not either, the answer was simple: like it or not, Douglas should marry Lady Juliette Devereaux. It was an oddly unattractive idea; Lady Juliette was quite right—Douglas Candlesby wasn't up to her weight. But if she weren't interested in the damned young idiot, why did she keep snatching him off like that?

Douglas Candlesby's return, alone, put an end to this line of thought. Mr. Candlesby was greeted by smiles of approbation from his doting mama, and by a decided coolness from Miss Isobel Fonthill. Douglas, undaunted, flung himself gracefully at her feet and endeavored to draw her into conversation, but she so coldly rebuffed him, and talked so pointedly to her sister, that finally Althea excused herself and wandered over to the pianoforte, where Mr. Anthony Devereaux was desultorily picking out a tune.

"May I join you?" Althea said. "We might play duets, although I warn you I am but an indifferent musician."

Mr. Devereaux must have replied in the affirmative, as Jack heard the tinkling strains of a popular four-handed melody begin a moment later. It formed a cheerful counterpoint to the tender scene unfolding across the room: Miss Isobel, deprived of her sister's support, had relented, and Mr. Candlesby now sat beside her on the settee, deep in conversation and oblivious to his mother's pointed glances. It was altogether a sweetly peaceful scene and should not have been a sight to wring anyone's heart, let alone to cause such a chill as fastened on the Marquess of Barham.

Only Lightfoot Bobby Gressingham had told Jack to the penny what Isobel Fonthill would bring, and Jack knew it wasn't enough.

Juliette slept far into the next morning and awoke feeling unaccountably languid. She had only a little more of this selfish freedom to look forward to—the arranging of Douglas Candlesby's affairs was a small matter for one accustomed to management and command. It didn't occur to Juliette that it was exceedingly odd for a young lady of twenty to be arranging matters for a gentleman four years her senior. She had never had anyone to turn to for support and protection; it was her place, as mistress of the manor, to provide it. If she was accustomed to deference, she was also accustomed to service and self-sufficiency.

She stretched and yawned luxuriously, casting a knowledgeable eye at the late-morning sunlight. Why, it must be nearly nine o'clock! She had never lain abed so late before this Season, when she had merely made the night her day, putting in as many hard hours of work as she did at Chaceley—with as little leisure for her own concerns.

But for yet another few weeks, she could do as she pleased; no servants would look to her for guidance, she could amuse herself with her friends. Why, then, this feeling of restlessness and discontent? There was absolutely nothing wrong with her life, Juliette told herself crossly as she rang sharply for Mattie. She was not some silly girl, she was Lady Juliette Devereaux, Mistress of Chaceley, and all her affairs were in perfect order—or would be very soon!

"And how is Miss this morning?" said Mattie as she entered with Juliette's chocolate and biscuits.

Juliette favored the loyal abigail with a bright smile. "Why, I am very well, Mattie. Isn't it the most perfect day?"

"It's that new horse," said Mattie darkly. "I don't doubt you'd find a blizzard perfect were a new horse arriving. Just like my lady—oh, how you do take after her, my lovey!"

"Horse?" said Juliette blankly. "Oh, yes, Lord Templeton is sending Oriflamme to me today, I believe. Set out my rose morning dress, Mattie, and take that chocolate away."

When Juliette went down to breakfast she learned that Lord Ralph had offered to show the party some sport and taken the men off with guns, dogs, and bearers. Juliette almost wished she were with them; it was one of those blue-and-gold days that are supposed properly to belong to summer, but which never really appear until the fall. Helping herself to a generous portion of kidneys, bacon, fried bread, tomatoes, and coddled eggs, she could look across the lawn to the ornamental water, a glowing sky-reflecting blue edged about with waterlilies that had not yet succumbed to the autumn chill. She longed to be out of doors, to fly cross-country at the gallop, but the opening of the hunt season proper was still far off. All one would get now was cubbing. Normally Juliette found the introduction of the young hounds to their work of intense interest, but today that, too, seemed stale and flat.

The peace that had been so welcome only an hour ago was now oppressive, and the unaccountable restlessness seized her again. She started nervously at a sound behind her, but it was only Althea Fonthill, coming in rather late to breakfast. She was dressed simply, fittingly, and modestly in a morning robe of pale cerulean muslin decorated with tiny knots of silk flowers. Juliette thought it bland, and was sure her deep rose silk with the ruffled gauze overdress was by far the prettier.

"Juliette!" said Althea happily. "I thought I should be left quite alone, and I am very glad for your company. But you are generally up long before this—is your headache better?"

Juliette had almost forgotten the excuse she had used to flee the rest of the evening after her unsuccessful interview with Douglas. Reminded by Althea's remark, she hastily pronounced herself quite cured. "I, too, thought I should be alone at breakfast," she added in a tone that made Althea say,

"Oh, dear—shall I take myself away again? You will be quite undisturbed then, I think, for Isobel is writing letters, and Mama and Lady Hawkchurch and Lady Ralph are examining the herb garden, and as for Miss Gressingham—" Here Althea paused and shuddered dramatically. "*She* is in the library reading improving tracts, and I dare not venture in for fear of being read to."

Juliette smiled, rather wistfully, and said, "No, please do stay, Thea. I—I need your advice."

This was such a novel announcement from Lady Juliette Devereaux that Althea took a moment to gather her resources, gaining time by ringing for Wiggins to bring her a pot of tea and some toast that had not yet attained a state of fossilization.

Once the tea had arrived and the servants departed, Juliette had apparently forgotten that she had solicited Althea's advice. Althea, to fill the silence, offered up the topic much on her own mind.

"I must say, Juliette, that I am quite glad to know that you have no interest in accepting Douglas Candlesby's suit—even if he were to offer—or I should be quite distracted to think that my baby sister had stolen him from under your very nose."

"What?" said Juliette, her attention yanked suddenly back to the here and now. "Thea—you don't mean Douglas and Isobel—?"

Althea nodded. "You did not see them together last night because you retired early with the headache, but it looks perilously like a match to me! Only imagine, Juliette—not once did he make a pretty speech to her or ask if he might dedicate a poetic effusion to her. He simply glowered at everyone who came near, and when I teased Belle with it later—oh, how she blushed! But I shall have the truth out of her, never fear, and if he can be brought to the point Mama will be so pleased—and so shall I, if she can make a suitable match and a love match at the same time."

"Oh, but this is dreadful!" Juliette burst out.

"I *beg* your pardon?" said Althea stiffly.

"Oh, Althea—you said there must be money for a suitable match. Well, there isn't!"

That morning the Marquess of Barham, reverting to military habits, was up with the dawn, as much to escape further conversation with Lord Ralph as from any desire to observe the beauties of the sunrise. If the Duckmanton grooms were startled to see a member of the Quality up and about at that unwonted hour they concealed it admirably and soon had Cavalier saddled and brought round. Not half-an-hour after arising, Jack had Cavalier under him and was trotting through a world made silver by the early frost.

Like Lady Juliette, the Marquess, too, was restive and out-of-sorts with the world. He had grown increasingly dissatisfied with both himself and his way of life even before coming to Sussex; the respectable atmosphere of Duckmanton only exacerbated the feeling.

If he had any sense, or any decency, he would depart immediately. He could simply keep riding, and no one would miss him overmuch—least of all his much-tried hostess, Lady Ralph Candlesby. But he had forfeited all claims to decency long ago, and as his pockets were very much to let, he could only hope Lady Ralph's nerves would hold out another fortnight. Then he would, with only a little aid from Dame Fortune, be plump in the pocket when Sultan won the St. Leger, and he could join Drewmore's party of pleasure, and that would see out the year. As for what he would do then—

His hands tightened on the reins; Cavalier tossed his head to make his objection to this unwarranted interference known. Jack smiled ruefully and relaxed his grip, patting Cavalier's neck apologetically. "Sorry, old boy. If I had the sense you do, I wouldn't be in this damned mess."

Cavalier shook his head and snorted, and Jack laughed. "Too true," he said. "Of course," he added meditatively, "if I had the sense that managing little Lady Juliette has, I'd be in a worse one, so all things considered—"

He stopped, reining Cavalier to a halt. To extricate himself—and, incidentally, Douglas—from *this* imbroglio would take something like twelve thousand pounds cash. According to Robert Gressingham, who made it his business to know such things, Lady Juliette Devereaux would bring more than five times that when she finally bestowed her heart and hand. She might not be as rich as "Golden Ball" Hughes, but as far as he could tell not a stick nor stone of her inheritance was entailed, and the moment she married it would go to her husband.

Juliette had categorically refused to consider

Douglas Candlesby as that husband, and Jack now was glad of it. For why, after all, should Candlesby take that appealing prize when Jack himself would put it to so much better use?

For if he married her, he could raise loans fast enough on those glittering expectations—by God, the money-lenders would fall all over themselves to advance him the blunt then! He could buy back those blasted post-obits from Douglas, and then, by heaven, he would redeem Owlsthorne from his father's ruinous clutches if he had to drag the old devil through every court in the country to do it.

True, Lady Juliette had also declared that Jack himself was not-at-all what she looked for in a husband, but he dared swear, he thought with some amusement, that he could be. Oh, of course she feared for her precious Chaceley, but lawyers could see most of that estate safety tied up for her children; there would be quite enough income to let Jack come about and support himself in comfort, if not in luxury. Doubtless Lady Juliette would be delighted to have a pupil for her theories on management. In return, Jack would undertake to choose her dresses for her.

She was too serious by far, but that too could be remedied, and he'd not yet met the young lady who'd turn up her nose at the eventual title of Duchess. Even with his tattered reputation, there'd been many willing to chance his reformation for the pleasure of being called "Your Grace." Yes, it began to seem that Lady Juliette Devereaux was very much what he looked for in a wife. It remained only to convince that self-possessed young lady that they would suit; Jack fancied, somehow, that she was not as entirely immune to his manly charms as she so obviously liked to think.

"Lady Juliette, 'how stands your disposition to be married?' " Jack quoted to the frost-bright air.

Cavalier, tired of standing here while his master made ridiculous remarks, pawed the ground vigorously. Jack, conscious of an odd lightness of heart, urged the black charger to a swinging canter and let him have his head. As long as he was this far along, he might as well pay a visit to Temple Down. He was sure his prospective bride would prefer horses to jewels as a wedding gift.

It would be inaccurate to say that Miss Fonthill understood all of Lady Juliette's impassioned explanation of Douglas Candlesby's folly, post-obit bonds, principal, and annuities, but she grasped quite clearly that the situation was serious. "Oh, dear," she said when Juliette stopped and looked entreatingly at her. "I must confess, Juliette, that it sounds very bad indeed."

"Oh, Althea, it is worse than that! For when the principal comes due it will be the *whole*, and that after Douglas has been paying outrageous interest for years. And if he does not, they will have him in court—or in prison."

"That would be exceedingly awkward," said Althea, "especially if he is married to Belle. Certainly Mr. Candlesby must be made to see reason while there is still time for him to make a recover."

"And so I have told him and told him! But he will not, and—and I am not precisely sure what to do."

"Nonsense, as you yourself would say. You always have a plan, and you know that in this case I must help you, unless it is totally ineligible. Do tell me what it is."

"It is all Lord Barham's fault," said Juliette roundly. "And I shall go to him and tell him so!

And then I shall insist that he speak to Lord Ralph."

Miss Fonthill looked down at her empty plate, biting her lip. After a moment, she remarked, with commendable steadiness, that Juliette's plan was only what she had expected of her. "But you must see, Juliette, that it is unlikely to—to work as you wish."

"I do not see why," said Juliette, frowning.

"Because gentlemen in general—and we must account Lord Barham a gentleman, if only by courtesy—do not like to be dictated to by females. And if he says no, what will you do then?"

"Well, I—" Juliette began decisively, and stopped. Althea was quite right; if the Marquess chose not to behave as she wished, what could she do? This was not Chaceley, after all—she could not have him thrown out of the house.

"Perhaps if you laid the matter before our cousin? Mr. Devereaux has a great deal of sense, you know, and—"

"*Tony?*" said Juliette in disbelief. "Oh, no, Thea—he would only tell me that any of Barham's to-do's was not my concern—and that I should come away to Fakenham with him—and that I *will* not!"

Althea considered this for a moment. It hardly boded well for Mr. Devereaux's matrimonial destiny—such as he had confided to her—that his prospective bride thought so little of his problem-solving ability. Still, that confidence was not hers to betray—Mr. Devereaux must make his own declaration. "Of course, a gentleman who has developed a *tendre* for a lady is a trifle more inclined to do as she says, even without the adoption of physical force," Althea continued. "So with your permission, Juliette, failing Mr. Devereaux's in-

tervention, I shall lay all before Belle. There is
no need to tease Mama with it just yet—and perhaps, if matters progress as I think they must, she
can bring Mr. Candlesby to follow what I am persuaded is the wisest course, and tell his father the
whole."

However, if Althea had no faith in Juliette's ability to bend the Marquess to her will, Juliette had
even less in Isobel Fonthill's ability to influence
Douglas Candlesby to a sensible course of action.
On the other hand. . . . Juliette abstractedly began
to chew on a piece of toast, which, having been
passed over for others for too long, was cold and
stiff with this prolonged rejection.

No, one could not expect reason from Douglas,
however besotted with Isobel he might be. Althea's
conversation, however, had given Juliette a new
and attractive notion of her own. It remained only
to consider how this infallible plan might best be
put into execution

The park at Temple Down, shaded by its surrounding trees, was still shining with frost as Jack
rode up the broad avenue. The sight of the sprawl-
ing stables, a-bustle with the peaceful tasks of early
morning, had the odd effect of dampening Jack's
good spirits and making him wonder what he was
really doing here. He and Harry Templeton were
not on terms of easy intimacy, and grandiose plans
to marry an heiress were hardly enough to justify
imposing himself further on Lord Templeton in the
guise of prospective purchaser.

He was guilty of air-dreaming quite as badly as
any silly chit of a girl. This mortifying realization
made him rein Cavalier in sharply. Fortunately, it

was not too late to remedy the matter; he would simple ride straight back to Duckmanton.

This admirable plan was almost instantly thwarted by the appearance of Lord Templeton himself. By nature an early riser, this morning the Viscount had gone to the stables to personally oversee the disposition of the horses Lady Juliette had bought the day before, accompanied by a brace of his eldest son George's foolish and affectionate spaniels. As he left the stableyard to return to the house and breakfast the spaniels, espying a stranger in their midst, thundered forth crying battle.

Strategic retreat was impossible; Jack found his mount surrounded by two floppy-eared dogs of apparently murderous inclination. The spaniels bounced and bayed; Cavalier lowered his head and sniffed inquisitively, only to jerk back again as one of the spaniels, in a veritable frenzy of battlelust, licked his nose.

If Marcus Templeton were surprised to see so early and so unannounced a visitor to his stables, he gave no evidence of it. Marcus, having raised three sons to adulthood, was tolerably conversant with the ways of young men who considered themselves dangerous. Lord Barham, stiffly erect upon his black charger, bore the look of one who would not take kindly to impertinent questions this morning, and who was, moreover, in the mood to find almost anything an impertinence.

As Marcus had no desire to embark on the tedious and fatiguing business of being thought impertinent by a touchy young buck half his own age, he merely nodded a greeting and adjured Jack to tell him what the head of the House of Templeton could do for the son of the Duke of Owlsthorne.

"Nothing whatever, sir; I am sorry to have disturbed you. I was riding, and did not realize I had come so far along the avenue, and your dogs did the rest. I beg you will excuse me."

Lord Templeton toyed briefly with the notion of accepting this and allowing Jack to remove himself, but he was a kind-hearted man and young Barham looked as if something had touched him on the raw this morning. "Not-at-all, I am glad of the company. George is still in London visiting my sister, and Harry was, I am very much afraid, out raking last night and oddly enough had no interest in joining me this morning. Come along, if you will—I was just looking over the horses Lady Juliette bespoke; they are to go to Chaceley today."

Jack hesitated, then condescended to accompany Lord Templeton on his rounds. As the young animals were paraded in front of them, he was forced to admire Lady Juliette's judgment in matters equine, if not in matters sartorial. Clothes sense she might lack, but his little wood-nymph had a great deal of horse sense. He said as much to Lord Templeton, who sighed and agreed.

"Yes, she does—Sebastian taught her well."

Jack raised his eyebrows. "You don't approve, sir?"

"Let us just say, Lord Barham, and I feel that a daughter should be raised as a daughter, rather than as—"

"A son?" Jack suggested with a wry smile.

"An estate agent," said Marcus Templeton flatly. "And I'm afraid he did my goddaughter no great service thereby."

"Surely her mother—" Jack began, remembering Juliette's remarks about that Success whom she had so hoped to emulate.

"Little though you would think it to hear Juliette go on about her," said Marcus dryly, "her mother died before she was a year old. She was Sophia Halford, you know, and a cousin of my first wife."

"She was very beautiful, I collect?"

"Very beautiful and very willful, and when Sebastian Devereaux offered for her at the end of her second Season the Halfords breathed a sigh of relief that was doubtless heard in Paris."

Considerably startled, Jack tried to make this information jibe with what Juliette had let fall about her much-admired mother, whom his poor little wood-nymph apparently considered the pattern-card of perfection. "What happened to her, sir?"

Lord Templeton told him, and then allowed himself to be cozened into revealing enough about Lady Juliette's subsequent rearing to bring a look of indignant sympathy to Jack's face. Marcus Templeton was most reprehensibly amused by Bad Lord Barham's interest, and rather more aware of its cause than was the Marquess himself.

"But you will not wish to stand here listening to family gossip all day," Lord Templeton finished. "No, no, it's very polite of you, but I've no wish to bore you."

"I assure you, sir—"

"For nothing, I am convinced, is more tedious than listening to long stories about persons in whom one has not the slightest interest." Marcus smiled. "Now, you'll stay to breakfast, I hope?"

Jack looked startled. "I—you're far too generous, Lord Templeton!"

"You're far too much in awe of your own reputation, Lord Barham; while I have more sense than to throw my daughters in your way—you'd put too many damn-fool romantic ideas into their silly heads!—none of them will be downstairs at this hour. Be a good lad and come along, and save me from my own company."

Either Marcus Templeton usually made a solitary breakfast at this very early hour, or the admirable Euphemia, well-warned by the servants, had discreetly absented herself. Jack spent most of the meal considering the information Marcus had imparted about the Devereaux family in general, and Lady Juliette's upbringing in particular; it was, in Jack's opinion, no way to raise a lady. No wonder there was that wistful look in those deep green eyes. . . .

He did not realize how thoroughly occupied he had been in gathering wool until Lord Templeton's use of his name called him sharply back to attention. "I beg pardon, sir?"

"It's nothing to do with you, of course," Lord Templeton went on imperturbably, as if he were quite accustomed to having his conversation so thoroughly ignored. "But I thought as you'd some experience with intractable horses, you might be able to offer advice. To hear Harry tell it, at least, some of your replacement mounts in Spain were little better than wild things, but you did wonders with them. So perhaps you can suggest some course to take with Vulcan. It's doing no good keeping him penned up in the stables. He upsets the other horses, not to mention the grooms." Marcus shook his head. "I'm too soft; I should have had him destroyed years ago."

"That would be a criminal waste of good horseflesh, and I hate waste." Jack sat up straighter, and his eyes gleamed. "Lord Templeton—I think I could ride Vulcan."

"Ride him?" exclaimed Marcus, startled. "You're mad, boy."

Jack shook his head. "No—or at least, no madder than necessary! Any horse can be ridden—by the proper person, and that's what Vulcan needs—some hard riding to take the tricks out of him."

"And you think you're the proper person to ride him?"

Jack shrugged, as if the matter were of no particular interest; Lord Templeton, regarding him shrewdly, suddenly laughed. "Well, perhaps you are at that. Very well, Lord Barham, you may try—but mind, I'm not having that devil rampaging all over the county with my saddle on his back."

"I'll use mine," said Jack quickly, ignoring Lord Templeton's implication that Vulcan would instantly deposit him in the nearest ditch. "Would you care to place a small wager on the outcome, sir? I back myself to back Vulcan. As you plainly think I'll break my neck, shall we say my Cavalier if you're right against Vulcan if you're wrong?"

Marcus Templeton lifted an eyebrow. "You seem to place very little value on your neck, Lord Barham."

"Cavalier needs a good home, and my neck, Lord Templeton, is of precious little value at the best of times. Shall we adjourn to the stables?"

The Templeton grooms were unenthusiastic about the prospect of approaching Vulcan. Jack, to the eternal gratitude of the stable staff, spurned all assistance in favor of handling the big stallion himself. Vulcan regarded him with a rolling eye, but Jack's prowess with half-wild cavalry mounts had not been exaggerated; after a brief contretemps in the loose-box Vulcan had not only been persuaded to stand for saddling, but was regarding Jack with wary caution.

It had not been an easy task, however, and both man and horse were wet with sweat by the time Jack led the quivering Vulcan out into the yard. As they cleared the stable doors, Jack felt the stallion collect himself to lunge. He had expected that, however, and before Vulcan could decide whether it would be more amusing to run over Jack or to scatter the watching grooms, Jack was in the saddle. Vulcan, stunned by this unexpected development, stopped dead for the instant Jack needed to settle himself in the saddle.

"Get out of the way!" he yelled at the goggling audience, and the grooms obediently scattered as Jack set his heels to Vulcan's heaving sides.

Startled—for on those rare occasions when a human dared attempt to ride Vulcan, they were more in the habit of trying to rein him in than to urge him on—the big stallion sprang forward and up, twisting as he went. Jack, to everyone's astonishment, rode out Vulcan's spirited attempt to fold himself in half and then urged the stallion on once more.

Vulcan needed no more encouragement. He shot out of the stableyard at a dead gallop, sliding on the cobbles and nearly swiping Jack off at the entryway. Lord Templeton, watching from the relative safety of the tack-room, winced, but Jack weathered this valiant attempt on the part of his mount to murder him without apparent difficulty. The stableyard was safely cleared; a few moments later horse and rider were out of sight.

There was a second's awed silence, almost instantly broken by a babble of voices laying long odds that neither the mad stallion nor his even madder rider would be seen in these parts again. Marcus Templeton himself felt that would be too much to hope for; he contented himself with remarking mildly that he was surprised at so much leisure so early in the day. The stablemen scattered almost as rapidly as they had for Vulcan, and Marcus, casting a last glance in the direction Jack had taken, strolled up to the house, there to sit on the veranda that overlooked the stables and await further developments.

Vulcan tried to take the bit in his teeth as he bolted, but Jack was by far too canny a horseman to allow that; Vulcan might run as he liked, but Jack kept control of the reins. It was the only thing that stood between him and the nearest overhanging branch—even Vulcan had to respect a good sharp yank on a double curb.

But branches aside, the stallion was given his head. Jack had a pretty shrewd idea that bolting was only one of Vulcan's many little tricks. Very well, the stallion should run. Jack set himself to the task of keeping his seat and enjoying the ride; Vulcan, flying madly along, was the fastest thing it had ever been Jack's good fortune to meet.

The wind of their passage whipped Vulcan's mane into tangles and made Jack's eyes water. The sheer speed and power was almost intoxicating.

But even Vulcan could not keep up such a pace forever—or even for long. As he slowed his pace, the stallion's ears flicked back and forth, and Jack knew he was contemplating mischief.

"Oh, no you don't," said Jack, and tapped Vulcan firmly with his riding crop.

Vulcan, outraged, leapt forward in a dead run once more. After a few moments, he slackened his pace, only to be whipped up to the same frenzied gallop. This time the stallion tried to slow down almost immediately, snorting and shaking his head fretfully.

"Sorry, old fellow," said Jack, and drove him on again. Vulcan had too much energy and too many tricks, and Jack knew his only chance was to ride the horse to the brink of exhaustion . . . "And hope it doesn't kill both of us," he told Vulcan, digging his heels harder into the tiring stallion's sides.

Several hours later Jack rode the crestfallen Vulcan—at a gentle walk—through the archway into the stableyard at Temple Down. It took only a hint that his rider was interested in halting to bring Vulcan to a standstill; his breathing was no longer labored, and his sweat-soaked coat had dried on the long walk back, but the stallion's muscles trembled with fatigue.

Jack, swinging down from the saddle to greet Lord Templeton, sympathized deeply with Vulcan. His own legs were none too steady under him. "Well, Lord Templeton, I have returned with my neck intact," said Jack, catching Vulcan's reins immediately below the bit and rubbing the stallion's rumpled neck. "I told you all he needed was a bit of exercise."

"So I see," said Marcus Templeton dryly. "Congratulations, Lord Barham, you've won yourself a horse. Might I enquire just what you're going to do with him?"

This brought Jack's head up, a flush darkening his features. "Don't be ridiculous, sir," he said haughtily. "You never accepted my wager."

"By silence and implication I most certainly did, and you will do me the favor, Lord Barham, of *not* treating me as your equal. I object to bad manners, particularly in the younger generation."

The Marquess, who was almost as accustomed as Vulcan to being treated with fear and trembling, was struck dumb by this plain speaking. Then, with an almost visible effort, he swallowed his anger. "I beg your pardon, sir. But I—I cannot accept Vulcan, although it's very kind of you—"

Lord Templeton waved him to silence. "Stop arguing with me, boy. You've won your wager—and if you call it kind to saddle you with a horse whose temper will have you thrown out of every place your own won't, and whose keep will be the ruin of you besides—I don't. But I do admit it'll be a relief to hand Vulcan over to someone who seems to be able to handle him."

As if on cue Vulcan bumped his head into Jack's chest and began to rub vigorously, sending Jack staggering back a step before he braced himself. "You're more than generous, sir," said Jack, uncomfortably conscious of the fact that he sounded more sulky than coldly dignified. "But I must confess I have no place to keep him. You can hardly expect Lady Ralph to welcome his presence in the Duckmanton stables!"

"The stables at the Temple Down Dower House are empty now. You may keep Vulcan there if you like. You'll have to provide your own groom, of course."

"Of course," agreed Jack with a grin. "And you must tell me, Lord Templeton, how I may best repay this—extravagant kindness."

"By removing Vulcan from my stables with as little delay as possible, for one thing," said Marcus Templeton promptly. "And as I have said, it's not kindness. I believe in like to like, Lord Barham, and better for you to have Vulcan than someone who would be missed."

Chapter
SIX

After breakfast Juliette wandered back and forth, all a-twitch. Not only was she contemplating her new plan for bringing the Marquess of Barham to his senses and his knees, but Oriflamme was to arrive today; these attractive distractions made it impossible for Juliette to embrace any program of entertainment, or even to sit still for more than three minutes together. Fortunately Althea, recognizing danger signs, forcibly removed Juliette to the library to bear her company and keep her out of the clutches of the rest of the house party. She knew that Lady Hawkchurch, at least, would surely have quizzed Juliette about her restlessness, and Juliette was in no mood to speak softly.

So Althea sat calmly stitching on her fancywork, while Juliette paced back and forth and eventually settled down with a copy of the *London Almanack*, admiring, in a perfunctory sort of way, what Althea could only regard as the most ineligible dresses.

Finally Juliette closed the volume with a sigh. "It is no use. I shall die of boredom if I sit here another minute, but what else is there to do? Oh, Althea, you are too good to stay with me like this, when I am persuaded you are as bored as I!"

"I, bored? Well, if I am, boredom is far preferable to many other states, and besides, I have my fancywork to occupy me. Embroidery with colored threads is so much more enjoyable than plain sewing of shifts and petticoats, don't you think?"

"I don't know," said Juliette, glancing yet again at the mantle clock and tapping her fingers impatiently on the arm of her chair. "I do not know how to sew."

"You cannot sew?" Althea was dumbfounded. True, she had never seen Juliette occupied with her needle, but she had thought only that Lady Juliette disdained the gentle art. It had never occurred to Miss Fonthill that any young lady of quality would lack this skill entirely. "But Juliette, surely your governess . . . ?"

"Oh, I daresay Miss Foljambe tried, but I was not a clever pupil, so when I was fourteen Papa sent her away, saying I could manage very well on my own. And so I did—I have ridden to hounds since I was in short skirts!" she finished proudly.

Miss Fonthill privately doubted that any proficiency in the hunt field would attract the suitor Juliette claimed to require, or replace the social graces and accomplishments she unfortunately lacked. Riding to hounds! And not her own father's pack, either, but the local Squire's! No respectable unmarried female did such a thing—it was considered dashing conduct in a matron. Reputation aside, few ladies cared to risk the certain falls that attended upon jumping fences while riding sidesaddle. Did Juliette's father have *no* concern for his daughter?

Sternly, Althea admonished herself for such uncharitable thoughts. But really, when one thought of poor Lady Juliette, who wished so much to be "all the crack" as her mother had been, and hadn't the least idea of how to go on—!

However, Miss Fonthill had a great deal of self-control, and contented herself with saying mildly, "I daresay you have—only it is not always hunting season, you know, and there are times when I have found it quite useful to be able to efface myself behind my embroidery hoop!"

"Really?" said Juliette seriously. "When?"

Althea smiled a little at the gravity of Lady Juliette's expression. "Oh, when Mama's callers are very dull, I can meekly concentrate upon a pillow cover and not have to think what to say. And when Belle has callers and Mama does not wish to be bored to death with their chatter, I sit virtuously in the corner and stitch away, harmless as a little mouse, and as little regarded, I promise you! Fancywork is such a useful social grace. If you like, I could teach you some stitches."

Lady Juliette appeared to consider the matter intently for a moment, then nodded decisively. "Yes, if you please! I should like that above all things."

This took Miss Fonthill aback; she had made the offer only out of automatic politeness and had never expected Juliette to accept. It struck Althea suddenly that perhaps Lady Juliette was rather lonely; certainly there would be little companionship of her own sort for a young lady who spent her time managing an estate and riding to hounds!

So Althea's pretty workbox was plundered for silks, needles, and a second length of linen, and soon Althea was painstakingly instructing a grimly determined Juliette in needlework, much as she had once instructed her young sister Isobel.

"I shall find the hunt field dreadfully flat after this!" Juliette announced in mocking triumph nearly an hour later. A line of uneven stitches straggled across the rumpled piece of linen as visible proof of battle engaged. She set the cloth in her lap, mindful of the needle, and added ruefully, "I am said to have excellent hands, but this—"

Althea laughed at Juliette's aggrieved expression. "It will come with practice—you did not learn to ride in a day, did you? And perhaps your great-aunt can show you how to go on, if you wish to continue with your needlework. You go to her at the end of this week, do you not?"

"Not if I can help it!" said Juliette in genuine alarm. "I tell you, I had rather face anything than Madame!"

Althea looked startled. "But Juliette—I know it was she who particularly wished you to go to London, and of course she must hope for you to marry well. Surely she will not think it your fault that you did not have an offer you wished to accept."

Juliette looked down and twisted her hands in her lap, looking very like a small child caught out in some mischief. "Oh, no, but . . . but of course she wished me to have a successful Season, like my mother's!"

"Well, then, perhaps she will take you to Bath for the Little Season," suggested Althea. Lady Juliette was plainly quite agitated, so soothing words were in order. "Or to Brighton, perhaps?"

"I have been to both Bath and Brighton, and I am done with the Season in any size or shape!" Juliette declared fiercely. "I shall *not* go anywhere but home to Chaceley! Besides, the Squire's young hounds will be entered to fox soon, and I wish to be there for the cubbing. The Alworthy Hunt may have only bag-foxes and a trencher-fed pack, but I daresay we have as tolerable sport as any in the country," she finished proudly.

"I daresay," Althea agreed, frowning. "Juliette, whatever are you talking about? It sounds so—so slangy."

Juliette looked at her in astonishment. "Why, I was only telling you about Squire Alworthy's pack—fox hunting, you know, Thea. You should try it, it is the most exhilarating sport imaginable!" Then Juliette looked eagerly at Althea. "Oh, Thea, do come to Chaceley with me for the holidays. I should so love to have you, and I know we could find something in the stables to suit you, and we would have some famous sport. I cannot wait to show Maria Alworthy the way on my Oriflamme!"

"I am very much afraid," said Althea, "that Mama would have a spasm were I even to suggest that I ride to hounds. My consequence is not great enough to support eccentricity, you know! But I should like very much to see Chaceley, and I will come if it can be managed. Only think, if Mr. Candlesby does fix his interest with Isobel, there is every possibility that we will be asked to remain at Duckmanton for an extended period—but *that* would mean that Mama will turn out to have me wed too. I should not mind that so much, only I am certain her hopes will turn upon a brown curate."

Juliette was diverted for a moment by the thought of Althea married to such an ineligible commodity. Then her mind turned to the substance of Althea's statement. "Douglas! Oh, Althea, has Isobel prevailed upon him about the bonds?"

Althea seemed to droop a little. "I do not think so. Belle will not even admit that she had formed a *tendre* for him, and will say only that if she must be poor, she'd as lief be poor in a fine house in the country with servants and coal-fires on every grate."

"Well, there is a great deal of sense to that," Juliette agreed, and Althea frowned. "But Juliette—" she began, only to be interrupted by the entrance of a footman, who informed Lady Juliette that her new mare had arrived.

Juliette leapt up with a glad cry and Althea resigned herself, interjecting only the *caveat* that it was almost time for luncheon.

"Oh, bother luncheon! How can you think of food at a time like this?"

With that, Juliette was gone, leaving Althea to hope that Lady Juliette would at least change into a riding habit before flinging herself upon Oriflamme's back, to wonder how Douglas and Isobel's problems could be solved and when Anthony Devereaux would declare his suit for Juliette's hand, and to hope that the Duckmanton cook had once again made that delicious gooseberry fool for the midday meal. As none of these matters came under Althea's immediate control, she contented herself with folding her embroidery away preparatory to investigating the question of the fool.

As she laid her silks neatly in her workbox, the library door opened once more, this time to reveal the tall, muscular form of the Marquess of Barham. He was dressed for riding, and bore an indefinable and interesting air of having recently engaged in great exertions.

"Miss Fonthill!" he exclaimed upon beholding her. He glanced quickly around the library. "My apologies; I had no wish to disturb you."

Althea set the last skein of silk in its place and closed her workbox. "You do not disturb me in the least, Lord Barham." Then, as the Marquess showed every sign of being about to dash off, exactly as had Juliette and probably in the same direction, she added, "Do, please, come in. I have no wish to drive you from the room."

Lord Barham surveyed her for a moment, then grinned at her, his amber-gold eyes seeming to dance. "I'm sure, Miss Fonthill, that your presence would have rather the opposite effect."

"How—how very kind of you to say so, my lord," said Althea doubtfully.

"I'm never kind," the Marquess informed her, coming into the room and closing the door behind him. "I speak, my dear Miss Fonthill, nothing but the truth, which is one of the reasons I'm so unpopular."

Althea considered this a moment. "I should think it would be," she said, regarding him a trifle nervously. Miss Fonthill had been very well brought up indeed; consequently, her innocent curiosity about such an ominously intriguing figure as a Gazetted Rake was intense, and such a chance to speak with him might not come again, for Mrs. Fonthill had strenuously discouraged her daughters from any more contact with this unwelcome fellow guest than was strictly called for. After all, what harm could he do her here?

"None whatsoever, unless I were an idiot as well as a rake," Lord Barham agreed.

This display of divination made Althea gasp and clutch her workbox, flushing hotly.

"Nor do I add the practice of black magic to my other crimes," he went on, pulling a large leather chair near to Althea's and lowering himself gracefully into it. "I'm merely a dab hand at interpreting the expressions that flit across the faces of pretty innocents." He slouched back in the chair and ran his fingers through his dark hair. "Very well, Miss Fonthill; I am here. You may look your fill upon the wicked Marquess. Don't forget to take notes for your sister's benefit," he added, with a sudden quirk of his lips that might have been either a suppressed smile or an expression of irritation.

It was quite the outside of enough for any man to be that knowledgeable about the workings of the female mind! Mama had been quite right; being alone with a rake was clearly a mistake. Setting her mouth in a prim and virtuous line, Althea put her workbox aside and rose to her feet; Lord Barham laughed, somewhat ruefully.

"Someday, Miss Fonthill, I shall achieve a life-long ambition and be able to speak nothing but tactful and fatuous commonplaces. My apologies, and do sit down again. I wish to speak with you, and this will doubtless be my only chance to see you alone—if I were your mother, I wouldn't encourage my company either." The Marquess smiled and pointed at the chair Althea had just vacated.

Miss Fonthill, a fair-minded girl, could quite understand why Lady Juliette found Lord Barham both attractive and disturbing. When he smiled—

"It's about your sister," the Marquess added as she hesitated, and Althea, faced with a plain duty that made her continued presence obligatory, sank back into her chair and folded her hands in her lap.

"My sister, Lord Barham? Whatever do you mean?"

"It cannot have escaped your notice, Miss Fonthill, that your sister and Mr. Candlesby seem well on the way to an understanding. In fact," he added, "it can't have escaped anyone's notice, Douglas being what he is! Dissimulation is not one of his talents."

Althea considered and discarded several tactful, fatuous, and commonplace replies. If Juliette had little faith in Isobel's ability to make Douglas Candlesby act sensibly, Althea had none at all in the success of whatever plan Juliette had so plainly been contemplating at the breakfast table. Lady Juliette's abstracted, cunning expression as she had eaten cold toast could only mean forthcoming disaster.

So, since Lord Barham was here and apparently approved of plain speaking, Althea said, "I will not pretend to misunderstand you, Lord Barham. Yes, I believe Mr. Candlesby will ask for Isobel's hand, and I must confess, I do not see what is to be done, for Isobel's portion is very small, and unless the bonds are paid Mr. Candlesby needs must marry very well indeed. But I understand that Mr. Candlesby cannot possibly pay off the bonds, and I suppose you cannot either, or I am sure you would not have asked him to sign them. So you do see, Lord Barham," she finished hopefully, "that something must be done?"

"What I see," said Lord Barham in a soft voice that somehow had the effect of making Althea shrink back in her seat, "is that someone has been very busy indeed on my behalf." His eyes narrowed. "Who told you this touching story, Miss Fonthill? It cannot have been Douglas; the boy hasn't the brains to be worried. Well?"

"I—I cannot tell you that," said Althea, with as much firmness as she could muster.

The Marquess rose to his feet in one fluid motion. "You don't need to, Miss Fonthill; I rather think I can figure it out. She must have badgered the whole out of Douglas and has been busily meddling ever since. I must—yes, I think I really must—provide her with more to do with her time and energy."

Althea, shaken, made a valiant effort to say that she had no notion what he was talking about; the Marquess, smiling in a way that put Althea forcibly in mind of Lady Juliette's expression at the breakfast table that morning, leaned down to chuck her under the chin. "Don't worry, Miss Fonthill, I shan't ask you to perjure yourself. Just tell me where I may find Lady Juliette and I shall leave you in peace."

"Where Lady Juliette is I do not know," said Althea, scarlet-faced, "but her new mare arrived not an hour since."

"Good girl," said the Marquess, smiling down at her. "And don't worry about your sister's forthcoming nuptial bliss; I'll settle the matter. Far be it from me to stand in the way of true love."

He had reached the library door before Althea found her voice. "Lord Barham!" she said in alarm. "What are you going to do?"

"Nothing drastic, I assure you," he said as he flung open the door. "Merely wring Lady Juliette's neck, beat some sense into Douglas Candlesby, and solve the little matter of those bonds."

"Lord Barham—" Althea jumped to her feet, eager to get at least one hard fact out of the conversation. "What will it take to redeem them?"

The Marquess paused in the doorway. "Twelve thousand pounds," he said. "Good afternoon, Miss Fonthill."

The door slammed shut behind him, leaving Althea, stunned, to fall numbly back into her chair once more. Twelve thousand pounds! She'd never heard of such a sum; if that was what must be found it was hopeless indeed for Isobel and Mr. Candlesby. Where could Lord Barham possibly—

Althea drew a sharp breath as the answer struck her. It had seemed to her that Lady Juliette was not indifferent to the Marquess; for his part, a penniless rake could hardly be indifferent to Lady Juliette's prospects. The "little matter" of the bonds could be easily solved did Lord Barham marry Lady Juliette. Twelve thousand pounds would be a large bite out of even the Devereaux fortune, but, with a bit of management, it could be handled. Yes, the more Althea thought on it, the more it seemed that that must be what Lord Barham had in mind.

She thought of seeking out Juliette to warn her, but some instinct told Althea that the bearer of this information would not be met with the gratitude that one might think she deserved.

Nevertheless, someone must be told. Remembering the emerald flash of Juliette's eyes as she spoke of the Marquess, and the hot golden glow in Bad Jack Barham's eyes as he spoke of Lady Juliette, Althea reluctantly set aside the craven wish to let two such obviously capable adversaries manage their own affairs. Anthony Devereaux was here— and he was Juliette's closest male relative. He must hear of this, even if it would cast her in the unfavorable light of a gossip and a talebearer.

Fortunately for the peace of Duckmanton, the Marquess and Lady Juliette were not to meet that afternoon. True, Lord Barham had left Althea's presence with every intention of wringing Lady Juliette's meddlesome, interfering neck. But he was intercepted by Lord Hawkchurch and Mr. Gressingham, who demanded his opinions, which he had already given on numerous occasions, on the probable outcome of the St. Leger; by the time he won free and reached the stables, Lady Juliette and Oriflamme were long gone.

Balked of his prey, and unwilling to undertake a wild-goose chase after her, Jack attempted to hunt down the hapless Douglas Candlesby, only to discover that that worthy had absented himself with Isobel Fonthill. Twice deprived, and in a vile temper indeed, Lord Barham retired to his room to brood upon the perfidy of Fate until it was time to change for dinner.

It took Althea some time to find Mr. Devereaux. The moment she emerged from the library, she was pounced upon by Lady Ralph, who had a long and rambling recitation of hideous troubles—which kept returning, somehow, to her devout wish that "poor dear little Isobel" should not suffer any of these extreme fates. Althea was at least as clear of vision as Lady Ralph, and it was quite obvious that Douglas Candlesby had lost his heart in earnest—and to a girl of whom his mama could not approve. It was a great pity, thought Althea as she listened, that she could not tell Lady Ralph that she too thought the match was a bad idea—on the grounds that she did not wish Isobel to marry someone even more impoverished than she was—but Juliette had been quite right; the only two people who could present the matter of Douglas's indebtedness to his family were Douglas himself or the cause—Lord Barham.

So Althea listened and agreed as Lady Ralph explained that she feared for poor dear little Isobel, of whom Lady Ralph was exceedingly fond, and that she should take more care of herself, as she was becoming quite burnt to the socket, and would surely endanger her health if she continued in her gadabout ways (the translation being that Miss Isobel was spending far too much time in Douglas's company for his mother's peace of mind), and that it was a great pity that Lady Juliette was reluctant to put herself forward more when Douglas was engaged in extending the courtesies of a host (meaning that Juliette used any excuse to avoid Douglas). Since both of these things were the simple truth, Althea had no trouble in being conciliating, though she wished desperately to find Anthony Devereaux and lay her troubles before him. At last Lady Ralph, feeling she had accomplished something, disclosed to Althea that Mr. Devereaux was keeping Lady Hawkchurch company in the conservatory, and Althea gratefully vanished in pursuit of him.

Mr. Anthony Devereaux did not have an embroidery hoop to protect him, but he was possessed of a fund of idle chatter which served much the same purpose—and having lived all his life beneath the shadow of Madame Solange Devereaux, did not find the dowager Lady Hawkchurch particularly intimidating. Anthony Devereaux was that *rara avis* indeed, the perfect houseguest, and had instantly intuited that his place was at Samantha Hawkchurch's side, if both Juliette and Barham were going to be interesting. With his knowledge of the aches of old bones, he had suggested that the orangery might be a pleasant place to sit; with his knowledge of ancient history, he drew Lady Hawkchurch upon that most delightful topic, the scandals of her youth.

"—oh, and aye, and everyone knew that Christian—Lord Warltawk to you, young man—was quite mad (your Lord Byron, with all his everlasting airs and graces, is a tame puppy beside him), but when he ruined Selene Clarendon's boy, and then married the daughter. . . . Married, ho! Won her in a card game, after persuading young Peregrine to stake her *and* her dowry on a flip of the cards. But why am I telling all this to you, young man?"

"Perhaps," said Anthony, "because I am delighted to disclaim any ownership of 'my Lord Byron' as you say, Lady Hawkchurch. His poetry is overrated—"

"Overrated is it? Overripe, I should say! When I was a gel, there wasn't any business of banning books of poetry as bein' too warm for polite company! But that's neither here nor there. Selene was such a lovely thing; we were all madly jealous—who'd've thought I'd outlive her? Good lord, young man, that must be forty years gone and more—I wasn't even out when Warltawk was banished to France."

"They had to let him return eventually."

"Oh yes—came back at the height of Bonaparte's ravings and died last spring. Over a hundred he was—so don't let anyone tell you that wickedness ain't its own reward!"

"In that case, dear Lady Hawkchurch," said Anthony innocently, "dare I be presumptuous enough to assume that you have been very, very, wicked indeed?"

Lady Hawkchurch gaffawed and thumped her cane on the tiling. "Ah, Devereaux, you're quite wasted on the modern generation—but I think it still has an interest in you, hey?" Lady Hawkchurch pointed with her cane, and Anthony turned to see Althea Fonthill hovering on the doorstep indecisively.

"Oh, I do beg your pardon, Lady Hawkchurch,"

said Miss Fonthill. "I did not wish to impose myself on you. That is—"

"Spare me your roundaboutation, girl—d'you think I'm green enough to suppose you've come to see me? Oh, run along, young Devereaux—youth must be served. As for me, I'm deaf as a post; always have been."

Anthony smiled in answer to the glint in Lady Hawkchurch's eyes as he rose gracefully from his seat. "As to that, Lady Hawkchurch, I am quite certain you hear everything you ought." With a tiny bow, he made his way to Althea's side.

"And how are you today, Miss Fonthill? From your presence, may I collect that Oriflamme has been delivered and Julie is safely away? You are very good to keep her out of trouble, you know."

Althea smiled faintly. "You make it sound as if it were an onerous task, when I am persuaded you know it is not. Oh, Mr. Devereaux—you do care for Lady Juliette, do you not?"

"Oh, yes," said Anthony warily, "I do care for Julie—little though you'd guess it—and that question, my very dear Miss Fonthill, always prefaces the most appalling disclosures. Do go on."

So saying, he conducted Althea to a marble bench in sight but out of hearing of the conveniently deaf Lady Hawkchurch. That lady nodded and smiled sardonically upon the pair of them before busying herself with a small book of improving homilies she had brought with her.

"You see," said Althea, twisting her lawn handkerchief between her fingers until the lace edging was sadly pulled, "to do so I must betray a confidence—though Juliette ought not to have told me, I am glad she did—and speculate in the most odious fashion! I— It is really very foolish of me to indulge in a fit of missishness, when I have already made up my mind to be brazen." She looked up at him helplessly.

"We shall just have to be brazen together, Miss Fonthill," said Mr. Devereaux, trusting Lady Hawkchurch to be blind at need, as well as deaf, and taking one of Althea's hands in his. Rather than being offended by his forwardness, Althea took comfort from his concern, and grasped his hand tightly. "Now, do begin at the beginning, and never mind how muddled it is. I am used to hearing about Juliette's scrapes, and will not find any detail too irrelevant or fantastic."

Althea Fonthill took a deep breath and marshaled her resources. "It begins with Mr. Candlesby knowing the Marquess of Barham, I think," Althea began. Haltingly, with much back-and-forth, she related the tale as she understood it—that young Mr. Douglas Candlesby had guaranteed a ruinous loan for Lord Barham, who could not, would not, repay. This had been bad enough, but then Juliette had found out both about the loan and that Douglas's affections were engaged by Althea's sister—"who cannot know what it will mean when the loan falls due, Mr. Devereaux—Juliette tells me it could be prison!"—and had pledged herself to right the matter and bring the Marquess of Barham to a sense of his own culpability.

"And I am afraid that now he knows that Douglas has told Juliette—oh, my wicked, wicked tongue; I had thought he knew already, and when I told him, he said the most horrible things!"

"Such as?" prompted Anthony. He knew already that this was quite the worst scrape Juliette had ever been involved in, and made her Town fooleries pale in comparison.

"He—he said he would *thrash* her, Mr. Devereaux—
and then he went off looking for her, and—Juliette
is not indifferent to him, you know," Althea admitted painfully. "It is not her fault, she cannot com-
prehend, and—he said he would redeem the bonds,
somehow—but it will take *twelve thousand pounds*,"
she finished in a whisper.

"Where in heaven's name does Bad Barham
think he can raise that kind of money, unless . . ."
Anthony looked at Althea. "He cannot be thinking
of Juliette?"

Althea withdrew her hand from his to worry at
her handkerchief once more. "I have told you, Mr.
Devereaux, that she is . . . not indifferent. She told
me he was quite the most infuriating man she had
ever met, in fact, and—she said she had a plan!"
Althea finished miserably.

"Good lord—my dear Miss Fonthill, I salute your
fortitude. Had I been in possession of this information, I'd be a nervous wreck! In fact I am, now
that you have told me—I shall be quite the romantic hero, with pallid countenance and trembling
hands. The only thing that puzzles me is what
grounds can Julie have for thinking she can bring
him to his knees? Ordinarily I would assume she
was relying on news of her fortune to carry all before it, but as Juliette Devereaux has never been
able to tell a bouncer in her life, I don't imagine
she would be able to start now."

"I— But Juliette *is* a great heiress," Althea said
in confusion. "That is—oh, I do not wish to say that
she has acted like an odious Cit, forever telling one
precisely how much money she had, but she is so
proud of Chaceley, that one cannot help understanding . . ."

Anthony Devereaux fumbled in his pocket, withdrew his spectacles, placed them on his nose, and peered at her intently. "Mistress of Chaceley," he said flatly. "Lord, Miss Fonthill—does she think Maria intends to let her rule the roast and keep the keys?"

"Keep it? Who is Maria? Is that Maria Alworthy the Squire's daughter? Of the Alworthy Hunt—with its bag-fed hounds and foxes in trenchers? The one Juliette intends to 'show the way' on Oriflamme?"

"The one Juliette's papa intends to marry," Anthony said brutally.

"Marry!" Althea cried. "You mean—Juliette's father—"

"Is about to enter parson's mousetrap again. Yes. But don't tell me she doesn't know—half the county knows, and is going to the wedding—they are to be married sometime in November, I believe. They have been betrothed since the grouse-hunting."

As Althea stared at him blankly, Mr. Devereaux hurried on, using words as a cover for his own feelings. "Uncle went to shoot over Squire Alworthy's land and was so pleased with his bag that he presented him with a set of Mantons and offered for Maria."

"Do you know her well, Mr. Devereaux?" Althea said. She knew it was an inane question, but what else could there possibly be to say?

"Oh, quite. She is younger than Julie, and Julie has bullied her for years. She will be glad to get some of her own back, I promise you."

"Juliette does not know—she cannot, Mr. Devereaux, for you are right; she is quite impossibly truthful, and all she has said to me is how happy she will be to return home to Chaceley."

Anthony groaned aloud, and buried his head in his hands, to the disorder of an already disorderly *coiffure.* "Uncle Sebastian has already hailed his solicitor down from London to draw up the marriage lines, and Maria wants Juliette for her bridesmaid! And—oh, lord! If Uncle hasn't told Juliette, ten to one he hasn't told Madame either! For I came here straight from Chaceley upon her written orders, and she didn't mention it!"

Mr. Devereaux raised his head from his hands and regarded Althea with an expression of fascinated horror. Althea said valiantly, "Well, how—how interesting, to be sure!"

"I can see, Miss Fonthill, that it falls to me to tell her. It will break her heart for certain—and what is to become of her?"

"You— You did say you intended to marry her, Mr. Devereaux," Althea prompted with unaccountable reluctance.

"And of course nothing would delight me more," said Anthony with mendacious gallantry, "but it is generally considered good form for the bride to agree to the wedding, and—oh lord, Julie is going to have strong hysterics for certain."

"Perhaps it would be better if I told her, Mr. Devereaux?" Althea ventured.

"I could hardly ask it of you, Miss Fonthill— though by the offer you prove yourself either a true friend to both of us, or unacquainted with Julie in her takings. No, I'll tell her—quietly, after we leave here. She really can't keep a secret, you know, and there's no reason to make her look like a fool by telling her here where everyone will instantly guess the news and Miss Gressingham will recite improving homilies. Poor Julie!"

Mr. Devereaux shook his head, sadly, so plainly at a loss that Althea took his hand and squeezed it. He covered it over with his other and patted it in empty reassurance. They were both children of the modern age, and well acquainted with the fickleness of fortune—where a minor event, far removed on the family tree, could strip one of inheritance in an instant. The moment the ring was on Maria Alworthy's finger Juliette Devereaux would cease to be a great heiress—the nearly inevitable son and heir would claim all but what had been settled on Sophia Halford's daughter.

"I'll go and give the orders to the servants," said Anthony at last. "And make up some tale for Lady Ralph. And then, Miss Fonthill, I shall hide somewhere where Julie can't find me!" Watching him depart, Althea could only think that a greater trouble than Juliette's disinheritance had happened, but she was unable to put a name to it.

It was only as the wicked Lord Barham entered the drawing-room rather later than was truly courteous to his hostess and saw the party gathered there that he remembered that the Templetons were dining at Duckmanton that evening. Lord and Lady Templeton were standing before the fire, exchanging civilities with their host and hostess, and Harry Templeton was listening politely as Lord Hawkchurch pompously explained what he looked for in a good heavy hunter. The rest of the company bore that faint air of restlessness that afflicts even the most congenial of parties when the announcement of dinner is imminent, and is the more pronounced when all guests are not quite in charity with each other.

"Lord Barham!" Lady Ralph exclaimed upon beholding him in the doorway. "Well, now we may go in to dinner—and you do know the Templetons, do you not? So sad that dear Deborah could not be here as well, but under the circumstances—"

"Such a dreadful cold," Lady Templeton interjected hastily.

"And so unexpected an ailment, too," said Jack, looking rather thunderous.

Lady Ralph began to flutter helplessly, and Harry Templeton took Jack by the arm and led him aside, saying in an undertone, "Be reasonable, old man— you can't expect m'mother to let Deb be seen in your company. Dash it, the chit ain't out yet!"

"Doubtless," said Jack in a dangerously calm voice, shrugging off Harry's clasp, "you know your sister's character better than I."

Harry Templeton's face darkened. "Now see, here, Barham—"

At that moment the butler announced in dignified, if stentorian, tones, that dinner awaited their pleasure, and Jack felt a light, firm touch on his arm. He looked down to find Lady Juliette Devereaux looking up at him, her green eyes full of determination and a flirtatious smile curving her lips.

"Lord Barham," she said, "you may take me in to dinner, if you like."

"I'll take you, Julie," said Harry Templeton instantly, but Jack was already tucking Lady Juliette's hand through his elbow.

"Sorry, old man," said Jack, his tone mocking Harry's, "but as you know, I never disappoint a lady. Come along, my Cruel Fair; our good hostess won't have a peaceful moment until I deposit you in the dining-room with your reputation still intact."

Harry Templeton hesitated, his arm held out, but as Lady Juliette merely glared at him and clung to Lord Barham's arm, Harry abandoned the field and allowed himself to be assigned as Miss Gressingham's guide to the dinner-table.

"Damn the man," said Jack, half to himself, as he and Lady Juliette followed the others towards the dining-room. "Does he expect me to ravish you between here and dinner?"

Lady Juliette made a choking noise, and Jack apologized blandly for the use of such strong language in the presence of an undoubted lady. This pretty speech had the odd effect of making Lady Juliette glare at him; then as suddenly smile, the elusive dimple appearing in her cheek. "What nonsense!" she declared scornfully. "As if there would be time!"

Jack was surprised into outright laughter. As Lady Juliette looked up at him, her brows drawing together, he said, "My pretty innocent, there would be time and to spare. No, don't bother to blush and gasp indignantly, my pet; I know perfectly well you haven't the least notion what I'm talking about. Young ladies of quality," he went on, grinning down at her and patting her gloved hand, "have such lurid imaginations. I'm sure it comes of too much novel-reading. In any case—"

"I never read novels!" snapped Juliette. "And you are the most presumptuous man I ever met!"

"Then you haven't met very many, my sweet. Now, assuage my curiosity; why have I been chosen for this singular honor?"

"Lord Barham, I have something I most particularly wish to say to you!" Lady Juliette drew a deep breath, an unwary action which gave Jack a chance to admire the delicate curves of her bosom, displayed to great advantage by the *décolletage* of a vivid crimson evening dress. The gown was by far too sophisticated for a girl in her first Season, and the color and trim wildly unsuitable, but the rich hue made her skin look even whiter by contrast.

"Do you?" said Jack, letting his gaze travel upwards from her bosom to her throat. "No, no, my pet—not emeralds with that dress, I beg of you. Haven't you got a garnet set or some such thing?"

"But these are the Devereaux emeralds!" she protested, looking startled. "They were brought from France by my grandfather—saved from the Terror."

"I don't care if they were saved from the Black Hole of Calcutta," said Jack callously. "They may go with your eyes, my sweet, but with that dress— no."

"Many people," said Lady Juliette with great dignity, "have admired this combination excessively."

"They must have been color-blind. You should stop listening to that abigail of yours, child; good-hearted she may be, a lady's dresser she is not."

"And you know all about what a lady should wear, I suppose?" said Juliette, with a toss of her head that made her ebony curls dance.

"My dear child, I do. Now, Lady Juliette, what was it you particularly wished to say to me? As a gentleman, I'll grant you the first shot—for I have a number of things I most particularly wish to say to *you*!"

Lady Juliette tilted her head to look up at him, looking intrigued, but as they had, by that time, entered the dining-room, Jack was forced to relinquish her with what grace he could muster.

That evening's dinner was to linger long in Lady Ralph's memory as one of the great social disasters of modern times. It was bad enough that Lord Barham's presence had forced dear Euphemia to deprive them all of little Deborah's company, and that the appalling man had come down nearly late to dinner and then cast out lures to Lady Juliette Devereaux. As for that young lady's arrant folly in succumbing to them—! Well, Lady Ralph knew what to think of that, and she would be very remiss indeed in her Duty did she not write to Lady Juliette's great-aunt and warn her as soon as might be.

Yes, all this had been quite dreadful enough, but there had been worse to come. For reasons Lady Ralph shuddered even to contemplate, Harry Templeton had snubbed Lord Barham quite shockingly over the first course, whereupon Lord Barham, doubtless under the influence of the wine, had abandoned all pretense at civilized behavior and commenced to say the most dreadful things—and at the dinner-table, too!

The Army had been the unwitting cause of this conversation debacle. The gentlemen had, toward the end of the first course, begun discussing Politics, which Lady Ralph could *not* like, and, as the second course succeeded the first, the Marquess of Barham had waxed more than eloquent on what the country was doing on behalf of the army which had served it so faithfully for twenty years—which was, according to my Lord Barham, nothing.

Indeed, though the mob had wished to draw Lord Wellington's carriage through the streets of London itself (and had succeeded with General Blucher's conveyance), the country had then—so Barham wished them all to believe—left its infantry to die of gangrene and plague in the Calais streets, with no medical attention, no back pay, and certainly no pension. It was Lady Ralph's opinion, later expressed to her husband, that if any of these shocking things were true, then Parliament and Lord Wellington would be dealing with them—and as she had had it straight from Lady Hawkchurch—who was bearing up as well as could be expected under the great tragedies that had oppressed her family—that her son said no such question was before the House, well, it followed naturally that Lord Barham's elevated ravings were merely moonshine and madness—and in rather poor taste besides.

Lord Hawkchurch had tried to put a stop to the Marquess's far too graphic description of the plight of the ex-Army. In young Lord Hawkchurch's opinion, much of this sorry state of affairs was sheer exaggeration—"For not to put too fine a point upon it, Lord Barham, one must admit that most of the soldiers were little more than rabble from the streets. One cannot expect such people to hold the same notions, or entertain the same feelings, as those of higher station," Lord Hawkchurch finished with solemn earnestness.

Lord Barham had directed such a look at Lord Hawkchurch as had made Lady Ralph, as she later explained to her husband at great length, feel quite faint with terror at what the Marquess might do next.

"I was unaware," Lord Barham had drawled, and in the most insolent tone, "that those of higher station suffered more intense pain when a leg was sawn off—or that they were left in more dire straits when abandoned where they stood by their government!"

Here Lord Ralph Candlesby had made a noble and dignified effort to point out to the Marquess that there were ladies present. The Marquess had merely smiled sardonically. "Yes, the tenderhearted ladies, who weep over a pet dog's injury and laugh and chatter while they toss a penny—if they remember to do so!—to those crippled scarecrows in tattered regimentals who sweep the crossings of every London street!"

There seemed to be no adequate response to this; Lady Ralph had hastily requested the butler to present the dessert course *immediately*.

"No one can deny that war is a dreadful business, Lord Barham," Miss Gressingham had finally said in sanctimonious tones. "Doubtless it was to spare you such distressing revelations that your father forbade you to enlist; it is always wisest to obey those in authority over one."

The Marquess had turned those lambent cat's eyes on the unwary Miss Gressingham, but before he could speak Lady Juliette had entered the fray.

"Nonsense!" the headstrong heiress announced sharply. "Lord Barham is quite right. That is no way to treat one's loyal servants, and surely our soldiers are the country's! Why, I would not treat any retainer of mine so, and—and I think it is a disgrace, and I shall have Papa write and tell our Member of Parliament so!"

Lady Hawkchurch had emitted a crack of laughter that boded no good for anyone's peace; Mrs. Fonthill had announced that she believed she had a sick headache coming on; the younger ladies looked at their plates and the gentlemen looked uncomfortable. Lady Templeton quietly announced that the ladies would retire and leave the gentlemen to their port.

Lady Ralph thankfully seized the opportunity to flee the scene of this social Waterloo. Never had she spent such a hideous evening; the tale would be all over the county before the cat could lick her ear!

And as the ladies rose to their feet preparatory to decamping with all due haste, Lady Juliette Devereaux directed upon the Marquess of Barham a look of such glowing and shocking approval that Lady Ralph quite decided that, fortune or no, Lady Juliette would not do for Douglas after all.

And so it came to pass that Lady Ralph Candlesby beamed approvingly upon Douglas as he moved to sit by Isobel Fonthill's side after dinner. Douglas, quite flustered by this change of tack, had asked his mama if she was feeling quite the thing. Lord Barham, mercifully, had gone off without a word to anyone, and Harry Templeton had vented his feelings by delivering to Lady Juliette a rousing scold on the impropriety of having anything at all to do with Bad Jack Barham. Lady Juliette's cousin, Anthony Devereaux, whose office this would logically have been, simply sat at the pianoforte and played in the most abstracted fashion—doubtless concerned for the crisis in Madame Solange's health that necessitated their hurried departure the day after tomorrow. Well, all in all, Lady Ralph would not be too grief-stricken at their going—it was a bad idea, as she had *always* told Lord Ralph, to attempt to marry for considerations other than true affection, and she was relieved that Douglas had given up the idea.

Chapter
SEVEN

So there *was* something one could lay to the Marquess of Barham's credit. Juliette had carried this warming thought to bed with her that night, holding it up as a talisman against Harry Templeton's horrid lecturings. What did *he* know of Lord Barham's true nature—and as for his sheer impertinence in telling her she hadn't the least notion of what she was about—well!

Her musings were interrupted by Matilda's arrival. The abigail bore a basin of hot water and a sorely tried expression. She bustled about laying out Juliette's things and fussing so that Juliette finally demanded to know what in heaven's name might be the matter.

"Oh, and nothing for some folks! We aren't here half-a-day, when it's Mr. Tony sayin' pack everything, and then a-changing of his mind, and then he turns around again and it's off termorrer and like as not he'll be a-changin' of his mind again just as I've got all your lovely gowns all packed away careful-like."

"Packed? Go? But I'm not leaving!"

Mattie looked at her and sniffed. "And didn't Mr. Tony give me my orders—yes, and to John Coachman and Tom Perkins—and to Lady Ralph Candlesby, as well, I daresay. Oh, lovey—don't fuss so—you was a-knowin' it'd be time to go to your great-aunt by-and-by."

"Yes—but not now! Oh, bother Tony—he hasn't got a brain in his head—and he won't even be up at this hour!" Juliette drew a decisive breath. "Well, there's no call to cry before I'm hurt, I suppose. I shall go riding, just as I planned—and I will talk to him once I've returned. But what can have possessed him? It is not like him to go and do things when I have specifically told him not to!"

Juliette was still mulling over Anthony's peculiar behavior, and wondering if perhaps she ought to discuss Lord Barham with him nevertheless, when she entered the stableyard. It was so early that the slanting light had barely cleared the rooftops; nonetheless Juliette found she was not alone.

"So I was right, as usual," said a cool voice. The Marquess of Barham stepped out of the shadows. "Good morning, Lady Juliette."

Juliette turned, startled, and then smiled. "Good morning, Lord Barham. I must confess, I am surprised to see you here at this hour." The renewed memory of his stirring words at the dinner-table the night before made her tone even more cordial.

The Marquess looked somewhat taken aback at the warmth of her greeting, then grinned at her, an engaging expression that made him look several years younger. "After my too-liberal potations last night, you mean? Alas, I fear I have a head hardened by many years of riotous living. I only hope I didn't shock everyone too deeply."

"You did not shock me at all," Juliette replied, "and if what you said about our veterans is true, it should be said, and loudly. And is it true what

Harry told Mr. Gressingham—that you have ridden Vulcan, and Lord Templeton has given him to you?" Juliette regarded him with warm admiration. "Harry was very vexed, but certainly he could not handle Vulcan at all!"

Jack laughed. "Yes, it's true—and what I'm to do with the horse I can't imagine. Among his dislikes are rocks, trees, lanterns, sheep, and other horses—and no, my pet, I will not sell him to you, so you may try and transmute that acquisitive gleam in your pretty eyes to some more feminine emotion."

"That is not what I was going to say," Juliette protested mendaciously, flushing a bit. She hesitated, then went on frankly, "I must confess, my lord, I had not thought so well of you before—"

"No? You astound me, Lady Juliette." The Marquess's eyes danced with the unholy amusement that always gave Juliette a burning desire to make him take her seriously.

"—but now I see that I may have been mistaken in my judgment of your character," she went on firmly. "So I wish to talk with you about a matter of great importance. I know all about the bonds Douglas Candlesby signed for you, and I cannot stand by and let you ruin him. And I am sure—"

Lord Barham's hand shot out to grip her arm; startled, she allowed him to pull her a step closer to him. "My pet, I won't even trouble to ask what possible business young Candlesby's affairs are of yours. But I beg you will moderate your voice in discussing them—or better still, cease discussing them at all!"

Juliette tried vainly to shrug off his hand. "I care nothing for Douglas Candlesby's affairs—but he is to marry Althea Fonthill's sister, and Althea is my friend and I will not see her hurt! Everyone knows the Fonthills are poor as churchmice—"

"The things everyone knows and don't scruple to say never ceases to amaze me," said the Marquess, shaking his head as if in dismay over the wickedness of the world. "But I am willing to stand corrected; if Miss Fonthill is your friend then of course her affairs are yours. And, as her friend, do try and impress upon her the importance of keeping a close mouth about the debt—although by now she has doubtless confided it to half the world and I might as well save my breath."

"Althea is no gossip," said Juliette hotly, jerking her arm free of his grasp and stepping back a pace. "And if you are so loath to have the matter known, my lord, it can only be from shame at your conduct, and I should think you would wish to set matters right!"

"My dear child, I can't," said the Marquess in a deadly flat tone. "And in this case, not only will talking pay no toll, but should your blasted prattling be repeated until certain parties hear of it, those bonds will come due *now*, and not in ten or fifteen years!"

This had never occurred to her; she regarded Lord Barham in horror. After a moment, he shrugged and laughed. "But come, Lady Juliette, I'm sure you had more pleasant occupations in mind when you awoke this morning—and at such an unfeminine hour, too." He surveyed her carefully from the toes of her boots to the crown of her dashing little hat. "And you've taken my advice about your habit, I see. Green suits you—as I'm sure you know, my little wood-nymph. Well, it's a lovely morning for a ride, to be sure, especially in such charming company."

"Thank you, but I do not require your escort," Juliette announced with what she intended to be icy dignity.

The Marquess grinned and flicked a careless finger over the tip of her nose. "Haven't you had enough of riding alone?" He leaned forward and lowered his voice to a confidential purr. "Why, my dear Lady Juliette, you might be accosted by some insolent stranger, and we can't have that, now can we? Besides," he added, "I had it from your own fair lips last night that you had something you most particularly wished to say to me, and I'm sure you should be forced to hold your peace no longer."

As Juliette tried vainly to think of a sufficiently lethal retort, the Marquess turned to call to the nearest stableboy. "Ho, there—saddle up Lady Juliette's new mare and my Cavalier, and be quick about it."

There seemed to be nothing a lady could, with dignity, do, but wait for the horses to be brought round. Juliette stood, tapping her boot with her crop, until the horses were let out a few minutes later. Oriflamme was curvetting playfully, arching her neck and looking at the sidesaddle on her back as if she'd never imagined such an article existed in the world. As she noticed Juliette, however, the mare's ears pricked forward and she whickered gently.

"Allow me," said Lord Barham with exaggerated courtesy as Juliette went towards the mare. Before Juliette could protest, he had tossed her up into the saddle and had swung himself onto Cavalier; Juliette was left with nothing to do but gather up the reins and urge Oriflamme sedately from the stable-yard.

Juliette had already formed a good understanding with the temperamental Oriflamme yesterday; the chestnut mare was, in the vulgar parlance, a right sweet-goer—once she had been convinced that Juliette was as strong-minded as she and would not indulge Oriflamme's fits and starts.

Now Oriflamme half-heartedly shied at the startling spectacle of a leaf in the roadway. Juliette easily sat out this foolery and then laughed and patted the coppery neck as Oriflamme craned her neck to sniff at the toe of Juliette's boot and regard her mistress with limpid brown eyes. "So you mean to try me again, do you," said Juliette, her voice soft and caressing. "But I am more than seven, and you shan't catch me out!"

She urged Oriflamme forward again, and looked over to her companion to find Lord Barham regarding her with a peculiar expression on his face. Juliette could not quite read it, but something about the way he looked at her gave her a giddy, fluttering sensation just below her breast. Her cheeks oddly hot, she looked down quickly and made a great play of adjusting her reins more suitably, thinking hard.

She believed she understood Lord Barham now. Plainly he was one of those incomprehensible people to whom everything must be made a jest, but she had listened to him last night, and had heard the distress in his voice this morning as he'd spoken of the problem of the bonds. Almost—almost she was willing to think he might be a good man at heart. True, he had a bad reputation, but so had Oriflamme had, and the mare was really the sweetest thing! Perhaps, were he shown how to go on properly. . . .

"I'd offer you a penny for your thoughts, my pet,"

said Lord Barham, happily oblivious to the trend of these, "but I lack even that small sum."

"I—I beg your pardon," said Juliette, startled from her contemplation of the Marquess's potential rehabilitation. Then she frowned. "Oh, surely you must have a penny, my lord!"

"My sweet, you're too literal-minded," the Marquess told her. "But in this case I exaggerate very little. Perhaps after the St. Leger—" He shrugged.

Juliette reined Oriflamme to a halt. "Oh, Lord Barham, you are not depending on a *sure thing*, are you?" she demanded.

Barham laughed and reached out to grasp Oriflamme's bridle and urge her forward again. "So indignant on everyone else's behalf, even mine? Thank you for your concern, sweetheart. Yes, I must confess all my inconsequential monies are placed squarely upon Sultan's back—and you need not harangue me on my folly. I freely admit that it's the act of an idiot or a desperate man. You may choose for yourself which label applies to me."

It seemed to Juliette that there was a note of courageous mockery in the Marquess's voice, and that directed at himself. She glanced at him and he grinned at her and shrugged, and Juliette's original plans to force Lord Barham to her will dissolved, to be replaced by a shining new design.

"Lord Barham!" She pulled Oriflamme to an abrupt halt once more; the mare bounced once to indicate her displeasure at this and then subsided, heaving a sigh and blowing loudly through her delicate nostrils.

The Marquess reined in Cavalier. "Lady Juliette!"

The sardonic note remained, but Juliette was no longer to be deceived, and smiled at him happily.

"Lord Barham, I have discovered how all our problems may be solved!"

"You terrify me," said the Marquess. "Dare I ask—?"

"Oh, do stop joking," Juliette begged.

The Marquess's eyebrows rose, and he waved a hand as if granting permission for her to speak. "My humble apologies, my pet. Do go on; I await your revelation with bated breath."

Juliette fidgeted with her reins, trying to collect her thoughts. Finally, her cheeks pink, she stared down at her twisting fingers and said, "I think, my lord, that the best—the most sensible course—would be for me to-to m-marry you." She had intended this to be a simple statement of fact, calmly presented, but unfortunately for her dignity it had degenerated into a breathless, stammering whisper.

There was what seemed like a year-long silence, broken only by the restless stamping of the horses and the rustle of wind through the trees. Finally Juliette risked a look over at the Marquess; there was an oddly stricken look in his eyes. Juliette grasped at her courage and went on. "I—I know it is not proper for me to ask you, my lord, but I have no patience with such scruples when it is a plain matter of everybody's good! For you see—"

"For God's sake, stop!" said the Marquess, swinging Cavalier around and moving him towards Oriflamme. "Does insanity run in the Devereaux line, darling?"

Juliette regarded the Marquess open-mouthed with shock. "No, of course it doesn't!" she told him indignantly after a moment. "Why do you ask that?"

"Because you seem to have run mad," said the

Marquess. "Now, let us have a pleasant canter through the trees and forget this nonsense."

"It is not nonsense!" Juliette drew a deep breath. "I think it would answer admirably, Lord Barham—and only think what a wonderful stud Vulcan will be for the Chaceley stock!"

"And you think the same can be said for me? I'm honored." The Marquess's wry smile made Juliette's face go hot, and after a moment he said more gently, "My dear child, have you thought about my reputation?"

"Yes, and it seems to me to be quite ridiculous!" Juliette declared, recovering her countenance. "Everyone is very ready to criticize you, my lord, but as I told Lord Templeton last night, when *he* did so, people *will* say a horse is a bad horse when *they* are only bad riders! And—"

She broke off, flushing indignantly, as the Marquess doubled over with laughter. "Stop!" he said, after he recovered himself. "My dear little innocent, you can't possibly have the least notion of what you are saying! Now, come along and we'll have a pleasant canter and be back to Duckmanton in time for breakfast."

"Indeed, I am not so innocent as all that, and I have every notion what I am saying," Juliette assured him. "I have thought about it a great deal, my lord, and—and I am certain it will do very well."

Lord Barham regarded her with an indulgent, if wary, smile. "Will it? And how will you like it when I—as a Gazetted Rakeshame, you will perhaps recall—run through your fortune and leave you ruined as well?"

Juliette smiled indulgently in her turn. "Oh, of course the marriage settlements will be drawn up so that that will be out of your power, my lord. I shall loan you the funds to redeem your bonds and free Douglas Candlesby of the debt, and matters will be arranged to leave you in funds as well. But certainly the management of my affairs will remain in my hands."

"Oh, will they?" said the Marquess in an odd tone. As Juliette, sensing danger, gathered up her reins, he urged Cavalier so close to Oriflamme that his leg pressed against Juliette's; she fancied she could feel the heat of his thigh even through the cloth of her riding habit. "So your brilliant plan is that I marry you and be given an allowance and do as I'm told, is it? Oh, no you don't," he added, catching Oriflamme's reins and forcing her to stand as Juliette would have moved on. "For once, Lady Juliette, you're going to listen to reason—someone else's reason!

"No, I'm not going to marry you, Lady Juliette—although God knows someone should, and soon, and take a horsewhip to you daily!"

White to the lips, Juliette managed to get out, "But—but I thought—you would have a rich wife, and I would have—"

"A husband for your precious Chaceley? Well, if this is the way you mean to go about it you'll find one soon enough—but it's not going to be me, my lady; I draw the line at that!"

"But—"

"You little fool, what sort of a husband do you think I'd make for you? You seem to have some romantic notion that I can be redeemed—by the love of a good income, if by nothing else—but men don't change their natures, pet. As for this charming notion that I'd do as I was told once the settlements were signed—in heaven's name, child—what makes you think so? Settlements or no, do you realize the legal rights I'd have over you once the ring was on your finger?"

He jerked on Oriflamme's reins as if to emphasize his point; the mare half-reared and Juliette yanked the reins back from his hands. "Let go of me this instant! How—how dare you—"

"Talk to you this way?" said the Marquess. "As you're so fond of saying, my sweet, it's for your own good." Then he laughed and looked her up and down with a calculating expression that made Juliette turn scarlet. "Of course, if you'd care to marry me on *my* terms—well, that might be another story altogether."

"You stay away from me! I—I wouldn't marry you if you were the last man on earth!" Juliette cried, slamming her heel into Oriflamme's side. The mare, freed from restraint, sprang eagerly into a canter which quickly stretched into a gallop. It was not fast enough to keep Juliette from hearing the steady pounding of Cavalier's hoofbeats as the Marquess came after her.

Juliette touched her crop to Oriflamme's side and the mare, nothing loath, lengthened her stride until the wind whipped Juliette's cheeks to tingling brightness and her veil floated behind her like wings. But Cavalier, under the Marquess's expert handling, caught up with the fleet mare and remained just behind, despite Juliette's best efforts to lose him, as they fled down the long ride that led back to Duckmanton.

At the end of the ride they were faced with a low wall and the long stretch of lawn between the ornamental water and the main house. Oriflamme could leap like a deer; Juliette set her to the wall, but even as the mare gathered herself Cavalier flashed past and was swung around hard to bar the way. The Marquess seized her bridle and dragged the plunging mare to a halt.

Breathing hard, Juliette lashed out with her crop, but the Marquess easily snatched it away. For an instant she had the mad thought that he was about to use it on her, then he flung it to the ground.

"Let go of my horse this instant!"

"And let you go careening across Lord Ralph's lawns? That's hardly the action of a thoughtful guest, Lady Juliette."

"It's no concern of yours where I ride! And I do not wish for your company, so you may leave me in peace!"

The Marquess grinned, teeth flashing white. "I thought we'd agreed that young ladies who rode alone were asking for trouble? Now let me give you one more piece of advice, my sweet: you're far too young and far too pretty to indulge in eccentricities. You seem to think that your fortune and position give you unlimited license, but take it from one who knows, my child—fortune can vanish overnight and position—well, let us just say that that, too, can be illusory." The Marquess seemed to be looking somewhere beyond her; against her will, Juliette found herself listening intently.

"But reputation—ah, that, my pet, is a more fragile possession than all the rest." There was a moment's stillness, then Oriflamme began to dance nervously and the mood was broken.

"You're a fine one to talk of reputations!"

"So I am—who better? And yours isn't so secure as you like to imagine."

Juliette tossed her head. "And yours is?"

"Very." The Marquess's lips twisted in a wry smile. "There's nothing so liberating—for a man— as having no reputation. But it's a different story

163

for a woman, my sweet, which is deuced unfair but the way of the world. A word to the wise, Lady Juliette—or even to you—"

"Thank you very much, but I don't need your advice!" Juliette snapped. "Only let go my horse!"

"Certainly," said the Marquess, releasing Oriflamme's reins. "And you might start your program of maidenly virtues by riding quietly back to the stables with me like a good girl."

"I will not," said Juliette, knowing even as she spoke that she sounded like nothing so much as a spoiled child, but unable to stop herself. "I'll ride when, and where, and how I like, Lord Barham— and I never want to see you again!"

"Suit yourself," said the Marquess, a predatory gleam in his amber eyes. With that he leaned over and swatted Oriflamme's rump; the mettlesome mare, needing no further encouragement, shot forward over the low stone wall and went careening across the velvet-smooth greensward.

Juliette, mortified, fought desperately to rein Oriflamme in, with but indifferent success; her temper was not in the least improved by the sound of the Marquess's laughter following her across the lawn.

So Lady Juliette wished to marry him—or rather, she wished to buy a complaisant husband and thought his debts would bring him to heel, damn the little minx! As he rode off on Cavalier after watching Oriflamme leave hoofmarks across half the Duckmanton south lawn, Jack cursed himself for an idiot for not taking the child up on her ingenuous offer. Damn it, he'd been scheming to marry her not a day ago!

But recent events had conspired to ram it home

to him that he was no fit husband for a well-bred heiress, no matter how capable and efficient she thought herself. And when Lady Juliette had looked at him with that innocent determination, that pleasure at her own cleverness in solving a thorny problem, that odd softness in her brilliant emerald eyes, Jack had realized that he simply couldn't do it. It has been a more painful renunciation that he had anticipated.

But his little wood-nymph deserved better; and while it was true that few of the young sparks of the *ton* were up to her weight, there were many worthy men around who could take good care of both Lady Juliette and her fortune. She would not find them if she continued in her present course of egregious folly, however. Someone must take Lady Juliette in hand and give her a lesson sharp enough to shake her out of that cursed self-confidence. The next scoundrel she set her fancy upon might not have his own ridiculous scruples. In fact, it was all too likely that he would not!

Swearing vehemently, Jack set his heels to Cavalier's sides and sent his surprised mount back down the shady ride at the gallop. The devil fly away with respectability; he'd go over to Temple Down and work off his temper by exercising Vulcan.

Somehow she would make the Marquess of Barham take her seriously—and stop laughing at her! She would make him humbly beg to marry her, and to pay off the bonds, and say that she was right. She would then spurn him utterly, and—and once that was done she would— past this point even righteous anger refused to carry her; Juliette was only sure that she would, somehow, make Lord Barham very, very sorry indeed.

As Lady Juliette was unused to indulging in excesses of sensibility, it never occurred to her that some of these admirable aims were mutually exclusive, nor that the Marquess, as already proven, was unlikely to submit as tamely to her dictates as she wished to imagine.

Her furious mortification was not slaked in the least by confronting Lady Ralph and Lady Hawkchurch in the front hall as she came in from the stables, nor by the expression of barely controlled distress on Lady Ralph's face when Juliette begged pardon for the damage to the south lawn.

"Thought it was the huntin' field, did you, m'gel? In *my* day a lady kept to a lady's place, miss! Sporting's a man's business." Lady Hawkchurch emitted a sharp caw of laughter at her own wit.

Juliette bowed her head to conceal her far from lady-like emotions. This was all Barham's fault—come what might, she would be revenged upon him. No one could treat her like that, and laugh at her to boot! And when she thought that she had almost admitted to a certain fondness for the man—! Face burning with humiliation, Juliette ground her teeth, and stalked off in the midst of Lady Hawkchurch's lecture to find her cousin and make it very clear to him that he, at least, was not to trifle with her.

But Anthony Devereaux, true to his protestations of cowardice, had taken himself off to Temple Down early that morning to spend a quiet day far from Juliette's wrath. Having been lectured by Lady Juliette on the proper treatment of servants often enough, he was reasonably certain that she would not whipsaw them by countermanding his orders—instead she would lie in wait for him and force him to countermand them!

It did not take Juliette long to come to the same conclusion. She was far from admitting he had won, however; her sulphurous thoughts were entirely directed to showing the wicked Marquess of Barham how very, very foolish he had ever been to cross her.

Filled with these agreeably bloodthirsty musings, Juliette gave Mattie no trouble over the preparations for leaving. Trunks that had been packed could be unpacked, in Juliette's opinion, and she had more urgent concerns. If Tony was denied to her, it was the work of a moment to discover where Althea was, and to hurry off for a council of war.

But Althea, as it turned out, was occupied—sitting at her needlework with her sister and Miss Jerusha Gressingham while Mrs. Fonthill occupied the chaise in the corner.

Lady Ralph's sudden approval of Isobel had been lost on none of the Fonthills, and Althea had been subjected to a trying evening—after the ladies had retired—of listening to her mother build cloud-castles on the hope that Douglas would offer for her sister.

"—and then you know, my love," her mother had gone on, "we must find a husband for you, for you cannot think you would wish to make your home with Belle, and exist only on the edge of her happiness."

"Indeed, Mama, nothing could make me happier. It is a far more comfortable thought than of marrying just to marry. But do remember, all is not settled yet, and—something might happen, Mama, we must not be too previous." But Mrs. Fonthill had made light of Althea's *caveats*, and Althea hardly dared say more. In her heart of hearts, she could not believe that having to scrape and manage would be so very bad for Belle—though it would of course disappoint Mama—and if only Lord Ralph were aware of his son's peccadillo, surely, surely, debtor's prison would not result!

The following morning, despairing of her ability to talk sense to her mother or prudence to her sister, deprived of Mr. Devereaux's agreeable company by his visit to Temple Down, and guiltily sure her knowledge of the Comte de Devereaux's betrothal would show on her face the moment she spoke to Juliette, Althea had accepted Jerusha's invitation to sit and stitch.

It was always better to spend time in Jerusha Gressingham's company than not, Althea reflected, as she made certain Isobel joined them. The more hard information Jerusha possessed, the more inconsistent her gossip became, which was the only thing that had saved many a reputation. Miss Gressingham spoke as if she were on the most familiar of footings with people whose names and reputations she knew only from the Gazette; conversely, she was never at all certain of any fact pertaining to her closest friends. Therefore Althea sat and stitched, and listened to Jerusha pillory the absent Lord Barham—with the none-too-occasional aside on Lady Juliette's folly in making up to him so shamelessly.

Althea had just begun revolving in her mind for the third time the best way of ensuring that Douglas Candlesby make a clean breast of things to his papa when Lady Juliette burst into the room. Juliette looked distracted and dangerous, but not, fortunately, like either a rakehell's jilliflirt or a disinherited heiress. Althea rose to this challenge as well.

"Oh, here you are, Juliette; have you come to sew with us? Miss Gressingham was only this instant saying how she wished for your company, and I still have your workpiece in my sewing box."

Juliette's mouth dropped open at this pretty speech, but in an instant her sense of self-preservation asserted itself.

"Why Althea, I should adore that above all things! Do say I may join you, Miss Gressingham."

Which, as Althea reflected, wouldn't fool anyone, but Jerusha could hardly say so, now, could she?

Chapter

E I G H T

The rest of the afternoon would have been far
worse, had not Douglas Candlesby been the racing-
mad scion of indulgent parents. Lord Ralph had
paid well to have the news of the St. Leger brought
by special messenger, and this worthy arrived at
Duckmanton just after nuncheon, to impart his
news with an air of great importance which was
actually justified, for the results were stunning.

Sultan, the odds-on favorite, had never even
reached the course, having broken down during a
morning gallop. The race itself had actually been
run *twice*—for several horses had not gotten away
with the field, and the first race was declared a false
start.

After considerable disagreement, a second race
had been run which had been started by a helpful
spectator, as Mr. Lockwood, the starter, had thrown
down his flag and refused to perform this office. The
first race had been won by one Antonio, and the
second by Sir Walter, and nobody, the messenger
finished with relish, knew what the final result of
the imbroglio would be.

The house party thereupon commenced an excited argument, interrupted as the entire tale was

told over for each new arrival. The heated discussion was not in the least hampered by the fact that not one of them had any real information on the matter under discussion. The Doncaster Racing Club itself had cravenly referred the question to the Jockey Club, and hoped to have a reply within a few weeks, when all questions of wagers could be settled.

Lady Juliette, her emotions still agitated past reason or sense, cared not whether the St. Leger had been won by Antonio, Sir Walter, or the disobliging Mr. Lockwood. She had room for only one thought: Sultan, upon whom Lord Barham had wagered what little capital he had, had not even started. The Marquess would now be desperate indeed—and Juliette dared swear he would be more amenable to her proposals!

Anthony Devereaux spent an agreeable day in exile at Temple Down. He had, naturally, kept the information of Douglas's hideous folly strictly to himself, but had heard some little account of the Wicked Marquess from Juliette's godpapa. It was a great pity, as Marcus had said, that Juliette did not have less money and Jack less reputation, and Anthony had sat mumchance again, for though Juliette was no longer an heiress, Jack's reputation continued to grow, and all things being equal, there could be no hope of a match there for all the future dukedoms in England.

He had then confided to Lord Templeton that, while nothing at all had been settled, it was nearly a sure thing that he would be marrying his cousin sometime in the next few months. Instead of the routine felicitations he had expected, Marcus Templeton's reaction was very different.

"Good lord, Anthony—I thought you had more sense than that. Whose bright plan was this—no, don't bother to tell me; it has the stamp of the *ancien régime* all over it. Well, I shan't wish you very happy, if that is what you are expecting, since you won't be."

"But—why?" said Anthony, startled into bluntness by this plain speaking.

Marcus had sat back in his chair and reached for the Cato they had been discussing. "Why won't you be happy? Because Devereauxes—do pardon my vulgarity—should marry for love. My goddaughter fancies herself an estate manager in petticoats; which is as much folly as you thinking yourself a cool, dispassionate intelligence, untouched by romantic nonsense; yes, I see I've touched you on the raw."

"Leaving my dreadful secrets aside," said Anthony with forced lightness, "we must be practical. I can afford to waste my life among my books wishing for, er, love, but Julie can't. She's my cousin; I'm fond of her; Madame particularly wishes the match; and I am certainly more eligible a *parti* than Bad Barham. I shan't turn her out in her shift, squander her substance, or interfere with her ideas on farming. Beyond that"—he shrugged—"love is a luxury for Cits. I shall go back to my books, and Julie to her plow. We shan't trouble anyone else."

"Ah," said Marcus, with a speaking glance to where Euphemia Templeton's portrait hung over the fireplace. "Well, it is plain to see you have not met the woman to change your mind—and so long as you do not, you, at least, should almost be content. But when will you give up the notion that Solange Devereaux can run your life better than you can? You are more than seven, you know."

172

"Were I more than seventy-seven, I should not give up my notion, sir, until I also give up the notion that I like peace and quiet above all things as well. It suits Madame, it is not intolerable, and I am a lazy fellow, as well as a coward."

Marcus did not agree, but spoke no more on the subject, wondering if Anthony knew how much he had revealed with his blithe assumption that a hasty marriage to the first man who could be forced to take her was Juliette's only hope. And as there was no recourse for the polite and considerate guest save to return to his hostess's table for dinner, at length the cowardly Mr. Devereaux took his leave to ride back to Duckmanton, and Marcus sat and pondered.

He had expected alarms and excursions; instead he received three versions of the St. Leger debacle—Douglas Candlesby's, Lightfoot Bobby Gressingham's, and Juliette's—within moments of his arrival, and the predatory smile that played on Juliette's lips when Mr. Gressingham revealed that the absent Lord Barham had lost considerable money on Sultan was nothing Anthony Devereaux could like. Throwing caution to the winds, he had done his best to see Julie alone but had been balked at every turn; finally he had departed to change for dinner. Perhaps Miss Fonthill would be able to shed some light on his cousin's strange behavior.

Miss Fonthill, it transpired, was equally baffled—though she was able to contribute the *on-dit* that Juliette had ridden Oriflamme across the lawn this morning, cutting it up badly, and had followed this by snubbing Lady Hawkchurch. While this had only put the seal on Lady Ralph's approval of Isobel as a potential daughter-in-law, it was so unlike Juliette as to destroy any joy Althea found in the happy outcome. Still, as Mr. Devereaux had said, the morning would see them far from the fatal lures of Jack Barham, and Juliette would soon be distracted by the news of Maria Alworthy's betrothal. He then allowed himself to hope that Miss Fonthill would do Little Fakenham the honor of paying a call upon Juliette there sometime in the near future, and by the time Althea had disentangled this syntax, the gong had summoned the company in to dinner.

Lord Barham too was at dinner, though one would not have thought it was the same rake, so doucely did he respond to Lady Ralph's inquiries as to his future plans. He also bore up wonderfully well under Lightfoot Bobby's long discussion of the amount of money Barham had lost, nor did he put himself forward by attempting to speak to Lady Juliette, who had cast him one volcanic glance before subsiding, eyes downcast.

Juliette herself sat and thought intently all through dinner, and hardly had the ladies withdrawn when she rather breathlessly explained to her hostess that she must retire early in order to make an early start in the morning. Lady Ralph was all mournful kindness on the undoubted trial and disaster to befall her on her journey, and Juliette was gone long before Mr. Devereaux appeared to seek speech with her.

She knew now how she would handle the Marquess; the St. Leger fiasco had left him penniless, and he would be forced to agree to her every proposition, lest he lose what little acceptance he still had. She hurried upstairs to her bedchamber, where she pounced upon Mattie, who was engaged in folding down the bedcovers.

"Mattie, you must deliver a message to Lord Barham at once!"

"That I won't, Miss Julie," the abigail declared firmly. "Now, miss, you let me get you out of those things and brush your hair like a good girl."

"Oh, yes you will," Juliette informed her with equal stubbornness as she scribbled a few lines on a sheet of notepaper. She folded it and held it out to Mattie. "I am not a child, Mattie, and you will do as I say! Now go and give him the message, and be quick about it, for I shall need you here tonight!"

It was relatively peaceful upon the terrace, and Lord Barham had taken refuge there to smoke a cigarillo and contemplate his future. After three seconds cogitation, he concluded that, for all practical purposes, he *had* no future. He supposed, idly, that he might go soldiering again—they must need cavalry officers somewhere, he supposed—and Vulcan alone would be enough to terrify any enemy. But he lacked the wherewithal to buy in, and lacked the taste for enlisted life.

Jack leaned back on the carved stone railing that marked the edge of the terrace, looking at the lighted windows of Duckmanton. He normally despised the seductive lure of the "might have been," but tonight he couldn't help himself. Living beyond society's sanctions was always a lonely life, if a merry one, but it took money to brazen it out, and his resources were now at end.

"I should have taken her up on it," Jack said to the brisk night air, then smiled ruefully and shook his head. Oh, well, he supposed he'd come round again—somehow.

As he straightened and began to stroll towards the house, a stout female figure marched towards him, rigid with what his practiced eye instantly recognized as disapproval. "Be you the Marquess of Barham?" asked the female, glaring at him.

"I'm afraid so," said Jack, tossing his cigarillo away. "What is it?"

"Here," she said, thrusting a piece of paper at him. "But mark my words," she added darkly, "no good will come of it, and what she's about to be writing to Marquesses at this time of night—and if you lay a finger on one hair of her head, my lord, I'm warning you—"

"My good woman," said Jack, unfolding the missive and tilting it to catch the light from the house, "I don't know who your mistress may be, but it wouldn't be her hair that would interest me. Now run along and let me read this in—that damned little idiot!"

Swiftly he scanned the paper again; it still carried the same message. Lady Juliette Devereaux would be very much obliged to my Lord Barham if he would do her the honor of waiting upon her tonight—in her bedchamber—after the household was asleep. These last lines had been heavily underlined. Jack read it once more and then began to tear the paper into very small pieces; he handed the resultant confetti to the sullen abigail.

"Very well," said Jack, "far be it from me to disappoint a lady. Now run along and tell her to burn that!"

The woman bobbed a curtsy and tromped back to the house. Jack lit another cigarillo and prepared to wait.

When the house was dark and quiet, Jack made his way through the corridors to Lady Juliette's room. The hour was late, and he was half-prepared to find that his lady fair had fallen asleep, but a streak of light showed under the door. Well, as he'd said, he hated to disappoint a lady; besides, he was agog to discover just what Lady Juliette thought she was doing. That she had a plan to revenge herself upon him for refusing her offer was fairly clear to Jack; what that plan might be he couldn't imagine.

A more prudent and less curious man would have withdrawn to his own room to sleep the sleep of the just. Jack, hardly hesitating, rapped softly on Lady Juliette's bedroom door and entered the room.

The room was well-lit with candles, and Lady Juliette, wrapped in a voluminous combing-robe of sea-green tabby silk lavished with Dutch lace, sat before her dressing table as if caught in the act of preparing for bed. As her shining ebony hair was still arranged in neat curls, and the foot showing unwarily below the combing-robe still wore a gilded kid slipper, this attitude of *négligé* lacked, to Jack's critical eye, a certain air of verisimilitude. Nevertheless, he smiled at her as he pulled the door closed behind him and turned the key in the lock. Lady Juliette, who had begun a coy smile in return, looked startled.

"So we shan't be interrupted, my sweet," Jack explained as he came towards her, pausing briefly as he passed the massive mahogany wardrobe to push its doors, which stood most oddly ajar, tightly shut. Muffled sounds of objection came from the wardrobe; Jack ignored them and advanced upon Juliette.

"And now, my dear little wood-nymph, I'm quite sure we shan't be interrupted, as I know from sad experience that those things are deuced hard to open from the inside."

Lady Juliette's expression had become one of outright apprehension. "I-I'm sure I don't know what you mean," she stammered, leaping to her feet and clutching her robe more closely to her.

"Spare me the time-wasting protestations, I beg of you," said Jack. "Just tell me plainly—why did you ask me to come to your room—of all the stupid places—and in the middle of the night? I won't even venture to comment on that ridiculous garment you're wearing over your clothes—and pray, sweet Juliette, do not tell me that any number of people have admired it excessively, or I shall be forced to entertain an even odder idea of your conduct than I do now."

Before she could move, Jack had laid hands upon her and deftly peeled off the combing-robe and let it drop in a pool of silk to the floor. As Juliette, her cheeks flaming, shook his hands off and tried hastily to smooth out her evening dress, Jack continued heartlessly, "Doubtless you have a very sensible plan, my pet, and I'm all afire to hear it."

From the glare Lady Juliette directed at him, the plan involved his immediate and painful demise; she looked so like a rumpled and indignant kitten that Jack couldn't help grinning at her. Lady Juliette set her chin.

"If you do not marry me at once, and on my terms, Lord Barham, you will be ruined!" she announced triumphantly.

"Behold me terrified," said Jack. "Do gratify my curiosity, my child—just how do you intend to accomplish this?"

It cannot be said that Lady Juliette's ensuing explanation made all instantly clear; halfway through it Jack laughed outright. This made Lady Juliette actually stamp her foot in frustration and completely lose sight of her original objective—the remainder of her discourse concerned itself primarily with the multitudinous flaws in Jack's character.

"—and I shall scream and you will be found here and thrown out of the house!" she finished. "And no one will ever receive you *at all* again!"

"Say, rather, that no one would receive *you* again, my pet!" Jack said. "Such an incident could only enhance my reputation—such as it is; I've been dismissed from any number of bedchambers, usually by the husband of the lady in question. But say no more," he went on, holding up a hand as Juliette opened her mouth again. "Since your mind appears to be quite made up, so be it. Name the day, my sweet."

Apparently taken aback, Lady Juliette stared up at him. "You—you mean you will do as I say?"

"I'll marry you, at any rate, as you seem to wish it. Where shall we have the banns called?"

"Banns?" said Juliette, as if she'd never heard the word.

"You don't want to wait? My sweet, I'm touched. Very well then, a special license it shall be—if you've the blunt to pay for one that is. You are of age, I take it?"

"Well, I—yes, or I soon shall be." Lady Juliette sounded increasingly shaken. "How—how much is a special license?"

Refusing to take pity upon her, Jack shook his head. "It doesn't matter if you're not of age, darling. No, I'm afraid there's nothing for it but Gretna Green. Be a good girl and let the poor abigail out of the wardrobe and have her get you into a riding habit. If we leave tonight we can reach the Border within the week, I daresay."

"A *week*?" said Lady Juliette in horror. "I can't be alone with you for a week!"

"Thank God, the light of comprehension dawns at last! Now come here, my little innocent, and I will give you some advice." As Juliette tried to back away, Jack swooped her up into his arms and settled himself on the edge of the bed and Juliette upon his knee. Ignoring her violent struggles, which disconcerted him not at all, he began.

"You invited me here tonight with the admirable intention of teaching me a lesson—no, don't bother to deny it; we both know it's true. Well, my child, I am about to return the favor, and you should stop writhing about in that enticing fashion and pay attention to your elders.

"Lesson one: I am far larger and stronger than you are, and it is vastly unlikely that you can overwhelm me by physical force—nor am I chivalrous enough to let you hit, kick, or bite me, dear heart, so you may as well stop trying. Now, the only thing that keeps me from doing any number of things to your charming self is that protection of Society which you are presenting yourself as wild to cast off."

Lady Juliette gave Lord Barham to understand that she required no one's protection and despised Society; Jack sighed.

"Yes, all it means to you, my sheltered little miss, is that you must be polite to tiresome people and attend parties at which you are not the adored center of attention—but can you even begin to imagine how little you would care for the sort of parties at which you were? The wrong sort of parties, my pet, which do *not* end with hand-kissing over the supper table, but, rather, here—" Jack made as if to roll over onto the bed with Juliette, and she gave a little shriek of quite unfeigned terror. As a determined thumping commenced from the depths of the wardrobe, Jack straightened and looked squarely into Juliette's frightened eyes.

"Well, you do have some sense of self-preservation after all; my compliments."

"You—you horrible man! Let me go at once, or I *shall* scream!"

"Not before I'm through with you—and do try to bear in mind, precious, that it is you who will be ruined if anyone finds me here tonight. Now, I have several more things to say to you, Lady Juliette, and then I shall take my leave."

Juliette made another valiant effort to do him severe physical damage. "I shan't listen!"

"Lesson two:" Jack went on imperturbably. "Stop trying to be twice the man your mother was."

Juliette gasped indignantly. "How dare you mention Mama!"

Jack grinned. "As you already know, I dare the most amazing things. But back to the sainted Sophia Halford, belle of the 'nineties. Allow me to point out, my child, that that was a quarter-century ago, and times have changed. Furthermore, I have it directly from Viscount Templeton that your mother was wild to a fault, and spent two exhausting Seasons upon the Town before her family managed to snare your father. Her dress and behavior are hardly fit models for you. I suggest you allow someone like Miss Fonthill to do something about that appalling wardrobe of yours; with all your money it's a pity you have no taste in clothes, but at least you can look like a young woman of quality and not a high-flyer!"

"You—you—" Juliette quivered in outrage. "How dare you tell lies about Mama! Mattie was with her, and she's told me—"

"If Mattie is that stout and worthy body who is even now trying to tunnel her way out of the cupboard, she can barely have been into her 'teens when the sainted Sophia held sway, and her testimony is of doubtful value."

Juliette yanked one hand free and tried to slap him, a move Jack countered easily. "One more thing, and then I am done and you may vilify me to your heart's content. Doubtless you've been told your mother died in childbed, or some such fairy tale—well, she didn't! She died trying to take a high-perch phaeton with a unicorn hitch around the gate-house turn at Chaceley at the gallop. It was an unruly team, and one she'd been forbidden to drive, of course. The horses all had to be shot, so Lord Templeton told me."

Lady Juliette stared at him with a stricken expression. "She—she didn't!"

"Oh, yes, she did, my child. So stop trying to emulate her—you have twice her looks and, the evidence of your current undignified position to the contrary, six times her brains. So, if you truly want that worthy husband for Chaceley, I advise you to consider well what I have said, and act accordingly."

There was one last loud thud from the wardrobe, and a considerably rumpled and breathless Matilda tumbled out and advanced upon the bed. "You unhand Miss Julie, my lord, or I'll—"

"I think," said Jack, smiling ruefully, "that this is our cue to kiss and part, my sweet." So saying, he tightened his arms and carried out the action, paying no heed to either Juliette's desperate wrigglings or Mattie's steady blows with a feather pillow.

At last, as this assualt had no effect upon the Marquess, the abigail dropped the pillow and fled to the doorway, intent upon seeking outside aid. As she pulled the door open, Jack released Juliette, who sprang from his lap, panting and disheveled.

"Oh, you—you vile man! I—I wish I had never invited you here in the first place!" she declared with disastrous clarity as the door swung wide, only to fall silent, her eyes widening in horror, as Lord Ralph Candlesby, closely followed by Miss Jerusha Gressingham, strode into the room.

"I thought I heard a noise, and naturally I roused Lord Ralph at once," said Miss Gressingham, staring in virtuous distress at the tableau before her. Glancing at Jack, she put a hand to her throat, as if to make sure that her dressing-gown were securely and modestly fastened. "Oh, my poor dear Lady Juliette—how dreadful for you!"

"Oh, lord," said Jack, quite as appalled by this development as was Juliette. "Well, so much for good intentions, Lady Juliette—although I shouldn't describe this room as hell, precisely. But you need not scream again, for, as you see, you have been rescued in the most timely and theatrical fashion." He stared hard at Juliette, willing her to take another's lead for once in her life.

"Oh—oh, dear," Lady Juliette moaned faintly, and put her hands to her cheeks.

Lord Ralph was clad in dressing-gown and night cap, and carried a dueling-pistol in his hand. Now he pointed this lethal object at Jack. "That will be quite sufficient, Lord Barham."

"More than," Jack agreed, as Lady Juliette was taken into Mattie's fiercely protective embrace. "Ah, well—these attempts to ravish heiresses never prosper, you know." He bowed mockingly in Juliette's direction. "A thousand apologies, my dear, I was quite carried away by your beautiful fortune—which is why, of course, I sought to carry her away," he told Lord Ralph. It wasn't much, but it was the best Jack could do. If Miss Gressingham had heard Juliette's touching farewell, which was all too likely, the tale that the *ton* would hear would not be that of a foiled abduction—which would be bad enough, God knew!—but of an assignation. Damn the woman and her noises!

"Lord Barham," Lord Ralph began in a half-outraged, half-apologetic tone, "I fear I must ask you—"

"To leave the hallowed halls of Duckmanton," Jack finished for him. "By all means, Lord Ralph, let us proceed with my expulsion without delay."

"If you will excuse me, Lady Juliette, I will see Lord Barham to the stables," said Lord Ralph. "Miss Gressingham will perhaps—"

Miss Gressingham nodded and moved to comfort Lady Juliette, giving Jack a wide berth and pulling her skirts aside as she passed him, a gesture Jack had never expected actually to see outside the precincts of Drury Lane. "Of course, Lord Ralph. Oh, my poor dear Lady Juliette, the shock to your feelings—!"

"Well," said Lord Ralph, the pistol wavering, "I—er—I wish you a very good night. Now, Lord Barham—"

Jack, his mouth twisting in a wry smile, bowed mockingly to the company at large and removed himself from the scene of the crime. He was not able to resist one last backward glance, and so saw Lady Juliette shake off both Matilda and the solicitous Miss Gressingham and fling herself, crying bitterly, onto the bed.

It was not to be hoped for that the curtain would come down quickly on such an entertaining scene. Miss Gressingham dispatched Mattie to rouse Mr. Devereaux at once, and Mattie, with great good sense, summoned Althea as well.

Within a short time both had arrived; Althea took one look at Juliette, well on her way to the most violent hysterics, and sent Mattie again for Mrs. Fonthill's laudanum drops. Then she attempted to calm the sobbing victim while Mr. Devereaux was made the repository of Jerusha's tale.

It was quite dreadful; Miss Gressingham, as she told him several times, had no idea why she had roused Lord Ralph, or what she had seen, or what had been going on in Juliette's bedroom, though she was quite clear on the hour and the cast of characters. Anthony listened with a sinking heart, and when Miss Gressingham paused to draw breath he ruthlessly and fulsomely congratulated her on her sapience, her wit, her delicacy, and her tact while compelling her toward the door. Raining a last fanfaronade of compliments upon her, he swept the returning abigail into the room and closed the door in Miss Gressingham's face.

"I'm a-having of the laudanum drops right here, Miss Althea," Mattie said importantly. Juliette's tears had faded to wracking sobs of the sort that could go on for hours.

"Give me six drops in half a glass of water, please, Mattie," Althea said briskly. "Oh, what can have happened?" she asked of no one in particular.

"Don't cry, Juliette—it will be all right, I promise you. Just drink this, my love, and you will have a good sleep, and you need never see Lord Barham again, and—"

"No!" said Juliette, trying to push Althea away and struggling to sit up. Her gaze fell on Anthony Devereaux. "Tony—oh, what are you doing here?" she demanded, covering her tear-flushed face with her hands. "Leave me alone!"

Mr. Devereaux, so far from doing that, leaned over the bed and drawled, in an irritatingly affected voice that Althea had never heard him use before, "Tell me, Julie, is it true what Miss Gressingham says; that you invited the wicked Marquess of Barham to your rooms to elope with you? Tut, tut, tut—trading on your expectations in that wicked fashion; the more so when you haven't got any."

"Mr. Devereaux!" gasped Althea in stunned outrage, but Anthony knew his cousin very well. His bizarre expertise had its effect; Juliette thrust Althea away and sat up. Her chest heaved alarmingly as she struggled to control her breathing, but when at last she looked up at her cousin her gaze was steady.

"Be a Trojan, cousin," said Anthony, sitting down beside her on the bed. "I shall tell you all the worst in a lump, just as I did when your hunter was shot, and then you will drink this and sleep." He put an arm around Juliette's shoulders and took the glass from Althea's hand. "I came here directly from Chaceley, and Uncle Sebastian is to marry Maria Alworthy sometime in November. It is all settled, and there is nothing to be done. In the face of that, Bad Barham hardly matters, does he?"

Juliette turned appallingly white, and Althea

clutched at her ice-cold hands in real consternation. Anthony held the glass against her teeth, and Juliette obediently gulped down the sleeping draught. Then she began to laugh with a sharp note of hysteria that made Anthony wince.

"Oh—then it has all been for nothing! You see, it's true—I did invite Lord Barham!"

Althea stared at her for a moment, then said quietly, "Dearest Juliette, you know that I am fond of you—are you quite sure you wish to tell us anything more?"

"Oh, yes," said Juliette, under the compulsive urge to confess all and be absolved. "You see—"

It cannot be said that either Anthony or Althea found Juliette's explanation either comprehensible or convincing of anything other than her extreme misery. "Oh, why could you not have told me sooner, Tony?" Juliette wailed, and Anthony looked grim. "Lord Barham would never have behaved so had he known! Maria is not yet twenty—and I will *not* be her bridesmaid and I will *not* call her Stepmama!" Juliette seemed to crumple up, and looked so miserable that Althea, put her arms around her again.

"I—I am sure Miss Alworthy will not expect you to call her that, my love. Why, you have been on terms before, have you not?"

"Maria will be impossible," said Juliette, on the verge of renewed tears. "And doubtless that is my fault too, for I am sure I should have been nicer to her, even if she *hasn't* got any seat—for she does take her falls well, you know."

"That is—is an excellent trait, of course," Althea agreed, her voice quavering only slightly. "And I'm sure you were never uncivil to her, Juliette!"

"And worse than all—oh, Althea, what shall I do? I—I—I shall not be received, now!"

"Madame will receive you, Julie—and we shall go to Fakenham just as soon as you can travel. Your trunks are all packed, you know—we shall break the news of Uncle's wedding to her together; won't that be fun?"

"I cannot go to Madame," said Juliette, in low exhausted tones.

"Forgive me, Juliette, but I think it would be a very good thing for you to go to your great-aunt's," said Althea.

Lady Juliette suddenly clasped Miss Fonthill's hands. "Oh, Thea—do come with me! If—if you come, it will not be so bad. Please say you will!"

"Yes, Miss Fonthill, please do come." Anthony Devereaux was as collected as if he were not in an hysterical woman's bedchamber in the middle of the night, with her abigail glaring poisoned daggers at him from the doorway.

"Of course I shall come, if Mama will allow it." Miss Fonthill knew it would be difficult to persuade her mother to allow her to visit such a notorious young lady as Juliette was proving to be, but didn't doubt her ability to do so in the end. "I am sure it would be very convenient for Mama to have me safely bestowed elsewhere for a time."

"Then you will come?" The laudanum was beginning to take its toll; Juliette's head lolled limply against Althea's shoulder.

"I shall ask Mama directly, and I am sure she will say yes. Now we must get you to bed, Juliette, so say good night to your cousin and let Mattie see to you."

* * *

Anthony Devereaux was standing in the hall when Althea stepped out a few moments later.

"My heartfelt gratitude, Miss Fonthill, for your aid and succor, and I apologize devoutly for involving you in this appalling muddle. If I could decide precisely who to take a horsewhip to, I should hire someone to do it on the instant. Perhaps to me," he said with a sigh, leaning back against the wall. "Pay me no mind, Miss Fonthill; I know you are eager to retire, and I am simply indulging in such an excess of sensibility as a cool dispassionate intelligence should properly abhor. If only I *had* told her—"

"If only Lord Barham had stayed out of her bedroom!" Althea snapped acidly. "Do place the blame where it belongs—you only wished to save Juliette's dignity, but that—that *man* wished to ruin her!"

"Yes. Well, good night, Miss Fonthill. I daresay I am off now to let Lord Ralph congratulate me on what a narrow escape we have all had, and then to put off our preparations for leaving another day. What a joy a country house party is, to be sure." With a sketchy bow he strode off down the hall.

Chapter
NINE

Upon awakening late the next morning, it was Juliette's devout hope that the events of the night before would be proven nothing but a nightmare brought on by an excess of spleen. Failing that, she could only wish, without any hope at all, that no one would ever speak to her again. This, she knew, was unlikely in the extreme; people would speak to her, and at great length, and she knew she would deserve every critical word.

In the harsh light of day, she found it hard to imagine what she could possibly have been thinking of—to invite Lord Barham to her room like that—! Juliette fell back against the pillows and pressed her hands to her temples, as if to drive away memory. Oh, how could she have—she, who so prided herself on her common sense! She had never experienced such a state of agitation before; perhaps she was sickening for a brain fever. And worse than all, the things Lord Barham had said to her— Juliette wondered sickly whether they could possibly be true.

Well, none of it would matter. Tony had said they were leaving—she would go away to Fakenham, for

Chaceley, too, was to be taken from her—a fitting punishment for her pride and willfulness.

She was occupied with these Gothic thoughts, and the slight headache that is the aftereffect of a dose of laudanum, when there was a light scratching upon the door. "Go away," said Juliette faintly.

In response to this, the door opened and Althea Fonthill marched into the room. Regarding Juliette with a sympathetic yet reproachful expression, she continued past the bed to the window and threw open the heavy velvet curtains, allowing the late morning sunlight to stream into the room.

"Well, and you have slept quite long enough; it is time to be up and doing; Mr. Devereaux has explained to Lady Ralph, and we shall leave tomorrow instead of today, but that is no reason to spend such a lovely day in your room!" Althea rattled on, with slightly forced cheerfulness.

Juliette stared at her as if her calm, sensible friend had run quite mad. "I have the headache," she suggested at last.

"Very likely you do, and I'm sure I'm not surprised," said Althea, advancing upon Juliette with a determined gleam in her soft gray eyes. "But this is *not* the time to suffer an attack of the vapors— not with Miss Gressingham and Lady Hawkchurch ready to dress you for carving upon every table in England!"

"What?" cried Juliette, sitting bolt upright.

"Miss Gressingham is denying absolutely—oh, Juliette, you know her way!—that what Lord Ralph interrupted was not an abduction, but an elopement. So you see, Juliette, that if you lie abed with a headache today you merely proclaim yourself steeped in guilt. Now do get up!"

"I can't," Juliette said weakly. "Oh, Althea, how can I possibly face anyone?"

"You must," Althea told her implacably. "Juliette, if your reputation is not to be utterly shattered in this one moment, you *must* appear—and hold yourself as a very pattern-card of virtue." Althea sat down upon the bed beside Juliette and smiled wanly.

"Now, I have already told Mama that Miss Gressingham is merely jealous of you and completely misinterpreted the unhappy mischance that brought Lord Barham to your rooms. Everyone knows that Miss Gressingham has been pleased by nothing since her fiancé was killed in Spain, so *she* should be quite easy to discount. Lady Hawkchurch is more difficult, but it seems Mr. Devereaux is quite her chum, so she will temper her disagreeable remarks for the sake of your relationship—oh, Juliette, you should *not* have snubbed her yesterday! But we will not talk of that, if you please! And since Lord Barham himself held you blameless, I think—" Here Althea drew a deep breath, and continued, "I *think*, Juliette, that we may bring you off yet. But *not* if you are to cloister yourself moaning in your bedchamber; to absent yourself at this juncture would be fatal!"

"I am not moaning!" snapped Juliette, then surprised herself by bursting into tears.

"There, there, my love—of course you are not—and it is very too bad about—What I *should* say, is that Mr. Devereaux has also been telling everyone about your father's engagement, since it is nearly news enough to stop anyone thinking of—of such an *unimportant* person as the Marquess of Barham!" Althea finished bravely.

"Oh, Thea," said Juliette with the ghost of a

smile, "I am sure I do not deserve as true a friend as you! And—and will you go with me to Fakenham?" she finished timidly.

"Of course," said Althea bracingly. "I have already settled it with Mama—who is daily expecting a happy disclosure from Belle and so has no time for me—and now that Lord Barham is *quite* ruined, you know, I am sure Douglas will tell his papa the whole. So perhaps that will be all right, although that can hardly be a *great* deal of consolation to you. And now I think you should be up and dressed, for it will soon be time for luncheon and you must be there. Let me ring for your abigail and then we will find you a suitable gown for the occasion."

Althea turned to the trunk—one of six—that remained. The others had been packed and strapped the day before, in preparation of the journey to Fakenham; this one remained to receive Juliette's night robe and dressing-gown. Althea peered into it hesitantly.

"Althea," Juliette said in a small voice, "was Lord Barham right?"

"Right about what, Juliette?" Althea asked, turning back.

"He said—" Juliette flung back the covers and joined Althea in front of the open trunk. "He said my clothes were horrid."

Althea bit her lip, and said "Did he?" in an admirably steady voice. Then she put an arm around Juliette's shoulders and hugged her warmly. "Well, they are not horrid, precisely, but they are not, you know, quite what—what a girl in her first Season should wear!"

"Oh," said Juliette with unaccustomed meekness. "Well, then, is there anything here that I can safely wear to luncheon, Thea?"

The two girls gazed into the depths of the trunk, Juliette hopefully, Althea with increasing despair. Where, oh where were the demure frocks in pastel challis and muslin that would mutely proclaim the inviolate innocence of a young maiden?

Lady Juliette Devereaux's clothes fairly trumpeted the fact that their owner was a rich and headstrong young woman with no one to say her nay. Walking-dresses in emerald and maroon and puce; morning robes of butter-yellow and deep violet and grass-green silk; evening-dresses of every too-dashing cut and hue. Present Juliette in any of these and the gossips would crucify her.

After much searching, Althea stumbled upon a cream kerseymere round dress; true, it was over-trimmed with floss *and* knots of multicolored ribbons, but that could be remedied, and then the gown would do for today. Althea pulled the kerseymere from the trunk; there would not be an evening-dress here, but somewhere in Juliette's overflowing wardrobe must be something that could be altered to serve as a vestal garment tonight.

By now Matilda had made her appearance, and was fussing about Juliette, loud in her protests of Lord Barham's villainy and demands for the punishment of her innocent lamb's tormentors.

"For it's a right lot of jealous old cats they are, Miss Julie, and no mistake, and put up with them you shouldn't. Why, Miss Sophia would have given them the right-about for such impertinence, and that's the home truth!"

Cold with alarm, Althea interrupted hastily, for if Lady Juliette took it into her head to call Lady Hawkchurch impertinent, Juliette might as well put a period to her existence and have done with it. "This is the dress you should wear today, Ju-

194

liette—once the trimmings have been removed it will do very well."

"Whatever you like, Thea," said Juliette, looking listlessly at the kerseymere gown, but Matilda was not to be so easily won.

"Why, whatever can you be thinking of, Miss Althea—t'would be like a-cutting the flowers off a rosebush, it would, to take off all those nice bits o'ribbon!" Sure of her backer, Mattie looked to her mistress for confirmation, only to be betrayed.

"Do as Miss Fonthill says, Mattie."

"A simple style is more—more suited to the country," Althea explained kindly. "And then you must open the trunk of Juliette's evening-dresses, Mattie, so that we may find her something to wear tonight. I shall loan you a lace shawl if you do not have one, Juliette, and I'm sure you will do very well."

Sniffing with disapproval, Matilda took the cream kerseymere and swept from the room.

Still regarding her despised wardrobe, Juliette heaved a deep sigh. "Althea, are all my gowns quite—quite notorious?"

Althea smiled faintly. "It is not the gown but the wearer that makes for notoriety. Still, they *are* too elaborate for the country, you know."

Eyes bright, as if with unshed tears, Juliette burst out, "He was right—everyone was right! And now I have ruined everything!"

"Hardly that. Now, you shall have a cup of chocolate before Matilda brings your dress back, and then we shall go down to luncheon together."

"Yes," said Juliette drearily, and made a valiant attempt to smile. "After all, if I can face a rasper in the hunting field, I should be able to outface Miss Gressingham, don't you think?"

"Of course you can!" said Althea stoutly, and gave her friend an encouraging hug.

By the time luncheon was over, however, neither Juliette nor Althea was sanguine about Lady Juliette's future in polite society. The first person they had met upon leaving Juliette's room was Miss Gressingham, and that lady's well-bred withdrawal was impossible to mistake. After congratulating Lady Juliette upon her happy escape in tones that indicated all too clearly that Miss Gressingham knew Juliette considered it nothing of the sort, Miss Gressingham had gabbled some unconvincing excuse and hastily left them.

"Well, of all the bad manners!" said Althea roundly, as Miss Gressingham's blue challis demi-train disappeared around the corner of the gallery. "And as for her offering you that revolting book of sermons—!"

But worse was to follow. Lady Ralph did not speak to Juliette at all and Lady Hawkchurch's remarks were so sharp-edged that she might as well have saved her Janus-tongued kindness. Lord Hawkchurch delivered himself of a long and pompous monologue on the joys of filial obedience and right conduct; Isobel Fonthill turned wide eyes upon her, obviously agog for details; and Douglas Candlesby was too mortified to do more than stammer a greeting and then apply himself to his food. It was left to Mr. Devereaux and Miss Fonthill to carry the conversational ball, and since her friend and her cousin could hardly have done anything but champion her innocence, their testimony lacked a certain weight. True, Mrs. Fonthill and Miss Gressingham also made valiant attempts at conversation, but the former was too easily flustered and the latter too mournful to lighten the funereal atmosphere.

Mr. Gressingham alone seemed not to feel the oppression, but as his contribution to the day's delights was to treat Juliette with a kind of encroaching particularity until Anthony Devereaux offered to have him drowned, it cannot be said that his attention was of any consolation.

By mid-afternoon Juliette had a sick headache of shattering proportions. To have been catapulted overnight, and through her own headstrong folly, into a position where she must submit to such treatment would have overset an older and wiser female than she. She wished only to lie down, preferably for the next several weeks, and never see anyone again. But Althea was adamant in her insistence that to retire from the field of battle would be fatal.

"Althea, I cannot sit in the drawing-room and listen to Jerusha Gressingham one more minute or I shall go mad!" Juliette looked as if she were about to burst into tears.

Althea admitted that Juliette had reason for this outburst. "For if she says one more time that, whatever *others* may chose to do, the out-of-the-way is simply not her dish of tea, I shall strangle her myself!"

"Why, Thea!" Juliette, despite her troubles, looked at Althea in surprise; Miss Fonthill was generally the most amiable and soft-spoken of young ladies.

Althea looked contrite. "I am sorry, Juliette; I should not say such things. But when I consider that this is all her fault in the first place—"

"Oh, please!" Juliette begged, and Althea humbly asked her pardon.

"But still, my love, you must not go back to bed. Why do we not go and look through your trunks, and see what Mattie may have found for you to wear?"

Juliette brightened a bit at the chance to remove herself from company, and quickly stood. "Oh, yes, Thea—I am sure Mattie will have found the perfect thing!" Juliette headed for the library door, completely though momentarily distracted by the promise of action.

Althea heaved a sigh as she followed Juliette from the room. She had not realized how exhausting trying to keep Juliette's social standing intact would prove.

And then, as if Juliette's woes were not enough, there was a question of Isobel, Althea mused. Matters would be a great deal simpler if only she could be sure that Isobel *would* be unhappy later. To be sure, it was unpleasant to be poor, but the Misses Fonthill were accustomed to make and scrape. Mama was determined that the family fortunes must be recouped by good marriages, but Isobel already knew what it was to be penniless. If she still wished to marry Douglas Candlesby and live in a cottage, was it right to prevent her?

And in the end, all problems brought Althea's thoughts right back to the cause of all the trouble in the first place. Oh, if only the Marquess of Barham had never been born—then none of them would be in this horrid mess!

Matilda, crossly denying any ability to choose a dress to Althea's tastes, had unpacked a number of them and laid them out for inspection. Althea quickly dismissed most of them as impossible to make over in time for dinner, and settled on a pink satin frock done *en la mode Russe*—slightly behind the times now in 1819, but with the signal advantage that the multicolored satin appliqué flowers could be removed from the hip, hem, and neckline quickly, and the extreme *décolletage* need not matter since Althea's lace shawl would serve as a cloak of virtue.

"Now, Juliette, have you any *white* gloves? I will own that colors are very dashing—"

"But they are not-at-all the thing," Juliette finished with a wry face. "Oh, Thea, people said so over and over, but I never dreamed they were right!"

Dinner that evening passed off with such smoothness that it was hardly recognizable as a Duckmanton meal. Before anyone else could broach a topic of conversation, Mr. Devereaux seized the conversational bit firmly between his teeth and sent the topic of Sebastian Devereaux's forthcoming marriage firmly into play. None of those present knew the bride or were over-familiar with the groom, but this did not, of course, prevent an engrossing discussion of the matter.

The news served as a pretty excuse for Lady Juliette's imminent departure; a gloss to the tale of Solange Devereaux's ill health. That Miss Fonthill was to accompany her was then presented to the company for its delectation; Miss Fonthill, without a blush, contributed the tidbit that Lady Juliette was to serve as Miss Alworthy's bridesmaid and that Althea was to help with the wedding preparations.

This intriguing gambit meant, of course, that the ladies monopolized the conversation for the rest of the meal. What with Lord Barham's absence and

Mr. Devereaux's presence the company was as decorous as might be hoped for, and Juliette and Althea escaped any after-dinner inquisitions by excusing themselves to oversee Althea's packing. This had the additional advantage of preserving Althea from her sister's questioning as well.

As they were to leave at such an early hour, Miss Fonthill was to share Lady Juliette's room for the night. As they settled themselves for sleep, Juliette said, "I am so *very* grateful, Thea—for I know I could not have faced today without you."

"Don't be silly, of course you could." Miss Fonthill blew out the candle. "Go to sleep, Juliette—and pray, do not worry, I am sure it will all come right."

There was a silence, then, just as Althea was falling asleep, Juliette spoke once more. "Thea? What do you suppose happened to Lord Barham?"

"Oh, really, Juliette! I must confess, I neither know nor care, for he has behaved very badly indeed to you. Now do, I beg of you, go to sleep."

Juliette subsided, but not to sleep. She had had far too much agitation in the past twenty-four hours, and her mind refused to rest. And of all her unruly thoughts, the one that troubled her the most was that of the Marquess of Barham, turned penniless out of doors in this bitter autumn weather.

Chapter
TEN

It was a sad fact, which would have vexed Juliette very much indeed had she been privy to it, that the Marquess of Barham was the veteran of far too much catastrophe to let it interfere with his comfort. Upon his expulsion from Duckmanton, he had simply taken himself and Cavalier to the best accommodations circumstances afforded—the Dower House stables at Temple Down. There he had rolled up in a horse blanket and slept the dreamless sleep of the scoundrel, trusting that the morrow would provide some solution to his difficulties.

For one who had learned to forage in the Peninsula, the English countryside was a well-stocked larder. As Lady Juliette lay in laudanum-induced sleep in her bed at Duckmanton, Jack was breakfasting on roast rabbit and thinking that now he was well and truly at the end of his resources.

There was nothing more he could do for Lady Juliette, either. It was too much to hope that last night's folly would remain secret—he could only hope that she would be able to ride out the ensuing storm. There was one ray of hope; she had enough in the way of fortune to compensate for a certain amount of tarnish to her reputation. She might be able to buy that complaisant husband after all.

Jack swore and went on to consider the matter of Mr. Candlesby's bonds. There was nothing to be done there, either. Perhaps Douglas would have enough sense to go to his father when the money-lenders began dunning him—which they would directly when Jack's latest escapade was known. If Jack was entirely beyond the pale, the shylocks would want their pound of flesh.

He could do nothing to halt the inevitable, and could make no reparations—beyond his apologies, which he doubted would be welcome.

No, he must do now as he should have done five years ago: go to his father's solicitors and see what the old devil would pay for Jack's promise to quit England forever. Perhaps he would go to India and become a nabob; there were fortunes to be made with John Company. Perhaps he would simply shoot himself. There must be someone who'd loan him the money for the bullet!

But before putting either of these plans into execution, there were arrangements he must make. Jack rose to his feet and began kicking dirt over the small fire, wondering if there were any way he could arrange to shave this morning before paying a call.

Marcus Templeton was at his usual early and solitary breakfast when a footman came in bearing Lord Barham's card. Marcus looked at it and his heavy dark eyebrows rose. "Well, send my lord Barham in."

The footman gave his master to understand that Lord Barham would not come in. His lordship would, however, greatly appreciate the favor of an interview with Viscount Templeton at once.

"So? Damned young fool. Very well, tell him I'll come." Getting to his feet with the aid of his cane, Marcus made his way stiffly out to the front steps. There he was confronted by an unshaven and rather raffish-looking Lord Barham. Marcus raised an eyebrow at this apparition, but made no comment.

"Good morning, Lord Templeton." The Marquess's voice was harsh, and he seemed to be very much on the defensive. "Forgive the intrusion, but I would greatly appreciate the favor of a private word with you."

"As you see, I am entirely your servant, Lord Barham. Perhaps you can enlighten me—is it the new fashion to hold such conversations upon the threshold?"

The Marquess flushed. "As to that—I must tell you frankly that I am no longer welcome at Duckmanton, and have no wish to force myself upon you. So—"

"So you thought this private business might be better conducted as a Cheltenham tragedy for the benefit of the servants? Come now, man, in a year that's seen one of my sons elope with his cousin's bride, don't you think I'm dead to shame? For heaven's sake, give your horse's bridle to James, here, and come into the breakfast-parlor before I freeze to death."

Lord Barham looked sullen, but obeyed. Despite the Marquess's best efforts, Marcus refused to open discussion until they were seated at the table and fresh coffee had been procured and poured.

"And now, Lord Barham, do not hesitate to tell me how I may serve you. I don't suppose you sought me out merely to confide that you're no longer received by Lady Ralph."

Somewhat to Marcus's surprise, Lord Barham swallowed this with a fairly good grace. "No, sir, I did not. With your permission, I should like to present you with my horse—Cavalier, that is, not Vulcan. It has been borne in upon me that I shall have difficulty keeping one horse, let alone two. Cavalier's trustworthy and steady, and deserves better than I can give him. Will you take him, Lord Templeton—as a gift, you understand!"

Marcus regarded Lord Barham steadily for a moment. "I think I must break a promise to myself and ask you why you are no longer welcome at Duckmanton, Lord Barham," he said at last.

Barham rose abruptly from the table and walked over to the window to gaze out at the lawn. "Very well, if you will have it! Last night I tried to abduct Lady Juliette Devereaux from her bed with the aim of dragging her to Gretna and forcing her to marry me. Unfortunately, I was interrupted."

There was another long pause; eventually Marcus merely said, "Indeed?"

The Marquess rounded on him. "That is what happened, Lord Templeton—as anyone there will tell you!"

"You don't seem the sort to engage in half-baked abductions," Marcus commented mildly.

The already high color in Lord Barham's cheeks darkened still further. "About the horse, Lord Templeton?"

Marcus sighed. "Oh, very well, take him round to the stables; I shall keep him for you as long as you like. You know, if this Banbury tale of yours gets about it will be the worse for you, my boy. Where are you going now?"

"Oh, to the devil, I suppose—I usually do," said the Marquess with a laugh. The laughter had a bitter note to it; Marcus looked after him, frowning thoughtfully, as Lord Barham turned on his heel and stalked out. After a moment, Marcus rang for the footman and demanded paper and pen; this being produced, he began to compose a long and comprehensive letter to Solange Devereaux.

The old and very well-established firm of Pendray, Monmouth, Gloucester, and Scire, Solicitors, was located just outside the Temple precincts in the City of London. It was late afternoon as the tall man on the energetic bay stallion rode up to their door.

Jack Barham had been several days on the road from Duckmanton to London, having neither the funds nor the inclination to travel faster. He had pawned the last of his remaining jewelry on the way into the city, and between that and what he had won gaming at Duckmanton, he had enough to keep himself and Vulcan in reasonable comfort for a few days.

That grace period would be long enough, Jack hoped, to arrange his fate. Doubtless his father was still enough out of charity with him to pay for his absence, but having no desire to be left standing at the gates of Owlsthorne Hall and denied admittance, he had come to the family lawyers. They would be more likely to be reasonable and turn loose of the monies in question in any case.

The most immediate question in Jack's mind as he pulled up before the door, however, was how to dispose of Vulcan during his visit. The stallion could hardly be left with any of the street urchins loitering about so hopefully—even as well-exercised as Vulcan now was, one toss of his massive head would send a child over the rooftops!

As Jack pondered the question, his eye lit upon a well-built man in a disreputable-looking but still recognizable uniform tunic; he swung down from Vulcan's back and beckoned. "You, there—soldier! If you can hold this horse for half-an-hour there's a shilling in it for you."

The man stopped lounging against the lamp post and hurried over, face brightening. "Yes, sir! There's not a horse living can get away from Ned Sykes, I promise you!"

"This one might," said Jack, handing over the reins. "If he gives you any trouble, Ned, just clout him a good one from me." Having done the best he could for the safety of the London streets, Jack swatted Vulcan's neck lightly before striding up the worn stone steps and thumping furiously with the large brass knocker.

The door was opened by an elderly law clerk who seemed unsurprised to see Jack and ushered him in without even inquiring as to his business. Another clerk standing at a high desk in the outer office looked up at the jingling of spurs.

"Ah, Your Grace—we've been expecting you. I'll inform Mr. Pendray of your arrival."

Jack's eyebrows rose. "I beg your pardon, but you've obviously mistaken me. I'm the Marquess of Barham."

The wizened party behind the desk adjusted his spectacles and peered at him intently. "Yes, yes," he agreed testily. "The son of the late Duke of Owlsthorne."

"The *late* Duke?"

Instantly the clerk's expression changed to one of deep concern. "But—but we wrote to you, Your

Grace—at your club—Did you not receive the letter? Your father died some ten days ago."

Within Mr. Pendray's inner sanctum it was very dark, and nearly as cold as the street outside. There was a strong odor of sealing wax and turpentine, and fainter scents of sawdust and old leather. Jack shifted uncomfortably on the hard chair and tried to give his attention to the solicitor's words. After the first flush of shameful relief at the news of his father's death had subsided, Jack felt a dawning optimism. Something might, after all, be saved out of the wreck of the Owlsthorne affairs.

"Of course, as your lordship—I beg your pardon, Your Grace—is well aware, the estate is in some disorder."

Snapping back to the here-and-now, Jack said dryly, "Mr. Pendray, you have a veritable genius for understatement. We both know damned well the old devil ran the place into the ground."

Mr. Pendray winced, and covered the action with discreet cough. "As Your Grace says, but the late Duke's affairs are in a state of—ahem!—some confusion, and it is as yet impossible to ascertain the true condition of the estate. Naturally Your Grace will wish to go and see for yourself.

"Now, as to the monies available—"

"Money?" Jack laughed outright. "Oh, come now, Mr. Pendray—my father swore he wouldn't leave me so much as a brass farthing. Are you going to tell me he miscalculated?"

The solicitor looked affronted. "No, Your Grace; as previously mentioned, that is unknown at this time. I was speaking primarily of the bequests made by the late Duchess to Your Grace."

Jack stiffened. "My mother? But—what the devil—?"

Mr. Pendray, apparently satisfied that he had his noble client's serious attention at last, sat back in his chair and commenced to polish his pince-nez with the tail of his coat. "Well, Your Grace, as you were not in the country upon the lamentable occasion of Her Grace's death, nor did you come for the proving of her Will, it was felt that all matters pertaining to you should be held in abeyance against your return.

"Naturally, this information was conveyed to you in a letter; when you did not respond to it, or indeed, to subsequent letters, we of course ceased to pursue the issue."

"Sent them care of my father, did you?" said Jack carelessly. "Damn it, man, did you think he'd forward them to me?"

"As your address at the time was unknown, Your Grace, there was no other course for us to follow." Mr. Pendray looked accusing.

Jack shrugged. "I suppose not. But you say Mama left something for me? I must confess, I can't imagine what. You know she sold her diamonds to buy my colors and outfit me as a proper little dragoon— what else can there be?"

Another little cough; Mr. Pendray placed his pince-nez just above the tip of his nose and looked down at the papers on his desk. "Now, let me see, Your Grace—ah, yes, here we are. Now, while the late Duke made a number of extreme demands on the estates, naturally his wife's marriage portion was not affected. As there were no daughters of the union, it was your mother's wish that her dower property and curtesy rights vest in you. In addition, there are some pieces of jewelry which were Her

Grace's personal property, as well as a few keepsakes." Mr. Pendray sat back and removed the pince-nez; he looked cautiously pleased with himself.

"How much?" said Jack sharply.

"I beg your pardon, Your Grace?"

"Come, man, how much is my mother's bequest worth?" Jack leaned forward, willing a favorable reply.

"Oh—ah—well, Your Grace, you understand that this can only be a rough estimate—" Mr. Pendray rustled some papers about, frowning. "But I should say—something in the neighborhood of between four and five thousand pounds. Properly invested—"

"Never mind about that—how soon can it be turned into cash?"

It took some time for Jack to convince the scandalized Mr. Pendray that he was in earnest, but at last the solicitor capitulated and promised His Grace the monies as soon as might be. Jack then took his leave and, lighthearted for the first time in days, went down the steps with considerably more enthusiasm than he'd gone up.

In the street, Vulcan and Ned Sykes awaited, regarding each other with wary respect. Both looked relieved to see Jack; Vulcan's ears pricked forward and he neighed softly.

"Well, Ned Sykes, I see you made good your promise to hold him," Jack said, his voice vibrant with cheerfulness. "By the way," he added as he took the reins back from the ex-soldier, "what's an able-bodied man like you—"

"Doing holding the Quality's horses for a living?" Sykes interrupted bitterly. "Aye, you could see it if I were a cripple, that's plain. But there's too many able-bodied men, sir, and not enough jobs to go round, and that's the round tale."

Jack swung himself into the saddle and then fumbled in his pocket. "Well, Sykes—what were you, a sergeant?—here's something for your trouble with this beast of mine, and my card. Look me up if you're ever in Kent—Owlsthorne Hall—I may be able to find something for you."

The ex-soldier goggled at the yellow boy Jack bestowed upon him; it was one of Jack's last guineas, but he didn't grudge it. "Yes, sir! Thank you, sir!" Drawing himself up to attention, he saluted.

Laughing, Jack returned the salute and set his heels to Vulcan's sides. Life seemed wonderful once more; a week or so in London while Pendray arranged matters, and all Jack's problems might be solved at last.

It took three days for the Devereaux party to travel from Duckmanton to Little Fakenham, the village from which Fakenham took its name. It was an article of faith in Little Fakenham that the tiny Stuart manor house possessed a priest's hole which had once hidden the future King Charles the Second's favorite spaniel, and had later been the headquarters of conspirators against good King George the First.

As the coach rattled up the drive to the manor, Althea almost wished Mama had forbidden her the pleasure of this visit. They had made a late start that morning, for Juliette had dawdled over every aspect of their preparations; both Juliette and Anthony were grimly silent. Althea correctly assigned the blame for this to a strong reluctance to face Madame Solange; she herself quailed at the prospect of facing a dragon formidable enough to cause the lion-hearted Lady Juliette such qualms.

A butler in powdered peruke and elaborately gold-laced scarlet jacket awaited at the door. He bowed stiffly to Anthony and informed him that Madame wished to see Lady Juliette and Mr. Devereaux.

"Now?" said Anthony.

"At once, sir," replied the butler.

Lady Juliette clutched at Althea's arm. The carriage ride had not agreed with Juliette and she looked quite exhausted. "At once?" said Althea. "Oh, but—"

"Tears, threats, pleas, and entreaties vain, all vain," said Anthony dolefully. "Fear not, my dear Miss Fonthill; it is generally better to get this over with so we can go back to quailing timorously in our bolt holes. Right, Julie?"

"I have known you all my life and you have *never* made any sense!" snapped Lady Juliette with a show of her old spirt.

"Well, then," said Anthony equably. "Miss Fonthill, I shall beg you to bear us up in our hour of trial—you may draw some of Madame's fire, and I'm sure she would never forgive us if we kept you from her."

Madame Solange's drawing-room was decorated in the strikingly modern *chinoiserie* mode; it would not have been out of place in the most up-to-date London townhouse. Its owner, a ghost of Georgian elegance, seemed oddly out-of-place amid its crisp geometric designs.

"Well, so you have arrived at last." Madame rose to her feet as they entered, and Althea saw with a shock that the much-feared dragon was less than five feet tall and of a delicacy of structure that made even Lady Juliette appear almost coarse beside her. Madame Solange's creamy skin had surely never known a moment's exposure to wind and weather, and her exquisite and delicately hued gown could be meant for no more serious exertion that choosing which invitation to accept. Her luxurious hair, a dramatic silver-white, was worn in a charming but slightly old-fashioned style, and her vivid eyes were the darkest shade of blue.

Though Devereaux family legend had it that Madame had been smuggled from Paris at the very height of the Terror, she carried no trace of France in her speech; it was only a hint of charming mystery that clung to her like exotic perfume. It was this indefinably regal air that had caused Anthony's father, the irreverent Armand Devereaux, to dub her "Madame," and the royal sobriquet had clung. There was a hint of the gracious elegance of the past about her; one looked involuntarily for hairpowder, or jeweled heels and bosom bows, not the modern dress of the nineteenth century.

"Well, child, have you seen what you wished to?" Madame said, and Althea flushed slightly. "No, Juliette, don't sit down—I'll not have your travel dirt all over my drawing-room. Anthony, perhaps you will be so kind as to make the proper introductions?"

"This is Lady Juliette Devereaux, Madame; she's a great-niece of yours—"

"Don't be impertinent, Anthony, you haven't the wit for it."

"—and perhaps you will allow me to present Miss Althea Fonthill. Miss Fonthill, our great-aunt, of whom we have told you so much. Miss Fonthill is a friend of Juliette's, Madame, and Juliette has invited her to be her guest."

"How very kind of Juliette," said Madame dryly. She seated herself in a rustle of silks and inspected the three young people before her. "Now, Juliette, you are to give me—briefly—your news since your departure from your cousin Markham's in Bath and then go and change for nuncheon." She fixed bright eyes on her great-niece. "I do not scruple to inform you that I have had letters from Helena Candlesby, Samantha Hawkchurch, and Marcus Templeton. They are unanimous in decrying your particularity towards the late Marquess of Barham, and I await with interest your version of events."

"The—the late Marquess—?" Juliette's ivory complexion had taken on a ghastly green undertone, and she swayed dizzily, putting a hand to her throat.

"For heaven's sake, sit down, child—I will not have you fainting on the floor. Anthony! Bring your cousin some brandy."

"Lord Barham is not dead—" Conventional modes of address somehow seemed to lack the proper respect; Althea, defeated, fell back as had so many others, on the family nickname as the most appropriate mode. "Surely Lord Barham is not dead, Madame? Why, he was in great good health not a week ago."

"No one said he was—but as his father died a fortnight since, there is no more Marquess of Barham until the new Duke of Owlsthorne gets him an heir." Madame's eyes were fixed intently upon the shaken Lady Juliette; to Althea's amazement there seemed to be a glint of approval in their lapis depths. "Now, Juliette, if you are over your fit of missishness, perhaps you will indulge me with your explanation."

Under the influence of a liberal draught of brandy, Juliette's color had markedly improved, but at this injunction she looked greatly alarmed. Anthony came to her rescue.

"It would save time, Madame, if Juliette knew what you had already heard. Then she need not defend herself from accusations that have not yet been made."

Madame did not deign to reply to this; she merely fixed an unwinking gaze upon the hapless Juliette.

Trapped, Juliette began haltingly, "I—you see—oh, Madame it is nothing—only that—"

Madame reached out to grasp a ribbon-bedecked carved ivory cane. Without speaking, she rapped its silver tip sharply on the floor.

"Lord Barham tried to elope with me from Duckmanton, and—and Papa is to marry Maria Alworthy," Juliette said in a rush.

There was the awful silence that obtains in the seconds before the most select sort of natural disasters.

"Undoubtedly you will explain these interesting confidences in your own good time, Juliette. And now Dimity will show you to your rooms. We dine at nine o'clock, Miss Fonthill; we do not keep country hours here at Fakenham however much it may please our neighbors to do so. You may ask Dimity for anything you require, of course."

"Thank you, Madame," said Althea, with an almost involuntary curtsy.

"Now you girls may go, for I know you are fatigued, and I wish a few words with Mr. Devereaux. I shall see you both at nuncheon, when I shall expect the news from Duckmanton."

The door had barely closed behind Juliette and Althea when Anthony turned accusing eyes on his great-aunt. "I say, Madame, that wasn't very subtle of you—"

"Juliette, my dear Anthony, is not a subtle young woman," said Madame. There was a self-satisfied smile curving her lips; it was the expression that always made her undutiful great-nephew think of china cats.

"It was a low trick to play on poor Julie, anyway. Is Owlsthorne really dead?" Mr. Devereaux was not perhaps quite so terrified of his great-aunt as popularly believed; but Solange Devereaux's nature, never outgoing, had been molded by the disappointment of all her hopes into a rather venomous fondness for the surviving members of the family, and she could not bear to be accused of kindness.

"He is, as you would know if you ever troubled yourself to read the *Gazette*, child. The notice appeared two days ago. Now, what is this about Maria Alworthy? Isn't she the local squire's girl, or some such thing?"

"I had hoped Uncle Sebastian had written to you—"

"If you did those books of yours have finally addled your brain—as if Sebastian would dare consult me after he bungled so badly with his first marriage! Are you quite sure there is to be a wedding and not some other arrangement?"

"You shock me, Madame. No, it is a wedding; I believe they will call the banns in a few weeks, though the date has not been determined as yet."

"I cannot say Sebastian's taste in women has improved with age. However, I shall write to the young person and say all that is amiable. Now, what about Barham? The truth, child, and not whatever outrageous lie Juliette will try to foist off on me at nuncheon."

Anthony ran his fingers through his hair as he thought, an action that caused no appreciable damage to a coiffure already far from elegant. "Though you will find it hard to credit, Madame, I don't know. Though I have had Miss Jerusha Gressingham's version of course, she has changed her tale three times in the telling, and insists she does not know what in the world the truth could be. Barham apparently said—so Lord Ralph says—that he was attempting to elope with Julie, and all Julie will say is that she invited him to come to her. Any time I dared raise the subject on our journey she either burst into tears or called me dreadful names. Having been ninnyhammered from Three Bridges to Richmond, and gudgeoned from there to Watford, I am no wiser than when I began. Barham behaved shockingly, from all accounts, and it is clear that he *was* in her bedroom. Ought I challenge him to a duel?"

"Must you try to be clever before noon?" Madame then regarded him with a narrow azure gaze that made Anthony feel a bit of a ringing welkin himself. "So Juliette is ruined and penniless. Well, sir, when do you call the banns for?"

"The banns, Madame?" said Anthony, quite as if he had not himself told both Althea Fonthill and Marcus Templeton that this was to be his fate.

"Yes, the banns—you may hardly marry Juliette without."

Anthony shifted uncomfortably beneath Madame's inspection. He did not know why he felt this sudden reluctance. It was, after all, his destiny to cloak his cousin's sins in the mantle of matronhood. Nevertheless, a resolve too new-born to subject to

Madame's reaction made him sit traitorously silent.

"Indeed?" Madame said at last. "Well, there will be time to speak of that tomorrow. Now go away and send Saunders to me; I need to think."

ELEVEN

Though Madame had extensively renovated Fakenham's main rooms when she had taken possession, she felt that the upper story, which was seen by no one but the Family, was very well as it was. Here there was no trace of either Georgian elegance or modern modes. The bedchamber into which Althea and Juliette were ushered contained massive furniture of time-blackened Tudor oak and was further enhanced by paneled walls, heavy velvet and brocade draperies in a deep and brooding crimson, and several large chests that should, by rights, have contained the bodies of trapped brides.

As it had been Juliette's room at Fakenham since she was a child, this air of ancient gloom bothered her not at all; Althea looked about her with bewildered curiosity.

"My!" she said after a few moments inspection of the bedchamber. Then she untied her bonnet and set it upon the nearest chest, remarking, "You did not tell me I was to be presented, or I should have brought hoops and ostrich feathers."

Juliette stared at her for a moment, then hugged her and laughed. "Yes! It would have been the very thing—but you should have brought one of the ridiculous wide gowns such as Mama wore when she was a girl! Mattie tells me that she would sometimes be called to help lace Mama into them. I do not know how they could move!—but I am persuaded Madame would think it ideal!" Then Juliette stepped back, looking anxiously at Althea. "Oh, but I was ready to sink! Do—do you suppose it is true?"

Althea did not pretend to misunderstand her. "I daresay it is quite true that Lord Barham is now the Duke, for I cannot think of any reason for your great-aunt to deceive you—although you know her better than I, of course."

"Well, Madame does a great many peculiar things, but she has never told a bouncer yet," said Juliette. "So Lord Barham is now the Duke— Althea! Douglas Candlesby will wish him to redeem the bonds now, and—"

"Oh, Juliette, haven't you had enough of Mr. Candlesby's affairs? We can only hope he will disclose the whole to Lord Ralph, as he should have done from the beginning. Perhaps, with Belle's help, he still may."

"But Thea—will Lady Ralph permit him to marry Isobel then? Surely she will want another heiress for him—"

"I *think* that Lady Ralph is 'off' heiresses now, and will be happy to see her son married to a biddable girl. Not that Belle is a biddable girl, but she can act the part."

This sally was greeted with giggles from Juliette, more from sheer relief at having survived her first interview with Madame than from any real appreciation of Miss Isobel's virtues. "Well, and I am sure she may," Juliette said at last, sobering. "But—oh, Thea, what *am* I to do?"

"Why, doubtless you will do just as Madame wishes." Having met Madame, Althea herself was sure of this. "I must say, Juliette, that your great-aunt is most—most singular!"

Juliette sighed and nodded. "Oh, yes, and I must confess that I have always wished *I* could be so—so elegant and poised! She makes me feel like the veriest gawky farm-girl whenever I am near her!"

Althea sympathized with this; Madame Solange had had that effect upon her as well. "Why is she called 'Madame'; do you know?"

"Oh, my Uncle Armand—Tony's father, you know—named her that. I am not quite sure why— it has something to do with France, I believe." Juliette, English to her marrow, had no interest whatsoever in the doings of those most incomprehensible people. "She raised both Papa and Uncle Armand when her brother Raoul died (he was the Comte de Devereaux then, before the title went to Papa), then raised Tony when Uncle Armand and his wife died, since Papa did not yet have an establishment. We Devereaux are a monstrously unlucky family." Juliette gave a shaky laugh. "I have been unlucky this year, have I not, Thea? There was my Season, and—and Lord Barham, and now Papa is to marry and—and—Maria is sure to give Papa a son—and I am sure I hope she may—and Chaceley will go to him."

Here Juliette assayed a smile; it looked very unconvincing to Althea's critical eyes. "It would have been a monstrous joke if I *had* eloped to Gretna with Lord Barham, would it not? Why, by the time we stood by the anvil I would have been penniless, and he a Duke!"

"Juliette!"

"No . . ." Juliette wiped her eyes, dampening her

gloves considerably. "I am done being a watering pot, I promise you! And it is not so bad as all that, for I shall still have Ashdene when I am of age—it was Mama's and it is mine outright. But I do not think I shall wish to live at Chaceley when Papa has married, and I cannot stay here!"

"Do take off your bonnet and pelisse, love, and let us ask Dimity for a nice *tisane* for you," Althea entreated. Juliette's other problems were beyond immediate solution; Althea perforce fell back on the old standbys. In Althea's experience any disaster was rendered more bearable were one only made comfortable.

"Nonsense!" Juliette said decidedly, with a flash of her old style. "I do not need a *tisane*, Thea, and I have only myself to blame for everything. Do not worry over me—I shall be content enough in the end." With that she took a deep breath and turned a determinedly cheerful face to Althea, who was saved from the need to reply by the arrival of their trunks, a darkly muttering Matilda, and a redoubtable individual known as Saunders.

Saunders, Madame's ferociously excellent dresser, promptly took command, ordering the trunks flung open and contents removed. She then swept the contents of Juliette's wardrobe with one sulphurous glance and announced that Lady Juliette would wish her to make a few alterations in her gowns.

Mattie bridled, Althea quailed, and Juliette, after drawing a fiery breath to defend her wardrobe, recollected herself and meekly agreed.

Saunders then examined Althea's more meager stock of gowns; she sniffed but said nothing. Althea felt ridiculously relieved to have passed muster.

Much to Mattie's dismay, Saunders then began

directing the process of divesting the two young ladies of their travelling clothes and preparing them to appear at nuncheon. By the time they were pronounced fit to be seen, both Juliette and Althea were in a fair way to regarding Madame as the lesser of two evils.

Nuncheon was a small exquisite meal served in a small exquisite room—yellow this time—by a forbidding butler and two footmen clad in the most elaborate livery Althea had ever seen. Madame, apparently, clung firmly to the royal style in more than her name. Amid all this Buhl and Sevres delicacy, Althea was almost afraid to move lest her large and lumping self destroy the air of exquisite fragility.

Her feelings were soothed in part by the appearance of Mr. Anthony Devereaux, resplendent in fawn-colored trousers and mustard-gold coat which gave the blond Mr. Devereaux a strong resemblance to a badly managed field of wheat. To cap his sartorial derelictions, he wore about his neck not yards and yards of snowy-white linen, but an oxblood Belcher neckcloth. Althea began to suspect it was as much an affectation as anything here, since Mr. Devereaux's dress had been perfectly unexceptionable, although far from dandified, at Duckmanton.

Catching her look, he gave her a knowing smile. "It's no good at all trying to compete with Madame, you know; I think of myself as a sort of counterpoint, perfect in my small way. Besides, think of all the time I save not requiring a valet and three strong footmen to assist me into my coats in the morning. Unless of course you are an admirer of the Dandy set, Miss Fonthill? If you are, I may be forced to reconsider my position."

"Why, Mr. Devereaux," said Althea, raising her eyebrows and glancing towards the head of the table where Madame sat in state, "how can I believe you would pay the least attention to female conversation?"

"Oh, Lord," said Anthony resignedly, "bested at last."

Madame affected not to notice this by-play and was dedicating her energies to her wayward greatniece. "Tell me, Juliette, did you enjoy your Season?"

"No, Madame." Juliette's eyes were downcast and she wore a penitent expression that would have suited a postulant nun.

"And why was that, miss? Since you did not consult me, I imagined you had everything arranged to your satisfaction and would by this time have done me the courtesy of informing me of your choice of husband. As it is. . . ." Madame let her voice trail off suggestively and Anthony looked up with a guilty expression.

"I have decided I do not wish for a husband." Juliette's voice was almost inaudible. "The suitable men are bores, and the interesting men are so monstrously unsuitable!" Juliette sighed deeply.

"If you persist in thinking of a suitable husband as one who can be yoked to a plow when the horse fails, I don't wonder you've found nothing to suit. Not that this paragon's views on land management matter now that Sebastian is to marry. How odd it is that in all the time since the matter was decided, no one thought to write and inform me," she said, with a darkly speaking glance at Anthony.

Anthony looked unconvincingly remorseful and

wisely said nothing. "Never mind," said Madame, imperturbably continuing her monologue. "Now you must tell me what you did at Duckmanton."

There was a long silence, which Juliette finally broke. "I bought a horse, Madame."

"A horse. Good heavens, child, how could I have expected that, with you staying next door to the Templetons and Marcus preparing for the autumn sales. I am astounded. Did anything else of note happen while you were there?"

"Sultan did not start in the St. Leger," supplied Anthony helpfully. All three ladies at table glared at him.

"I *think*—Lady Ralph may have had hopes that I would marry her son, but Mr. Candlesby had formed a *tendre* for someone else."

"And so you quite sapiently refrained from casting out lures to Mr. Candlesby. Do go on, Juliette."

But at that point Althea was unable to bear it any longer. "You—you must not allow your good nature to be trespassed upon, Madame. Our news is stale indeed, and I—I am persuaded that there are any number of things you wish to disclose that will be of far more interest."

"Oh, bravo, Miss Fonthill," said Anthony Devereaux in an undertone.

"Are there?" said Madame, with an eagle's brilliant gaze fixed on Althea. "Well, perhaps you are correct. In the first place, Miss Fonthill, I hope and trust you will be stopping with us for some while, as I will be giving a ball in a month's time— November first—at the Fakenham Assembly Rooms to commemorate Juliette's return. That will give you girls time to provide yourselves with what the modern generation considers suitable dress. It will be a small affair—no more than a hundred couples—

and though I am persuaded it will not be so grand as what you are used to, still, one likes to remain on terms with one's neighbors by giving them some small entertainment now and again.

"In the second place, Juliette, I further hope and trust that you will give some consideration to Miss Fonthill's good opinion when choosing your future course of action, and conduct yourself over the next month in a way to bring credit upon your family. We will have no repetition of the behavior that forced me to send Anthony to find you, shall we, Juliette?"

"No, Madame," Juliette mumbled.

"Very good. Now, if we have all completed nuncheon, I should like to see you, Juliette, and you, Miss Fonthill, in my parlor. Anthony may run along and make himself useful elsewhere."

"Now, Juliette," said Madame implacably, when she had both girls at her mercy in the *chinoiserie* parlor, "I will reserve your well-deserved scold on the infamy of your conduct, for I see that you will hold I have been proved right, but I must have accurate information about this Duckmanton scandal. Not that the truth will play any part in the scandal broth that is brewing, but I should like to know for my own peace of mind. You will tell me, without roundaboutation, how it came about that the Marquess of Barham was discovered in your room."

"I had invited him there, Madame." Juliette whispered to the floor.

Madame did not seem particularly surprised by this. "And was there a reason that you invited him?"

Tears had collected on Juliette's lashes and

spilled down her cheeks. "I wanted to make him sorry—" she began.

Half an hour's stringent questioning elicited little more, except Juliette's earnest hopes that the new Duke of Owlsthorne was suffering dreadfully wherever he was, that she was very sorry, and that she would hereafter devote to virtuous spinsterhood a life which was to be the very patterncard of propriety, abjuring hunting, horses, and every other pursuit inappropriate to a fallen woman such as Juliette knew herself to be.

"Well, then," said Madame. "You may begin this admirable program by occupying yourself with needlework. You never did a sampler, miss; I suggest that as a suitable project. You will oblige me by taking Proverbs 31:10 as its text. And now, Juliette, you may go. I shall send Miss Fonthill to you later." Dismissed, Juliette thankfully fled the room.

Although burning to know the text of the recommended verse, Althea did not quite dare ask. However, Madame, apparently very well pleased with herself, saved her both the pangs of curiosity and the trouble of enquiring.

" 'Who can find a virtuous woman? For her price is far above rubies.' That should put an end to Juliette's mopings once she reads it. Purity is not a becoming affectation, and she does not carry it off well.

"Now you may come and sit by me, Miss Fonthill. I would find it most useful if you could favor me with a candid recitation of Juliette's London Season. Oh, do stop gawking and come over here, child. Contrary to any fancies my grand-nephew may have instilled into you, my bite is hardly ever fatal."

Thus encouraged, Althea seated herself beside

226

Madame. "To begin with what you already know, Madame, Juliette made her debut under the sponsorship of Mrs. Hector Bastingstoke—"

Three-quarters of an hour later, Althea, wrung dry, was allowed to make her escape. She felt, oddly, more heartened than otherwise by her exhausting interview; it was plain that Madame would fight with the fury of ten tigers for her greatniece's reputation. This task would be made easier by the fact that Madame, absent from the haunts of the *ton* these fifteen years at least, was nonetheless still a powerful figure within its confines. Tongues would wag, but with Madame Solange's version of the scandal, and with Juliette safely wed and reformed in character, this too would pass.

The only remaining puzzle was the identity of Juliette's prospective and vitally necessary husband. Althea turned the matter over in her mind as she ascended the stairs. Madame had not mentioned Mr. Devereaux, which was odd as Althea understood the matter to have been all but decided, contingent upon Juliette finding someone she preferred during her Season. Since Juliette had not, and since she must now marry at once—preferably before Maria Alworthy did, in fact—it must be Mr. Devereaux. Althea felt a pang of denial, and roundly scolded herself for air dreaming. What would Mama think to find her practical daughter entertaining the most unsuitable notions of a man who had treated her with the greatest of kindness—and no more? Or if there had been more . . . surely it was very too bad of Anthony Devereaux to pay particular attentions to any other damsel when he was nearly betrothed to his cousin. And her concern over the match was only for Juliette's happiness. Juliette could never be happy with her cousin, whose every remark she took as utter nonsense—and poor Anthony, with no one to appreciate his jests.

Unfortunately for Althea's peace, Anthony Devereaux was coming down as she was going up, and her lips curved in an unintended smile at his questioning look. "I have just come from Madame," she said in answer to the unspoken query, "and she assures me that matters can be brought about."

"If Madame says it, it is as good as done, and so we may cease troubling our puny intellects about the matter. Now that Juliette's reputation has been saved and her future assured, let me offer my humble, if insincere, apologies for bringing you to this house of woe. If I had known you were to be embroiled in one of Madame's grand strategies, I would have discouraged your company. On the other hand, if I had known anything of the situation when I arrived at Duckmanton, I would probably simply have gone on riding until I got to Land's End, and never stopped at Duckmanton at all."

He made as if to take her arm, and Althea, in confusion, shrank back. "Where is Juliette?" she asked, to cover her blunder. She could feel her cheeks burning and prayed that Mr. Devereaux would think it only agitation over her interview with Madame. It was so very nearly the case, after all.

"Juliette is writing a letter to Maria to welcome her into the collective Devereaux bosom. You need not worry about the contents," Anthony prattled on imperturbably, "as it is entirely unlikely that either Uncle Sebastian or Maria Alworthy will pay the least attention to the post while preparing for the first meet of the season; when we go for the wedding, I can retrieve the unopened missive and burn it. And now, Miss Fonthill, what have I done that you should regard me as if I were an avatar of one of the less reputable demigods?"

The ruthless change of subject caught Althea entirely by surprise. "D-done?" she stammered, her cheeks flaming a deeper scarlet. Anthony took her firmly by the arm and led her to the seat on the landing.

"It cannot have escaped the meanest intelligence, Miss Fonthill—or even mine—that something must have happened to cause you to give me such a *very* conscious look. As I do not believe I have done anything to disgust you during nuncheon, it must be the result of your interview with Madame. Whatever the cause, I deny it categorically, but I would appreciate the opportunity to frame a refutation." Anthony regarded her encouragingly.

Althea took a deep breath and a firm hold on her feelings. "I am sure you have done nothing to give anyone a disgust of you, Mr. Devereaux, and have quite mistaken the matter. What I mean to say is— have you not yet spoken to Juliette about your wedding? You must, you know, before she is too set upon another course."

Mr. Devereaux regarded his nails. "Did Madame tell you that we were to marry?"

"No, of course not; how infamous that would be in her. But she did discuss the wedding, and—" At that moment the door across the landing from the seat Althea and Anthony occupied slammed open and Juliette was among them, a high color in her cheeks and a fire in her eyes that improved her looks immensely.

"Above rubies!" she said wrathfully. "Mattie! *Mattie*! I want my green habit—at once!"

She swept past them. Anthony regarded her retreating form and shrugged. "Perhaps, Miss Fonthill, you would care to choose a book from the library to occupy you? It is right through that door, you know."

The longer Jack had stayed in London, attempting to unravel the tangle of his father's affairs, the more pressing it began to seem to go home at last. He must look at the books, see the tenants, think what could possibly be done with the estate to rectify a decade's ill-use. At last he gave in, telling himself that it was the only sensible way to evade his creditors, and set out for Owlsthorne Hall.

The ancestral home of the Dukes of Owlsthorne was located in the fertile sheep country of the Kentish downs. Until recently, Jack's mode of life had discouraged nostalgia; he only realized how much he had missed his home country when he crested the last low rise and saw the Downs spread before him. Mile after mile of verdant green just beginning to take on the silver-dun hues of winter, like a sea of earth—scant of trees but thickly dotted with the weirs, hedges, and stiles that were the mark of rich agricultural lands. . . . Jack sat and looked silently for a few moments, then, picking up the reins, he sent Vulcan forward at a brisk trot.

As he drew near to the Hall, the countryside looked very much as he remembered it, and he was able to persuade himself that whatever depredations his father had made, they had not touched the land itself.

This fantasy lasted until he arrived at the lodge gates.

He shouted for the porter, but no one answered. A moment's inspection showed him the lodge had not been occupied in some time. The gates were rusted shut, but it was a simple matter to put the vastly interested Vulcan at the low wall, and soon he was trotting up the drive through the park.

The drive was weed-grown and rutted; obviously the damage of many spring rains had been allowed to go unrepaired. On either side the high uncut grass lay in mare's-nest drifts. But it was the sight of the Hall itself that made Jack's heart sink.

The house had been beautiful once. Built in the symmetrical four-square style of an earlier day and faced with the local gray stone, Owlsthorne Hall had stood, austere and gracious, as a symbol of home and respectability in Jack's memory.

Now the fountain at the end of the drive was choked with leaves and weeds, and cracked by winter's ice. The bluestone drive had been washed away by storms, or carried off by vandals and gipsies. Riding closer, Jack could see broken windows where the shutters had fallen or been torn away. The brass fittings of the regal entry doors were green with verdigris and neglect.

"Dear God in Heaven," said Jack in a husky voice. He spurred Vulcan around to the back of the house, where the peacock-inhabited terraces of his childhood led down to the formal gardens that had been planted by his great-grandfather.

All was an impenetrable welter of thorns. Even his mother's rose garden had vanished.

Turning Vulcan abruptly and with little regard for his mount's temper, Jack cantered back to the front of the house. Pendray had said there was a caretaker at the Hall—and the late Duke had been living here. Surely there was someone about the place?

After tying the aggrieved Vulcan as securely as possible, Jack took a deep breath and strode up the steps. Disdaining the corroded knocker, he pushed open the door.

The entry hall was barren and musty, lit only by the wan light filtering in through the filthy and broken windows that ringed the gallery above. Unheated damp had brought the hand-painted Chinese paper from the walls in bulging, mildewed strips. Jack put his gloved fingers to wainscoting milky with damp-rotted varnish, then, mouth set, strode into the Great Hall through the dirt and leaves that littered the black-and-white marble floor.

The Great Hall was stripped almost bare; only a few random pieces of furniture remained, dusty and draggled. Jack swore silently; he had seen ruined cities and sacked towns in Spain, but Owlsthorne was his, and this was England, and he should not be standing in the cold and silent shell of a proud manor *here*.

Unable to bear the silence any longer, he thew back his head and shouted. "Ho! Ho, the house! Ho!"

The echoes had not died away when there was a scuffling, as if the mice in the walls had been joined by larger brethren. Jack turned toward the sound, to surprise a thin, stooped figure of a man shuffling toward him in carpet slippers, with a dim lantern held high in one hand.

"My lord?" quavered the relict, gazing upon Jack. "Oh, praise be, you do be my lord—it's the young master come home again!"

* * *

232

"But where is the caretaker? Pendray said there would be a caretaker here."

The servants rustica was at least warm and dry; it was here Baldrick had conducted Jack. He had been a stablehand at Owlsthorne Hall when Jack had been in residence, and on the verge of being pensioned off then; what he was doing wandering about the house *en deshabille* was a mystery to Jack.

"As to that, sir, I dessay he meant me—we've done for His Grace, the missus and me, since our Mr. Knowton were carried off nigh two years back."

"But the other servants. . . ?" In the normal course of things Baldrick and his missus would have been pensioned off to a small cottage on the estate years ago—he would certainly never have been body-servant to Jack's father.

"Oh, Your Grace, t'weren't no other servants after Her Grace died! Pensioned 'em off 'e did, and right 'andsome, too, though it would fair 'ave broke your heart to see them go—some of them at least."

Jack, unravelling this, took it to mean that the traditional enmity between the servants brought from London and the ones whose families lived in the village had not been one whit abated by misfortune.

"And then were all sort of people about the place—'e sold off the stables, sir, every horse, and the furniture from the 'ouse. Were mad for money, 'ee; savin' your present Grace's pardon."

"But—" Jack threw up his hands in despair, a gesture he'd read about but never thought to perform. Plainly his father had converted everything he could to hard cash, and then wasted that.

"—and I come to him, I did, I said, 'sir, what's to become of me and the missus?' and 'ee said—that's

His Grace as was, sir—and 'ee said I might go to the devil and please myself, but then 'ee said I might bide 'ere as long as may be, and then when our Mr. Knowton sickened for the influenza—"

"Never mind that. Come along and show me the stables, then see if your missus can find me something to eat and a place to sleep."

"But—You'll not be wishful to stay, surely, Your Grace?"

"Why not? It's my Hall now."

"Then you'll be wishful to have your father's rooms," said Baldrick, serene in the knowledge of what was due the Quality. "I'll just go and find the missus, and we'll have sheets aired and everything fine as may be quick as cat can lick her ear."

"There are sheets? You astound me, Baldrick."

"Oh, aye, o'course there be sheets, Your Grace— although the best pair, mind, they went into the ground w' His Grace as was."

"Damn," said Jack regretfully. "They were probably the only undarned ones in the place."

Baldrick looked scandalized. "Well, o' course they were, Your Grace, as was only right and fitting, and missus and me knows what's due—"

"Yes, yes—but now, about the stables? My horse," Jack added with a wry grin, "won't want to wait all day, you know."

Tugging his forelock in the approved style, Baldrick ventured it as his opinion that if it were that there big bay 'orse as was His Grace's, he were a right mettlesome one at that. He then shuffled out. Jack, torn between grief and laughter, went to see to Vulcan before the ancient Baldrick tried to attend to the matter and cut a life of loyal service untimely short.

The situation seemed to be about as bad as it

could be—there was no way yet to tell whether it was past remedy. But he'd made his bed—someone had, at any rate. And now he would have to lie in it.

Life at Fakenham—which had long since been dubbed "the Jewel Box" by Anthony, who was no more reverent than his father Armand had been—was far more agreeable than Althea had been led to expect. There were shopping expeditions to the town of Little Fakenham for trims and furbelows to furnish their ballgowns, walks and drives and rides upon the very quiet horses the stables were able to furnish, the pleasant toil of inscribing and directing all the invitations for Madame's ball, and the occasional highly amusing social call. All in all, the round of pleasure at the Jewel Box was the perfected exemplar of that exquisitely leisurely life Althea thought she could easily come to adore. It was therefore quite one week later that Althea came to her senses and realized she had not heard one word of betrothal—from Anthony, Juliette, or Madame.

She knew it was wretched vulgar curiosity that made her so concerned, but she was also conscious of time slipping away, and with no banns called in the church in Little Fakenham that Sunday, Althea wondered if Madame were actually waiting for Anthony to declare himself.

Her suspicions were confirmed when, upon returning to the house, Juliette announced it as her intention to ride. So far from attempting to discourage her from this inappropriate Sabbath pursuit, Mr. Devereaux announced himself intent on accompanying her. Althea watched them ride off, and was sure that Mr. Devereaux must be choosing this agreeable venue for his proposal. The knowledge made her feel ready to sink through the floor, or fling herself on her bed and weep.

It had been borne in upon her, as Miss Fonthill was an honest soul, that Mr. Anthony Percival St. Devereaux Devereaux, so far from being the incomprehensible idiot of Juliette's retailing, was a man to whom Miss Fonthill could not remain indifferent. It was the worst sort of luck for her to meet him only as her best friend's fiancé, but what was the steel corseting of Society for, save to allow one to surmount these Golgothas with serenity?

She had said nothing for which she must blush; Mr. Devereaux's attentions to her had been nothing improper. Though she knew him to have reservations about his match with his cousin, she was not so vain as to fancy herself the cause. He might look—if not as high as he pleased, then certainly round about—for a bride; whether he and Juliette thought to suit or not, there was nothing in it to concern her.

Only he will be so unhappy if he is married to Juliette—and so will she! Striving to ignore this warning voice, Althea turned from the window and went to read improving texts.

Both Oriflamme and Traveller were fresh; Juliette and Anthony indulged their mounts with a good gallop down the ride before drawing the horses back to a walk.

Anthony had spent the week in what Madame would surely have called "an expense of spirit in a waste of shame"—and the fact that he was well aware of it did nothing to make his temper the sweeter. He knew very well that the next act of the farce was his proposal of marriage to his cousin Juliette, and the fact that Madame had not pressed him further on that subject since his return made it, he knew, no less imperative.

He had come up with any number of logical, sensible reasons to marry Juliette, including the fond theory that she was a reformed character, since her behavior following the mock-abduction from Duckmanton was rife with such signals to the hopeful eye. However, even a reformed Juliette Devereaux was not a Juliette he could bear to marry.

So the Devereaux should marry for love, he thought wrathfully in Marcus Templeton's direction. Very well, he would be delighted—only show him the way to accomplish this amiable aim while not flinging Juliette to the wolves. Marriage would at least provide her with a respectable roof over her head when Maria was queening it at Chaceley. If only Miss Fonthill had not accompanied Juliette to Little Fakenham—or, better yet, never come to Duckmanton at all. As for that unconscionable cad Barham—

I only wish the black-hearted devil HAD run off with Julie, thought Anthony with uncharacteristic passion. Unfortunately, the same scruples that had him out here now trying to think how best to propose to Juliette would not have allowed him to leave her to Bad Barham's mercies.

Juliette seemed blissfully ignorant of anything other than the delightful weather, and was chattering away almost as naturally as if her future did not stand in such a perilous balance. "Do you ride with the Alworthy Hunt this season, Tony?"

"Oh, *damn* the Alworthy hunt! Name the day you will marry me, Julie, and let's put an end to this!" said Anthony savagely.

Juliette goggled at him. "Marry *you*, Tony?" she said in patent disbelief.

Anthony pulled Traveller to a stop. The brown gelding tossed his head violently, catching his rider's mood. "Yes. Marry me—or live at Chaceley under Maria's roof. It is all Madame's idea, cousin—so you see it must answer!"

"I own I see nothing of the sort—and I see no reason to keep the horses standing while you explain it to me," Juliette responded, touching Oriflamme to a walk. "It is quite easy to see when you are cross, Tony—because you do not go on and on—and one can easily understand what you are saying. You do not think Madame's plan will suit."

Anthony continued to gaze at her. "My . . . my sincere and quite simply expressed apologies," he said at length. "Must I take it then, that you are to dash my nascent hopes—confound it, Julie—you can't *do* that—"

"Oh, Tony, you don't want to marry me!"

"Well of course not, but lord, Julie—"

Mr. Devereaux was unable to get any further, as his unregenerate cousin was laughing so hard she had to clutch at the saddle for support.

"Oh, I knew I should get you to talk sense sooner or later, Tony—you should see your face! But for heaven's sake—if I had the least intention of marrying you, do you not think I should have done it from Chaceley and saved myself the expense of the Season? Come now! Madame has had that maggot in her head for ever so—and though I never dared tell her, it will not suit. You shall tell her, Tony."

"Oh, lord, won't I just?" Anthony said in wonder. "And choirs of angels shall be nothing in it, for her reply. But we both know that you'll have to marry, after—you'll have to marry now. What you wanted before two weeks ago was someone to help you run

Chaceley—and you haven't got Chaceley anymore, so—"

"But I have Ashdene—I shall take Mattie and go there—and surely among all the Halfords and Markhams there must be some distant female connection who will come live with me! For I tell you plainly, Tony, I would not marry you if you were the last man in England—I had rather go live in the—the Black Hole of Calcutta than that!"

"Where did you ever hear of the Black Hole of Calcutta, Julie?" said Anthony curiously.

"Oh, Barham said he wished my emeralds at the bottom of it, so I suppose it is someplace in France. Oh, how I *despise* him!" cried Juliette, but the words had a forlorn ring.

"We shall contrive somehow, Julie. And if I ever see him—I shall shoot him for you, if you like."

Juliette reached across and patted him reassuringly. "I should not ask you to do that—for you wouldn't be any good at it, you know—and he was right. About everything." Juliette hung her head slightly as the color ebbed and flamed in her cheeks, then collected herself. "I only think, Tony, that it would have been a very good thing if I had been penniless sooner; since I am sure we would all have behaved more sensibly." With that remark, she touched Oriflamme up into a trot, leaving Anthony to stare after her, for once completely at a loss for words.

It is not a quick and simple process to impoverish a great estate. The old Duke's bailiff still lived nearby and proved cautiously happy to see Jack. It did not take long for him to impart to Jack precisely how matters stood: very badly indeed, but not hopeless.

The Hall itself was quite empty of anything save bats and fieldmice—anything Jack might possibly sell to raise income had been sold already, and as no one had yet conceived the notion of entailing furniture, the house, from loggia to lumber-room, was stripped bare. The sole exception was the late Duke's bedroom, an island of ramshackle comfort in a stark and rather Gothic house.

The unentailed property had been sold, as he had expected, and the tenants driven from the Home Farm. Leases, as they expired, were not renewed, and without gardeners or gamekeepers the estate that remained soon took on the aspect of a wilderness. In addition, it was mortgaged well past the hilt.

The only bright spot in all of this was that, strangely enough, Jack's own credit in the village couldn't be better. The Old Duke, as he was already being called, had been intent upon ruining his estate; in aid of this amiable ambition he had even resorted to the unheard-of device of paying tradesmen in cash and on time. Thus Jack was able to eat upon tick; with the state of the lawns there was no lack of fodder for Vulcan. He awaited only the advice of his lawyers as to the final disposition of matters. The entail would have to be broken so the property could be sold.

It was the only sensible course. And, as Jack himself had played a great part in bringing Owlsthorne to this pass, he had no right to indulge in pangs and heart-burnings—neither about the loss of the Hall nor that other loss that seemed more acute as time passed.

Jack knew he spent far too much time brooding over the affair of Lady Juliette, but he had little else to do for the time being but sit and wait—and wonder.

Poor little wood-nymph! Perhaps there was some way to find out whether she had survived that disastrous discovery or whether Society had decided to cut her dead. He had done what he could, but he knew it was far from enough. If she had any sense, she was by now safely restored to the bosom of her family—

But Juliette *had* no sense. He, of all people, should know that. And she certainly had no idea of how to go on at a daggers-drawn house party of that sort. Cold with sudden apprehension, he damned himself for a thousand kinds of fool. Despite the conventions he should have written to Solange Devereaux himself and told her—well, *his* version of the truth. He knew Juliette's stiff-necked pride; she'd probably told them all to do their worst, been turned out of Duckmanton the very next day, and gone home to her precious Chaceley to hide from the only person in England who had a ghost of a chance of helping her.

He found the thought of his sweet centauress condemned to a life of joyless penance the final, unforgivable straw. He would go to Solange Devereaux, by heaven, and force her to see reason and save Lady Juliette if it was the last thing he did.

Chapter
TWELVE

The news from Duckmanton was frequent and favorable—the house party had broken up but the Fonthills had been asked to remain indefinitely, and Mama was in hourly expectation of a proposal from Douglas Candlesby.

Althea had long since resigned herself to her sister's impoverished future, since somehow, during her stay at Fakenham, the thought of wresting a lover from his beloved had become an action too heinous to be considered. She had been quite puzzled when Anthony and Juliette's Sunday ride produced no disclosure—then appalled as Juliette made the entire dinner-table free of the hilarious joke that Anthony had offered her his hand in marriage when as all the world knew, he had no idea whether corn or barley did better in marginal land. Fortunately they were dining strictly *en famille*, and Althea had been surprised by the look of warm approval Anthony bestowed on his cousin until she realized that Mr. Devereaux must have been dreading making the same disclosure. Oddly, Madame did not hurl the lightnings, merely remarking in arid tones that it was fortunate indeed that banns had not been called, and announcing it as too much to hope for that Anthony would contrive to announce his engagement at her Winter Ball.

Any persuasion Mr. Devereaux employed upon his cousin to that end was invisible to the enquiring mind in the days that followed; Juliette spoke only of her plans to remove *en chaperone* to Ashdene following Maria's wedding—to which Madame said that obviously Juliette would continue to please herself in this as in all things—and continued to treat Mr. Devereaux with a familiarity bordering on rudeness. As he responded in kind without the least trace of resentment, Althea could find nothing to resent herself, although she did think it odd.

There was nothing odd in Mr. Devereaux's treatment of herself, either, except that Althea, having helplessly lost her heart to the polysyllabic moonraker, could not fathom the intent behind it. Mr. Devereaux treated her with such fond particularity that it was with difficulty that Althea forced herself to treat him with no more than ordinary civility. He had not declared himself. She might be mistaking the matter. How could he even consider marrying anyone else while Juliette espoused this ridiculous scheme to go and live on her mother's dower property? No, Althea believed in an ordered world, and someone so kind, so conscientious, so amiable as Anthony Devereaux could not leave his cousin to be a despised recluse.

Anthony had offered much the same opinion to Madame on that Monday morning. Juliette's declaration at the dinner-table had dumbfounded him—though he had come as close to loving her in that moment as he ever could, knowing the gallant bravery it had taken—as he had hoped for more time to prepare his arguments. The feline being well and truly out of the haversack, however, he went the next day to confront Madame.

"Julie won't have me," he said without preamble. He sat down and disheveled an already tousled head. He spread out his hands. "She says she won't have me if I were the last man in all England."

"I must say, you are bearing up beneath the crushing weight of your sorrow rather well," Madame commented. "How distressed you must be, after prosecuting your suit so assidiously."

"I didn't," Anthony said flatly. "She said we wouldn't suit. She was right."

The expression on Madame's face obviously presaged a crushing remark about the unreliability of youth in the modern age, but instead she smiled. "So you 'will not suit.' I suppose you are now hoping that I will do some piece of sorcery to rescue the pair of you from your squeamishness and folly? It is most peculiar, but I do not see your Miss Fonthill shrinking from the difficult decisions *she* is forced to make—and with her sister marrying the worst sort of wastrel as well: an amiable one."

"Has Douglas offered for Miss Isobel, Madame?" Anthony asked, hoping to divert the conversation from a discussion of Althea.

"I had it from his doting mother by this morning's post—and now you may stop lowering at me, sir—as if it were my fault that you had ever offered for Juliette, and been turned down into the bargain."

Anthony took a few moments to mull this over. "While one always hopes to be of some little use in the world, one had best get all the facts before meddling. Now I myself would have been ready to swear, Madame, that you had intended a match between Julie and me last March."

"And where are the snows of yesteryear? Acquit me of serving mutton as lamb, teaching an old dog new tricks, and locking the barn after the horse has been stolen. March has nothing to say to October. Now, if we have been sufficiently literary, great-nephew, oblige me by being useful to the extent of taking this note to Lady Thunderfields, and leaving me to do for Juliette what you will not."

So matters had stood through October, as the leaves turned and fell, and morning frost became more frequent and longer lingering. Mr. Devereaux was amiable but not forthcoming; Juliette was forthcoming but not truthful; and Althea dissembled. It hurt to lose your heart, when you had nothing to offer but that. On this particular morning, with a ball and dinner party to occupy the afternoon and evening, Althea was afflicted with idleness, a state deadly to those suffering from agitation of the spirit or the heart.

She wondered again, as she had so often, what motive had really been behind Barham's visit to Juliette on that fatal night. If Juliette had invited him, he must have known it was a trick—only a soul deaf, dumb, blind, halt, and imbecile could have thought otherwise, and Barham was not that. No, he was clever, and at this healing distance, Althea thought his heart must be good as well. He had said, after all, that he meant to do something about the bonds (as well as wring Juliette's neck). Had he but stood his ground and revealed that Juliette had sent for him, she would have had to marry him, practically upon the spot, for no one could live down such a scandal otherwise. Juliette's fortune would have been his. And a Duke's coronet covered a multitude of sins.

Only they hadn't known that he was a Duke and she no heiress. And if they had, it would have kept them just as far apart—despite what Althea had come to suspect as the true reason for Juliette's mad scheme.

But talking, as Althea had said many times, paid no toll. A far better occupation of her idleness would be in thinking of tonight's entertainment. The ball itself was to be held at the Assembly Rooms in Little Fakenham, but the dinner that was to open the evening of Madame's triumph—which Anthony Devereaux persisted in referring to as a Restoration Comedy, a witticism lost on everyone save Althea—would be held at Fakenham. Fortunately Saunders had taken all in hand, and in addition to cowing Mattie into some sense of the current mode and salvaging the best part of Juliette's wardrobe, she had contrived to provide for both Althea and Juliette quite the most maidenly and becoming ball dresses that any young lady could unreasonably wish for.

At three of the clock in the afternoon of November first, 1819—a mere six hours before dinner, since Madame, as she never tired of informing the world, did not keep country hours at the Jewel Box—Juliette and Althea were attempting to occupy themselves until it should be time to dress. Althea was stitching vigorously away at a piece she hoped to include in Isobel's *trousseau*, and Juliette was dutifully reading aloud from *Persuasion*.

Lady Juliette was no advocate of novels, holding them to be nonsensical time wasters. However, rather than attempt embroidery, she had yielded to Althea's urgings that she would find Miss Austen's books as commonsensical as even Juliette could wish. Juliette had been doubtful at first, but had at least been brought to agree that, if one must read novels, Miss Austen's were not nearly as silly as most, containing not one Wicked Duke, Lost Heir, Haunted Castle, or, indeed, any of the other ingredients that rendered modern literature ridiculous.

Still, even the well-measured words of *Persuasion* could not hold Juliette when the sound of carriage wheels on gravel arrested her attention.

"Oh, Thea—who can that be? It is far too early for guests!" Abandoning the volume without a second's hesitation, Juliette bounced to her feet and over to the window. She pulled back the curtain and uttered a strangled squeak. "Oh, it cannot be!"

Althea hurriedly put down her sewing and joined her, but all she saw was an undistinguished four-horse equipage.

"Oh, look, Thea, there is Brownie, and Topper, and Slowcoach—it is *Papa*!" And in a swirl of skirts Juliette was bound for the front door.

Althea, following more sedately, met Mr. Devereaux coming out of his study. "I hear the sound of Julie in full cry, Miss Fonthill—dare I ask the reason?"

"Papa!" Juliette cried, even as Althea began to speak.

"Never mind," said Mr. Devereaux, taking Althea's arm. "Forward; I believe that familial duty calls once more."

They reached the front hall just in time to witness Juliette's enthusiastic embrace of a short stocky man with broad English features, who was nonetheless the Comte de Devereaux. Despite all she had suffered from his sins of omission, Juliette seemed very fond of her father. He patted her shoulder, and seemed not so much disinclined to suffer her greeting as baffled at the reason for it.

"Here, girl. Here, now. Let me get a look at you, Juliette," he said.

Juliette stepped back and glanced around, meeting Anthony's pellucid azure gaze. She turned pink and bobbed a hasty curtsey. "Papa, I am so glad to see you—and may I present Miss Althea Fonthill? She is my dearest friend."

"Delighted," said her father, taking Althea's hand and giving it something between a salute and a shake. Now that Juliette had stepped back, Althea could see that he was dressed as plainly and as quaintly as any country squire, and if he did not wear the hair-powder and rouge of an earlier generation, well, it was a very near thing. "Delighted," he repeated. "And here is our Maria—Juliette, say hello to your mama-to-be."

Maria Alworthy was a strapping young lady, with a high color and bouncing chestnut curls, for whom the adjective "healthy" might have been coined. She had already handed her pelisse over to the nearest footman, and she looked so out-of-place in a girlish and slightly outmoded pink muslin frock that for an automatic moment Althea thought of mutton dressed as lamb, until she realized that a plow horse in racing harness would be more accurate.

"Oh, pshaw, Sebastian—how you do go on!" Maria said, giving the object of her affections a playful shove. "As if me and Miss Julie haven't been as close as two peas in the same shell ever since she could first sit on a horse!"

"But, Papa," Juliette went on, dismissing Maria as thoroughly as that young lady did her, "what are you doing here?"

"Why, we've come to your ball, of course. When Madame wrote and said the evening would not be complete if I did not come to dine and dance and bring Maria as well, well, what could a father do, eh?" He pinched Juliette's cheek affectionately.

Juliette's face was what is properly termed a study; Maria Alworthy merely looked smug, as well she might. Anthony Devereaux set Althea firmly aside and, athletic as a salmon, made his way to Sebastian Devereaux's side and shook his uncle's hand. "We're so glad you're here, Uncle—you can hardly imagine! And you too, Maria, of course—how Madame has been longing to welcome you personally into the jolly old collective bosom since she heard. And have you met Juliette's dear friend Miss Fonthill? She has been a tower of strength to us these past weeks."

"How he do go on! It's as good as a play, it is," said Maria enthusiastically, looking to Althea for support in this conviction. Althea flicked a glance at Juliette, and saw her friend's color had deepened alarmingly.

"Oh, yes," said Anthony encouragingly. "Quite as good as a play. Now, it desolates me to withhold from you Madame's society for any length of time whatsoever, but allow me to bestow you, Miss Alworthy, and your admirable abigail, upon our Mrs. Dimity, who will take you off so you can refresh yourself after your exhausting ordeal."

In all probability Maria had not understood a word he'd said, but she did understand the presence of the housekeeper. With a final burst of affability all round, Maria allowed herself to be conducted off into the upper reaches of the Jewel Box.

"And you, Uncle," said Anthony without an appreciable pause for breath, "If you'll just take your-

249

self off to my study, I can offer you an excellent brandy and a rather fine Horace; I'll be along in just a tick."

Sebastian Devereaux, nothing discomfited by this cavalier attitude on the part of his nephew, took himself off as requested.

"I swear, Julie, Madame didn't tell me they were coming," Anthony said quickly as soon as his uncle was out of earshot.

Juliette emitted a strangled wail. "Oh!" she gasped. "Oh! Oh! Never mind, Tony, it was as good as a play!" She clung to Althea, shaking with a strong emotion Althea, after a moment's alarm, identified as hilarity.

"Don't," Anthony begged in stricken accents, "If you send me off, I shall never be able to face Uncle."

"Oh, I shall die," moaned Juliette, sinking to the stairs, "or say rather, I will bid fair to bust a gusset."

"Poor Mr. Devereaux," said Althea, in a voice that shook only slightly.

"Too kind, dear Miss Fonthill," said Anthony manfully, "But it is quite all right. I have known Maria forever, and she is a good soul. Only Squire did not want any of his daughters to become what he considered missish and over-gentle."

"I would say he had succeeded admirably," said Althea after a moment.

By now Juliette had her feelings under control and was able to rise. "Oh, but she will suit Papa down to the ground, you know—he never pays the least attention to what anyone says, so he will not notice that Maria is not missish nor over-gentle. I am reconciled to his marriage, Thea, truly I am— oh, my poor ribs!—just think of Madame!" Juliette hugged herself, giddy with the release of tension. "Do come along, Thea, Tony must go to Papa and we must go to Madame, so she does not think we are hiding. Only think, Thea—Madame has never met Maria!"

"Oh, dear," said Althea weakly.

"Yes, indeed," said Anthony with fervor. "Do not, I beg of you, desert us in this our hour of trial, my dear Miss Fonthill!"

"Of course I shan't," Althea replied calmly, digging into her reticule and handing Juliette a handkerchief with instructions to wipe her streaming eyes. "And now I think we had best go and—and tell Madame that her first guests have arrived."

Madame had been reticent in the extreme regarding the guest list for dinner—a circumstance that had aroused all of Althea's newly sharpened suspicions. However, as she had no control over the matter, and Madame was easily capable of getting the best of her in any encounter, she did not confide her fears to either Anthony or Juliette. It was not, after all, as if they would be seeing the new Duke of Owlsthorne at table that evening, and no one else could possibly be as bad.

It was to be admitted that Althea's thoughts were very much with her new gown, and all other matters received but perfunctory attention in any case. The underdress was a pale coral satin, rescued from a gown that had made Juliette's skin look chalky, but had the happy effect of making Althea glow as if with inner radiance. The overdress of cream gauze was one of Althea's Fakenham purchases. Three tiny pearly buttons closed each diminutive puffed sleeve, and slippers and gloves were of cream colored kid.

Earrings, necklace, and bracelets of coral completed the outfit, and a cream-colored ribbon was threaded through her soft hair. Lady Juliette, who was half-distracted, admired the ensemble excessively, declaring that Althea looked as pretty as an apricot meringue. Althea accepted this compliment gravely, remarking that she was quite fond of apricots; she could not help wondering whether Mr. Devereaux was also partial to the dish.

Still, Althea was quite satisfied with her appearance. She made, she felt, a pretty compliment to Juliette's sea-foam pale beauty, and for once Althea thought she might not look entirely no-how beside her companion.

Lady Juliette's gown was breathtakingly beautiful and managed, by some miraculous feat on the part of the noble Saunders, to match both Juliette's tastes and the reigning mode. A satin underslip of the palest leaf-green was veiled by an overdress of white embroidered gauze *en la mode français*, and the bodice, bound beneath the bosom with a wide band of dark green velvet, left shoulders bare. Juliette wore no jewelry except her strand of virginal pearls.

However delightful the gowns, they needed time and to spare to get Juliette turned out. The dress she had approved in every particular two days before was now seen to be far too daring, the pearls perfect not an hour ago were now vulgarly overlarge, and at last, near tears, Juliette demanded a lace shawl be produced, to cover shoulders and bodice, which had been discovered to be by far too *décolleté*.

"Oh, Thea—surely you do not think I can go to the ball like *this*?" Juliette's tragic tones suggested that her attire was scandalous enough to have her thrown into the nearest magadalen on the spot.

Juliette looked perfectly charming, and Althea drew breath to say so, but Saunders interposed herself between the two girls. "I dare say Miss Fonthill is too polite to ask you to hurry your dressing, Lady Juliette, so we will tell her you won't be a minute more, shall we?" Without waiting for an answer, she shepherded Althea to the door and opened it. "Pay her no heed, miss; it is only nerves. She will go on much better if you are not here." Before Althea could reply, she was out in the hall with the bedroom door firmly shut in her face.

After that, there was nothing to do but descend to the drawing-room where Madame and Mr. Devereaux were waiting to greet their dinner guests. Althea, her mind occupied with Juliette, did not take heed of the vision awaiting her at the foot of the stairs until she was beside it, when she stopped and blinked in surprise.

Mr. Anthony Devereaux was, as his great-aunt was to say acidly, impersonating the magpie, but Madame had never approved of the reforms in gentleman's dress advocated by Mr. George Brummel. Conversely, it was unlikely that the Beau would have been willing to take any credit for the extreme form of his famous rational dress which Mr. Devereaux had affected for the evening.

From his patent kid slippers with their discreet silver buckles, to the white silk stockings molding rather excellent calves, to his satin knee breeches, nip-waisted coat, smooth severe cravat, and brilliantly pomaded flax-pale locks, Anthony looked every inch the aristocrat in starkest black-and-white. Althea bobbed him a curtsy that was not all mockery as she reached the foot of the stairs.

"Miss Fonthill, you are a radiant vision of love-liness, and quite suffice—but I admit to a lively cu-riosity as to Juliette's whereabouts."

"I thank you, Mr. Devereaux; you, too, look very well indeed. Juliette is still being dressed. It was thought that my presence represented an impedi-ment, and so I came down. I hope I am not too early?"

"No one has arrived yet, if that's what you mean, but Maria and Uncle Sebastian are with Madame already. In fact, I have been cravenly waiting in the hall until someone arrived, as Madame is less likely to vent her feelings in company. There is safety in numbers, you know."

"You do not think she will approve your dress, Mr. Devereaux? But how could you? It is 'slap up to the echo,' as I believe the phrase is."

"I see you have been too much in Julie's com-pany, and are in sore need of a refining influence, Miss Fonthill, so we may be glad that Miss Alwor-thy is to be among us tonight. I confess I could not resist this *toilette* when I thought of what Madame might say, and as I think it much nicer to compli-ment lovely ladies' dress than to compete with it, my decision was rendered easy."

He had taken her arm as he spoke, as if to escort her into the parlor, but instead of proceeding he simply drew her closer to him. "No, stay a moment. I have something I wish to say to you, Miss Font-hill. I—"

"Oh, *there* you are, Mr. Anthony! Don't be stand-ing around in the hall like that. Madame Solange has been wondering where you were!" Maria Al-worthy's triumphant vowels rang off the marble parquetry and Anthony jumped back guiltily.

"Your servant, dear cousin-to-be," he said, bowing. He offered his elbow, at a punctilious distance, to Althea.

"Good lord in heaven, what *are* you got up as, Mr. Anthony?" demanded Maria in high glee.

Juliette still had not made her appearance some quarter-of-an-hour later, but Anthony's suggestion to Madame of conveying to Saunders a dose of laudanum for use as she thought best was sharply vetoed, and Anthony retired penitently to a seat by the fire next to Althea, complaining mildly that no one ever appreciated his humble efforts to be helpful.

"I do not know who we are to welcome here tonight," he added in an undertone, "but I hope they may all have been buried in the country for ever so."

"And not have heard any of the latest *on-dits*? So do I—but do you know, Mr. Devereaux, I am very much afraid that that may not be the case."

"Sir Vivian and Lady Thunderfields, and party," the butler announced, as if on cue.

Althea stood, turning in the direction of the announcement, and came face-to-face with Jerusha Gressingham.

It was an unfortunate fact of life that Mr. and Miss Gressingham, while making their home in Town, did visit extensively during the winter months. It was twice unfortunate, though equally factual, that Mr. Robert Gressingham had a character that could kindly be termed "rackety," and his sister accompanied him, out of the strongest sense of family duty, through the entertainments of a slightly fast and disreputable crowd.

It was also true that Madame, who had a regrettable taste for scandal when her own family was

not the subject, was quite likely to invite Sir Vivian
and the young dasher he had married to Fakenham
any time they were in residence, along with whatever flash crowd they were entertaining. Letitia,
Lady Thunderfields, was always glad to oblige Madame with scurrilous gossip.

Miss Gressingham stared back at Althea, and a
faint smile of self-satisfaction tucked in the corners
of her mouth. Miss Gressingham was the slave of
duty and never embarrassed by the company she
kept.

Althea darted a worried glance at Mr. Devereaux, but his manners were impeccable and his expression bland as he came forward and begged the
privilege of presenting everyone in the room to anyone they might not already have been presented to.

Throwing herself on the pyre of Christian charity, Althea intercepted Miss Gressingham's beeline
toward Maria Alworthy and drew her over by the
fire. "Why, Miss Gressingham," Althea said with
deep insincerity, "How wonderful to see you again.
Do come and tell me all you have been doing since
last we met."

A few moments later, Lady Juliette made her entrance, looking the picture of chaste, well-bred innocence. The effect was slightly marred by Lady
Thunderfields's expression of amusement, and Robert Gressingham's over-warm greeting. Lady Juliette, keeping her temper with admirable firmness,
quietly withdrew her fingers from his clasp and
went forward to greet Madame's other guests.

They were, when all had arrived, thirty for dinner, and it was the most elaborate meal Althea had
yet eaten at Fakenham. There was hot fruit soup,
duck with orange sauce and almonds, venison and

hare, pork and apple tartlet, and all manner of jellies, preserved fruits in spirits, cremes, cakes, and vegetables well disguised in spicy sauces.

The sauces, however, could not compete in pungency with the atmosphere. The Comte de Devereaux was at the foot of the table, with Maria on his right, Juliette on his left, and trouble on every side. Conversation was not flowing as smoothly as one might like; it tended to eddy in treacherous whirlpools across the table, especially among those luckless souls not protected by the Sevres epergne.

Madame's chair was specially built to make up for any deficiencies in her size, and gave her the air of looking down on an assembled multitude. As she felt free to direct conversational sallies at any of her guests from this height, the effect was rather that of Jove hurling the lightnings.

It was easy enough to see what the criterion for the selection of this guest list had been. One must be impeccable, either in reputation—thus Sir Vivian, the local Justice—or connection—such as Baron Rolvendon, one of Sir Vivian's guests. The added advantage of inviting the Thunderfields party, foot and horse, was that Jerusha Gressingham came with it, and it would look very odd indeed for Miss Gressingham to brand Lady Juliette the harlot while accepting invitations from her great-aunt when Juliette was under the same roof.

"I did not know you were to marry until Lady Juliette's last day at Duckmanton, Count Devereaux," Jerusha Gressingham said as soon as the soup course was served. "Your daughter was very naughty to keep secret such a momentous piece of news."

"Yes—Sebastian did surprise all of us, didn't you,

257

Nephew? But I daresay it is his English blood that makes him flighty."

Judging from her expression, Miss Gressingham was about to wonder aloud that she had always thought there was French blood in the Devereaux, and mention that the French were well-known to be a skimble-skamble lot, when Sebastian forestalled her.

"Flighty. Hum. Nonsense, ma'am, you'll pardon my saying. Good blood, English. Maria's English. Sound as a drum." The Comte, whose interests were evenly divided between Nineveh and Tyre and Quorn and Pycheley with very little to spare for inessentials, returned to his soup.

Madame, balked of her first target, started fresh game. "One supposes you are looking forward to becoming the mistress of Chaceley, Miss Alworthy. Perhaps you hope to become as a mother to my great-niece?"

Maria, proving that she possessed a certain instinct for self-preservation, agreed cautiously that she looked forward to her installation at Chaceley.

"How nice for dear Juliette, who has stood so long in need of a mother's guidance." This was Miss Gressingham's contribution.

The Comte bestirred himself once more. "Here now. What? Mother? Sister, surely. Almost the same age, what?" He frowned, thinking. "In fact, Julie's a bit older—aren't you, m'dear?"

As neither Maria nor Juliette cared to have this awkward fact mentioned, they were momentarily united in perfect charity. Both looked daggers at the oblivious Sebastian Devereaux.

"Don't despair, Maria, I'm sure you'll have something to mother before long," said Anthony consolingly.

"Oh yes—a dear little boy to inherit Chaceley!" gushed Miss Gressingham. "You are looking pale, Lady Juliette. Oh, I hope I have not said anything wrong?"

"When is the wedding to be, Miss Alworthy? Surely it will be the social event of the Season." Viscount St. George, another of Madame's guests (Althea had not yet decided where his impeccability lay—reputation or lineage) came to the rescue of the floundering conversation.

"Season? Oh, no, your lordship. It's the end of this month that the Count and I are marrying—we felt it best to get it over with as soon as possible and not wait for June."

"Oh, but why ever not? Unless . . ." Miss Gressingham produced a mortified silence, and the talk at the upper end of the table ceased; that at the foot provided far more interest.

Flustered, Miss Gressingham looked around and put a guilty hand to her lips. This action not unnaturally riveted everyone's attention on her last words; silent speculation was plainly about to begin.

"And how did you find the Nineveh Hunt, Uncle?" said Anthony, ruthlessly forcing a change of topic.

"Nineveh Hunt?" said his uncle. "Hum. Not a member. Don't rightly collect where it meets, but— oh, I *see*! A joke, is it, young Anthony? Oh, I say. Very good. Nineveh Hunt. Must try that on Squire."

"Naturally, Miss Alworthy, you wish to marry as soon as may be in order to be able to present your younger sisters next Season. You do have sisters, do you not?" said Althea hopefully.

"Five of them," confirmed Miss Alworthy, "and

proper cautions all—but that's hardly the reason I'm wishful to marry so soon—"

"It is fortunate that you are able to make the best of it, Miss Alworthy," said Miss Gressingham earnestly.

Lady Juliette set down her spoon; there was a ringing chime as it hit the edge of the plate. "*I* think it shows a—a great deal of sense!" she declared, regarding Miss Gressingham with emerald-hard eyes. Althea groaned inwardly; Juliette's defense of her step-mother-to-be was all that was admirable in the way of family loyalty—but there was no denying that to cross swords with Miss Gressingham now was unwise, to put it mildly.

"Well, I've got my Duty, there's no denying," said the agreeable Maria. "But it seemed to me that with marrying in November, as I am, I should be lightened by November-next at the latest, and well up for another winter's hunting with nary a bobble."

"Oh, dear," Miss Gressingham plainly found such forthright talk indelicate. "My dear Miss Alworthy, I hope you may not have misconstrued my little pleasantries! I did not mean to suggest that there was anything in the least previous about your wedding date."

"And how not, with my Sebastian being married before? But you'll see. I'll get him licked into shape all right and tight."

"Do tell us about some of your more famous runs, Uncle," Anthony urged, with the air of one making a last-ditch defense of the ramparts. "From Marathon to Waterloo. Hunting in the Agora. All that sort of thing."

The Comte considered this for a moment; the assembled company seemed to hold its breath in anticipation. "If more females took up healthy outdoor pursuits and spent less time hiding under pianofortes, there'd be a lot less unhappiness in the world," Sebastian Devereaux finally announced, and returned quite contentedly to his dinner.

Chapter
THIRTEEN

However much he wished to come to grips with Lady Juliette's fearsome relative, it seemed impossible for Jack to abandon Owlsthorne Hall immediately, and in the end it was several weeks before Jack left for London. Each step in the rehabilitation of the Hall had instantly demonstrated another dozen matters that needed to be set in train; Jack, used to the hand-to-mouth existence of a dedicated rogue, found the process more exhausting than chasing the French had been.

After voluminous correspondence between Jack and the firm of Pendray, Gloucester, Monmouth, and Scire, a satisfactory compromise had been reached with the Owlsthorne bankers. His Grace's bank, based upon assurances from His Grace's solicitors that His Grace intended to work like a Trojan to bring himself about, had cautiously agreed to advance certain meager sums of money and to extend the more pressing of the mortgages. This largesse had allowed Jack to hire some workmen from the village and begin the most urgent of the repairs to the Hall.

At last, however, Jack felt that he must go up to Town himself; the legacy from his mother awaited him in the useful form of almost five thousand pounds cash, and there were certain other matters that only he could attend to. On this jaunt he proposed to travel in effete comfort and take the stage. Vulcan was not a horse who took well to the confines of London, and, as the doughty Ned Sykes had chanced all on the possibility that the open-handed swell had meant what he'd said, and shown up at the Hall some two weeks after Jack's arrival, Jack had no qualms about leaving the stallion.

Once arrived in London, Jack first met with his bankers and the useful Mr. Pendray. Both bank and solicitor strongly discouraged an attempt to break the entail; it was the learned consensus that such a proceeding might take years and finish the ruin the old Duke had begun so well. On the other hand, they warned His Grace against undue optimism— but as they also seemed willing to extend His Grace's credit for the time being, Jack thought there might be more hope than this gloomy warning would admit.

Certainly most of his other creditors had drawn back, momentarily mollified by his elevation to ducal status, and willing to watch and wait in hopes of a better return on their investments than Jack's sojourn in debtor's prison. So, affairs financial being well in train, Jack promptly did some investing of his own, restocking his sadly depleted wardrobe and even purchasing a trunk to pack his new purchases in.

These matters having been taken care of, Jack, once more looking the part of the successful man-about-town, set off to cautiously elicit news of Lady Juliette's fate. Pendray, Gloucester, Monmouth and Scire had been quite willing to produce Solange Devereaux's direction for him, but before he made any further moves he wished to scout out the state of the gossip. It didn't take long to discover that gossip there most certainly was, but as he figured so prominently in the tales, and was such a good shot, few people were willing to favor him with details. Lady Juliette was known to be visiting her great-aunt; beyond that his informants were generally admirably reticent.

Abandoning this line with little regret, Jack agonized briefly over whether he should limit himself to a strongly-worded letter or simply appear in person and demand an interview. Very little time was needed to decide that the entire matter was both too delicate and too awkward to confide to paper; besides, once he stood on the doorstep it would be more difficult for anyone to either ignore him or say him nay.

So Jack composed a short note that rather curtly informed Lady Juliette's great-aunt that His Grace of Owlsthorne expected to be in the vicinity of Little Fakenham the last week in October, and would do himself the honor of calling upon her then. This task done, Jack turned his attention to the last call of duty in his dish: the post-obit bonds signed by Douglas Candlesby.

The amount of the indebtedness totaled slightly over twelve thousand pounds; the amount Jack had originally received for the pledge a little over four. In possession of the cash from his mother's legacy, a stout walking stick, and the promises of a few favors from some individuals of high estate who were once more willing to stand his friend, Jack set out to recover the bonds Douglas Candlesby had so incautiously signed in what now seemed another lifetime.

The moneylender's was easily reached; agreement with the fellow, not so easily. The interview was long and unpleasant, but, as Jack pointed out with a smile that seemed to alarm his opponent, by accepting his generous offer the repayment of at least the principal was guaranteed. Jack then casually mentioned how salubrious the air of the Continent could be . . . in the end, the documents were in his possession—damning signatures, dangling seals, and all.

This act of redemption, which Jack persisted in describing to himself as quixotic, left him dependent upon the grudging generosity of his bank. Nevertheless, he felt oddly lighthearted—even if deuced light in the pocket!—as he strode off to make arrangements for a journey to the village of Little Fakenham.

Jack liked to think of himself as imperturbable; certainly beyond surprise by the respectable element of society. But it must be admitted that when he found that the best room in Little Fakenham's premier hostelry, the Arm and Hammer, had been reserved for his use by Solange Devereaux, his eyebrows rose. As the Arm and Hammer also bore the distinction of being Little Fakenham's only hostelry, he made this unnerving discovery quite soon after his arrival.

Over a dinner quite tolerable for its kind, and a bowl of hot rum punch enjoyed in solitary state in a private parlor, also courtesy of his absent benefactress, he was baffled to find the fact that the locals treated him with the sort of breathless deference reserved for the more favored demigods. True, he *was* a duke, but he knew well enough that the lower classes were exacting enough to insist that a duke be accompanied by sufficient ducal display to enliven a dull day, and his current state fell lamentably short of this requirement. It was rather puzzling.

The following morning brought a note, scented with *chypre* and inscribed in an old-fashioned script. It informed him, in terms quite as peremptory as his own had been, that Solange Devereaux of Fakenham would give him tea at four o'clock; a carriage would call for him at three. Stare at it as he might, the stiff cream paper with the embossed crest would surrender no more information than that.

By the time three o'clock chimed, Jack was heartily glad to discover that the vehicle sent to fetch him was a closed carriage. He had ventured on a tour of the village to pass the time, and the looks cast at him by most of the passersby had made him feel more and more like a druidical sacrifice. He had finally decided that the interest taken in him by Miss Devereaux must be to blame for this phenomenon—he could hardly feel that either his title or his tailoring was enough to account for it. Apparently the villagers held her in as much superstitious awe as did her unfortunate great-niece.

The carriage conveyed him to a tiny Jacobean manor house. Jack squared his shoulders and went forward purposefully into the fray—only to be conducted into a charming salon with painted walls, where a tiny woman of a fairy-tale exquisiteness bade him sit down. After regretting that the young people were all out on a pleasure jaunt that afternoon, so that he must make do with the poor company of an old and querulous lady, she then proceeded to feed him malmsey and sugared almonds and converse upon the pleasantness of the weather in a sweet, aimless fashion until Jack was ready to throttle her.

At last, just as he was about to resort to the extreme of raising his voice, she set down her teacup and fixed him with a commanding gaze. "But you will not have come here merely to indulge a feeble old woman, my lord Duke."

Jack was by far too wary to be caught in the trap of either agreeing with this or denying it. "Surely any man must be delighted to indulge so charming a hostess?"

Solange Devereaux inclined her head ever so slightly, and continued as if he hadn't spoken. "So to spare us both whatever affecting farrago you planned to amuse me with, I shall tell you at once that I have had a letter from Viscount Templeton. He tells me that you are in love with my greatniece, and she with you. He does not approve, of course—the young are so conventional." Madame, a bare ten years Lord Templeton's senior, shook her head over the follies of youth.

Jack turned a rich shade of maroon, trying vainly to frame a response to this outrageous statement. "Why, that damned meddling, interfering—" He leaped to his feet; Madame regarded him with feline equanimity. "Allow me to relieve your mind—it's not true. My only interest in Lady Juliette was her money, and *she* is too sensible and virtuous to—"

"You should stay out of the playhouses, boy, and stop trying such tales on a defenseless old woman. Now, if you've done, allow me to return the favor and ease your mind: Juliette is no longer a great heiress."

The maroon faded to white as Jack stared. "But— You don't mean to tell me that her father believes those malicious lies put about by a lot of jealous old maids— He can't have disinherited her?"

There was a rustle of silk as Madame, apparently satisfied, settled back in her chair. "My dear Owlsthorne, please do me the courtesy of seating yourself, and try to be less theatrical. Take another glass of malmsey—or Pelham will bring you brandy if you require something stronger. Yes, I believe you do."

Conversation was perforce suspended until the butler, apparently expecting the summons, had come and gone, leaving behind a decanter of brandy on a silver tray. Under the compulsion of Madame's rapier-sharp gaze, Jack poured himself a generous glassful and tossed it off, then sat down again, his expression almost sulky.

"My, with such manners and address, it is little wonder you have won my great-niece's heart—no!— I will not have any more of your ill-considered interruptions until I have put you into possession of all the facts."

Forestalled, Jack set his mouth and prepared to hold his peace. He'd decided throttling was too good for her; Solange Devereaux required horsewhipping at the very least.

"To begin with, we shall settle the matter of Juliette's inheritance. You may not be aware, as it has not yet been generally announced, that her father, afflicted no doubt by the brain fever, has decided to marry a Maria Alworthy, daughter, if one can credit it, of the local Master of Hounds. As the young person is younger than Juliette, and in the most robust health—" Here Madame shrugged. "While the children have not, as yet, been born, there is every likelihood that they will be produced in the fullness of time. In short, Juliette can no longer be considered a great heiress, although she may yet be fortunate and remain an only child. Do I make myself clear so far?"

Jack considered and rejected several replies. "Go on."

"Very well. Do pay close attention, Your Grace, as this next matter may prove somewhat taxing to your intellect. When Miss Alworthy is mistress of Chaceley, Juliette will no longer wish to live there, nor will she be eager to make her home with me." She regarded Jack unblinkingly, as if daring him to make any of the retorts that had risen immediately to his mind.

Satisfied that she had his docile attention, she continued. "So she must make her home with another of her relatives, or she must marry. No matter how many sons her step-mother chooses to produce, Juliette will still have a small estate in the north, a bequest of her mother's. She will also bring a tolerable sum when she marries. But this dowry will not be great enough to erase memories of the unfortunate episode at Duckmanton—"

"As to that, Madame Solange, I can explain—"

"I imagine you could, young man, but why tax yourself? I have already had the truth from my erring grand-niece, and a number of entertaining fictions from many others."

"I must at least tell you that she is entirely blameless in the affair!"

Madame laughed, a sound almost irritatingly like chiming bells. "My dear Duke, I told you I have had the truth from Juliette. Still, it is admirably chivalrous in you to say so. Now do let me finish. I find I simply cannot adjust to modern manners; interruptions put me off."

Thoroughly rolled up, and entertaining a deep

sense of pity for Lady Juliette, Jack subsided once more.

"However, I see that you agree with me that Juliette's reputation requires mending, and that with all due dispatch. I take it, Your Grace, that you are now prepared to make the gesture that best darns rents in the garment of a lady's chaste reputation?"

Jack stared. After a moment, Madame thumped the Aubusson carpet with the tip of her cane. "Come, come, man—are you prepared to make reparations and marry my grand-niece?"

Playing for time, Jack poured himself another generous libation of brandy before answering. "Madame, allow me to say that nothing would bring me to let Juliette throw herself away on a worthless fellow like myself."

"In my day," said Madame acerbically, "one did not call a dukedom worthless! And, as ought to have been borne in upon you by now, young man, there is very little left for Juliette to throw. In fact, if you will not have her, I fear I shall be forced to make her cousin Anthony do so, which will make them both quite cross, as *she* has now already refused him once, and I have every reason to believe *he* intends to offer for Althea Fonthill. Now, leaving your character aside, is there any other reason you cannot support a wife?"

Jack laughed bitterly. "Any number of them! Good God, the dukedom's mortgaged to the hilt, and my pockets to let—and my character cannot be left aside! If you wish to reinstate Lady Juliette in Society, I doubt that marriage to me will accomplish it!"

"You will allow me to be the judge of that, young

man. Now, as to your debts, to Mr. Candlesby and others—"

"Does the whole world know?"

"We have already established that my grand-niece cannot keep secrets from me. I have spoken to your bankers and your solicitors—they are also mine, and were quite forthcoming once they realized you were contemplating marriage with my family—and find their reports highly encouraging. You will no doubt be gratified to know that they seem moderately convinced of your desire to reform. Doubtless your affairs can be brought round in time; Juliette's dowry, while not great, will be of help to you."

The prospect was too tempting; Jack firmly suppressed the enchanting vision of Juliette as his wife. "And do you suppose she will consider being Duchess of Owlsthorne sufficient compensation for foregoing all the elegancies of life—even many of its comforts—perhaps for years?"

Madame looked him up and down in a considering manner that made Jack feel that he ought, by rights, to blush. "Doubtless you will be able to make it worth her while somehow," she said dryly.

Jack struggled with his emotions for a moment, then surrendered and laughed. Madame sat back and waited placidly until he had begun to sober and wipe his eyes.

"I see you have all arranged—have you decided on the number and sexes of our children?"

"You are too previous," Madame reproved him. "Now, I am giving a ball in Juliette's honor tomorrow evening. You will oblige me by attending; here is your card of invitation. If you win her consent, the engagement can be announced at the ball—if you do not, your presence there, on terms with our family, can only be of help."

Jack obediently accepted the card. "Not win her consent? I thought you had all arranged?"

"Don't be impertinent, young man—and I am by far too old a lady to be taken in by that smile of yours! Matters are never neatly arranged in affairs of the heart—and Juliette is unused to dealing in them at the best of times."

She held out her hand. "Now you must go. I am endeavoring to keep you a secret, lest Juliette do something interesting and cause further scandal."

Bowing to the inevitable, Jack kissed her hand and was escorted back to the carriage for return to the Arm and Hammer.

Chapter

FOURTEEN

The Little Fakenham Assembly Rooms occupied an extremely old and extremely ugly building that was situated at the opposite end of the village green from the Arm and Hammer. It was rumored to have been built on the site of a Saxon *witenagemot*—however unlikely this might be in Hertfordshire—or, conversely, to have been a hay barn dating from the time of William the Conqueror.

Whoever had built it, whenever it had been built, it had been built to last. The ground floor was constructed entirely of large blocks of granite, faced with the local reddish stone; the interior was generously covered with thick coatings of horsehair and plaster, and half-timbered in fine old English oak. In Jacobean times a second story had been added to the massive building, in the beam and plaster fashion common to the day. This addition had given the structure a certain distinction, if only that of being the largest ugly building in the neighborhood.

As the village grew and prospered, the building had served many purposes, and been unsatisfactory for each. It had once been an inn, but the opening of the more comfortable and convenient Arm and

Hammer, some eighty years ago, had led to the almost instant close of the hostelry. It had defeated generations of shopkeepers; it was impossible to cut larger windows in the ground floor walls to better display wares, or to triumph in any way over a building that seemed in turns too small, too large, too near to Town, too far away, too cold, too stuffy, too old, and without a sense of history. Even the most optimistic merchants had finally abandoned it for more advantageous locations nearer the post road inn, and the looming structure had fallen vacant.

In 1812 the visionary Mr. Samuel Watling of London, much struck by the building's manifest possibilities, decided to emulate Beau Nash and transform Little Fakenham into such a fashionable watering place as Bath had become. Not one whit discommoded by the lack of hot mineral springs in the vicinity, Mr. Watling had promptly bought up the lease on the building, re-christened it the Fakenham Assembly Rooms, and taken up a subscription from the local gentry to renovate the place. The ground floor was to become a fashionable gentlemen's club; the first floor, a series of dancing and supper rooms to rival Almack's.

To this end, artisans were summoned from London and the entire facade was refaced in white Italian marble, with ornamented stringcourses in porphyry, and tasteful and extremely elegant bronze sphinxes were placed at the corners of the roof. The Egyptian motif was continued throughout the interior; plaster reproductions of lotuses and crocodiles were added to cornices and lintels; any wall not covered with Jacobean oak paneling was papered in a very fashionable wallpaper. It was gilt and viridian, and had been smuggled from France at great trouble and expense to the determined Mr. Watling.

The remodeling complete, Mr. Watling had taken great care over the furnishings and appointments of the Assembly Rooms. When the decorating was done, delicate gilded chairs upholstered in brocade striped to match the papered walls, and graceful tables supported by Greek urns, completed the look of sophisticated refinement for which he had striven.

The ballrooms were a guarded success, with country dances held regularly twice a month. But the elite gentlemen's club Mr. Watling had established went bankrupt within a twelvemonth. There were very few young gentlemen in this part of the country who would not rather dash up to Town for their pleasures, and those who didn't preferred to drink and dice at the Arm and Hammer.

Mr. Watling at last was forced to abandon his dream. He returned to London, after selling the Assembly Rooms to the newly-formed Ladies Committee of Little Fakenham.

The Ladies Committee, composed of the guiding female lights of the local gentry, had been unable to decide what to do with the ground floor until recently, for no decision could be made without the unanimous agreement of the Committee. Then, with a burst of inspiration, the Committee had realized what must be done: the ground floor should be converted into a fashionable array of little shops. Away with the Little Fakenham Gentlemen's Club—welcome the Little Fakenham Universal Bazaar!

Unfortunately, due to an inexplicable inability of the local workmen to properly understand the wishes of the Ladies Committee—a problem in no way alleviated by the fact that the decision to create the Bazaar was the first and last time the Committee agreed upon anything—work on the Universal Bazaar proceeded very slowly. It had, in fact, come to a grinding halt some months before the night of Solange Devereaux's ball.

Mr. Anthony Devereaux had retailed the history of the starcrossed Assembly Rooms to Miss Althea Fonthill during the drive, but even so she was not prepared for the apparition that was the Assembly Rooms by moonlight. At her comment, Mr. Devereaux helpfully pointed out that the Rooms had done much to promote sobriety in Little Fakenham, as many a young buck in his altitudes had, upon exiting the Arm and Hammer during the full of the moon, become convinced that the Assembly Rooms were actually chasing him. These high-flown unfortunates usually, according to Mr. Devereaux, came to grief in the Fakenham Ditch.

Althea smiled at these drolleries, but even so was not completely distracted from her worries over Lady Juliette. Madame had planned this evening as the opening salvo of Juliette's rehabilitation in the eyes of the Polite World. Well, what Madame intended would doubtless come to pass—Althea had a great faith in Madame's steely whims. But even if it did carry Juliette safely back into the arms of respectability, what was she to do then?

Lady Juliette had been wondering very much the same thing over the past four weeks. From the moment she had heard of dear Papa's coming marriage, the weight of responsibility for Chaceley had been lifted from her shoulders; dearly though she loved her home, she could not deny that there was

276

a certain relief mixed with her sense of loss. But now she must think of her future very differently.

To begin with, she knew she must leave Chaceley soon after the wedding. It would be Maria's right to govern Chaceley, and it would be monstrously unfair to both Maria and Papa for Juliette to keep the reins in her own hands. Juliette knew herself well enough—and was honest enough—to admit that watching Maria in her own place would gall unbearably.

But live with Madame she would not, and her plan to live at Ashdene with a chaperon was, Juliette admitted to herself, not very appealing. Still she supposed it must be—since the alternative, marriage to Anthony—was just as unappealing, if more hilarious. Marry Tony—and have the two of them make each other miserable? If she had learned nothing else in the aftermath of her Season, she had learned better than that. No doubt she would manage to content herself. She had very few alternatives, with no money and too much reputation.

As did so many thoughts, this brought Lord Barham—or, rather, His Grace of Owlsthorne—to mind. Removed from his provocative presence, Juliette had been forced to admit that his advice, however vexing she had found it, had been sound; she would have valued it now. How he would have laughed to find that she no longer needed what he had called "a husband for Chaceley!"

She could not help wondering where he was and what he was doing—doubtless efficiently bartering his title for a suitable marriage settlement, and no silly sentiment about it. And there was no use whatsoever repining over it; she would probably never meet the man again. Whatever Juliette needed or wanted, *he* still must marry money. If he would not have her when she was a great heiress—

Fortunately, the carriage drew up before the Assembly Rooms just as her eyes began to sting, and further indulgence in sensibility was rendered impossible by the usual furor attendant upon arrival at one's own ball.

Whatever one might think of Madame's high-handedness, no one could deny that it was precisely what was needed to make an entertainment run smoothly. The gentlemen did not disappear into the card-rooms leaving the ladies to stand and gossip; the musicians did not refresh themselves to the detriment of their playing.

Madame, enthroned in state at one end of the first of the series of rooms, kept a baleful eye on events. She was aided in this by Miss Gressingham, who had greeted her hostess and announced that she did not dance. Madame had then ordered Miss Gressingham to sit by her and tell her all the news, told Anthony that he would like to dance with Maria Alworthy, and efficiently procured partners for Juliette and Althea. Those bidden to dance meekly proceeded to the floor as the orchestra began the strains of a sprightly country dance. Madame did not approve of the waltz.

Waltzing or no, Althea found herself enjoying the evening immensely. She did not lack for partners. Her dance card was quickly filled by young gentlemen who were unsophisticated enough to take honest pleasure in standing up with an agreeable young lady and who had not yet learned to despise dancing utterly in favor of more dissipated pursuits.

Althea tried to keep a watchful eye on Juliette,

but soon found this impossible. Rather than having one good-sized ballroom, the Assembly Rooms were composed of a series of small rooms connected by archways. As more and more guests arrived, and the floor became crowded, Althea began to feel as if she were trapped in a maze.

So when Anthony Devereaux appeared from no-where to ruthlessly cut out her partner of the moment, Althea smiled upon him even more warmly than usual. "And how do you find our Assembly Rooms, Miss Fonthill? Although the real trick, as you must know by now, is to find your partner once you have been so unwary as to set foot beyond the first archway."

"They are not quite in the common way," she admitted as Mr. Devereaux deftly whisked her out of the set and led her off the floor, chatting quietly as he did so.

"I have sought you out, my dear Miss Fonthill, because even Madame can hardly fault my attention to my partner for the next set. Espying you at last, I found it meet, good, and entirely admirable to rescue you from the clutches of that cow-footed oaf, and suggest we sit it out. If you have been as diligent as I, you will be glad of the rest."

"I feel as if I have been dancing for hours—I have quite lost track of the time!"

"It is nearly midnight, when I shall escort you in to supper, if it please you—please say that it does, or Madame will assign me elsewhere, and her choice is sure to fall upon either my cousin—who is got up like Vice Avenged and is acting the part, you will have noticed—or Miss Gressingham, and that I cannot support. Gressingham green doesn't suit my complexion. Come to that, it doesn't suit Miss Gressingham's. Why do you suppose she wears it? Ah, I have it! She wished her complexion to match the chairs!"

"Oh, don't, I pray you, Mr. Devereaux! You will make me laugh, and that would be too dreadful!"

"I cannot think your laughter would be in the least dreadful, Miss Fonthill. But let us away from this entrancing spectacle—I shall serve as guide and mentor and reveal unto you the many facets of great historical interest which these hallowed halls possess."

"—and it was upon this very spot that King Alfred opened a bakery; it closed again three weeks later, as he made a dreadful muddle with the cakes. This is also the site of the demises of Williams Conqueror and Rufus. Under those stairs—" Anthony pointed, "—you will find the bodies of both the Little Princes of the Tower, and directly over here Robert Bruce did something with a spider."

"It was Robert Gressingham," Althea said tartly as they walked on, "and he has swallowed a spider."

"You astound me, Miss Fonthill. However, youth must have its fling, and as Bobs cannot reach the roofs of the village from here, all he can do is try riddles with the sphinxes, if he can reach them." Anthony Devereaux set down his borrowed candelabrum on a pile of masonry. They were among the clutter of the ground floor of the Assembly Rooms; the music and noise from the dancers came faintly from the floor above.

Anthony gestured, indicating the odd mingling of half-finished booths and the remains of the elegant appointments of the defunct gentlemen's club. "No one can understand why the work on the Bazaar does not proceed with more dispatch. All that is needful is for the foreman to read the collective mind of the Ladies Committee at the moment that it makes it up and before it changes it again. Very puzzling. On the other hand, if the work is delayed until spring, there is no telling what might be the outcome. I've thought of suggesting they remodel it along the lines of Astey's Amphitheatre, with equestrian shows. What do you think, Miss Fonthill? Will it do?"

"I think Mr. Gressingham is not the only one who is in his altitudes tonight, Mr. Devereaux," said Althea placidly, lifting the Holland cover from a settee and seating herself. "But do tell me why you brought me here—we haven't much time, if we are to make our appearance at supper."

"I," said Anthony, "have less time than that— and I haven't the courage to do this twice. Good lord, it seems I haven't the courage to do it once, Miss Fonthill. You would be very well advised to wash your hands of me and go back upstairs before your absence is remarked."

"What, before my poor feet have stopped aching? And as you have promised to take me in to supper, I fear I must remain, for where else would I find a partner on such short notice? The kindness of Viscount St. George, you know, can be tried only so far."

"Very well, we must try to muddle through. My dear Miss Fonthill . . ." Anthony stopped, looking harassed. "Miss Fonthill . . ." he began again.

There was a sudden tingling in Althea's veins. She clasped her hands very tightly in her lap and managed to make her voice steady. "Yes, Mr. Devereaux?"

"Good heavens, what a hash I'm making of this," said Anthony ruefully. "Miss Fonthill—

Unfortunately I am very much as Julie has described me to you, and—but—" In a brisk and businesslike fashion Anthony turned towards her, dropped to one knee beside the settee, and seized her hands in his. "Miss Fonthill, would you do me the honor—the privilege—the very great favor—of becoming my wife?"

He had finally conquered the ministrations of his valet, Althea noted distantly. His flaxen hair, carefully pomaded and curled for the evening, had returned to a state of nature at last and was, as usual, falling over his eyes.

"I—If you are not serious, Mr. Devereaux, I pray you will get up and we will say no more about this," Althea said faintly, and made a feeble effort to pull her hands away.

Anthony remained where he was and retained possession of her hands. "I am serious, actually," he said in normal tones. "Unfortunately, it is my curse not to ever seem able to say anything serious seriously. 'Miss Fonthill, I wish to marry you.' 'Miss Fonthill, though we have known each other only a few short weeks, I love you and I hope you will become my wife.' It doesn't work. *I* can't even believe it.

"However, if I were to say, 'dear and radiant goddess, complete my life and make me the happiest of mortals,' I know I'm sincere—only no one else seems to."

Althea turned her face away, though her hands remained firmly in Anthony's grasp.

"My dear Miss Fonthill? Althea? Do please consider an offer made with heartfelt sincerity. I know I am not dashing, nor particularly handsome. I cannot offer you a title, and my fortune is comfortable merely. I am known to have an odd and incomprehensible sense of humor and no particular taste in horseflesh, but I should try very hard to make you happy."

"But what about Juliette?" Althea's voice was low, and she kept her face averted.

"Juliette?" said Anthony blankly.

"Yes, Juliette. Mr. Devereaux, I am—am deeply sensible of the honor—"

"Bother the honor! My dear, I know I rushed into this without proof of your affections or approval from your family, but—well—when I saw you this evening I knew I must put it to the touch before you went back to them. You'd be sure to be beseiged by men of far more polish and address than I, and—my dear Miss Fonthill, you're the only person in the county who laughs at my jokes; what could I do? Now, what has my cousin to do with anything?"

Althea, much gratified by this avowal, kept her head, although with some difficulty. "Mr. Devereaux, you know how poor Juliette is situated; she must marry someone, and—and I know your great-aunt intends it to be you. I—I am very fond of dear Juliette, and—and I would not wish you to marry to disoblige your family."

Anthony stared at her, then seized Althea's hands and drew her to her feet. "Miss Fonthill, may I be blunt—candid—brutally frank? I don't care what Madame intends, I am not going to marry Julie. She refused me, as you know—the only sensible thing she's ever done. If I marry anyone, my dear Miss Fonthill, it will be you—or no one." He peered at her anxiously. "Is it to be no one, Miss Fonthill? I do not wish to disgust you with too-fervid protestations of my sincerity; it's deuced awkward. Now, if I only were a hero from a Gothic romance I should simply kiss you into submission at this point and take your consent for granted, but as I am not, say, the Duke of Owlsthorne—"

"Bother the Duke of Owlsthorne!" Althea's voice was firm and she faced Anthony squarely. "I do not wish to marry a hero from a Gothic romance, Mr. Devereaux."

"Then—Miss Fonthill, will you make me the happiest of men?"

"Probably I shall not—but I will marry you, Mr. Devereaux. And—oh, Anthony! Juliette may make her home with us!"

Mr. Devereaux was momentarily distracted from his joy at her acceptance of his suit by the horrific vision so conjured, but he proved the depth of his affection by actually smiling as he said, "My dear, I am sure that will be delightful, and the happiest of solutions." He raised her gloved hands to his lips and slowly kissed them, one after the other.

"My reward for virtue above and beyond the call of duty," he explained gravely as Althea blushed. "Now, shall we rejoin the others and make our intentions known? For if we remain closeted here alone much longer, Miss Fonthill, I'm afraid I cannot vouch for the continued propriety of my conduct." Althea turned toward him and surprised an expression in his eyes that augured well for their future together.

She turned even pinker and put her hand on his arm. "In that case, Mr. Devereaux," Althea said primly, "I am sure we should return to the ballroom at once!"

Chapter
FIFTEEN

In the rooms above, Lady Juliette Devereaux was managing the evening with the same magnificent competence she brought to all endeavors. At least, this was what she kept telling herself, in the hopeful mental tones of one who does not believe that the unexamined life is not worth living.

After all, she had survived the dinner party; her dance card was full; no one had pulled their skirts aside as she passed. Madame had apparently triumphed once more. Juliette supposed drearily that her reputation was, if not shining, at least not tarnished. Now she need only decide what to do with the rest of her life.

It was near midnight, and Juliette, who had not eaten much at dinner, and was looking forward to refreshment more substantial than a glass of punch, suddenly realized that she had no one to take her in to supper. This was a singular oversight on Madame's part—she had organized everything else about the evening with the ruthless skill of the experienced tyrant.

Juliette shrugged off this oddity and looked about for Anthony, with an eye to demanding his escort to supper. After a moment, she saw Anthony and

Althea making their way through the crowd. Althea's hand was tucked rather possessively through Anthony's arm; his head was bent towards her and they were blissfully and obliviously exchanging comments that apparently greatly pleased them both. A sudden suspicion lanced through Juliette; it was confirmed by Althea's hot blush as she looked up and saw Juliette staring at them.

Althea tugged at Anthony's arm and his head came up. He blinked vaguely at Juliette. "Oh, hullo, Julie. Having fun?"

"Not as much as you are," replied Juliette with a venom that surprised her. She pressed a hand to her cheek. "I'm sorry, Tony—I don't know what's the matter with me—and I'm sure I wish you two very happy."

Neither Althea nor Anthony wasted breath in denials. "I'm sure we shall be," Anthony told her, with a fond glance at the radiant Althea. "As for what's the matter with you, Julie—you're hungry, that's all."

Juliette gave a shaky laugh. "Yes—and Madame has somehow neglected to provide me with a partner for supper. I had hoped—"

"His Grace the Duke of Owlsthorne!" announced the footman at the main door in the carrying tones of Stentor.

Juliette spun around, hand going to her throat. It was true; Jack stood in the doorway, tall, broad, and handsome in a coat of claret velvet. Juliette turned pale. Jack smiled and bowed.

His Grace of Owlsthorne had certainly not expected, at this late hour, to be announced by a leather-lunged serving knave laboring under the delusion that it was his duty to make himself heard the length and breadth of the Assembly Rooms. However, it had served one useful purpose: no man of Jack's considerable experience could mistake Lady Juliette's reactions. The lady was not indifferent to him—Jack had feared that she might, not unnaturally, have developed a distaste for him after their last encounter at Duckmanton.

Smiling, Jack strode forward, only to be confronted by Jerusha Gressingham in her self-appointed capacity as Madame's assistant hostess. Apparently Jack's elevation to Grace had returned him to favor in all quarters.

"Oh, here you are, Your Grace! How kind of you to honor our poor country entertainment—you will be looking for Lady Juliette, of course—dare we hope an interesting announcement is due in that quarter as well? How charming if she and her new mother-in-law were to make it a double wedding!"

Jack always enjoyed watching a master craftsman at work; Miss Gressingham's ability to unhesitatingly unveil the most devastating item of gossip in her armory precisely where it would do the most harm fascinated him. Had he indeed been interested in Lady Juliette only for her money, news of her father's remarriage would surely have made him veer off.

Jack, smiling sardonically, bowed over Miss Gressingham's hand. "Miss Gressingham, you have once again bested me with your razor wit. Now, if you will excuse me—?"

Lady Juliette was still standing as if mesmerized beside Althea Fonthill and her cousin Anthony. As Jack approached, the color flooded back into Juliette's face and a glow of pure joy seemed to light her from within. "Oh—Lord Bar—I mean, good evening, Your Grace!"

Decidedly Lady Juliette was too forthright to be in the mode for young ladies, but Jack was in no mood to be critical of such a flattering welcome. Casting an expert's eye over her attire, he grinned as he bowed over her hesitantly outstretched hand. "Well, my centauress, someone of taste has had the dressing of you, that's plain enough. My compliments, my dear Miss Fonthill—I'm sure Lady Juliette owes all to you. Mr. Devereaux, how nice to see you again, and I shall be willing to listen to anything you wish to say to me after I have spoken to Lady Juliette."

"You mean about calling you out, I imagine, Your Grace. Well, set your mind at rest; in addition to the fact that we have no quarrel, Miss Fonthill has just done me the honor of consenting to become my wife and I am sure you are here at Madame's invitation."

"Oh, Anthony, do talk sense—" The simple act of speech made Juliette flush scarlet to the roots of her hair. She did not seem to notice that Jack still held her hand.

"My sincerest felicitations to you both, and I'm sure you'll be ecstatically happy together," said Jack absently. "Mr. Devereaux, if you will grant me the loan of your cousin—?"

"For as long as you like," said Anthony promptly. "Come along, Miss Fonthill—we must break the news to Madame." Taking Althea firmly by the arm, he bore her off, apparently nothing loath to leave his cousin in the hands of a notorious rake.

"Admirable man," said Jack. "And now, my little wood-nymph, I have something I wish to ask you. Is there some place we may speak privately?"

The light died from her eyes, and she uttered a strangled gasp. "Oh—you do not know! Your Grace, there—there is nothing you can wish to ask me now, I assure you!"

"My dear child, there most certainly is—and I shall ask you either privately or here in full hearing of what I am assured will be a most interested audience." He raised an eyebrow and regarded her curiously. "Now, surely this rabbit warren possesses some secluded spot to which we may repair?"

Juliette sighed. "Very well, Your Grace. Come with me."

Almost visibly drooping, Juliette led the way to an archway between two small chambers at the opposite end of the floor from the supper room. Heavy swags of velvet draped the little alcove formed by the arch and provided a modicum of privacy; as most of the company had by now converged upon the supper tables, it was unlikely that they would be interrupted.

Here Lady Juliette turned to face him, squaring her shoulders as if in preparation for a blow. "Before you begin, Lord Barham—Your Grace—"

Jack grinned. "I know—I'm having the devil's own time getting used to it myself. So, considering all we've meant to each other, sweeting, I suggest you call me Jack."

"Oh, don't!" Eyes tearfully bright, Juliette took a deep breath. "I don't know why you are here, Your Grace, but I must tell you at once—my father is to marry again!"

"My dear, I know that," said Jack gently. "It has no bearing on what I wish to say to you." He reached out and took her hand; it trembled slightly, but she did not withdraw it. "Once you did me the honor of asking me to marry you. I refused you at the time, but you were quite right, my pet. So now I am asking you to marry me."

Juliette stared at him. "But you do not understand! He is to marry Maria Alworthy, and she is younger than I, and will have dozens of children, and I shall have no more than a competence! I am not an heiress!"

Jack laughed and tried to draw her closer. "Does poor Maria know of the fate in store for her? My dear, I don't care if your step-mother has a hundred children. Now, when shall we be married?"

Lady Juliette yanked her hand free and half-turned away. "Never."

Baffled, Jack stared at her blankly. "I beg your pardon?"

"I mean I will not marry you." Juliette's voice was so low he could barely hear her.

Putting his hands on her shoulders, an intimate gesture Lady Juliette did not repudiate, Jack said quietly, "I don't suppose it would make any difference to you if I told you I'd redeemed Candlesby's damnable bonds for him? Duckmanton is safe, the wolf driven from the door, conjugal bliss assured—he is still making up to Miss Isobel, isn't he?"

"Oh, yes." Lady Juliette didn't sound as if she cared overmuch. "I—I suppose the bonds cost you a great deal of money?"

"Pretty nearly every shilling." Jack pressed her shoulders and turned her to face him; Juliette looked down at the floor. "I see I shouldn't have told you about paying the bonds," he added ruefully. "Once you were willing to marry me to get them paid; I might have turned the same trick twice."

She lifted her head and smiled slightly. "But it was very bad in me to have done that, and—and it is unkind of you to remind me."

"My dear child, you know full well I'm not a kind man," said Jack calmly. "Now, why these sudden qualms? If it's the thought of your family, let me tell you at once that I had the most amazing interview with your great-aunt yesterday, and she says you must marry either me or Cousin Anthony. As Cousin Anthony has prudently taken himself out of the matrimonial sweepstakes, it must be me." He smiled. "I have wit, charm, title, address, and the consent of your family. What more is needed?"

He bent towards her to kiss her; Lady Juliette uttered a groan of pure despair and twisted out from under his hands, turning to bury her face in the swagged velvet hangings. "But you have no money!" The words were somewhat muffled by the green velvet, but not enough.

"But darling, I have never had money. I've made no secret of that."

To his surprise, Lady Juliette rounded on him like an angry cat, eyes sparkling and cheeks flushed. "But now you are Duke, and you have Owlsthorne to think of! Indeed, you should always have been thinking of it! You must know what it will take to make it what it was before—"

"Oh, lord!" Torn between anger and laughter, Jack compromised by backing Juliette into the alcove and putting his arms around her, ignoring her half-hearted attempts to shove him back. "Always estates with you! How any woman who looks so enchanting can have so practical a brain never ceases to amaze me. For heaven's sake, darling, consider yourself for once!"

"Someone must be sensible, and—and I have only myself to blame for my situation. I have behaved badly and am well-served for my folly. Now you must let me go, before someone sees!"

"And am I also to be well-served for your folly?"

Juliette looked up at him, her green eyes wide and puzzled. "What do you mean?"

"I mean, my dear, that I love you, and I wish nothing more than for you to be my wife. As for the rest, we'll muddle through somehow."

Shaking her head, Juliette put her hands on his chest as if to hold him off. Jack tightened his arms to pull her closer still.

"You are not to kiss me," said Juliette hastily. "I—I cannot let you throw yourself away on me. Now let me go at—"

As irritated as any other man to have his own arguments thrown back in his face, Jack put a stop to them in the time-honored fashion. Lady Juliette made no pretense of not responding to his lips, but when Jack finally lifted his head her lashes were damp with tears and he knew with a sinking heart that her mind was made up. However painful the sacrifice to them both, Lady Juliette would not condemn him to what she considered a life of poverty and regret.

Jack could cheerfully have shaken his obstinate darling until her teeth rattled. Her scruples, however noble in the abstract, were damnably inconvenient, and he was suddenly unsure of his ability to coax her round. "Juliette—for heaven's sake, sweetheart, don't tell me you mean to defy that incredible great-aunt of yours?"

Juliette blinked and made a brave attempt at a smile. "Madame does not care what becomes of you, Your Grace—only of my reputation! But—but I care! And so—and so I will not marry you. You must go and marry a great heiress, and thank heaven for your narrow escape!" The corners of her mouth quivered, but when Jack would have gathered her up again she wrenched herself out of his embrace and backed slowly away.

"Juliette—!"

"No! Oh, go away, Your Grace—go away at once!"

"And then—oh, my dear Miss Fonthill, you will scarcely credit it, but I saw the most shocking thing! I had gone to seek out Lady Juliette, for I thought to have Robert take her in to supper—we must all support her, especially as she must feel herself wholly friendless—"

"Lady Juliette has a great many very good friends," said Althea. She snapped open her fan and began to ply it vigorously, hoping her irritation with Miss Gressingham did not show too plainly. It was unfortunately true that at this pass Juliette must be all that was conciliating; Althea, as her representative to Miss Gressingham, must be no less so.

"And I am sure she must be grateful, the case being what it is. But *then*, my dear Miss Fonthill, what should I see but Lady Juliette herself, closeted alone with the Duke of Owlsthorne—and he had his arms around her! Well, I had to resort to my vinaigrette at once!

"You must know I was very surprised indeed to see him here, but dear Madame Devereaux is so very cosmopolitan—and so I confess I was at a loss what to do! Naturally I made my presence known and His Grace took himself off at once—after using the most intemperate language, which only goes to show you, I am sure! I offered my assistance to Lady Juliette, but as she was obviously suffering from strong hysterics, I guided her to a chair and came to fetch you to her, Miss Fonthill." At the conclusion of this speech, Miss Gressingham, apparently awaiting approval, blinked myopically at Althea.

"Oh, dear," said Althea, after some consideration. She looked worriedly at Anthony; Miss Gressingham's recital did not sound promising.

"Oh, I say—" Anthony pushed ineffectually at his wayward hair and peered at Miss Gressingham. "That was very good of you, Miss Gressingham, but not necessary, don't you know—Julie's not sickening for brain fever, so you mustn't worry. Young ladies are very much like that, I believe, when they are first engaged."

Althea kicked him sharply upon the ankle. As she was wearing satin dancing slippers, however, this brutality had little effect.

"Oh! Oh, I see!" Miss Gressingham looked both relieved and vexed. "Then Lady Juliette is engaged to the Duke of Owlsthorne, Mr. Devereaux?"

"How can you doubt it? The engagement has been known in the family for some months, but is not to be announced until after my uncle's wedding—I know I can count on your discretion, Miss Gressingham." Anthony beamed upon her, Miss Gressingham, flustered, offered profuse congratulations and took herself off, and Anthony calmly returned to the consumption of lobster salad.

As soon as Miss Gressingham was out of earshot, Althea rounded upon him. "Anthony, how could you? Now everyone will know, and you know that Juliette must have refused him!"

"Oh, but I told her in strictest confidence," said Anthony sweetly.

Althea gasped and choked on a giggle. "Anthony, you mustn't tease Miss Gressingham like that! Sooner or later she is bound to notice and will be dreadfully offended."

"I doubt it," said Anthony complacently. "And as for Julie's engagement, as you well know, my dearest, it must be Owlsthorne or me and Madame has set her *imprimatur* on him, to my undying gratitude. Julie and Owlsthorne seem made for each other; if he'll only beat her daily I'm sure they'll get on. Now you'd better turn out and find her—between His Grace and Miss Gressingham she must, in the immortal words of my aunt-to-be, be well on her way to busting a gusset."

Chapter
SIXTEEN

Anthony Devereaux arrived at the Arm and Hammer a good half an hour before the early Mail to London. This was not so great a feat as it might sound for a young man the morning after a ball, for Anthony had not as yet been to bed, and so the earliness of the hour was of no consequence. Earlier still Anthony had escorted a quietly weeping Juliette and a solicitous Althea back to the Jewel Box; he had then slipped out during the ensuing confusion and come to the Arm and Hammer in search of the Duke of Owlsthorne.

Mine host greeted Anthony cordially, and seemed not in the least started by his knee breeches and evening coat. One expected these sights after a ball, and good custom, too—the common room, in fact, was still lively, even at the ungodly hour of half-past three.

In answer to his query, Anthony was informed that the Duke—if Duke you could call him, which the innkeeper begged leave to doubt—was drinking in a private parlor, and had not ten minutes since thrown a mug at the servant who had come in answer to his ring. This incident inclined the landlord's opinion more favorably towards the Duke as

"Real Quality," but he was denied the opportunity to consider this topic at length, for Anthony brushed past him in search of the Duke.

The private parlor to which he was directed was dark save for the light from the fire; Anthony's foot struck something that rolled, clinkingly, as he entered.

"Go 'way." The shape in the corner shifted and subsided, apparently lacking ammunition. Anthony turned and devoted his immediate attention to lighting the branches of candles on the mantlepiece.

This illumination revealed the shadowy figure to be the Duke of Owlsthorne, in the company of rather too many empty bottles of brandy. He roused himself and glared blearily at Anthony, then spoke with the painstaking articulation of the truly intoxicated.

"What, sir, do you mean by this . . . abominable interruption?" It was true that Jack had a head for drink hardened by many years of dissipation, but even he was not proof against the vast amount of good brandy he had ingested since he had stormed out of the Assembly Rooms some hours since.

Anthony recognized the signs of hard and fast drinking and his heart sank. While it indicated a laudable sensibility on His Grace's part, it also tended to militate against any rational conversation. Still, he must try. "I came to make you a proposal, Your Grace—are you sober enough to hear it?"

"Proposal! By God, I am . . . done with . . . proposals, Devereaux! Going back to London. Tell 'em to . . . chuck it all. No damn good, anyway."

Resigning himself to strong measures, Anthony rang and demanded a large bucket of cold water and a strong pot of hot coffee. When these items arrived, Anthony placed the coffee well out of harm's way and heaved the water over Jack.

Jack came to his feet with a roar, upending the table as he lunged for Anthony. But Anthony had not been the smallest in his class at Eton to no purpose; he dodged the first drunken charge with nimble grace and managed to evade Jack's avowed intention to draw his cork for some minutes.

At last Jack managed to, in the parlance of the sweet science, "tip him a settler." Anthony, recruiting his wits on the floor, wondered painfully if this had been one of his better ideas as Jack loomed over him, weaving slightly.

After a moment Jack crouched down beside Anthony, peering at him intently. "Why are we doing this?" he said in puzzled and considerably more sober tones.

"It was my idea—but I don't think it was a very good one." Anthony groaned and rubbed his jaw. "Help me up, will you?"

Willing to be obliging, Jack did so; as he was still rather unsteady on his feet, it was an interesting operation, but at last both men were upright once more. "What the devil happened to my clothes?" Jack demanded after a moment.

"I threw a bucket of water over you," Anthony confessed with becoming modesty.

Jack stared at him blankly, then brushed his wet hair back out of his eyes. Comprehension was returning, and he frowned as if in deep thought as Anthony poured out the coffee and handed him a cup.

"Here—drink this. And go sit by the fire, Your Grace—I don't want you catching pneumonia."

"Considerate of you." But Jack obeyed, and sat

moodily drinking coffee and watching as Anthony pulled up a chair and sat down across from him. "What are you doing here, anyway, Devereaux? Come to challenge me to a duel after all? By the way, if you expect me to apologize for hitting you, let me at once reveal that I'm not particularly sorry."

Ignoring Jack's sneers, Anthony merely rubbed his jaw again and said that honesty was accounted among the virtues. "And of course I haven't come about a duel. For one thing, it's illegal. For another, with me stretched dead upon the greensward and you fleeing for your life to the Continent things would be in an even worse mess than Julie's starts have tangled them."

"Well, it's a realistic child after all! Why do I have the pleasure of your company, then?"

"Very simple. I want you to marry my cousin Juliette." Anthony leaned back and sipped his own coffee, watching Jack over the edge of the mug.

Jack laughed; the sound was without mirth. "Why, and so do I—and I even bask in the benison of your great-aunt's blessing. But unfortunately my little wood-nymph has other ideas, damn her to hell." Draining the last of the coffee, Jack threw the mug into the fireplace; it made a satisfying crash against the grate.

Swallowing without a blink the picture of his managing little cousin as anybody's wood-nymph, Anthony shrugged. "Oh, Julie only thinks she has ideas—it's really only a lot of damnfool, half-baked nonsense taking up all the space in her head not allotted to horses and hounds."

"Spoken like a true relation," Jack commented. "Why don't you go away, Devereaux?"

Ignoring this, Anthony went on imperturbably.

"Miss Fonthill tells me that Julie's madly in love with you and has been for months—Julie denies it and also says that she will not marry you only to ruin your life—it was the most fascinating carriage ride home from the ball, Owlsthorne—pity you weren't there. Julie's a poor liar and a compulsive confessor; I'm sure you would have found it enlightening. But if she doesn't marry you, you know, she won't marry—and I don't scruple to tell you, Your Grace, that Miss Fonthill has asked her to make her home with *us*. Now, I'm fond of Julie, but—"

Jack stared, blinked, and then roared with laughter. When he had subsided, Anthony said aggrievedly, "It's all very well to laugh—you won't have the Death of Hope in white muslin staring at you across the breakfast table for the next forty years! And if Thea—Miss Fonthill doesn't think Julie will try to rule the roast—"

"She's young. She'll fall in love and marry someone else," said Jack without conviction.

"Either you don't know Julie, or you think I don't. No, Owlsthorne, I'm very much afraid it's you or nothing."

Jack shrugged, and his mouth twisted into a wry smile. "Then it's nothing, Devereaux. She's refused me absolutely—would you have me kidnap her and marry her over the anvil?"

"Well, yes, actually, if you think it'll work," said Anthony apologetically.

"Perhaps *I* should call *you* out," said Jack, shaking his head. "Besides, Devereaux, greatly as it pains me to admit it, she has a certain amount of right on her side; I'm not going to force her—"

"Heaven preserve me from the scruples of a reformed rake! Now see here, Owlsthorne, do you want Julie—me—Miss Fonthill—even you—all of us, in fact—to be miserable? I'll take it as read that you do not," Anthony added hastily. "Julie's notion is that she won't marry you because she's no longer a great heiress, and without a good bit of money you can whistle your ancestral lands down the wind, isn't that it?"

"That's quite enough, I should think. For heaven's sake, man, leave it alone, will you?"

"Now, let me a proposition unfold—and hear me out before you say I'm crazy, Your Grace! Julie's got a property from her mother called Ashdene that's hers absolutely. Suppose I buy it from her at—oh, not more than twice what it's worth—Julie will ask three times but I'm sure I can argue her down a bit. My wife and I will need some place to live, and Ashdene's quite tolerable and located reassuringly far from the Jewel Box. Would that give you and Julie enough to overcome your various ridiculous scruples?" Anthony leaned forward and regarded Jack anxiously.

"My dear Mr. Devereaux—are you bribing me to marry your cousin?"

"Certainly not," Anthony protested virtuously. "Such a notion never crossed my mind for more than half an hour. Now that that's settled, let me give you some advice on the best way of catching Julie—Madame never has understood her."

On Tuesday, the thirtieth of November, 1819, at ten-thirty in the morning, Sebastian, the Comte de Devereaux, married Miss Maria Alworthy in a quiet ceremony in the village church. The bride was attended by her five sisters and her new stepdaughter; the groom by his nephew and a bound volume of the Odes of Horace, which he was inexplicably still carrying as he took his place by the altar rail. Breakfast and a showing of the new Comtesse's most promising hunters followed the ceremony.

The celebration was enhanced by the formal announcement of Anthony Devereaux's betrothal to Miss Althea Fonthill. Althea, in her turn, was able to contribute the news of her sister Isobel's forthcoming marriage to Mr. Douglas Candlesby. Anthony, who had been made privy to this intelligence somewhat earlier, had already sent best wishes and the post-obits bonds confided to his care by Jack.

Madame was singularly restrained in her comments, merely remarking that it was obvious that Anthony took after his mother, a statement no one was unwary enough to inquire into. Juliette smiled wanly at Althea's warm assertion that she was to make her home with them and asked whether Althea wished Juliette to loan her a mount for the hunt upon the morrow. Upon Althea's declining this generous offer, Juliette then disappeared in the direction of the stables, and was not seen again until dinner time. She reappeared with red-rimmed eyes and an air of such spurious cheerfulness that, as Althea told her betrothed later, it quite made her teeth hurt to be at the same table with her.

Chapter

SEVENTEEN

The day of the celebratory hunt dawned clear and bright and unseasonably cold. The entire household, including, much to everyone's surprise, Madame, arose betimes to make their way to the meet. Madame had, so she declared, taken a fancy to see the hunt off; she was an old woman and expected her last years of crotchets to be humored. Mr. Devereaux and Miss Fonthill, having unanimously decided to forego the pleasures of the hunt, accompanied Madame in her carriage.

The Alworthy hunt was meeting, this frosty morning, at the Bird and Bottle, a comfortable inn with the twin advantages of a hunting-mad proprietor and a situation equidistant between Althorp Manor and Chaceley. At the innyard, Madame ordered her carriage halted where she might have the best view; it rather impeded most of the other horses, but no one dared dispute her suzerainty of the territory. Madame then sat back and regarded the proceedings with the air of a queen inspecting her troops.

As they sat, with two of the three shivering slightly—Madame seemed indifferent to the weather—Lady Juliette jogged up to them on Oriflamme. Impeccably correct in black melton cloth, with her high-crowned hat securely tied in place, Juliette made a striking picture as the skittish mare danced and curvetted over the hard-frozen ground.

The uninvolved viewer would have been forgiven his confusion at the sight of Lady Juliette Devereaux, disinherited heiress, her life in ashes and her one true love forever denied to her, making up a hunting party—but where another shattered damsel would have retired to her music and her fancywork to nurse her heartache bravely and without display, Juliette returned to the saddle. The effect was the same, and her reasons clear enough to those who knew her well.

"You should have come with us, Anthony—and you, too, Thea." Juliette's cheeks shone with winter roses from the chill. "We shall see some fine sport today, I dare swear," she added in dutiful tones.

"So do I," Anthony murmured, glancing past the hunt to the low rise that protected the Bird and Bottle from the harsh north winds. He had been doing this since they had arrived; Althea regarded him curiously as she tucked her hands farther into her muff.

With a little wave, Juliette wheeled Oriflamme and trotted over to join Squire Alworthy. Both Madame and Althea fixed demanding gazes upon Anthony. Anthony, looking meek, begged their indulgence for but one moment more and rose to his feet in the carriage. After a moment, he smiled gently and pointed.

Althea twisted round in her seat and followed the direction of the gesture. Her eyes grew wide.

Cantering over the crest of the rise was the new Duke of Owlsthorne on Vulcan.

"Oh, my," said Althea inadequately.

"Sit down, boy!" Madame snapped. "We all see him."

Anthony, paying no heed to this command, lifted his hat and waved; the Duke checked Vulcan briefly. Secure of his audience's attention, Anthony pointed the hat in the direction of the Squire. The Duke touched his own hat in acknowledgment and salute and let Vulcan continue his powerful canter down the hill.

"Why, Anthony!" said Althea. "You are—"

"Ensuring a happy ending for all concerned," Anthony informed her placidly, and sat down facing the ladies once more.

"Play-acting!" Madame snorted. "In my day, matters would have been settled without all this nonsense!" She leaned forward to tap her driver with her ivory cane. "Move along, man—there's nothing more of interest to see here."

"Oh, come now, Madame, don't you want to see the end of the last act?" said Anthony.

"The farce, more like! Oh, very well—but one more minute only, mind. I've no wish to contract pneumonia."

Given this tacit permission to stare to their hearts' content, Althea and Anthony turned their attention to the drama unfolding before them. The hunt had begun to move off, a mill of horses and hounds that would soon sort themselves out into pack and field. Juliette was in the vanguard, talking quietly to the Squire. The Duke of Owlsthorne had reached the rear of the mass of riders and begun to edge the big bay stallion through the crowd.

Then Lady Juliette, turning to address some remark to a rider behind her, saw His Grace and Vulcan. Oriflamme came to an abrupt halt, shaking her head as if her tender mouth had been jabbed. Vulcan stopped in his turn, pawing vigorously; His Grace swept off his tall hat and bowed as deeply as is possible on a high-couraged horse.

It was plain to the onlookers in the carriage that Lady Juliette quite simply lost her head. As Vulcan began to move forward again, she brought her crop down sharply on Oriflamme's gleaming flank; the startled mare leapt into the air like a young doe and cleared several couple of hounds in one bound. As she landed, Juliette used her crop once more, and the mare took off at the gallop, heading due north.

The hunt had barely had time to assimilate this appalling breach of etiquette when Vulcan charged through in pursuit, scattering riders and hounds. Before either rider had disappeared from view there was pandemonium; saner heads prevailed in the end, and no more than half-a-dozen of the more rowdy element followed in the attempt to see the result of this unexpected match-race. As their horses were quite unable to keep up with the Templeton firebrands, however, these hopefuls came trotting back to the Bird and Bottle in time to move out with the hunt, which eventually started off again not more than forty minutes later.

By that time, however, Madame, grown tired of waiting, had ordered her carriage back to Chaceley. She glared impartially at Anthony and Althea during the drive, but this did not prevent Althea from leaning forward to ask softly, "Oh, Anthony—do you think Juliette will be all right?"

"Do you doubt it?" Mr. Devereaux answered, in a low but fervent voice. He looked rather harassed.

"But this had better be the *dénouement*, that's all I have to say—I am but a weak and feeble man, and my delicate constitution can't take much more of this!"

"Are you completely out of your mind?" Jack sounded somewhat breathless as he finally brought Vulcan alongside the wildly excited Oriflamme's flank a great many miles later. "Damn it, Juliette—pull up!"

The mare was visibly flagging after the long run, but her rider did not seem to notice. "No!" Juliette cried and set the mare at the low stone wall at the edge of the heavily-plowed field they had just laboriously galloped across.

Jack swore and dug his heels into Vulcan's lathered sides. The stallion responded gallantly. The added burst of speed let Jack bring Vulcan up beside Juliette's mare, so close that Juliette's skirts brushed his leg; Jack leaned to the right and pulled Juliette from her saddle. "Oh, no you don't, my girl!"

He had intended to heave her across the saddle-bow in front of him, but he was tired, she struggled, and Vulcan, discovering forgotten energies, made it known in no uncertain terms that he disapproved of such equestrian acrobatics. Vulcan and Jack went up and sideways; Juliette landed upon the ground in a disheveled heap.

She leaped up instantly as Jack worked to regain control of Vulcan, calling for Oriflamme. But the mare, freed of a rider's burden, had also developed new wings. With a buck and kick, she cantered up to the wall, popped over it, and took off into the nearby woods. Juliette, betrayed and abandoned, spun around to confront her pursuer.

Her hat was long gone and her hair a mad tangle; her cheeks had been whipped vivid scarlet by the winter wind. The once immaculate habit was blotched with mud, particularly at the rear of the skirt. She had also, at some point, lost her whip, a fact which Jack, regarding her expression, could only feel was fortunate.

He trotted Vulcan up to her and pulled up, unsure whether to laugh or murder her. "For heaven's sake, Julie—"

"Go away!"

Jack grinned. "And leave you here in the middle of nowhere? My dear child—"

"I can take care of myself!" Juliette declared, backing away. She tripped over the deep furrow and sat down hard.

Her outraged expression made up Jack's mind for him. He laughed.

"Oh, how dare you?" Juliette gasped. "Just look what you have done—and I shall never catch Oriflamme now!"

"And after all the carrots you've plied her with, too—but then, there's no gratitude in this wicked world, is there?" Jack grinned, rubbing Vulcan's neck. "Besides, I'm not the one who led this merry chase. If you'd simply waited to find out what I wanted instead of taking off like the proverbial bat, your devil-to-go wouldn't be halfway to Scotland by now. By the way, sweetheart, are you planning to sit there all day? Not that you aren't a most decorative sight, but I feel strongly that at this time of the year it isn't healthy."

Juliette glared at him, her bosom heaving under the influence of strong emotion in what he considered a most charming traditional fashion. "I thought I told you to go away—and you may stop—stop *smirking* at me!"

"I may, and then again I may not," said Jack, swinging down from the saddle; he looped Vulcan's reins over his arm and moved forward. He bent and grasped Juliette's arm and pulled her lightly to her feet. "No, no, don't thank me, sweetheart—I'd do as much for any damsel in distress. Now for the lord's sake, Juliette—what made you dash off like that?"

"The same thing that made you follow me, I dare say! I cannot imagine what you want!"

"Can't you?"

Juliette's mouth quivered, then firmed. "No, I cannot! I have nothing to say to you, Your Grace."

Jack regarded her speculatively, and flung Vulcan's reins back over his head. "Oh, but I have a number of things to say to you, my pet. Now, as this noble beast objects, among other things, to carrying double, and as I don't think I can trust you not to gallop off if I led you—and as I most particularly wish a private word with you, sweetheart, and feel that trying to hold on to both of you and make you see reason is far beyond my poor powers—" As Lady Juliette looked on in blank astonishment, Jack released his grip on Vulcan's bridle and swatted him hard on the rump. The stallion half-reared, tossed his head several times to assure himself of his freedom, and then disappeared after Oriflamme.

"Are you mad? You can't do that!"

"I just have," Jack pointed out kindly. "Now, I suggest a pleasant stroll in the brisk winter air—preferably in the general direction of Chaceley—while we talk."

Juliette ignored his outstretched hand, stalking

past him towards the edge of the field. Jack laughed and caught up with her in three strides, catching her hand and drawing it through his arm.

"A few weeks steady walking in that direction, my dear, and you'll be in Edinburgh. I always try to keep some grasp on my direction, no matter how attractive the activity in which I'm engaged—and Chaceley is that way." He pointed. "Now come along like a good girl; there's bound to be a farm somewhere where we can hire a gig."

"You are the most vile, despicable, odious man alive," said Juliette half-heartedly, trying to yank free, but his grip was firm, and she subsided. "I will not argue with you," she declared with great dignity. "You may take me home, Your Grace, and then we shall say farewell."

"You're not tall enough for noble speeches, darling. Leave them to Mrs. Siddons. My, isn't it a lovely day for a walk in the country?"

Juliette abandoned her air of tragic calm and glared up at him; Jack grinned.

"That's better. Now, sweetheart, why will you not even talk to me? After all, I've gone to a great deal of trouble over you—and at least this time we shall not be interrupted—and certainly not by Miss Gressingham charging up demanding to know 'what in heaven's name is going on!' I should have thought it was quite clear even to the least perceptive, actually," he added in a tone of fond reminiscense.

Juliette blushed, choked, and giggled, and Jack pressed her hand. "Now, my dear Julie . . ."

"Oh, don't! I—I collect that you intend to—to renew your suit, Your Grace, and I am persuaded that it will not answer! And . . ."

"And you have no money," Jack finished for her.

"My dear, I am not interested in whether you're as rich as Golden Ball or come to me in your shift—in fact, the later prospect's rather intriguing! However, I'm sure we'll come to it sooner or later—that shocked expression's not very convincing, darling, do give it up—but this is hardly the weather for such delights."

"Oh, you are impossible!" said Juliette crossly. She stumbled against him; the full heavy skirts of her habit and the narrow pointed boots were singularly unsuited to cross-country hiking.

"Too true," said Jack with no trace of regret. He stopped; Juliette halted beside him and looked up questioningly, only to let out an outraged squeak as he swept her up into his arms. "Now don't wriggle, darling, or I might drop you in the mud—again. I promise I'll put you down again as soon as we're out of this blasted field—and just to prove what a reformed character I am, I even undertake not to ask awkward questions while you're in such a vulnerable position. What the devil do you suppose they grow in it, anyway?"

After a moment's struggle, Juliette accepted the inevitable; her head dropped to rest against Jack's shoulder. "Mangel-wurzels, I think," she said dolefully.

"Good God," said Jack comprehensively. He settled Juliette more securely against his chest and began the trek to the other side of the field.

Several hours later Juliette began to be afraid that they would be lost for the night. The early winter's dusk had been deepening for nearly an hour, in a lowering fleecy fashion that promised more snow. The weather suited Juliette's mood; true to his word, His Grace of Owlsthorne had carried her in silence to the edge of the field and set her upon her feet. In the long cold walk since then, he had been a charming companion, if one cared for that sort of inconsequential chatter—he had said not one word that Juliette could take amiss, nor had he raised the subjects of either money or marriage.

Juliette was very cross indeed, and several times felt herself on the verge of tears; doubtless it was the cold and fatigue, and the soreness of her feet, that made her feel so drawn. The miles that had passed so swiftly under Oriflamme's flying hooves took on an entirely different measurement when one was walking. She shivered, wishing that Jack would forget he was a reformed character once more. It had been so much warmer in his arms!

"Hold hard darling—I think it's time to settle in for the night, and this looks a likely place to bivouac."

They had just pushed their way through a mass of bracken and come into a clearing. Juliette stopped dead, and her eyes widened as she gazed at the dilapidated barn before them. It had evidently not been occupied in a considerable time, nor were there any outbuildings attached to it—it was either the relict of a farm rendered derelict by the new Enclosure Acts or simply a barn built to hold an overflow harvest. "We can't spend the night here," she protested, swaying wearily. Almost she did not care, if only she might stop walking!

Jack put an arm around her shoulders. "I'm sorry, my pet, but you're looking at our resting place. We can't go on—yes, I know it's early, but we're not in a salon with a fire! It will get colder yet, though you'll hardly credit it, and we're likely to get lost if we wander about in the dark."

"I thought we were lost now," said Juliette drearily, not even bothering to try shrugging off his arm. "And it is all my fault, and now I *shall* be ruined, and not even Madame will be able to save my reputation, for everyone must have seen us ride off together."

"I think it very likely, sweetheart." Jack's voice seemed oddly unsteady. "However, there's a simple remedy: marry me, and no one will give a damn where we spent the night. Strawberry leaves are a sovereign remedy for all ills, so I'm told."

Juliette gasped, and a flash of anger warmed her briefly. "Why—you *planned* this, Your Grace! How dare you?"

"Oh, for heaven's sake, darling, come in out of the cold and then you may castigate me to your heart's content. But do, I beg of you, acquit me of courting death by freezing; if you weren't prepared to be reasonable I'd planned to take you off to a very comfortable little inn where I could ruin you in peace and quiet without peril to life and limb. Is it my fault you can't find your way home?"

He smiled down at her, his eyes ember-warm even in the dim light. "Now come along, Julie—unless you'd rather stand here all night? I do believe it's beginning to snow."

It would be ridiculous to refuse; in the first place, the infuriating man was quite right. In the second place, she was too tired, and her emotions were in too much of a turmoil, to do anything but obey.

Fortunately the doors were not padlocked. Juliette followed Jack in cautiously; it was far darker inside than out, even though a great deal of the fading daylight seeped through the cracks. There was not much in the barn: some old boards, a few small piles of hay, a couple of old buckets. It did not look promising to Juliette.

Jack appeared to think otherwise. "This should do nicely." He rummaged about in the pockets of his riding coat and pulled out a candle stub. Withdrawing a packet of lucifers from the same pocket, he lit the candle and set it upon one of the upturned buckets.

Juliette stared at him; Jack smiled, the flickering candlelight sparking hot gleams from his amber eyes. "I see you doubt, sweetheart, but trust me—I've lived rougher than this in Spain. I think those boards will burn, so if you will be so kind as to bring them over here, Lady Juliette?"

Apparently he knew what he was doing. Juliette could only approve such foresight. Wary of rats, she advanced on the abandoned lumber and carefully pulled out a number of the smaller pieces, thankful for the protection of her leather gloves.

By the time she brought the boards back, Jack had gathered up the scattered bits of hay—and very musty bits they were, too, as he cheerfully informed her—and dumped them in a heap. A wholly disreputable horseblanket had been thrown over the hay. Juliette wrinkled her nose in distaste, but said nothing. It would, she supposed, be better than freezing to death.

After breaking up the boards, Jack made up a nice pile of the resultant sticks, to which he added a few wisps of hay. He then used the candle to light the fire, carefully coaxing the flames along until they became settled and comfortable in their new home.

It seemed at once warmer and more cheerful; Juliette moved closer and held out her hands to the fire. Her moment of ease was short-lived. Jack straightened from his labors, stretched, and stood back to admire the effect. "Very nice," he said. "And now, my pet, to bed."

Juliette took an involuntary step back, and was suddenly so far from cold that her cheeks burned. "Oh—but—but it is far too early to go to bed!"

He grinned at her and Juliette promptly stared at the toes of her boots. "My dear child, I could a tale unfold ..." Then he sighed. "Never mind. However, allow me to alleviate your maiden fears; I have no intention of forcing my attentions on an unwilling woman in a barn in December. Bored or not, I'm not going to invite frostbite in such an egregiously stupid fashion; we are going to share a blanket, you and I, because that will ensure us both of warmth. I have no intention of nobly freezing while you enjoy the dubious pleasures of that blanket—especially as no one would believe I had abstained anyway." So saying, he flung himself down on the makeshift bed and patted the blanket beside him.

"Now prove that you're the sensible woman you pride yourself on being, sweetheart, and come to bed."

To Juliette's horror, her eyes stung as if she were about to cry; shivering though she was, she seemed incapable of movement.

Jack sighed. "Juliette, I promise I won't hurt you. Come and let me warm you."

As if in a dream, Juliette sank to her knees beside him. "I am *not* afraid of you," she announced. "It's only that—"

"That it seems very strange to you," Jack finished matter-of-factly, putting an arm around her waist and pulling her down beside him. He began tucking the blanket well around them. "And so it ought, my pet!"

Once snuggled beside him, the warmth made Juliette incautious. "It's not that—well, only partly—but I *am* so very hungry!" She had missed nuncheon, and tea, and was well on the way to missing dinner and breakfast as well; her stomach rumbled as if to verify her statement. Juliette was too tired and, now, too comfortable to be properly mortified.

"So much for my pretensions! Would you like ham or beefsteak sandwiches, sweetheart? Don't look so startled, my love, it's most unflattering; having brought you on this high treat, it's only my duty to feed you." He sat up and produced a paper-wrapped parcel from the capacious pockets of his coat. "There is also brandy, but I must confess that there is no tea-bottle."

"Ham, please," said Juliette meekly, struggling to sit up beside him. Jack presented her with the parcel; inside was a thick slab of country ham between two slices of bread well smeared with butter. Juliette, biting into it eagerly, was sure she had never tasted anything so delicious in her entire life.

"Courtesy of The Cunning Man in Whitchurch, where I spent the night. I'm sorry they're a bit crushed; I could hardly trust vital provisions to Vulcan, so I had to cram everything into my pockets. Now eat up so we may wrap up warm again. I'd forgotten how deuced cold roughing it is!"

Aided by hunger, Juliette rapidly finished her sandwich; fed, and with a strong draught of the brandy to warm her, she was content to be tucked up beside Jack once more. It seemed, somehow, the most natural thing in the world to be lying here in his arms. Certainly, Juliette told herself drowsily, it would do her no good to make virtuous protestations. He was quite right; after tonight no one would believe her anyway. But it hardly seemed worth troubling herself about.

Jack inquired, with an undertone of laughter in his voice, whether her ladyship were quite comfortable.

"Oh, yes!" Flinging all decorum to the winds, Juliette nestled closer. "I never realized you were so resourceful. I am very much afraid," she added contritely, "that I have had a very bad notion of your character. But—"

Tightening his arms around her, Jack chuckled. "On the contrary, my pet, you have had a very good notion of my character. It's my mind you don't understand. My love, I'm a bad lot, but I'm not an idiot, and I am certainly capable of providing for our comfort. Now, when we are married—"

Juliette shook her head, rubbing her cheek against the rough cloth of his coat. "We're not going to be married, Your Grace."

"My dear Lady Juliette, after this little escapade we'd better be, unless you are planning to enter a nunnery to expiate your sins!"

Juliette thought this over. "But I am not a Catholic."

"In that case, perhaps you will stop arguing with me, my literal-minded darling, and consider embracing your true vocation: marry me and you may manage Owlsthorne."

"You cannot marry me," Juliette explained patiently. "You wish to restore Owlsthorne, which is very proper in you, but for that you will need money."

"My love, I wish you will get this maggot about

money out of your pretty little head! Certainly it will require money, but what it chiefly needs is knowledge. When I should have been learning I was army-mad, and then I was off in Spain—well, anyway, I have the place now, and what am I to do with it? I've just been down to see it, Juliette—" His voice had hardened. Juliette tilted her head to see his face; the wavering light of the fire cast it into sharp planes and angles. "If I'd known what he was doing to it, I swear I'd have murdered the old man years ago. Some of the finest farmland in Kent gone to howling wilderness."

"Kent?" Juliette pushed back and propped herself up on her elbow. "Not the fen country?"

Jack yanked her back against his chest with a strength that left her a bit breathless. "Damn it, darling, stop letting in the cold air! No, Owlsthorne's northwest of there, towards Canterbury."

"But that's prime sheep country! Good heavens, what can your father have been thinking of?" Juliette said indignantly.

"Cutting off his son to spite his face, mostly," said Jack without heat. "Would you like to hear the rest? Let's see—it's mortgaged three times over, the unentailed property was sold to the last foot, the home farm gone to ruin, and the tenants driven off years ago. The entire place has gone back to thornscrub and rabbits."

"Well, that's to the good, anyway," said Juliette briskly, all traces of drowsiness gone. "At least the land has been rested! You should put it under sheep for a season, of course—it's the best thing for clearing it, and very little trouble—and then barley. And if you're willing to put the park under cultivation too—" Juliette broke off in confusion as Jack's body shook with laughter. "But it's nothing to do with me, after all," she finished lamely.

"My love, it has everything to do with you. Come now, if my charm, my address, my title cannot tempt you, can you not bring yourself to love an utterly run-down and ruined estate that you may manage to your heart's content?"

"Oh, but—" Juliette's automatic protest was cut off by his hand over her mouth.

"And for heaven's sake, darling, please spare me any more faradiddles about not being wealthy enough for me, or good enough for me, or any of the other pieces of nonsense I once was foolish enough to say to you! No, let me finish.

"It is true that a man overburdened with both debts and a bad reputation—that's me, my dear— does not ally himself with a gently-reared maiden of less than stellar expectations—that's you, by the way. The usual result is a vilely unhappy marriage and that condition politely known as 'genteel poverty'—I'd call it starvation myself, but I'm not a polite man. But we Favershams have never been gentlemen, and the Owlsthorne dukedom has been founded firmly for generations on the principle of getting our own way. And I wish to marry you for yourself—for your skills and abilities, and that practical little brain of yours. You are what I need, not money."

Jack pulled his hand away from her lips and smiled; the reflected flames danced in his eyes in the most entrancing fashion. "And I think we two would be most vilely happy, my dear. As to the other—well—I'm very much afraid, dearest Juliette, that you would have to forego yearly Seasons in Town. Do you think that would be too great a sacrifice?"

"Go to Town in the middle of the busiest time of year?" said Juliette, scandalized. "You must be mad, Owlsthorne, and I won't hear of it!"

Voice shaking, Jack begged pardon. "So you will marry me, my dear? Mind, I know it's only to get your hands on Owlsthorne Hall and Vulcan—by the way, if you ever set foot in his stirrup I will take your cousin's advice and beat you senseless—but—"

With an angry gasp, Juliette released her grip on his coat and sat bolt upright, shaking off the confines of the horseblanket. "Anthony said *what*?" she demanded wrathfully. "How dare he!"

"Damn it, will you stop doing that?" Before she realized what he was about, she was wrapped firmly against him and he was kissing her, and after a moment Juliette forgot all about Owlsthorne, Vulcan, and the perfidies of Cousin Anthony. There was nothing in all the world but herself and Jack.

When at last her head rested on his chest once more, Juliette drew a deep, shuddering breath. "I—But—"

"Yes, sweetheart?"

"We—we shall have to arrange for the sheep at once, Owlsthorne!"

"Not quite at once, I think," said Jack, and kissed her again.

"I suppose I am completely ruined now," said Juliette some time later, as she lay curled within the circle of Jack's arms and watched the dying embers of the fire. She did not sound much concerned.

Jack laughed and rubbed his cheek against her tangled hair. "Oh, not completely, darling. As a reformed character, I'm afraid that must wait until after the ceremony!"

"Well, it's about time you two showed up," said Anthony. "When Oriflamme came back alone yesterday I believe even Madame began to doubt her own infallibility. Good heavens," he added mildly, "where did you find that—er—"

Even Anthony's powers of eloquence failed him; he and Althea, who had come out to greet the returning wayfarers, stared at the conveyance before them in awestruck silence.

It was shortly before noon, and His Grace of Owlsthorne and Lady Juliette Devereaux, who had been missing and presumed dead to shame for over twenty-four hours, had just rattled up to Chaceley in a farmer's gig. This vehicle had, one presumed, once been new; the remains of several paint jobs in contrasting hues peeped at the unwary observer from the cracks and crevices. The animal drawing it was a draft horse of so ancient a standing as to deserve admiration for the amazing feat of remaining upright.

Althea recovered first, and ran down the steps. "Juliette! Where have you been? I mean—" She stopped, her cheeks awash with crimson.

"Good morning, Miss Fonthill; we spent the night in great discomfort and moderate chastity in a deserted barn some twenty miles from here. Hello, Devereaux; I see you are admiring young Rosinante here. I had to buy the beast to get the loan of the gig, but Juliette assured me I could undoubtedly fob him off on you. By the way, did Vulcan ever show up here?"

Paying little heed to any response this might elicit, His Grace vaulted down and turned to assist

321

Lady Juliette to descend. Her ladyship did not look nearly so distressed as one in her precarious moral condition by right ought.

Setting Juliette upon the ground, His Grace took her hand and turned to face the others. "And now, having won the fair maiden, I'm ready to slay the dragon—a bit backward, I'm afraid, but these things happen. Where is Madame Solange, by the way?"

Anthony made a resigned gesture upwards; they all tilted back their heads and stared at the window indicated. A practiced, or a suspicious, eye could see the brocade curtain twitch, as if jerked by an impatient hand.

"I am not perfectly sure," said Althea, "but I believe she expects us to spend the afternoon writing out the invitations for the wedding."

"Oh, I forgot to tell you," said Anthony, "Madame intends us to have a double wedding. I believe she has a theory that *our* undoubted virtue will expand to full the space available. On the other hand, perhaps she merely wishes to save money; she can have some of the most amazingly nip-cheese notions. By the way, Julie, will you sell Ashdene to Thea and me? We must live somewhere, you know."

Juliette's eyes lit up, and she looked speculative. "Well . . ."

"Oh, for heaven's sake, Juliette, you may talk about it later," said Althea. She put an arm around Juliette and hustled her off into the house, over her protests that she was not in the least fatigued.

When they were left alone with Rosinante and cart, Anthony stepped forward and held out his hand. "Congratulations, Owlsthorne. Will she let me have Ashdene, do you think?"

"Oh, I think so," said Jack, clasping Anthony's hand with the warmth of those who have weathered the same gale and survived. "But mind, Devereaux, I think you'll have to buy this horse as well!"

SPRING 1821

The breakfast parlor at Ashdene was a cozy apartment, and so situated as to be awash with light on a sunny morning such as this. Anthony Devereaux gazed fondly across the table at his wife as she worried at an aggressively sealed and rather thick letter which the footman had just deposited beside her plate.

Wrestling it open, she spread it flat and began to read the first of several pages crossed and recrossed in Juliette's sharply slanting hand. "I do wish she wouldn't cross her lines," said Althea, frowning. "After all, it's not as if Owlsthorne can't frank them for her!"

"Well, you know Julie—a sentence crossed is a sentence earned. What news from the hinterlands?"

"Oh—the sheep are doing very well, and she has great hopes of the barley—she says the winter sowing is nearly ready for harvesting, and she has high hopes for Vulcan's first colts ..." Althea puzzled over the next page, then looked up. "Something she calls the Dowager Rose Garden is quite promising. Do you have any notion what that might be?"

Anthony took the proffered page from her and

studied it intently. "It say 'Dowager's Rose Garden is coming back'—although since there isn't a dowager duchess, I can't imagine where it's coming back from. Does she say anything else?"

Althea glanced through the pages. "The roof in the West Wing has finally been repaired, and no longer leaks; she has bought Owlsthorne a pair of draft mares for his birthday—"

"Has she, by jove? I hope Owlsthorne can contain his ecstasy. Is there any more toast?"

Toast was passed; Althea continued to read. "Oh, there is a postscript, but I cannot quite make it out. . . . Anthony! Juliette says she too is expecting an Interesting Event in a few months and wishes us to come and visit! Do say we may go!"

"Whatever you like, my dear—providing all is as you say and the roof in the West Wing does not leak."

Althea smiled upon him as she folded Juliette's letter. "I must say, Anthony, that it has worked out very well—I am so glad that she married him after all!"

Anthony reached out and patted her hand. "So am I, my dear Thea, but there was never any doubt. Man proposes, Madame disposes. Their marriage was made in Fakenham."

Althea smiled, then said sharply, "Anthony! Do you think she intended all along for us—?"

"To the marriage of true impediments, admit no minds," said Mr. Devereaux piously. "There are some things into which it is better not to inquire. May I trouble you, my dear, for the jam?"

About
the Author

Rosemary Edghill lives in the Hudson Valley area of New York. This is her second book. Her first, TURKISH DELIGHT, was also a Regency Romance.

FANCIFUL FREEDOM OF FORM EMPHASIZED THROUGH **IMAGINATION AND EMOTION**

Marian Devon